The Bridge Over Flatwillow Creek

THE GENTLE HILLS

---◆◆◆---

Far From the Dream
Whispers in the Valley
Keeper of the Harvest
Some Things Last Forever

(All available in large print)

---◆◆◆---

The Bridge Over Flatwillow Creek
One Small Miracle

9710

The Bridge Over Flatwillow Creek

Lance Wubbels

BETHANY HOUSE PUBLISHERS

MINNEAPOLIS, MINNESOTA 55438

Published by Bethany House Publishers
A Ministry of Bethany Fellowship International
11300 Hampshire Avenue South
Minneapolis, Minnesota 55438

Printed in the United States of America by
Bethany Press International, Minneapolis, Minnesota 55438

Library of Congress Cataloging-in-Publication Data

Wubbels, Lance, 1952–
   The bridge over Flatwillow Creek / by Lance Wubbels.
     p. cm.
   ISBN 0–7642–2046–2 (pbk.)
   I. Title.
PS3557.U39B75   1997
813'.54—dc21

                                                  97–33852
                                                 CIP

To
Nils and Gloria Strom

For what you mean to us,
all the love and prayers,
the ceaseless giving,
the constant encouragement.
How does one
really say thanks?

LANCE WUBBELS, Managing Editor of Bethany House Publishers, taught biblical studies courses at Bethany College of Missions for many years. He is the author of *One Small Miracle*, a heartwarming novel about the profound impact of a teacher's gift of love on the life of one of her struggling students. He is also the compiler and editor of the Charles Spurgeon and F. B. Meyer CHRISTIAN LIVING CLASSIC series published by Emerald Books. He and his family make their home in Bloomington, Minnesota.

Contents

♦ Prologue   9

Part 1 ♦ Summertime

1 ♦ A Distant Rumble   15
2 ♦ The Rescue   24
3 ♦ A Proper Thank-You   33
4 ♦ Playing Hardball   42
5 ♦ Someone Who Cares   52
6 ♦ Speaking the Truth   61
7 ♦ A Chance Encounter   69
8 ♦ A Country Ride   78
9 ♦ A Sniveling Coward   88
10 ♦ A Closed Door   97

Part 2 ♦ Autumn Changes

11 ♦ The Bat Lady   109
12 ♦ A Silent Partner   118
13 ♦ From Bad to Worse   127
14 ♦ Doctor Doleful Lugubrious   136
15 ♦ Providence?   146
16 ♦ Big Daddy   156
17 ♦ How Could I Help but Love Him?   168
18 ♦ The Dingdong   177

Part 3 ♦ Winter Warmings

19 ♦ A Kiss in the Alley   189
20 ♦ When the Heart Goes Silent   200
21 ♦ Merry Christmas!   209

22 ◆ The Christmas Dream   221

23 ◆ Tracks in the Snow   231

24 ◆ Two Can Play the Game   241

25 ◆ Throwing Caution to the Wind   251

26 ◆ In the Night   261

Part 4 ◆ Spring Stirrings

27 ◆ Spring Is in the Air   273

28 ◆ The Angels Rejoice   282

29 ◆ One Rotten Apple Left   291

30 ◆ Cook the Goose   300

31 ◆ For a Lifetime   310

Prologue

"What do you think of him, Elsie?" Annie Harding asked her best friend, glancing up from the rocking chair where she was sitting. Elsie Dale was standing in front of the tall mirror, holding an open copy of the most recent *Life* magazine in one hand and pressing her stomach in with the other hand.

"I think I hate Mr. Charles Gibson for drawing these serials," Elsie muttered as she gazed down at the latest Gibson girl, then set the magazine on her old wooden dresser. "Look at how tall she is, how beautiful, that perfect hair . . . and her waist—she has no waist!" Petite Elsie stood as tall as she could, took a deep breath and held her stomach in, then pressed her fingers against the waist of her black skirt.

Annie laughed and shook her head. "Elsie," she said, "you know full well Mr. Gibson's model must have been poured into her corset. Besides, you already have the nicest figure of any girl in the county. And look at your hair—that lovely auburn color, all piled and pinned perfectly, just like a Gibson girl. How you can look in the mirror and complain is beyond me!"

"My lips. Look at my lips," Elsie countered, puckering at the mirror. "My lips are too thick. And I can't seem to hold my head the way she does. And look at her clothes! Don't you hate how boringly plain our clothes are?"

"This isn't New York City, in case you've forgotten," Annie said. "I don't recall seeing that dress style at Thatcher's Department Store."

"As if *you* need to be stylish," said Elsie, finally looking away from the mirror toward Annie. "You always look graceful, even in the plainest black dress. You're so lucky to be tall. And your lips are delicate and thin"—she gave the mirror another puckering pout—"and you never have to bite them to make them redder. And then there's that pale gold hair ... what do they call it? Cornsilk? I think I've got plenty to complain about."

"You didn't answer my question," Annie reminded her friend, "and I need to get home. Tell me, what do you think of him?"

"Stuart Anderson?" Elsie replied, her eyes still glued to the mirror.

"Yes."

Elsie shrugged. "I say, why bother, when you already have Arthur Simpson at your beck and call? Stuart is ... just Stuart. He's decent and reliable and ... nice-looking, I guess, but he's a ... small-town boy, and he'll never be more than that. If you knew him, you'd know there's no comparison to Arthur."

"I stopped and talked to Stuart the other day," Annie said, raising her eyebrows as her lips curled into a smile. "I think he's nice."

"And I think you're crazy!" Elsie exclaimed, finally turning toward her friend. "If Arthur hears that, he might think you're up to something with Stuart."

"All we did was talk for a bit," Annie said. "He just got home from college; he's working for his father this summer. Turns out he left for school just about the time my family moved here last fall. Too bad. I wish I could have gotten to know him in high school."

Elsie closed her hazel eyes and shook her head at Annie. "I've known you for almost a year now," she said, "and I still don't understand you. You have the handsomest, richest, most debonair man in town calling on you, and you turn your head toward some country bumpkin? Annie, Stuart Anderson works at the mill grinding feed for farmers! Arthur Simpson is a vice-president at Citizens State Bank, and his father *owns* the bank. Do I really need to explain the difference to you?"

"No, I'm not blind," Annie answered, still smiling. "And Arthur is ... well, you know how charming Arthur is. But he's also the first man who has sought my affections, and it seems a pity not to at least look around."

"Not a good idea," said Elsie. "Not when the man in question grew up in Chicago society and could have any girl he wants, here *or* there. He's so sophisticated, and he dresses so well!" She sniffed. "He must hate this little town. I wonder whatever brought them here?"

"His father said the price of purchasing our bank was just too good a deal to pass up," Annie said. "He went from running a large bank to owning his own small bank."

"Which Arthur will inherit someday."

"I suppose," Annie said. "But money isn't everything, Elsie."

"Maybe not, but you could certainly use some. Besides, you really like Arthur. Admit it."

Annie's big brown eyes grew soft. "I admit it. He *is* awfully nice to me, and Father likes him, which is a miracle in itself. I just ... I just don't want to make the mistake of falling for the first man who shows interest."

"My ma always says strike while the iron's hot," said Elsie. "But you let me know if you get tired of Arthur Simpson. I want to be first in line behind you." She turned to her mirror once more and sucked in her breath. "I'll bet he would buy me all the dresses that Charles Gibson could dream up...."

Annie laughed and shook her head as she stood to leave. "You are a piece of work, Elsie Dale. But I'll be sure and let you know if Mr. Simpson becomes available. By the way, when do you leave for home?"

"Friday!" Elsie moaned, glancing around her boardinghouse room. "I wish I could stay and keep my job here in town for the summer, but my mother says she can't handle all the farm work without my help. That means you and I will hardly see each other until school starts in the fall. Summers are so dreadfully boring on the farm. I can't wait till we graduate and I'm on my own."

"Just one more year," Annie said wistfully. "Who knows what's ahead?"

Part 1

•••••••••••• ✕✕✕✕✕✕✕✕✕✕✕✕✕✕✕✕✕✕✕✕✕✕✕✕✕✕✕✕✕✕✕✕

Summertime

Long before anyone came to Bradford, the stream was here, streaming and pooling, slicing its ribboned path through the mighty hills and lowly valleys. Even now, in the creek bank's cool shadows, it is easy to imagine the town is far away.

In this swirling world, all but hidden beneath the weeping willows and ancient oak trees that cluster its banks, the crystal creek seems to laugh at the summer sun that bakes the earth above. Here, the deep cold pools offer sanctuary to native brown trout, and the smooth, cool limestone slabs beckon visitors to rest beside the healing waters.

Here, in the pool's cool presence, it is easy to know that God is near.

Chapter 1

A Distant Rumble

"It don't matter what you say, woman. It never has," Andrew Sorenson barked toward the stoop-shouldered form silhouetted in the machine-shed doorway. With a thick, greasy hand he mopped the sweat from his broad forehead and stared at the nearly empty brown bottle on the workbench, then he squinted out the murky window at the flattened brown cornfield. "What's done is done," he muttered. "No thanks to you." He wrapped his huge fingers around the dark whiskey bottle, lifted it gently to his lips, and pulled one long last drink.

Gladys Sorenson's tightly drawn face showed no change from its somber, stony expression. Twenty years of living with the man had taught her never to let her husband see what she was feeling, but it did not keep her from standing her ground. "So now it's my fault that you're losing the traction engine, too?" she spoke slowly, deliberately.

"You . . . you just get outta here!" Andrew yelled as he suddenly reached back one of his long arms and flung the bottle at her with all his strength, striking the concrete base by the corner of the doorway. With the sound of the shattering glass, shards flew everywhere, but his wife remained motionless before him. The only movement in the shed was the lithe form of the farm collie escaping through the doorway with its tail between its legs.

"I can't take credit for the hail or the heat, if that's what you mean," Gladys finally replied after a long silence, then she looked down and carefully wiped some of the brown glass chips from her plain black cotton dress. "Maybe you should talk to the banker one more time. We ain't the only ones around here that had a bad year."

"You go talk to him if you want. Maybe cryin' real loud will help," her husband sputtered. "I begged that man once, and I ain't stoopin' that low again. Made a fool outta myself askin' for an extension on the loan. He already had a new buyer on the line before he even called me, and I'll bet he's doublin' his money on this deal. I either deliver the traction engine this afternoon for shipping to North Dakota, or he's comin' with a legal claim against the farm."

"We don't need no more problems with the law, that's for certain," she spoke without emotion, crossing her arms and straightening up. "We're lucky that judge didn't put you away after the last time you went on a bender. How much was in that bottle you just polished off, Andrew?"

"Not enough to keep me from droppin' by and havin' a nice chat with that bald-headed goose of a banker," Andrew replied with a smirk. He turned away from his wife's gaze and fixed his attention on the massive traction engine that stood silently beside him. "I'd like to get my fingers around his long skinny neck and squeeze as hard as—"

"You keep out of trouble, Andrew!" Gladys Sorenson broke in. "You hurt another man and the judge already told you he'd send you to the penitentiary. You think he was bluffin'?"

"I was drunk. I never meant—"

"And you'll be drunk today, just as soon as that liquor takes hold," his wife countered. "I'm sending Walter with you. You let him drive."

"I can drive this stupid—"

"Not if you're drunk, you can't," Gladys shot back, "and especially not when you get to town. That big ol' monster's hard enough to steer out here, and gettin' it over the bridge is gonna be a trick. You let Walter drive, I'm tellin' you. We can't afford no more trouble." Then she turned away from the shed door and was gone before the big man could protest.

◆ ◆ ◆ ◆ ◆ ◆ ◆ ◆ ◆ ◆

"Oh, Garrit, why can't you just go back to your room and play?" Annie Harding spoke softly to her eight-year-old brother, looking wistfully at her book and then stretching her arms and back. "Please. It's too hot out there today. We'll cook to death."

"Mother *said* you'd take me down to the river to catch minnows under the bridge!" the towheaded boy insisted, waving the small fishnet he clutched in his hand. He was barefoot, wearing shorts, a long-sleeved shirt, and his black cloth cap. "Mother said so."

"Can't you speak quietly?" Annie pled, hushing the boy with a finger across her lips. "I'll pay you a nickel if you stay in your room or find something else to do. Can't any of your friends play today?"

The boy flashed a grin, then shook his head no. "A dime . . . one slim dime . . . or I tell Mother."

"You little—" Annie cried, dropping her book and leaping from the crushed velvet davenport. She caught her brother by one sun-browned arm and tackled him to the shiny hardwood floor.

"Mother! Help!" screamed Garrit before Annie could plant her hand over his mouth. When she did, he tried unsuccessfully to bite her.

"You are a brat!" Annie whispered into Garrit's ear as the unmistakable clomp of her mother's shoes across the kitchen floor and the swoosh of the oak door opening into the dining room signaled impending doom. She let go of her brother and tried to quickly straighten the pale tendrils that had fallen out from her tortoiseshell hair clip. But she knew it was too late to cover up her dilemma.

"What in the world are you two doing now?" Dinah Harding called out even before she stepped into the opened living room doorway, still wiping white flour from her hands with her apron. Her expression clearly conveyed that she did not appreciate the break from her labors.

"Annie won't take me to the river like you told her!" Garrit exclaimed as he grabbed his mother's hand and tugged on it. Then he pointed his net at Annie. "She was trying to gag me."

"And he tried to bite me," Annie countered weakly.

"Annie Harding, you're seventeen years old," her mother lamented, putting an arm around Garrit and snuggling him up against her side. "I told you I wanted you to take your brother to the bridge to play, and if I have to tell you again, your father's going to hear about it when he gets home tonight. Now, put the book away and get some sunshine before the summer ends."

"Oh . . . it's just too hot, Mother," Annie complained. She picked herself up from the floor and shook out the wrinkles from her long white dress. "Even in the house here, with a breeze, I can hardly stand it."

Dinah Harding shook her head and pointed toward the front entryway. "You know full well how cool it is under that bridge on a day like today," she said with one of her rare smiles. "Go on now, enjoy it. Once school starts, you'll be wishing you could sneak down to the bridge. And leave the book here."

"But—"

"I want you watching your brother, not getting swept away to a dream world. The water's deep enough that you have to keep your eye on him."

"Maybe push him under," Annie whispered, picking up her book and slipping a velvet bookmark into place.

"What did you say?" her mother asked.

"She said she's going to push me under!" Garrit tattled, hugging his mother tighter. "Annie wants to drown me!"

"No, she doesn't," Dinah said as she pushed her gold wire-rimmed glasses back up higher on her nose. "Annie, don't say such foolishness. You never know when your words will come back to haunt you."

❖❖❖❖❖❖❖❖❖❖

"That's it, Mr. Bruss." Stuart Anderson tossed the last big gunny-sack of oats onto the back of the farmer's heavily loaded wagon. He wiped the grain dust from his hands and arms, then motioned to the older man, who sat patiently on the wagon seat. "Is that everything for you, sir?"

"Should keep me out of town for a spell." Mr. Bruss nodded appreciatively, then flashed a toothless smile. "You do good work, boy. 'Spect you must be figurin' on takin' over the mill and the store from your pa when you finish college?"

A gentle smile spread across Stuart's face as he shook his head. "No, sir," he replied, leaning one muscular arm against the back of the wagon. "I took a year out of high school to help Dad after we had the fire in the drugstore, but I don't think I want to do this for a living. Wouldn't want to run the drugstore for my father either."

"That was a bad fire," Edward Bruss said. "We're all lucky it didn't take the mill with it. I'd have to haul my grain six more miles. Don't think my ol' horses would 'preciate that in this heat. So, then, whatcha fixin' to be after college?"

"I'm hoping to go into the ministry." Stuart ran strong fingers through his sweaty black hair. His black eyes shimmered in the bright summer sunlight. "Least, that's what I've been planning."

The scruffy old farmer squinted his clear blue eyes and pressed his lips together. "Son, you can make more money running this here mill," he said, "an' do more for your fellowman besides. Wouldn't give a nickel for all the preachers I ever seen. All talk, nothing more. Never seen one of 'em who could do a lick of work. Don't go wastin' your life away like that."

"I surely don't want to waste my life, Mr. Bruss, and I appreciate your concern," Stuart replied. "But if it's the Lord's calling, and I believe it is, I'm confident He won't let me become a hypocrite."

"Like our town's fine Rever—"

"Please, sir," Stuart interrupted the farmer, holding up one hand and stepping away from the wagon toward the wooden stairs that led up to the mill office. "I'd rather we not become the judge of the man. God knows the truth of his heart, Mr. Bruss."

The farmer raised his dark bushy eyebrows and finally smiled. "Fair enough, boy," he said. "Maybe you got enough backbone to be a good preacher someday. But don't stick your head in the sand, neither. The reverend's a bad apple if I ever seen one, and you don't have to have religion to figure that out. Good day, boy. Tell your pa to give you the rest of the afternoon off. Tell him Ed Bruss thinks he's working you too hard."

The wooden wagon creaked heavily as the team of chestnut brown workhorses tugged against the load, and the large metal wheels rattled as they slowly began to roll down the street toward the old iron bridge that spanned Flatwillow Creek on the western edge of town. True to his manner, Edward Bruss was in no hurry to get home, and neither were his horses.

Stuart waved after the wagon and had turned to climb the stairs when he noticed young Garrit Harding racing down the street ahead of his sister, Annie. Over the summer months, he had seen the two of them go down to Flatwillow Creek many times. Now he stood staring after them, watching her climb gracefully down the steep embankment after her towheaded brother and then duck under the bridge. Peering carefully, he could make out two bright heads in the cool shadows.

"You gonna be gawking at that girl all day?" Stuart jumped at the voice and looked up to see his father's head sticking out the big office window. "Or should I expect that you're going to finish the feed inventory yet today?"

"I might just keep on gawking, if you're offering me a choice," Stuart replied with a laugh as his suntanned face took on a pink glow. "She's something, isn't she, Dad?"

"Maybe you shouldn't be such a chicken," his father teased. At thirty-eight, Robert Anderson had the same sturdy good looks as his son, although Stuart had inherited his mother's dark coloring. "Go on over there and talk to her. She's got nothing to do while she watches her kid brother. You can finish the inventory in the morning. Go ahead."

"Ah . . . phooey," Stuart mumbled, shaking his head with a crooked grin and turning to take the last three steps up into the office. "She's about as interested in me as a tree. I may as well spend my time working on inventories."

Robert Anderson turned in his swivel chair as Stuart opened the door. "She and the banker's son pretty thick, then?"

Stuart shrugged. "I don't really know for sure, but it looks that way. Who knows? We've only talked a few times."

◆ ◆ ◆ ◆ ◆ ◆ ◆ ◆ ◆ ◆ ◆

"Ma's gonna be real mad when she finds out you drove," Walter Sorenson was saying as he sat beside his father on the footboard of the traction engine. The immense steel machine shook the ground and belched great clouds of black smoke as it lumbered past the homes on the western edge of the town. Despite his mother's warnings, once they had gotten out of the sight of their farm, there was nothing Walter could do to keep his father from driving it. Even though he was as tall and nearly as broad as his father, the young man was still no physical match for his father, even when the older man was drunk.

"I ain't lying for you, Pa," Walter went on. "You better let me take her into town."

His father kept his hand on the long steel lever, and his red, dull eyes looked straight ahead. "You say one word other than what I done told you to say, and I'll beat you raw, boy. Just try me if you think things've changed. What your ma don't know won't hurt her none."

"As if you could hurt her any more . . ." Walter whispered, turning his freckled face away and letting the words be smothered in the roar of the steam engine.

"Once we get over that bridge, I got me a plan," Andrew declared with a loud laugh. "I'm gonna drive Big Bertha right up to the front of that bank's shiny glass windows and park her there. Seeing as that banker claims he's the real owner of this rig, seems to me he oughta appreciate me delivering it to the door." Then he burst out laughing again but did not bother to look at his son.

"You're gonna end up in jail again, Pa." Walter shook his head. "That banker don't like you, and you know that judge's got it in for you. You push him, and you're gonna get sent up. We'll lose the farm at the rate you're going."

"Can't be nothin' wrong with returnin' a man's property to him," Andrew Sorenson persisted with drunken reasonableness. Pulling hard on the lever again, he coaxed as much speed out of the mighty steam engine as he could.

◆◆◆◆◆◆◆◆◆◆◆

"Don't get so close to the deep spot!" Annie called out to Garrit, who was wading near the western side of the stream in water over his knobby knees. He reached out as far as he could to net an elusive school of minnows that was swimming past. "If you drop in that hole, I'm not getting my dress wet for you today," she added as she motioned to him from her perch on a slab of limestone beneath the iron bridge.

"Oh, there's a big one!" Garrit cried out, taking a long swipe through the clear cool water but coming up empty. "Shoot! I almost had him."

"How many minnows are you going to catch?" Annie called out above the din of the running, swirling water of Flatwillow Creek. "You already got a whole bucketful. The tomcat won't even be able to eat them all. Let's go home."

"Just a couple more," Garrit hollered back. "Why don't you go up and take a peek at that boy you're always watching for down at the mill."

"You be quiet," Annie ordered. A distant rumble caught her attention, though, and she turned to climb the steep, stony embankment to the street. Just as she reached the top, she slipped but managed to catch herself, then slumped to the hard ground. "These stupid wet shoes," she muttered, picking herself up quickly and dusting off her dress.

Looking down the street to the west, Annie saw an approaching traction engine and wondered how many housewives had been able to close their windows before the black smoke invaded their homes as the heavy machine passed by. "I hate those stinking engines. I don't know why they can't stick with horses," she said to herself.

Then Annie turned quickly and glanced to the east toward the feed mill. There, with his arms crossed in the big open doorway to the mill, stood Stuart Anderson. She gave a polite wave and a slight nod but turned to make her descent back down the slippery slope to the stream without waiting for the young man's response.

"Was he there?" Garrit called out as she held up her long skirt and leaped the last few steps to a big limestone rock that jutted up out of the stream.

"That's none of your business, shorty pants," she replied loudly, the roar of the oncoming traction engine nearly drowning out her voice.

"What's all the racket?" yelled Garrit, carefully lifting his net from the water and looking up at the rusty underside of the bridge, which was beginning to shake directly above him.

✦✦✦✦✦✦✦✦✦✦✦

Stuart Anderson stood in the cool shade of the mill doorway, all but oblivious to the smoke and rumbling of the huge traction engine coming down the road toward him. Annie Harding had seen him and actually waved! Who knew? Maybe he had a chance with her after all.

But his reverie was interrupted by his father's frantic voice on the landing above him. "That machine's too heavy for the bridge!" Robert Anderson was running down the wooden steps from the office, pointing down the street. "That machine's too heavy for the bridge! We have to stop it!"

Before the last words of his father's warning were out, Stuart was racing toward the bridge, waving his arms and yelling. The traction engine was already almost there, and through the billowing smoke, Stuart was not sure the driver could even see him.

"What's wrong with that idiot?" Andrew Sorenson growled, squinting ahead at the young man who was racing toward them. "I'm gonna run him over if he gets in my way."

Walter Sorenson had been admiring the fancy houses that lined the road near the outskirts of the town, but now he turned his gaze forward to see what his father was complaining about. He spotted Stuart just as the heavy wheels of the traction engine rolled onto the iron bridge. Then, before Walter could respond, the full weight of the engine suddenly bore down upon the first sixteen-foot span, and a tremendous cracking noise broke above the noise of the steam engine.

Walter grabbed the long steel lever from his father's hand and shoved it in, immediately stopping the engine. Enraged by his son's action, Andrew Sorenson shoved Walter from the footboard, knocking him to the heavy wooden beams that spanned the bridge's iron girders.

Stuart had nearly reached the other end of the bridge and could clearly see their danger. "Jump!" he screamed. "Jump for it!"

Whether Andrew Sorenson heard Stuart's warning or simply was too drunk to understand, he set the engine in motion again—and then came the crash! In less than a second the heavy machine had tipped backward, carrying the wide iron span with it, and plunged straight down into the deepest hole of Flatwillow Creek.

Chapter 2

The Rescue

At first it was impossible to see what had happened.

Screams from below and above the bridge were consumed by the terrible noise of smashing metal and splintering wood, and then all was still, hidden from sight by an ominous cloud of steam.

Stuart and Robert Anderson crept out on what remained of the iron bridge on its east side, clutching the twisted beams that had snapped in every direction when the first section of the bridge collapsed. Stuart inched his way ahead of his father, holding up his shirt to protect his face from the blinding, acrid steam. Hardly able to breathe, he heard his father coughing behind him.

"Look out!" Robert Anderson cried, Stuart felt the full weight of his father tumbling against the back of his legs.

As his own feet shot out from under him, Stuart reached back and grabbed the last metal I-beam he had held. The long, slippery wooden planks that covered the bridge's surface suddenly disappeared beneath his feet, and Stuart felt his body dropping over the bridge's edge. His wet hands clutched at the slick edges of the iron beam as they slid down, then his right foot suddenly caught hold of another metal beam below.

"Help!" Stuart cried as he dangled off the edge, barely able to keep from falling. His foot pressed desperately against the metal.

A ghostlike hand appeared through the steamy fog, wrapping its strong fingers around Stuart's left hand. "Hang on!" Robert Anderson yelled as he leaned forward and wrapped his other arm around his son's back. Steadying himself as best he could on the edge of the wet planks,

Robert reached down and managed to get the fingers of his right hand around Stuart's belt.

"Hurry!" Stuart gasped, his toehold on the lower metal beam beginning to slip free.

"Now!" Robert cried, pulling up with all his strength. Slowly, slipping and grasping, Stuart came back up over the edge of the bridge and collapsed beside his father in the hot steamy cloud that surrounded them.

"Are you all right, son?" his father asked with a groan, reaching his hand across to feel Stuart's face.

"Yes, I think so." Stuart tried to keep from coughing, although he couldn't stop taking in deep gulps of air. The solid planks beneath him felt like a bed, and his strained muscles began to relax. Then from below came another deep rumble of the traction engine, followed by a long hissing noise that faded once again into eerie silence.

Stuart rolled over and crawled alongside his father to the collapsed edge of the bridge as the last cloud of steam cleared away. Down below, the trout stream flowed tranquilly around twisted metal beams and broken wooden planks. The traction engine, still trailing wisps of steam, rested at an awkward angle in the deepest part of the stream. Beside it, the broad forehead of Andrew Sorenson reflected the bright afternoon's sunshine. Bubbles from the cooling steam engine swirled around his lifeless face and torso. The rest of him lay pinned beneath the engine.

Robert and Stuart Anderson looked at each other in shock. Then a slight movement to the left of the traction engine near the stream's edge caught their attention. From beneath a heap of broken wooden planks a small hand reached out and began pushing away small chunks of wood. The white-blond head of Garrit Harding suddenly emerged from the rubble, looking dazed and dirty but unhurt. He began to cry as he called out, "Annie! Annie, where are you?"

"Help!" another muffled voice cried out from somewhere on the stream's embankment on the opposite side of the traction engine. "Help me! I can't move."

"There he is!" Robert Anderson cried and pointed to a young man who appeared to be wedged beneath a large metal beam on the bank of the stream. "Must be Mr. Sorenson's boy. I'll see what I can do to help him," Robert called out as he began to climb carefully down over the edge of the bridge. "You help the boy find his sister."

Just then Stuart spotted a long swatch of pale hair swaying in the swirling currents around a snarl of metal beams in a deeper part of the stream, not far from the place where Garrit was crawling on the rocky bank. Quickly untying his shoes and pulling them off, Stuart got to his feet and jumped from the edge of the bridge into the deepest corner of the stream's pool. With a few powerful strokes of his arms, he managed to dive safely under the iron beams and then shot up to the stream's surface.

Gasping for air, Stuart spun in the water to where Annie Harding floated motionless against a spider web of bent iron I-beams. Her head was turned into the bridge's wreckage, and Stuart could not tell whether she was conscious, but it appeared that Annie's face was being held above the waterline by her long white dress, which was snagged between two of the larger beams.

"Annie!" Stuart shouted, reaching out for her right shoulder and pulling her cold white face toward him. Her eyes were shut, a nasty red welt crossed her forehead, and several cuts and scrapes streaked her cheeks. "Annie!" he called again, taking her wrist into his hand and feeling for her pulse.

"Is she dead?" cried young Garrit, who stood motionless at the edge of the stream. "Is my sister dead?"

"No!" Stuart called out in relief, having found a slow heartbeat. "She's alive, but we have to get her out soon. Go get help! Quick!"

Garrit turned around languidly, then stopped to look back again, seeming to understand Stuart's order but still dazed by the calamity.

"Hurry!" cried Stuart, watching the boy sluggishly climb the steep bank that led to the street above. Then Stuart reached for a beam above Annie and pulled himself up so that his face was above hers. Bending down, he listened closely. Above the gentle murmur of the stream's current, he was overjoyed to catch the first slight sound of her breath.

"Dad!" Stuart called out from beneath the iron wreckage. "Annie's alive, but she's unconscious! How's the boy?"

"His arm's pinned under a beam!" Robert Anderson yelled back. "As soon as some help gets here, we're going to have to see if we can force it up . . . or dig underneath his arm to free it. I think he's going to be all right, though. Can you wake the girl?"

"I don't know," Stuart returned, looking down into the young woman's delicate face.

"Try!" his father answered. "If some of that metal shifts, she'll be pulled under. And you have to get her out of that cold water."

Gently placing his fingers upon Annie's colorless cheek where it was not cut, Stuart tapped several times and spoke her name directly into her ear, "Annie." When there was no response, he tapped her cheek harder, then he put his face against her's and called out loudly, "Annie, wake up! Wake up!"

It was only the slightest of twitches, but Stuart was sure that he felt the muscles around Annie's eyes contract. He pulled his face away, but her expression was as lifeless as before. Placing his face against Annie's cheek again, he kissed her cheek and spoke directly into her ear, "Wake up, sweet beauty. Wake up!"

This time the results were unmistakable. There was an initial fluttering of Annie's eyes, then she took a deep breath of air that was followed by a long groan. Slowly her eyes opened and stayed open as Stuart continued to speak her name. Then she moved her right arm, and Stuart felt all of the muscles in her body suddenly stiffen.

"Easy now," he spoke calmly, looking directly into her frightened brown eyes and wrapping his left arm around her back to support her. "You've been hurt. I don't know how bad. We're still in the water, but you'll be all right as long as you don't panic. Trust me."

Annie blinked and looked around slowly, then she coughed and whispered, "Where's my brother? Where's Garrit?"

"He's fine," said Stuart. "He's gone for help."

"Good," Annie muttered, then she lifted her head and tried to stretch her arms. "My head hurts."

"You've got a big welt on your forehead," Stuart said, releasing his grasp of her a bit. "Do you hurt anywhere else?"

"My right leg," Annie replied as she pulled it up above the water's surface. Stuart reached out and pulled her dress back to the knee, unveiling a long cut that covered much of Annie's calf.

"That's a bad one," said Stuart, "but it doesn't look like you've broken anything."

"Can we get out of here?" Annie asked. She reached out and tugged on the piece of her dress that was caught between the heavy metal beams.

"Hold on!" Stuart warned. He grabbed her hand and pulled it back from the cloth. "That little chunk of dress saved your life, and it's holding you up now. Better wait for help. I think I hear someone coming now."

From the street above them, Stuart could hear the high-pitched shouting of Garrit Harding. That was followed by the booming voice of John Spenser, one of the town's blacksmiths, whose shop was just down the street from Stuart's father's mill.

"Where are they, boy?" Spenser called out.

"We're here!" Stuart yelled out before Garrit could answer. "Help!"

The blacksmith clambered down the steep bank of the stream toward Stuart and Annie. Without stopping to take off his shoes, he waded into the deep pool, dove down, and popped up on the outside of the wreckage. Wiping the water from his face and spitting out a mouthful of water, he said, "Can she move, Stuart?"

"I think so," Stuart answered. "She's hurt her head and cut her leg, but if we can get her out of this tangle of metal, we can make it to shore. Do you think we can get her through on your side?"

John Spenser surveyed the twisted metal before him and shook his head. "Maybe," he muttered, looking up at Stuart. "There's a spot over here that might let her through. Can you get close enough over there to help?"

"Sure," answered Stuart, loosing his hold on Annie with firm instructions for her not to pull herself free yet. Treading water over to where the blacksmith was pointing, Stuart saw the slender opening between two long vertical beams. "She'll never make it through here," he said quietly.

"She will if we can pry them farther apart," Spenser replied. Then he grabbed the two bars and tried to force them apart, but they didn't budge.

"Try to use your legs to push on one side," Stuart said. "I'll dive below and see if I can do the same."

Having given the order, Stuart plunged straight down into the pool, grabbed one cold iron beam, then pressed his feet against the other beam. With Spenser positioned to do the same above him, Stuart pushed with all his might. The beams spread apart ever so slightly. Running out of breath, he rushed to the surface and gasped for air.

"You did it!" the blacksmith proclaimed with a wide smile. "I think she can make it now."

"How?" Stuart questioned, trying to slide through the gap but unable to get his shoulder through.

"She's a bit narrower than you are, Stuart, if you hadn't noticed already," the older man said knowingly. "Trust me."

"That's right," Annie said in a soft voice as Stuart turned to swim back toward her. "Trust him."

"All right, all right," Stuart said, a half grin spreading across his face. Reaching around Annie to where her dress was still securely caught by the beams, he said, "Now, we just need to get you loose and out of here." With a hard tug from Stuart, the dress ripped free and Annie suddenly dropped down lower into the stream.

"Put your arm around my neck," Stuart ordered as he wrapped one arm around her back and treaded water with the other.

Annie did as instructed, and the two of them slowly made their way across to the narrow opening where John Spenser was waiting. The voices of townspeople could be heard above them now, and the sound of Robert Anderson calling out for help with the young man who was pinned beneath the iron beam gave Stuart another surge of energy.

Helping Annie into the opening, Stuart was relieved to see two more men diving into the water to join John Spenser. "Got her?" he asked as Annie slid easily through the gap into the strong grasp of the blacksmith.

"I got her, Stuart," Spenser acknowledged, pulling her toward him and taking her arm around his neck. "Good work."

By then the two other men had come alongside of Spenser and Annie, and with their help the injured young woman was easily brought to shore. Stuart remained treading water under the tangle of iron, watching as a large man on shore gathered Annie into his arms and feeling strangely bereft as the other man carried her up the steep bank and disappeared over the rim of the street.

"You stuck in there?" John Spenser called to Stuart as he sat on the bank of the stream and began to pull off his soaking shoes. "Need some help?"

"No, no. I'm fine," Stuart replied, shaking his head. "Just—just clearing my head."

He dove down in the water for the last time and came up beyond the wreckage of metal. Slowly he made it to the bank, climbed up on the rocks, and shook off some of the cold water as he looked around. More people had appeared, some gazing down from the road, some milling beside the stream. On the opposite bank, his father still knelt beside the other victim of the accident, while at least ten men on the steep embankment did their utmost to wedge smaller iron beams under the huge I-beam that held the young man prisoner. But the whole scene suddenly seemed strangely distant, as though he were simply watching and not a part of it. He glanced back up to the place where they had carried Annie off.

"Stuart, come and help!" His father's voice shook him out of his trance.

He waded across a shallow area and climbed the embankment to join his father. Stuart hardly recognized young Walter Sorenson, his face was so pale and his eyes held so much fright.

"We gotta get him out of here fast," Robert Anderson said. "He's losing a lot of blood, and I can't seem to find where it's coming from. If the men can lift the beam, I'll pull Walter out, but you have to get his arm out."

"What if—"

"On three, men!" Robert Anderson called out to the men who stood poised with their pry bars, cutting off Stuart's protest about the possibility of Walter's arm being crushed or something even worse. "One, two, three—"

With a huge thrust of their bars, the men were able to inch the huge beam upward.

"Now!" Robert Anderson called out to Stuart, who reached quickly under the beam and supported Walter's arm as his father lifted the young man away from the beam.

Walter screamed with pain at the movement, then passed out just as his limp hand cleared the beam. Stuart could feel more than one break in the young man's forearm as he tried to tuck it up close to Walter's body. The men up the line gave a great shout of success and let the big beam come crashing back down to the ground.

But as Robert Anderson rolled Walter's body closer to his chest and stood up, Stuart could see that the celebration was premature. Another broken bone in Walter's upper arm had punctured the skin and probably an artery; this was the source of bleeding that his father had not been able to find. The blood was already soaking his father's shirt and pants.

"He's bleeding bad!" Stuart cried. Looking to the street above, he spotted his mother. "Have you seen the doctor?" he called out to her. "We need Doc Jones!"

"He's taking care of Annie Harding," Marian Anderson yelled back. "They took her to his office."

"Run and get him!" cried Robert Anderson. "Tell him someone's bleeding to death down here."

"I don't think we have time for that," said Stuart, glancing at the pool of blood that Walter Sorenson had left beneath the heavy beam. "I think we've got to try to stop it now." Taking the young man's upper arm in his hand and studying the gush of blood flowing from the wound, Stuart probed carefully above the break and suddenly felt the surge of his heartbeat. Pressing down directly on what he hoped was the broken blood vessel, he was relieved to see only a trickle of blood seep out through the wound.

"Got it!" Stuart proclaimed, hardly daring to look up into his father's face for fear of losing his grip.

"Good!" Robert Anderson exclaimed. "Now, we have to try to get him to the doc. Don't let go, son!"

Slowly, with the help of two other men, they made it up the steep embankment and began their trek to the doctor's office. With every beat of Walter's heart, Stuart became more and more conscious of the life that was being held in his own hands. He searched the pale face, one he had seen many times over the years—now so strange and unfamiliar. "Hang on," he whispered. "Don't die on me now."

The fast clip-clop of a horse and then the sight of the doctor's buggy coming to meet the rescuers was met with shouts and exclamations. The doctor pulled alongside the group, then jumped down to examine the injured young man.

"Lay him down in the back of the buggy," Doc Jones ordered as he came around them. The men lifted Walter carefully, and Stuart climbed up beside him, never relaxing his grip on the severed vessel.

"Here, let me take it," the doctor said to Stuart, reaching long, delicate fingers to where Stuart's fingers were positioned. Stuart let go, and as he did so, a big gush of blood burst from the wound. "Got it!" the doc called out as the blood trickled back down. "Good work, son. I'll take him the rest of the way. Can somebody drive this rig to my office? Fast!"

Robert Anderson leapt to the front of the buggy, took the reins in hand, and snapped the leather across the horse's back. As the buggy lurched ahead, the white-haired doctor looked back and nodded at Stuart.

Stuart Anderson watched the buggy roll down the street toward the doctor's office, then he looked down and saw the blood that covered his hands and shirt. Slowly, he held his own wrist and felt the surge of blood through his veins. And for the first time he wondered at the amazing power that flowed within his own life . . . within Walter's life . . . and then of the life that so tragically lay at the bottom of Flatwillow Creek.

Chapter 3

A Proper Thank-You

"*T*hat's one nasty-looking infection," Doc Jones said, looking up through his silver wire-rimmed glasses after treating a short but deep cut on Stuart Anderson's shoulder. "You shouldn't have waited two days to come in. Better hope that iodine does the job."

"I'm sure it will," Stuart replied with a shrug. "I didn't even notice the cut till I got home that night. I have no idea how I got it."

Doc Jones rubbed his forehead and nodded. "You had plenty else on your mind, that's for sure," he said. "Annie Harding told me what you did for her, and I saw for myself what you did for the Sorenson boy. Folks are talking around town, you know. Story goes that you saved two lives. Blind Bill says he's going to run it in the newspaper."

"Oh no," Stuart protested, shaking his head with an embarrassed grin. "That's just a big story, Doc. People need something to talk about, I guess. I didn't save either one's life. I was just there . . . just did what I could at the time."

"You sure did," the doctor agreed. He sat down on his wooden stool and rested his foot against the opposite counter, making some of the glass containers shake that were sitting on top. "And it's not a rumor, Stuart. Blind Bill interviewed me, and he's quoting me that Walter Sorenson would have bled to death shortly, and Annie Harding would have drowned if her dress had pulled free before you got her out of the water."

"You didn't say that, did you?" Stuart wished out loud, squinting his eyes.

"Sure did, because it's the truth," Doc Jones said. "You responded in an extraordinary manner, Stuart. I talked with your father about it. Did he say anything to you?"

"No. Why?"

"Just curious as to what he thought," the doctor continued. "He tells me that you're planning to go into the ministry. That your idea . . . or his?"

"Yes . . . it's mine . . . well, my folks feel pretty strongly about it too," Stuart said. "Why? What does it matter?"

"I've been wondering . . . son, you ever thought of becoming a doctor?" Doc Jones ran his left forefinger across his lips and let his words sink in as Stuart shook his head. "I'm not suggesting you *shouldn't* go into the ministry. It's a noble calling. But I'd be remiss not to say something when I feel so strongly about it. Young man, the way you handled yourself in that emergency makes me think you'd make a very fine doctor. If you're interested, I'd do all I could to help you get started."

A short gasp escaped from Stuart's lips before he could catch it, then he chuckled quietly and looked out the tall glass window to the street. "I'm sorry, Doc," he said, glancing back and smiling. "I . . . ah . . . really don't know what to say. Your . . . um . . . your offer is very kind, but I could never be a doctor."

"Why's that? You could be a minister but not a doctor?"

"I . . . ah . . . my grandfather's a minister, the best I've ever met," Stuart muttered. "I've watched him, what he does, and I've felt for a long time that's what I'm supposed to do."

"That's good . . . and honorable," the doctor said. "I respect the ministry, Stuart, don't get me wrong. But what if God gave you a gift to bring healing through medicine? You wouldn't consider that something inferior to a pastoral ministry, would you?"

"No, sir," Stuart answered firmly. "Grandpa always said that whatever God calls a person to do, obedience to His call is all that matters. But I've never even thought about being a doctor."

"So, you are willing to consider it, then?" Doc Jones leaned forward and stared straight into Stuart's eyes. "You've got the gift, Stuart. Of that, I'm absolutely sure."

"Oh, I don't know about that, Doc. I guess I could pray about it," Stuart agreed. "But I can't even imagine doing what you do. I mean, God would have to show me something pretty special."

"What if He already has?"

"What?"

"What if what you've just gone through is a sign of what you're supposed to do?" the doctor asked, wrinkling his forehead. "You wouldn't want to settle for second best, would you?"

"No, but . . . you've . . . Do you talk to everyone who comes into your office like this?" Stuart asked, then broke out laughing. "I thought I was coming in for you to fix my shoulder, and you end up spinning my life around like a top."

"No, I don't do this with everyone," the doctor replied, laughing as well. "I'm no preacher, but when I feel I should speak to someone about their soul, well, I'm not afraid to speak of spiritual things. Preachers don't have a corner on that. Still, you're the first one I've ever talked to about becoming a doctor, and I've been at this for forty years. So don't take it lightly. You will pray about it, right?"

"I said I would, and I will," Stuart answered, pulling his shirt back on and buttoning it. "But I think you've given me enough to pray about for today . . . and tomorrow."

"By the way, did you stop by and see Annie Harding?" Doc Jones asked. He stood up and folded away the leftover gauze and tape.

"No, why?" Stuart asked, glancing up quickly from the button he was working on.

Doc Jones smiled and said, "Because she told me she was hoping you'd drop by her house. I think she'd like to thank you for all you did. She said she didn't get much of a chance after she was lifted out of the water. I'd recommend you head right on over there. You never want to keep a pretty young lady waiting, you know."

Stuart pulled his suspenders up over his shoulders, shook his head, and walked toward the door. "You're just full of advice, aren't you?"

"Sure am," Doc Jones answered. "Make sure your mother washes that cut out with salt tonight, you hear. It's going to burn a bit, but you have to do it."

"Yes, sir," Stuart replied. Then he pushed the wooden door open, walked quickly through the doctor's small front office, stepped out onto the sidewalk, and took a deep breath. "I can't believe that fellow," he whispered, squinting through the bright summer sunshine. "Me, a doctor . . ."

"Who you talking to?"

The high-pitched voice behind Stuart made him jump. Glancing around, he smiled at Garrit Harding, who was sitting on his wooden wagon in front of the doctor's office. "Just mumbling to myself," replied Stuart. "What're you doing?"

"Restin', as you can see," the white-haired boy said. "Mother sent me to get some sugar, but I'm tuckered out. Did your mother ever make you go to the store for her?"

"Sure. All the time," Stuart replied. "But we lived closer to the store. How's your sister doing?"

"Good," Garrit replied, scratching his ear and looking up at Stuart. "She keeps telling people that she's hoping you'll stop by so she can thank you proper. Want to come home with me and get it over with?"

"No, I don't think so," said Stuart, looking back down the street toward his father's mill. "My dad's probably expecting me back at work. You know how that goes."

"Yep," answered Garrit seriously, then he slowly stood up from his wagon and stretched. "My ma's expecting me with the sugar, so I better get on home, too. But Annie's sure gonna be disappointed when I tell her I saw you, but you couldn't come."

Stuart studied the young boy's look. "You really think she'll be disappointed?"

Garrit simply nodded and puckered his lips together.

"Why?"

"I already told you—she wants to thank you proper." Garrit picked up the handle of the wagon and started down the street toward his house. Then, in a voice that Stuart could barely hear, he added, "'Sides, I think she likes you."

"What?" Stuart called out, turning around and following the boy as he continued plodding down the sidewalk. "Garrit, what did you say?"

"I said I think she likes you," Garrit repeated nonchalantly. "Whenever she took me down to the stream, she'd always sneak back up to the street and stand there staring toward where you work. It took me a while to figure out what she was so interested in, but I spotted you one day and then I knew."

"Did you ask her about it?" Stuart pried as he walked alongside Garrit.

"Sure."

"What did she say?"

"Are you coming to my house now?" asked Garrit, stopping under a shady oak tree. "'Cause if you are, I was wondering if you might like to pull me in the wagon."

"I guess I can walk you there," Stuart conceded, reaching for the handle of the wagon as Garrit hopped in. "So, what did she say?"

"Nothing. She didn't need to."

"Why's that?"

"'Cause she got all red-faced, and she didn't never deny it," Garrit said with a triumphant grin. "Whatcha think 'bout that?"

Stuart shrugged his shoulders. "I don't know," he replied, glancing forward and lifting the wheels down from the curb. "Which way is closer?" he asked the boy as they crossed the street.

Garrit pointed right, then he said, "Did you know that Annie saved my life under the bridge? Like you saved her."

"No," Stuart replied, glancing back at Garrit. "What happened?"

"After Annie heard the bridge crack, she ran over and was trying to pull me out of the water when it all came down on us," Garrit said. "She pushed me out of the way, but then all that metal stuff came crashing down on her and pulled her under."

"But you were buried as well."

"Yeah, the wood fell down on me," Garrit replied. "That hurt. But I wasn't in the water. I wouldn't have made it. Guess Annie's a hero, too."

Stuart nodded and turned the wagon at the next street corner. "You're probably right," he said, looking toward a large white wooden house bordered by colorful flowerbeds.

"That's my house," Garrit stated. "Look, Annie's at the front door."

"Oh no," Stuart whispered. He was about to turn and walk away, but then he noticed that Annie had stepped back from the door.

"Now you gotta come in," Garrit said with a big grin as Stuart pulled on the wagon and walked toward the house. "She saw you."

Stuart didn't say another word until he stopped the wagon in front of the Harding house, but he kept his eyes focused on the front door.

Garrit had jumped out of the wagon with his bag of sugar before Stuart had even stopped.

"Follow me," Garrit called back, his short legs marching up the concrete steps, then he pulled the front screen door open.

"Don't you think I should knock or something?" Stuart asked, reluctantly taking his first step up toward the door.

"No!" Garrit said and giggled, stepping into the screened-in front porch as Stuart came through the door. "Annie saw you and probably went to comb her hair or something dumb."

"Shouldn't we let your mother know I'm here?" Stuart asked, pausing at the door.

"Mother's gone to my grandma's for a while," Garrit replied, ducking around the corner into the living room. Then he called out, "Annie! Stuart Anderson is here. Where're you hiding?"

"I'm not hiding anywhere," Annie's voice echoed out from the dining room where she had just placed a plate of sugar cookies on the table. "And keep your voice down, Garrit. Everybody on our street can hear you."

Stuart followed Garrit at a distance as the youngster swept through the dining room and quickly scooped up a handful of the white cookies.

"Don't take them all, you piggy!" Annie scolded, slapping Garrit's hand. Then she turned as Stuart walked through the doorway into the dining room. "We have company."

"There's lots more in the kitchen," Garrit said without remorse, but Annie wasn't listening.

"Miss Harding, forgive my manners for coming in without knocking. How are you?" Stuart asked, stopping as he reached the table, grinning from ear to ear. "You look much better today than when I last saw you."

Annie's blush brightened her smile. The angry welt that had marked her forehead was now only a scratch, and her brown eyes were sparkling. "I feel much better, thanks to you," she said quietly, holding up the plate and letting Stuart pull out a couple of cookies. "I'm delighted that you stopped by, even if it was thanks only to my brother. I never had a chance to thank you for . . . for saving my life."

"You saved *my* life," Garrit blurted out toward Annie, cookie crumbs flying from his mouth.

"Garrit!" Annie said sweetly but firmly, taking him by the arm and shoving him toward the living room door. "It's time for you to go play outside now." She lowered her voice. "And don't come in until I say so or . . . or I'll tell Father what really happened to the window in the back door."

Garrit looked back but didn't protest, and it was clear to Stuart that Annie had Garrit right where she wanted him. As the boy departed from the living room, Annie turned toward Stuart.

"I'm sorry," she said. "He's a nice little boy but a bit of a pest. Now, please come have a seat."

She led him into the living room and took a seat on the davenport, while Stuart gravitated toward a portly overstuffed chair across from her. Seeing the pipe on its side in the ashtray, Stuart assumed he was sitting in Annie's father's chair.

"For two days I've been thinking about what I'd say to you when I had the chance," Annie said, staring into Stuart's dark eyes. "And I still don't know what to say . . . how to . . . thank you. I was so sure that I was dead when those iron beams began to fall . . . then the water. I have no idea how my dress ever got caught or how I ended up in the deep part of the stream."

Annie paused, tilting her head back and sighing. The afternoon sun shone brightly through the window, highlighting a few pale gold tendrils that had escaped her pinned-up locks and glowed softly against her white blouse.

"Did you think I was dead when you found me?" asked Annie, looking at Stuart again.

"I . . . ah . . . I did at first," Stuart said haltingly. His first sight of that delicate face had been powerfully etched in his mind. "You were so pale, and I couldn't tell if you were breathing. Then I found your pulse, so I knew you were alive. When I heard you breathe, I couldn't help but shout out to my father that you were alive."

Stuart noticed Annie's lip tremble, then a tear slid down her cheek, and he suddenly choked up as well. He was totally unprepared for the rush of emotions that flooded his heart. For a moment, Stuart rubbed his forehead and tried to regain his composure. Annie pulled a white cotton handkerchief from a pocket and dabbed her eyes, looking a bit flustered as well.

"I do apologize for the tears." Annie spoke softly. "I've been more . . . well . . . emotional since the accident, and I seem to cry easily."

"No, no, don't apologize," replied Stuart, marveling at how deeply her tears had affected him. "Since I saw Andrew Sorenson trapped beneath his traction engine at the bottom of Flatwillow Creek, I find myself getting angry easily. I hear somebody complaining about how bad they've got it, and I want to tell them they should think about Walter's father."

Annie nodded. "I understand, and I'm glad you understand. Most people don't. Do you know how Walter is, by the way? I heard you saved his life as well."

"Please," Stuart said, shutting his eyes and shaking his head, "I only helped him and you for a few seconds. I certainly didn't save anyone's life, even if Doc Jones blabs around that I did. Walter's arm was terribly shattered. The doc said he almost amputated . . . and he's still not sure that Walter will be able to use the arm again."

"That's terrible," Annie said, then she took a deep breath. "Poor Walter. He lost his father, and now maybe his arm. . . ."

"If that big beam had fallen a couple inches over," Stuart said, "Walter would have lost even more. I've talked to him several times at the mill; he's a tough kid. I'll bet he does learn to use that arm again."

"Let's hope it's so," Annie said. She paused, straightening the cameo that hung by a gold chain around her neck, then she gave him a little smile. "Do you mind if I ask you something?"

"About what?" Stuart asked, fidgeting in his chair for the first time.

"About when you called my name when we were in the water," Annie continued. "Do you remember that?"

"Yes," replied Stuart. "I . . . ah . . . called your name several times before you woke up. I'm surprised you remember."

"It was like . . . I was caught in a dark, dark dream," said Annie, placing long slender fingers over her narrow red lips. "I couldn't get out, and I was so cold, but I heard someone calling . . . and calling . . . at first far away . . . then closer and closer. So close that I thought your cheek was right against mine and you were speaking straight into my ear. Isn't that strange?"

Stuart nodded at first, but then shook his head. "No," he said, his face flushing, "I did do that. Just as you said."

Annie looked down with a little smile on her face. Stuart couldn't tell whether she was enjoying his embarrassment or simply feeling embarrassed herself. "Your cheek was warm," she said softly. "It felt good when I was so cold." Then she looked up, and Stuart found himself gazing into her warm brown eyes. "I was also wondering if you said . . . what I thought you said."

"Oops," Stuart gasped, then he covered his forehead with his hand and felt his face warming to flame red. "I did say it," he spoke quietly.

"Hmmm," Annie said. "So I wasn't dreaming."

"No," Stuart said behind his hand. "That was just me."

"I've been wondering and wondering about it . . . whether you said it, whether I dreamed it," Annie said slowly. "And if you said it, I've been wondering if you'd dare tell me whether you meant what you said. No one's ever said anything like that to me before."

"Oh dear," Stuart groaned, hanging his head and covering his forehead again.

"I'm sorry if I've embarrassed you," said Annie with a little giggle. "And you don't need to answer. I just had to find out if . . . if it really happened."

Stuart broke out laughing and finally said, "Well, be assured that I said those words, and if you must know . . . I did mean them."

Annie had stopped laughing and now looked intently into Stuart's dark eyes. He stared back. For a moment neither one breathed.

Then, out on the front sidewalk, Garrit's voice broke the trance. "Guess who's in the house with Annie?"

"It's my mother!" Annie cried, jumping up from the davenport and peeking out the living room window.

Stuart jumped up, as well, unsure as to why he did or what he should be doing.

"Quick!" Annie exclaimed, turning around to face Stuart. "As I said, I really did want to give you a proper thank-you. And, well, I'm only returning what you gave me."

With that she took his face into her hands, kissed him right on the lips, and whispered in his ear, "Thank you, Mr. Anderson."

Chapter 4

Playing Hardball

"So you won't be coming home after church?" Marian Anderson asked, glancing over at her son. Then she turned back toward the hallway mirror and stuck another long pin into her black Sunday hat. "I wish you would have told me sooner. I baked a whole chicken, thinking you'd be here. Why didn't you say something?"

"I'm sorry," Stuart replied as his father came down the hallway past his mother, then joined Stuart in the entryway of their house. "I should have told you. It sort of . . . came up at the last minute and—"

"You were too embarrassed to tell your mother," Robert Anderson broke in. He reached out and quickly straightened Stuart's tie. "What happened when you stopped over to Miss Annie Harding's house on Wednesday, anyway? You've been acting funny ever since."

"Nothing happened!" Stuart blurted out, throwing up his hands in mock defense. "How many times do I have to say that? The doc said she'd told him that she was hoping I'd stop by so she could thank me for what I'd done. I did save her life, by the way. I bumped into her little brother on the street, went over to the house with him, and Annie and I talked about what happened. That's it."

"And Mrs. Harding suggested the picnic?" his mother asked. She backed away from the mirror and joined the men as they stepped out the front door.

"No, it was Annie's idea, but her mother agreed to it," answered Stuart as he walked down the sidewalk to the street. "What a beautiful morning to walk to church, eh?"

"Just . . . the two of you?" Robert Anderson asked slyly.

Stuart shook his head and said, "It's only a picnic, and as far as I know, it's *just* the two of us, but if you're so interested in seeing what goes on, you're welcome to sack up that chicken and join us in the park. Maybe we should invite her folks along as well. It's about time we all got to know one another," he added, waving his arms for exaggerated emphasis.

They all laughed and turned to walk down the street toward the church. The large white structure with its tall wooden spire was only two blocks from their house, and the three of them had always walked there. A cool morning breeze in the elm leaves overhead signaled the subtle shift toward fall, but the summer heat promised to have its way by the afternoon.

"I actually don't know the Hardings very well," Marian Anderson said, walking beside her husband and holding his arm. "It must be about a year ago now that they moved here. Dinah Harding and I have worked together at church a couple of times. She's so quiet . . . and pretty . . . and seems nice. Keeps to herself most of the time."

"I haven't had many opportunities to get to know her father, either," Robert said. "They say he runs his construction crew like it's his own little army. You have to have pretty thick skin to work for him, I hear. But he's a good builder, and they say he's honest to a fault. Was he home when you were there?"

Stuart looked back at his father and shook his head. "Just her mother," he replied. "And she didn't say much. I thought she seemed sort of nervous . . . like she was uncomfortable with my being there. So I didn't stay long."

"I wonder if they like living in a small town?" Marian wondered out loud. "Didn't they move here from Minneapolis? Must have been quite a change for them."

Just as the church bells began to ring, Stuart glanced back down the street and waved to a family who were just coming out of their house. "Still seems strange to see the Hendersons without David."

"It's been a long summer for you without him, hasn't it?" Marian said to Stuart. "Have they heard from him lately?"

"I don't think so. David's making pretty good money with the railroad out West, but they never know where he is. Last I heard he was in Missoula, Montana, wherever that is."

"Doesn't look like you'll see him at all this summer," Robert said as they crossed the street. "How long's it been?"

"Well, since I left for college last fall," Stuart answered. "But I didn't realize how much I missed him until I came home for the summer. Seems like there's nothing to do anymore without him."

"I felt that way when your uncle Willy moved out to western Minnesota," his father said. "He and I did everything together, just like you and David. But . . . well, I did get over it, and he managed to turn some prairie sod into a beautiful farm without me." He glanced pensively up toward the steeple that soared overhead. "That's just the way life is, I guess. It just keeps changing, and we have to keep changing, too. . . ."

As they approached the church, they greeted several families who were also ambling in the same direction, clearly in no hurry to trade the fresh morning breeze for the stale air inside the church. The tall, beautiful stained-glass windows were very efficient at stopping any movement of fresh air from the outside.

Stuart and his parents climbed the thick concrete steps, passed through the heavy wooden doors, and entered the spacious sanctuary, which looked about half full. Hat in hand, Stuart followed his mother and father as they walked down the center aisle and took their seats in a wooden pew toward the back. Several pews ahead of them, Stuart spotted the Harding family. Peering around the person in front of him, he could see Annie sitting next to her mother. He took a deep breath, rubbed his hands together, and noticed they were sweaty.

Stuart's attention was diverted from Annie Harding, however, when the pastor stepped out from behind the choir loft door and took his seat next to the pulpit. The Reverend Alexander Mackenzie had become an enigma to Stuart, and his appearance on the platform regularly stirred a litany of uncomfortable questions and feelings.

Tall and handsome, with polished manners and a marvelous speaking voice, the forty-year-old minister seemed the picture of what a congregation desired in a pastor. His sermons were pithy and brief, his visitations solicitous, and his tiny, pale wife kept a beautiful house and ran the Sunday school efficiently. Yet persistent rumors tarnished the pastor's image, even though no one had ever come forward with specific allegations. For several years, Stuart had heard whispers linking the pastor with one woman or another around town.

Stuart and his parents almost never talked about this issue, but he suspected it worried them more than they cared to admit. While not enthusiastic supporters of the pastor, they also insisted that it was unfair to judge or criticize anyone on hearsay. If no witness came forward, they argued, why should they believe the stories? Many parishioners evidently agreed with them, but that had not stopped the rumors nor the gradual decline in church attendance.

Stuart's own questions about the pastor had begun two years before, during a special Bible class the pastor held for the church's high school seniors. It had seemed to Stuart that Reverend Mackenzie focused almost all of his time and attention upon the five girls in the class, and occasionally he would lay a hand on a girl's arm or shoulder in a way that made Stuart uncomfortable. Somehow the gestures seemed inappropriate, although Stuart had to admit there was nothing that could be outwardly construed as anything but fatherly.

Having been away at college and under his grandfather's ministry for the school year, Stuart had returned to his home church with even more questions. Compared to the life and preaching of his grandfather, the Reverend Mackenzie's seemed shallow and uncaring. Stuart saw little of the intense love and compassion that his grandfather brought to his congregation, but he had also wondered if that might be something that came with maturity in the ministry. In any case, church attendance during the summer months had become strictly a matter of duty for Stuart.

Having nodded off several times during the pastor's message, Stuart was relieved when the last "Amen" was spoken and the benediction pronounced. He filed out of the pew behind his parents and lingered in the back of the sanctuary, doing his best to kill time. The plan was for Stuart and Annie to meet at her house and then go to the city park for their picnic. He wanted to make sure the Hardings arrived home before he got there.

Annie smiled and nodded at Stuart as she went by with her family, but much to Stuart's relief, she did not stop to talk. The last thing he wanted was to have his father and mother watching him with her. Now the Harding family was at the door, greeting the pastor, and Stuart noticed idly that the usually stoic Mrs. Harding was laughing about something. *That's odd*, he thought. *I've never seen her even smile before.*

"We'll see you later, son." Robert Anderson broke into Stuart's thoughts with a playful nudge. "Don't have too much fun," he joked.

After his parents left the church, Stuart stood and talked with a few friends before heading out alone to the Hardings'. It was only five blocks from the church in the opposite direction from his house, but the walk seemed much longer than that. The closer he got, the more his heart began to pound and the sweat began to pour.

As he rounded the last corner and the Harding house came into view, Stuart was surprised to see a stylish black mare hitched to a shiny new black buggy in front of the house. He was even more surprised when he saw Arthur Simpson stride from the house with a picnic basket on his arm. Stuart had met the banker's son only once since coming home from college, and that was merely in passing, but he recognized him instantly. Simpson was tall and muscular, with a handsome square face. His brown hair was streaked with blond, fashionably clipped, his light wool trousers neatly pressed, his hat pushed back at a cocky angle on his head. He lifted the heavy basket into the buggy as if it weighed nothing at all.

Then the front door opened and Annie emerged with a blanket in her arms. Spotting Stuart, she smiled and waved, then walked down the sidewalk and stood by the buggy as he approached. She had changed from her pink Sunday dress into a simple white blouse with balloon sleeves, dark blue skirt, and a straw hat with a wide blue ribbon. Stuart quickly pulled off his suit coat when he saw that Simpson wasn't wearing one, but he didn't see any graceful way to shed his stiffly starched collar.

"Mr. Anderson," Annie called out, hugging her blanket, "I'm so glad you could come. Isn't it a perfect day for a picnic?"

"Couldn't be better," said Stuart, still hoping that what he was seeing wasn't the way things really were. "Should I have gone home and changed clothes? It looks—"

"No, no," replied Annie. "You're fine. Mother would never let me wear my best dress on a picnic, and Arthur wears a stiff old suit all week at the bank, so he can't wait to get rid of his coat and collar. You have met Arthur Simpson, haven't you?"

Stuart turned toward Arthur Simpson and shook hands as graciously as he could manage. "Yes, we met earlier this summer, but I haven't seen you much since then. I guess you spend most of your time down at the bank."

Simpson nodded in return. "Seems like all my time is spent there these days—no rest for the weary, you know. But I do see you sometimes from my window; it looks out over your father's mill. It must be very hard work."

"It is," Stuart replied, rubbing the thick calluses that had built up on his hands over the summer weeks. "But it helps pay for college, if twenty-two cents an hour makes a difference. Besides, my father needs the help."

"So," Arthur said, taking the fluffy blanket from Annie and stuffing it in the back of the buggy with the picnic basket, "Annie tells me she asked you to join us today."

Stuart glanced quickly at Annie, who was still smiling, then replied, "That's right. But I don't want to get in your way if—"

"It's fine with me," the young banker spoke quickly, looking up at Stuart through narrowed eyes, then glancing over at Annie with a smile. "From what I've heard, I owe you a great deal of gratitude for saving my Annie's life. A picnic is certainly a small way to say thanks."

"I've already been thanked very amply," Stuart replied, looking straight at Annie, who blushed. "But I do appreciate the chance to go along on the picnic. Shall we go?" With that he offered his hand to Annie and helped her up into the buggy before Simpson could make it around to the front. Then Stuart walked around the buggy and stepped up, sitting on the right side of Annie while Arthur sat on her left and took the horse's reins in hand. The gleaming new rig barely rattled as the mare took off at a smooth gait in the direction of the city park.

To Stuart's surprise, the talk rarely lagged on the way to the park. Arthur Simpson proved a fluent and entertaining conversationalist, and he included Stuart by asking questions and soliciting opinions. Only as they turned in to their destination did Stuart realize that somehow, in his undeniably charming way, Arthur had managed to turn all discussion back to himself—his new mare and buggy, his responsible position at the bank, his former life in Chicago. *That's an impressive talent,* Stuart found himself musing, *to talk about yourself and yet somehow make people think you have an interest in them.*

The small city park was situated along the same stream where the accident had taken place, but nearly a mile north of the collapsed bridge. It boasted picnic tables, swings, a teeter-totter, and an immaculately maintained ball field, now enjoying a well-deserved Sunday rest. Several large oak trees clustered around the bank of Flatwillow Creek, which was wider and shallower here.

When they arrived at the park, Simpson pulled the buggy up as close as he could to a picnic table that nestled under a gnarly old burr oak tree. This time it was his hand that helped Annie down from the buggy. Stuart hefted the picnic basket from the back and carried it to the table while Annie covered it with the blanket.

"Why don't the two of you take a little walk while I get everything ready," Annie said as she opened the picnic basket and carefully lifted out a glass pitcher of cold tea. "It's very pretty down on the sandy point," she continued, "but you'll have to pull off your shoes."

Stuart really didn't want to walk anywhere with Arthur Simpson, let alone take off his Sunday shoes, but as the guest he didn't feel he could say no. Simpson finished taking care of his horse, then turned toward them.

"Yes, a walk would be nice," he said to Annie, "but I think I'll pass on the point until later . . . when you come with me and show me why you like it so well."

Annie smiled at him and went back to her work on the picnic table. Simpson marched down a thin worn path that led toward the stream, and Stuart followed. The loose limestone rocks in the pathway made it a bit of a tricky walk. Both young men had to watch their footwork closely.

When they reached the cool trout stream, Simpson jumped from one large boulder to the next until he was nearly halfway across. Finding a big flat stone that he seemed to like, he sat down and leaned back with his arms against the rock. Stuart followed suit and picked a rock next to the young banker and sat down very carefully, making sure he didn't soil his dress pants.

"That's a nice buggy you've got there," Stuart said, not quite sure where to start a conversation with Simpson. "Did you think about buying an automobile instead?"

"No, not yet," Arthur answered. "They're just too expensive—

couldn't see paying over fifteen hundred dollars when I could get a rig like this for so much less. Besides, the roads are too rough around here; they'd tear an automobile apart. Did you ever ride in one?"

Stuart nodded. "A friend at the university, his father had one. It shook and rattled and clattered and spit smoke and smelled awful. It was great fun."

"They are fun," Arthur agreed with an infectious grin. "My father was going to buy one until he decided to move here from Chicago. And I'm sure we'll have one before long. Why, wait a couple years and we'll be seeing automobiles everywhere, even here. Peace and prosperity, as President McKinley says, will change even this little whistle-stop of a town."

"We're hardly a whistle-stop," Stuart retorted. "We have nearly a thousand people living here in Bradford ... and we are the county seat."

Simpson raised his eyebrows. "So you still like it here after living in Minneapolis?"

"Oh, I don't care so much for the big city."

"Lots of people do," Arthur said, "myself among them. Why, people are flocking to the cities these days. Back in Chicago we topped a million in 1900. The way the immigrants are pouring in, who knows how high it'll get this year. The streets are teeming. There's always something to do, always money to be made. What a town!"

"So why'd you leave?"

Arthur Simpson's grin faded, and he shook his head. "It wasn't my choice, believe me," he said. "But at least I have my Annie here. You really didn't know about Annie and me, did you?"

"What?" asked Stuart, having heard him clearly but wondering if he also understood the pointed tone that accompanied it.

"I said that you must not have known about Annie and me before you came over to her house today," said Arthur. "You looked surprised ... like you weren't expecting company."

Stuart smiled and nodded. "No, I didn't know. But tell me, what is it that you want me to know?"

"Just that Annie and I have been seeing each other for the past five months," Simpson declared, sitting forward and leaning toward Stuart. "And I'm expecting that we'll be engaged by Christmas."

Rubbing his hand across his forehead, Stuart nodded, and all that came out was, "Hmmm." Then he looked back up the knoll at Annie, who remained busy attending to the food. Turning back to Arthur, he gathered his thoughts. "No, I didn't realize you two were so serious. And I . . . ah . . . didn't mean to step in the way, but I really didn't know. And you plan to get engaged during her senior year?"

"Why not?" Arthur shot back. "Most girls her age are already married."

"I just wondered," Stuart said. "Seems like you'd want to wait till she graduates, but that's your business."

"That's right," said Simpson, looking back at Annie. "And I'm not waiting that long. I want to marry her the minute she graduates."

"And she knows how serious you are?" Stuart asked.

"You're talking about my business again," Simpson said. "Why are you so interested, anyway? You got lucky and became her hero, but that doesn't mean she'd be sweet on you."

"That's true," Stuart replied, trying to piece together what Arthur Simpson was saying with the signals he thought he had received from Annie just the other day. "And I didn't say anything about her being interested in me. We just came together in a strange way, and . . . I . . . well, you can't blame me for being interested, can you? She's a beautiful girl. You're very fortunate, you know."

Arthur Simpson flashed a wide smile and nodded. "I certainly do," he said, "and she's one catch I won't let get away from me."

"So, she *is* as serious about your relationship as you are," Stuart repeated, wondering what response he might get a second time around.

"I don't care much for your meddling, Anderson," the young banker said quietly, leaning down and scooping some of the cool water into his hand. Then he reached up and carefully splashed the water on his forehead, sighing at the relief from the summer heat. "But I have good reason to believe she's falling in love with me, as I already have with her. Does that answer your question?"

Stuart nodded, although he still had doubts.

"Good," Simpson concluded. "So then, we have an understanding, correct?"

"Which is what?" asked Stuart, raising his eyebrows.

"That you'll stay away from my Annie from now on," Simpson said, his grin belying his serious tone.

Stuart chuckled and shook his head, then he leaned toward Simpson and said, "I'm not out to steal your girl, Mr. Simpson. And she asked me to come on this picnic, so I'm her guest. And I suggest you cut out the threats. Unless you have the paper work to show me, Annie isn't your property."

"I'll say this to you once, Stuart Anderson," Simpson said, squinting his eyes against the bright sunlight and squeezing his hands together tightly. "You try anything with Annie, and I'll make you pay. I mean it. I was a boxer in college."

"Oh boy," Stuart replied, chuckling and shaking his head again. Then he reached his right hand down into the water. "Mr. Simpson," he said evenly, "I've got something for you to remember as well."

"What's that?" asked Simpson, flashing another wide grin.

"I want you to remember that I don't like it when you try to play hardball with me, especially when I haven't done anything to warrant it," Stuart said, mimicking the banker's smile. "And since you're obviously feeling some heat here, perhaps you'd like to cool down a little more." That said, Stuart jerked his hand up and soaked Simpson's face with a large handful of the cold stream water. Then he jumped up and said, "I think I'll go see how Annie's doing. Care to join me, Mr. Simpson?"

Chapter 5

Someone Who Cares

"Annie, why do you think Grandma was such a grouch today?" Garrit Harding skipped down the sidewalk ahead of his sister, who was pulling his wooden wagon. One of his suspenders had slipped off his shoulder, but he didn't seem to mind. Then he stopped to kick a rock ahead of them and said, "I'm glad we don't have to haul food to her every day."

"Me too," Annie replied. "I'm not sure why she gets so grumpy some days. One of the reasons we moved here was to make sure Grandma was well cared for after Grandfather died, but I don't think she feels she needs all the help that Mother wants to provide. I wish they'd talk about it, but . . . they never will."

"Why?" asked Garrit, turning and looking up at Annie. "Could you pull me in the wagon? I'm getting—"

"You're getting nothing, buster," Annie broke in, shaking her head. "You are so lazy, I can't believe it. You conned Stuart Anderson into pulling you the other day, didn't you?"

Garrit smiled and rubbed his ear. "So why won't Mother and Grandma talk about it?"

"Because they never talk over anything important," Annie answered. "They just . . . kind of . . . get along." She stared off into the distance. "Neither one ruffles the other's feathers, even when something's really bothering them. So they pretend they're happy, but then take their frustrations out on somebody else."

"Like us," Garrit commented. "I think I'll tell Mother she should stop pretending."

"I wouldn't if I were you," Annie said.

"Why? You said—"

"I didn't say anything," Annie warned with a smile. "I've tried to talk to Mother about it, but it only seemed to make things worse. She said that Grandma Harding is Father's mother and that she could never speak to her mother-in-law like I said she should. I finally gave up and figured that the two of them have to work out their problems without my help."

"So Grandma keeps being grouchy with us until then?" asked Garrit.

"She's not always grouchy, Garrit," Annie said. "You know that. I'll admit that today was an especially bad day, but maybe something else is upsetting Grandma that we don't know about."

"I think next time we should ask her," said Garrit.

"You can try if you'd like," Annie offered. "I'm afraid that Granny would get upset with me if I tried to bring it up. But she might talk to you. She likes you."

"She likes you, too, Annie," Garrit objected as they turned the last corner before their house. "Grandma likes you."

"I was just teasing," Annie said with a laugh. "Plus, you're just a child, and little children can get away with saying anything."

Garrit turned around and squinted at his sister. "I am not a little—"

"Who's that coming out of our house?" Annie asked, pointing ahead to their front screen door. She and Garrit stopped in the shadow of the large elm tree they were passing and watched as a tall man emerged.

"Oh no!" Garrit said, jumping behind the trunk of the tree and motioning for Annie to join him. "That's Reverend Mackenzie."

"What did you do now?" Annie asked, refusing to follow him. "I'm not covering for you, Garrit."

"I got in trouble in Sunday school," confessed Garrit. "I'll bet Mrs. Redding talked to him, and now he's told Mother. Oh, I'm in trouble. . . ."

"Come on, he's heading down the street the other way," Annie said, stepping out of the shade and continuing down the sidewalk. "By the way, you'd be smarter to tell Mother first. She's going to be really mad if that's why he came here. I'll bet she's already pulling out the razor strap."

"Annie, you go in and find out for me," Garrit pleaded, running up behind her and grabbing her arm. "I'll go hide in my tree house. You can come and get me from the backyard when it's safe."

"You big chicken," Annie teased, taking his arm and dragging him toward the house. "It's time you learned to take your medicine like a man."

"No, you gotta help me, Annie," Garrit begged. "Please." The moment she let go of his arm, he took off running up their lawn as fast as his short legs could carry him.

Annie laughed and shook her head as Garrit disappeared around the corner of the house. Turning onto their sidewalk, she glanced down the street and noticed that Pastor Mackenzie was knocking on the door at the Sadler house. *Strange that he doesn't know they're out of town. Mrs. Sadler told everyone in the county that they're going to visit relatives in St. Louis*, she thought. *With every window in the house shut and the front door closed, you'd think he'd notice that no one's home.*

Pulling open the screen door and stepping into the house, Annie walked quietly through the entryway and stopped to listen for her mother. The soft rustle of papers in the living room drew Annie around the corner, and there she found her mother seated at the piano, looking through a small stack of sheet music.

"Mother," Annie asked, "are you all right?"

Dinah Harding gave a little jump, then turned around slowly and nodded. "I was fine until you scared me half out of my wits," she spoke softly, managing a slight smile. Her light brown hair was braided tightly and tucked in a bun at the back of her head. "How many times do I have to tell you not to sneak up on me? But why do you ask, anyway? Do I look sick?"

"No, you look fine," Annie said. "But you've barely touched the piano since we moved here, and now you're looking through your music." She walked over to sit beside her mother. "You used to play all the time. And I didn't sneak up. Didn't you hear the screen door squeak when I came in?"

Her mother shook her head. "I guess I was ... lost in thought. I didn't hear a thing, and I wasn't expecting you home for a while. Where's your brother?"

"Last I saw him, he was heading for the backyard on a dead run,"

Annie replied, moving to the chair next to the piano bench. "Grandma was on the warpath, so we didn't stay long."

"What was bothering her today?" Mrs. Harding asked, looking down at the music and continuing to finger through the dog-eared sheets.

"I'm not sure. Everything, I guess," said Annie. She ran her long slender fingers along the edge of the piano and studied her mother's soft brown eyes as they moved from page to page. "What are you looking for?"

"Just an old hymn arrangement that's hiding somewhere in this pile," her mother replied, not looking up. "Did she like the lunch?"

"I hope so, but it didn't sound like it," Annie answered. "She went into her 'I was getting along just fine before you moved here' speech. I wish you'd talk with her. Even Garrit doesn't want to go see her anymore."

"I told you before, Annie," said Dinah. "If you want somebody to talk with her, try your father. She's his mother, not mine." She looked up at Annie as if seeing her for the first time. "Where's your brother?" she repeated.

Annie shook her head and chuckled to herself, then she said, "He went to the magen-megan and vilta may da butter avachhaven."

"Where?" her mother repeated, wrinkling her forehead. "I thought you said—"

"You haven't heard a word I've said, have you?" Annie said with a laugh. "I already told you that Garrit's in the backyard. What's spinning around in your head, anyway?"

"Nothing much. I just can't find the music I'm looking for."

"I saw Pastor Mackenzie coming out of the house. What was he doing here?" asked Annie.

Her mother glanced up quickly and let the stack of sheet music drop into her lap. "He ... um ... just stopped by to ..." she paused, shaking her head, "to ... he heard that I play the piano, and he wondered if I'd be willing to play in church ... occasionally. At least over the next few months while Mrs. Higgins has her baby."

"And you said yes?" Annie asked, her brown eyes widening.

"What else could I say?" her mother returned. "I suppose I could have said that I'm sorry they have no one else to replace her, but I'm far too busy."

"This is marvelous!" exclaimed Annie, reaching out and taking her mother's hand. "You're much better at the piano than Mrs. Higgins or anyone else I've heard play at the church. I can hardly wait to see how surprised people will be."

"If I don't get practicing soon, you'll be surprised at how dreadful everyone thinks I sound," Dinah replied with a gentle nod of her head. "There's more rust on these fingers than can be taken off in a day."

"You'll do fine, Mother," Annie said. "I'll bet that Father—"

"You let me tell him myself," her mother interrupted. "Don't you be telling your brother, either. I want to break the news to your father at the right time, and your brother's likely to blurt it out."

Annie stared at her mother. "So you don't think that Father's going to be happy about this."

Dinah Harding shook her head solemnly. "I know he's not going to like it—at all. He's probably going to be angry with me."

"Why?"

Her mother shrugged and looked down at the pile of music in her lap. "Why . . . does he get angry about almost everything? I'm not telling you something new, Annie. You take your share of it."

"I know but . . . this is for church," Annie reasoned. "How can that make him mad?"

"Did you ever hear me play in the church in Minneapolis?" her mother asked.

"No."

"Your father refused to let me," Dinah said, glancing up at Annie.

"Why?"

"He said that my place is in the home and that if they really wanted my services they would have offered to pay me," her mother replied. "This time, though, I didn't make the same mistake that I made before."

"What's that?"

"This time I didn't ask your father," her mother replied firmly. "That will make him angry, too, but if I've given my word, he won't ask me to change it."

"Keeping promises is really important to him, isn't it?" Annie asked.

"Most of them, yes," Dinah Harding said, turning and looking out the window with a distant expression.

Annie sat quietly, still holding her mother's hand, knowing that further conversation about her father was unlikely, yet understanding something of what her mother was implying. Annie often found herself wondering if her father loved her, if he even liked her. It was easy to imagine that her mother struggled with the same thoughts.

"Has . . . has father always been so . . . so angry?" Annie spoke quietly.

Her mother took a deep breath, then she turned on the bench and looked at Annie. "No," she said finally. "When your father decided to start his own business, that's when I noticed the change. You were about three years old at the time, and of course Garrit wasn't here yet. But we were really struggling in those days, and we had to borrow some money from my parents. Anyway, your father decided that he needed to work much harder if he was going to provide for a family. So he did just that. For the next couple of years, you never saw him at all except on Sundays. He was gone before you woke up in the morning, and you were asleep before he got home again."

"Seems like he hasn't slowed down much," Annie said.

"Not much," Dinah replied, shaking her head and giving Annie a slight smile. "Not much. When he does get home, he's so tired that he's not fit to be around. I'm sorry for the way he gets after you and Garrit, but I think he forgets that he's not at work."

Annie nodded in agreement, and for a moment she wondered if she dared ask what had come to her mind. "Sometimes . . ." she said with a sigh, "I don't understand how you put up with it, Mother. When he speaks so cruelly to you or shouts at you, I get so angry. I think I would walk out."

"And not come back?" her mother asked, her eyes squeezed together like she had a headache. "Just leave you and Garrit behind? You know I could never do that, Annie. Besides, it's not that bad—most of the time."

"Do you think all men change after they get married?" Annie wondered out loud.

"No, I'm sure not," said Dinah. "My father has always been kind and gentle, and you know how he takes care of your grandmother. I can't imagine anyone more loving than my papa, but I think there are a lot of men like him. The secret is to find the right one."

"But how can you really know?"

"Are you wondering about Arthur?" her mother asked, finally managing a smile. "He's very serious about you, you know. Mrs. Benson thinks you'll be married before you graduate from high school."

"She does not!" Annie cried, blushing and laughing with her mother. "Tell me she didn't say that."

"Oh, she said it all right," Dinah answered, still laughing. "But then, she says that about every couple she hears is courting. She isn't right, is she?"

"No, of course not," Annie said. "I like Arthur, but I hardly think we're to the point of announcing an engagement. After all, he's only been calling for a few months."

"He does seem like a very fine young man," her mother said. "As far as I can tell, every girl in town is waiting for their chance, hoping you'll stop seeing Arthur. You'd better be careful, or some pretty young thing will steal him away."

Annie chuckled. "Mostly because he's the banker's son."

Her mother nodded. "And intelligent ... and handsome ... and charming. No wonder the other girls are jealous. I know *I* would have been!"

"Sounds like you've already made some decisions for me," Annie said, half teasing. "The trouble is, sometimes I feel like Arthur's doing that, too. It's almost like he expects he can buy me ... like his new buggy and horse. I don't want it to be like that."

"No, I wouldn't, either," her mother said. "But I think you're misjudging him, Annie. He's done nothing inappropriate, has he?"

"Of course not," Annie replied. "But it's ... so different being around Stuart Anderson. We laughed and talked and ... he seemed to listen to me. There's something special about him. And Arthur didn't like him much; I could tell. I mean, he was perfectly polite, but he always managed to sit next to me, and Stuart hardly got a word in. I suppose I shouldn't have invited them both to the picnic."

"Maybe Arthur knows something about Stuart that you don't," her mother said. "After all, you hardly know that boy."

"No, Arthur doesn't know Stuart any better than I do," said Annie. "They had only met once before the picnic. It's more like he wanted to keep Stuart away from me."

"Can you blame him, really?" her mother asked. "If Arthur doesn't want any other man to come between you and him, why, that just shows how serious his intentions are. Don't you think that's good?"

Annie shrugged her shoulders and laughed softly. "I suppose so. Arthur is very good to me, and everything you say about him is true, but ... well, I guess I do wish Arthur wasn't quite so serious."

"So you could get to know Stuart Anderson better?"

Annie stared out the window with a smile. "Well, you have to admit that Stuart also happens to be handsome, charming, intelligent, and—"

"And in college with a long ways to go, meaning he's poor as a church mouse," her mother interrupted. "Meanwhile, Arthur has a very good job *and* the keys to the bank. That's a mighty big difference, Annie."

"You already said that it was money that changed Father," said Annie. "Having a lot of money can't be that important."

"I said it was the pursuit of money that changed your father, or at least that's what I meant to say," Dinah replied. "It's one thing to grow up poor and spend every ounce of energy trying to become rich, and it's another thing to grow up rich and know how to keep it and use it. When you marry, you don't want to start out poor like your father and I did—not if you can help it. Then you end up spending the rest of your life scratching, skimping, and saving pennies. I wouldn't want you to have to go through what I did."

"And where does love fit into this?" asked Annie, gazing into her mother's eyes. "Or doesn't that matter, either?"

"Love's important, Annie," her mother said without hesitation. "But I reckon it's a lot easier to love a man who locks his office door at five o'clock and spends the evening with you than one who works sixty hours every week just trying to make ends meet. I've watched Arthur Simpson real close, Annie. That boy knows how to make money, and he's willing to spend it on what he really cares about ... and he has already showered you with gifts. I'm telling you, Annie, that young man cares about you. And whoever becomes his princess is going to be one lucky young lady."

"Do you really believe that?" asked Annie.

"I believe that to feel someone really cares for you is the most wonderful thing in this world," her mother said.

Chapter 6

Speaking the Truth

Stuart Anderson gently swished the foamy white soap from the long straight-edged razor, then he carefully tucked the blade back into its curved wooden handle and set it in the bathroom cabinet. He washed the remaining soap from his face, then stared into the mirror as he toweled himself off. "Pretty good shave," he whispered as he glanced from cheek to cheek and up and down his neck. "Now all I need's a haircut," he added, noting the scruffy dark hairs on the back of his neck.

Putting the towel back on its wooden rack and quickly cleaning up after himself, Stuart stepped out of the bathroom and walked down the long hallway with its shining pine floor to the kitchen. Earlier he had heard the front screen door slap shut when his father left for work, and he knew his mother would be in the kitchen. Saturday was the one day she did not go to her bookkeeping job in the mill office, and she loved to spend the early morning alone with a cup of coffee and a good book.

Quietly stepping through the doorway into the kitchen, Stuart stopped and turned toward the small table where his mother sat next to the open window. A light summer breeze rippled through the filmy white curtains and gently tugged at the corners of the book she was reading while a warm shaft of sun highlighted her black hair and high cheekbones. She wore a long white robe and crocheted slippers.

"Good morning, Stuart," she said softly without looking up from her book, then she turned the page and slipped her bookmark into the place. "It's your day off, and my day off, and I'm enjoying a rare moment with my favorite book," she continued, finally looking up at her son. "Why don't you head back to your bed and get some more sleep?"

"Can't," he replied, pausing to stretch. "I've gotten so used to waking up with the rooster that I can't get back to sleep. Besides, I hate to waste time when I have so few days left before I leave for school."

"Cup of coffee?" his mother asked, her pink lips turning into a smile.

"Sure," he said as she closed her book, then stood up. "What are you reading now? Looks like . . . *Sir Gibbie*. Am I right?"

"You remembered!" Marian stepped to the white kitchen cabinets and pulled out a coffee cup. "But I guess the book's worn edges give it away."

"*Wee Sir Gibbie of Howglen* by Mr. George MacDonald," quoted Stuart, sitting down at the table and squinting out through the sunshine into their large backyard. "How could I forget? Grandpa constantly quotes MacDonald in his sermons, and you have a whole shelf of his books here. How many times did you read me this story?"

"At least twice, I think," answered his mother as she poured him a cup of coffee. "You loved to listen to the story, and then you'd pretend that you were the speechless little vagabond, racing around the house like Gibbie did in his Scottish village. Sometimes you'd go all morning and refuse to speak a word."

Stuart laughed and pushed the chair beside him back from the table for his mother. "I always wished that I had a friend who was just like Gibbie," he said, taking the cup from her. "He always seemed like he was a creature from another world . . . almost too good and kind and forgiving to be real."

"That's the magic of MacDonald's writing," his mother said as she sat down and took her own coffee cup in hand. "Gibbie is so wonderful, such a picture of Jesus Christ, that you can't keep from loving him. Do you remember the old woman who lived on the mountainside and took Gibbie into her home?"

"Barely," Stuart said as his mother picked up the book and opened it to her marker.

"I was just reading this wonderful description of her," she said, gazing over the page and pointing to the section. "Here, read this. He's describing Janet Grant. Read it out loud for me."

Stuart took the leatherbound book from his mother's hand and found the spot on the page where she had pointed. He read:

"Not for years and years had Janet been to church; she had long been unable to walk so far; and having no book but the best, and no help to understand it, but the highest, her faith was simple, strong, real, all-pervading. Day by day she pored over the great gospel—I mean just the good news according to Matthew and Mark and Luke and John—until she had grown to be one of the noble ladies of the kingdom of heaven—one of those who inherit the earth, and are ripening to see God. For the Master, and His mind in hers, was her teacher. She had little or no theology save what He taught her, or rather what He is. And of any other than that, the less the better; for no theology, except the Word of God, is worth the learning, no other being true. To know Him is to know God. And he only who obeys Him does or can know Him; he who obeys Him, cannot fail to know Him. To Janet Jesus Christ was no object of so-called theological speculation."

"Amazing," Stuart murmured as he finished. He shook his head and looked up at his mother. "How could anyone write so beautifully?"

"I have no idea," his mother replied, "but I never tire of reading his stories. He could say more in one sentence than most writers can say in a whole page."

"Makes me want to be like Janet Grant," said Stuart.

"In what way?"

"Oh, that part about the Master being her teacher, or His mind being in hers. I . . . um . . . I sometimes wonder if I know anything about that."

"Stuart, what is it that's bothering you?" Marian asked, staring into her son's shiny black eyes. "Ever since the accident, you seem like something's eating you up inside. Want to talk about it?"

Stuart looked out the window again, focusing on nothing in particular, and rubbed his smooth chin. "Sure, why not? It's part of why I couldn't sleep this morning. If you can cure me, I can go back to bed, and you can go back to reading your book."

"I like that idea," his mother replied with a smile as Stuart turned to look at her. "Let me guess, though. I'll bet it's the same thing that's bothering your father."

"What?"

"You think that Doc Jones could talk to your father about your becoming a doctor and it wouldn't keep him up at night?" she asked. "Or me? You think we take this lightly?"

"No, but ... why didn't one of you talk to me about it?" Stuart asked. "Here I've been thrashing this thing over and over in my head. I don't know what I'm supposed to do with it. I wish the doc would've just kept his big mouth closed."

"Do you really?"

"Yeah, I do. It's none of his business, anyway. And I was so sure about the ministry, and everything. Doc knew that."

"Sounds like you're not so sure now."

"Well, I was," said Stuart. "But Doc asked me if I'd pray about it, even though I thought it was crazy, me becoming a doctor, and I have been ... praying ... and thinking ... and thinking ... and getting very frustrated."

"Maybe you better go back to praying," said his mother.

"Probably so," replied Stuart. "I thought that I'd go for a long walk this morning and give it another try."

"If it's bothering you so," she said, "you must feel that there's something to Doc's suggestion."

Stuart shrugged and looked away. "I don't know," he groused. "How do you know? It's so strange. . . . it's just that ... I've never felt anything like this before."

"Like what?"

"Like I was meant to help those people, Walter Sorenson and Annie Harding," Stuart explained, shaking his head. "It felt so natural. . . . I wasn't scared or nervous. And when I held Walter's arm, and I could feel the broken bones and the pounding blood ... his life ... in my hands, I liked it, Mama. Doesn't that sound strange?"

Marian Anderson shook her head no and leaned forward in her chair, then she reached out and gently massaged the back of Stuart's neck. "Sounds like ... something you better take seriously, son. You should have mentioned it to us before."

"What did Dad think when the doc mentioned it to him?" asked Stuart. "Dad didn't say anything to me, so I'm thinking he's not really pleased about it."

His mother smiled. "You know how proud your father is that you've been planning to become a pastor . . . like Grandpa."

"So he was upset?"

"No, just . . . surprised, I guess," Marian said. "Your father respects the doc way too much to not consider what he says."

"Would he be disappointed if I didn't go into the ministry?"

"I'm sure it would take him a while to adjust, but I don't think he'd be disappointed," his mother replied. "The only way you could really disappoint your father is if you forsake what you believe God has put on your heart. As long as you're following God's leading, your father will be a happy man."

Stuart tapped the edge of his coffee cup and nodded. "So, then," he said, "what did *you* think when Dad told you what the doc said?"

"What did I think?" Marian repeated slowly. "I guess I was surprised like your father."

"That's all? Just surprised?"

Marian Anderson sat back in her chair and crossed her arms. "That's a hard question, but . . . I guess I thought it was worth considering."

"Why?"

"Oh, I don't know if I should say why," his mother said. "It might sway your thoughts too much. It's important that you take full responsibility for what you do with your life, Stuart, and I don't want to get in the way."

"I realize that, but I'd really like your opinion."

"You're sure?"

"Yes. Why should I consider becoming a doctor?"

"I don't know about the doctoring, but I have had some wonderings about you and the ministry," she said. "And I grew up in a minister's home, so I know a little bit about it. Stuart, do you still feel the same way about public speaking that you did in high school?"

Stuart nodded and said, "I still don't like it. I can do it, and I'm not really scared about it, but it's not easy for me."

"Does that concern you when you think about becoming a pastor?"

"I guess it does," Stuart answered. "I'm aware of how often a pastor has to speak."

"And. . . ?"

"I assume that if it's what God wants me to do, He'll help me when I need it."

Marian Anderson raised her eyebrows and smiled. "I guess that's true, but what if it's always a struggle?"

"Then it's ... always a struggle, I guess."

"And you think that's something you want to do for your whole life?"

"What else makes you won—?"

"Not so fast," his mother interrupted him. "You didn't answer my question. You think that God might be wanting you to do something you dislike for your whole life?"

"I don't know, but that's His business, I figure."

"It is His business, but it seems to me that He works a little closer with us than that."

"You mean, you think that God's will for our lives matches up with what we're good at?"

"I think that happens a lot of the time. When you said that what you did for Walter and Annie felt *so natural*, those words sounded suspicious—like doctoring might be something God wants you to take seriously."

"What else, then?" asked Stuart.

"Okay, do you realize what it takes to remain as the pastor of one church for an extended period of time? I've wondered how much you feel you can change about yourself in order to do that."

"Such as?"

"Such as how you relate to people," Marian replied, puckering her lips and taking a deep breath of air. "Do you like working with a whole group of people, leading them, or do you prefer working with one person at a time?"

"Why ask me when you already know the answer?"

"To try to get you to think about it," his mother answered, tugging at the right sleeve of his shirt. "You're a doer, Stuart. You love to take a job and do it yourself, and you struggle whenever you have to wait for others and depend on them. You work wonderfully with people one on one, but so much of what you'd be doing in a church is with a group. I think that if you had to do that all the time, you might feel like you were being tortured for some evil deed you'd done."

"Maybe that ability would come with the territory?"

"Maybe. But that makes two mighty big maybes," she said. "You're also going to have to change the way you confront people. The way you do it now, I'm afraid your church would look more like a boxing hall than a sanctuary of peace."

Stuart laughed and shook his head. "You might be right. But you have to speak the truth to people, and not everyone is going to like that."

"Yes, you do speak the truth, and we taught you that," his mother agreed. "But a pastor must learn when to speak and when not to speak. Your grandfather says there's a gift to it, and I believe him. To speak to one another in love goes far beyond simply telling people the truth about themselves whenever you see it. Love must be patient and overlook faults, or the truth just becomes a club that we use to beat on people."

"So you think I couldn't change that about me?"

"I didn't say that," replied Marian. "I'm sure that God can help you mature in the way you deal with people. All I'm saying is that you need to consider whether you have a pastoral gift. Pastors are shepherds of people, you know. Being a shepherd is something in your heart, and it's either there or it's not there. And if it's not there, it would be dreadful to pretend that it was."

"But I do care about people, Mama. I want to help people, and I want to serve God."

"Of course you care, and you're good with people," his mother agreed. "But, Stuart, the ministry is not the only profession where you care for people—and certainly not the only one where you can serve God! There's also teaching and the law and . . . well, there's medicine. You have to think about *how* you are called to help and serve."

Stuart sighed and turned his gaze out the window again. The early morning breeze was gaining strength as the bright sunshine warmed the air. Stuart gently rubbed his clean-shaven face and said, "Where've you been hiding all summer, Mama?"

"What?"

"I've been home all summer, and you never said a word about this. Now I come down to have a nice Saturday breakfast—which I still haven't gotten, by the way—and instead I get enough questions to last a year. I thought you were on my side, not the doc's."

Marian Anderson laughed and pushed her chair back from the table. "You didn't ask for breakfast, if you recall," she replied, "but you did ask me what I thought. And no one in the world is more on your side than I am, with the possible exception of your father."

"I guess I did get what I asked for," said Stuart. "I think it's going to be a long walk that I take today. Maybe I'll just keep on walking."

"Two fried eggs and two pieces of toast?" his mother asked as she stood up and walked toward the kitchen cabinets. "Or oatmeal?"

"Eggs and toast would be great."

"I know it doesn't feel like it, Stuart, but this is good for you," his mother said, pulling a cast-iron frying pan from a cabinet and setting it down on a counter.

"How's that? I was quite happy with the way things were."

"And hopefully you will be after you get it all sorted out," she said. "But if being a minister is God's calling for your life, my questions and your own wonderings won't stand in the way of it. As long as you are seeking God with all your heart, He'll lead you, and what seems to be standing in the way will be driven back. Of that I have no doubt."

"Why is everything that goes wrong always so good for me?"

"Better to face it straight on now than to spend the rest of your life wondering, right?" his mother asked. "A lot of people never come to terms with God's direction at all, and their lives are that much poorer."

"Janet Grant did, but she was a character in a novel," muttered Stuart.

"She was a simple woman who lived in a highland cottage and was perfectly content to take care of her husband and family," Marian Anderson said, carving two thick slices from a loaf of yesterday's bread. "Whether you end up a minister, or a doctor, or a highland shepherd, God doesn't count one more important than the other. I don't, either, and neither does your father. This isn't about pleasing us, Stuart, or doing something with your life that will help make ours feel important. We want you to be happy in whatever you do."

Stuart Anderson simply nodded and continued to stare out the window.

Chapter 7

A Chance Encounter

Stuart Anderson crossed the street in front of his father's mill, paused to see whose wagon was parked out front, then continued walking west toward the partially destroyed bridge. Since the accident that had taken Andrew Sorenson's life, most of the wreckage had been hauled away, along with the crumpled traction engine, but no work had been done to repair the bridge. Local traffic had simply been redirected to the other bridge that crossed the stream on the north edge of town.

Walking quickly to the mangled structure, Stuart stepped around the metal guard rails and made his way carefully down the steep embankment toward the clear stream. In the morning shadows beneath what remained of the overhead bridge, his eyes struggled momentarily to adjust to the darkness, and then his foot caught on the jagged edge of a rock.

"Whoa!" Stuart cried, trying to catch himself as he lurched and fell forward. He managed to get his hands out in front of his skid and made a desperate grab at a big slab of limestone, pulling himself to a halt, but not before his left elbow bashed against the rocks. "Ow! That really hurt," he muttered as he slowly stood and dusted himself off.

"You're bleeding." A soft voice behind him caused Stuart to jump, then he spun around.

Annie Harding was sitting beside a large limestone rock several yards up the embankment, partly hidden by the rock and the shadows. She waved at Stuart and stood up.

"You scared me," Stuart said as she carefully made her way around the big rock and down the rocky path toward him. "I didn't see you."

"You didn't see much of anything," she replied with a small smirk. "I thought you were dashing down to rescue someone again."

Stuart shook his head. "Not today. Looks like I'm the one needing rescue." He twisted his left elbow around and studied the damage.

"That looks painful," Annie observed as she stepped beside Stuart. "Let me wash it off." She knelt down gracefully beside the stream and dipped her white handkerchief in the cool clear water.

"No, don't get my blood on your nice hankie," Stuart protested as she stood up.

"Nonsense," replied Annie with a big smile, then she took his sun-tanned arm in her hand and turned the elbow toward her. Carefully dabbing the wound, she wiped away the blood and dirt, then said, "That's a pretty deep cut."

"I'll be fine, thanks," Stuart said as she let go of his arm, although when he saw the cut, he knew it was going to be difficult to get it to stop bleeding.

Kneeling down again, Annie dipped the handkerchief back into the stream and gently swished the blood and dirt from it. Then she stood and squeezed out as much water as she could and turned to Stuart.

"I'm—"

"You just hush!" Annie ordered him, taking his arm and turning it again. Holding one corner of the handkerchief with her forefinger, she wrapped the cloth tightly around his elbow, then held her hand over the wound and pressed the handkerchief against it. Her cool fingers felt good against his arm as she slowly lifted her big round eyes and looked into his face. "Do you want to hold it now?"

"What? Oh yes. Sure," Stuart blurted out, momentarily flustered. His face felt warm as he pressed down on the damp white handkerchief and Annie lifted her hand away. "I . . . ah . . . this blood's going to wreck your hankie. I'll buy you a new one."

"It's old, don't worry about it," she said with a smile, then she sat back on top of a thick rock ledge. "Do you come here often?"

"No," said Stuart, leaning against a rock that faced Annie. "Never, actually."

"Just when I'm here?" asked Annie.

"No!" he retorted, shaking his head and grinning. "I mean . . . no, I didn't come knowing you were here. I'm sorry if I interrupted whatever you were doing. I wouldn't have thought you'd ever want to come back here."

Annie nodded. "You wouldn't think so, but I've been here a couple of times since the accident. Something . . . happened to me here, and it's not just that I nearly died. I can't figure out exactly what it is or what it means, so I come and sit and think about it. So far, I'm still waiting to understand."

"Is it like you got, well, a second chance to live?" asked Stuart.

"That's part of it, I'm sure," she replied, reaching up and pushing back some long pale tendrils from her face. "And I'm very thankful to God . . . and to you . . . for that. But it's more than that. This may sound strange to you, but I come here because . . . because God is here. I can feel His presence here . . . more than in any other place I've ever been."

"That's good news for me." The words were out before Stuart knew he had said them.

"What?"

"Nothing."

"I thought you said that it was good news for you."

"I did, but . . . well, it's hard to explain," Stuart said with a smile. "I didn't mean to interrupt you. I'm sorry."

Annie smiled back and shook her head. "No need to apologize. I really don't have much more to add about why I come here. I'm surprised you didn't think it was a stupid reason."

"Why should I?"

"Well, some people think it's strange to talk about God that way," Annie replied, leaning back on the limestone and kicking her heels against the front of the rock. "My mother thinks I'm wasting my time when I come down here. She says that the church is the proper place to worship God and that I should go into the sanctuary to pray. I haven't told my father about it, and I wouldn't let Arthur go into it when I told him why I was coming here. I know what they'd say . . . after they finished laughing."

"What would they say?"

"That I must have fallen off my rocker . . . or that I hit my head too hard in the accident."

Stuart nodded. "I know a lot of people think that way; I've met a lot of them at the university. But I'm just the opposite, I guess. I can't imagine believing in a God who doesn't come close to people. If I couldn't ever sense His presence, I don't think I could believe that there is a God."

"Why?"

"What kind of a God would He be if He left us to work out our lives on our own or left everything in our lives to chance?" asked Stuart. "I hate the idea that God stands outside this world with His arms crossed, refusing to communicate or to intervene in people's lives. I'm glad that Jesus Christ was never like that."

"You really believe that?" asked Annie, studying Stuart's face. "You're not teasing me?"

"No! Why would I do that?" Stuart protested, holding up his hands.

"I don't know," Annie said with a crooked smile. "But there's a lot I don't know about religion, and sometimes I feel like a blind person feeling my way around a new house. I'm not sure what's real and what's not real, or even exactly why I come here. I keep asking myself whether what I sense here is really God, or if it's just my imagination."

"I believe that God is everywhere," Stuart said, "but I do think there are places that He makes special for us."

"Is that why you're here?"

"What?"

"You said before that it was good news to you that I sensed God's presence here," Annie stated. "And when you were coming down the embankment, before you tripped, you were thinking about something pretty serious ... almost like you were troubled about something. Maybe we're both here for the same reason."

Stuart chuckled and looked out across the stream, then he nodded. "I think you're right," he said softly, glancing back into Annie's brown eyes.

"You sense God is here, too?" she asked.

"Well, not in the way you described it," he replied. "But this place ..." He paused, surveying the stream again. "Something very different happened to me here ... during the accident ... that has confused me. I thought that if I came back and spent some time praying here, maybe I could sort things out."

"Sort what out?"

Stuart ran his fingers through his thick black hair and shook his head.

"I'm sorry," Annie spoke quickly, "I don't mean to pry."

"No, it's all right," replied Stuart, standing up straight and taking a couple of steps to the water's edge. "It's just kind of a complicated story. I'm not sure where I'd start. Are you sure you want to hear it?"

Annie nodded, her expression serious.

"All right, then . . . and maybe it's not so complicated," Stuart began. "You remember on the day of the picnic that I said I was going into the ministry?"

"Yes," said Annie, "and I remember that Arthur thought it was a waste to spend so much money educating people for the pastorate."

" 'Not a good return on the dollar,' didn't he say? I don't think he's been impressed with the churchmen he's met."

"I thought that was a little rude of Arthur."

Stuart nodded his head in agreement, picked up a flat stone with his right hand, and with a quick throw he skipped it across a deep part of the stream. Then he turned to Annie and continued. "Ever since I was little, I wanted to be a pastor like my grandfather. He's the finest, most respected man you could ever dream of meeting, and the quality of his life matches his sermons. I always hoped I could help people in the same ways he does. That was up until the accident."

"Why would the accident change that?" asked Annie. "Seems like it would only strengthen your resolve. You helped in a wonderful way."

"But something was . . . different," said Stuart, shaking his head. "What I did that day felt so natural . . . and good . . . and it wasn't praying with people or talking to them or doing anything that a pastor would do. And afterward Doc Jones asked me if I'd ever thought of becoming a doctor."

"Had you?"

"Never!" exclaimed Stuart, bursting into a laugh. "I would have thought it was a joke, but I could still feel Walter's blood pumping through his veins."

"And you liked it," added Annie.

"Yes, I did," Stuart spoke firmly, glancing back at Annie. "And now I don't know what to do."

"So you came here to pray about it."

Stuart nodded and smiled. "That's pretty much it."

"And what did you hope would happen if you prayed?"

"I hope ... and I trust ... that God will somehow show me what He wants me to do with my life," Stuart replied. "I really need to know."

"You don't mean that He would speak out loud?" asked Annie.

"Well, that would be okay with me," Stuart said with a big smile. "But I was really thinking that He'd speak into the quietness of my heart and I'd ... just ... know."

"Has He done that before with you?"

"Oh yes." Stuart spoke softly but confidently. "Most of the times when I feel that God has spoken to me, it's when I'm reading the Scriptures. But sometimes it's more like He whispers into my heart and I just know it's Him."

Annie stared at Stuart, then she finally said, "I'm amazed that you would say it that way. It's exactly what I felt when I was here before ... that God whispered into my heart. But I've never heard anyone ever say that God does that, including our pastor. Do your parents believe that, too?"

Stuart chuckled, then he said, "I spent about an hour this morning talking with my mother about it."

"My goodness," Annie said, "my mother and I never talk about religion, even though she's doing a lot at the church these days. Your father—you talk to him about it, too?"

"Very much so."

"I'm amazed," Annie said, standing up and straightening her dress. "You're very fortunate, Stuart. I should be going, though. I'm keeping you from what you came here to do."

"No, I should be the one who leaves," said Stuart. "You were here first, and I have plenty of places on the outskirts of town where I can go."

"Oh, I won't be staying long anyway," replied Annie. "Arthur's going to pick me up here as soon as he finishes some work at the bank, and we're going for a ride into the country."

"Then I really better get moving," said Stuart. "Arthur might think that you and I ..."

"You and I what?" asked Annie, crossing her arms, then smiling.

Stuart smiled in return and rubbed his hands together. "I have this sneaking suspicion that he might think we're up to something behind his back. Meeting down by the river, out of sight like this, isn't exactly like bumping into each other downtown. And I don't think Arthur likes me very well anyway."

"I wonder why?" asked Annie, continuing to grin.

"I think he takes his relationship with you very seriously, Miss Harding."

"You think that Arthur considers you a potential threat?"

"I think he does," said Stuart with a nod, "but you'd have to ask him."

"And is he correct?"

Stuart stared at Annie for a moment, then burst out laughing and turned around to the water. He knelt down and ran his fingers across the surface, then he glanced back at Annie and said, "You're very straightforward, aren't you, Miss Harding?"

"You're leaving for college soon," Annie replied. "I don't have much time left to find out. Should Arthur be concerned, Mr. Anderson?"

"I suspect," said Stuart, standing up and tucking his arms behind him, "that he should be concerned about anyone you decide to kiss. That was quite a surprise to me, and I've wondered exactly what you meant by it."

"Just as I said that day. I wanted to thank you for what you'd done," Annie said, turning her head. "Should I have meant something more?"

"I had the impression that you did," Stuart returned, "but it's possible that I mistook your intent. It's not every day I am kissed by a beautiful young woman I barely know."

"And you said you meant the words you spoke when you rescued me," Annie said, pointing to the west side of the stream. "It's not every day I hear words like that."

"Have I given you a reason to think that I might say something to you that I didn't mean?" asked Stuart with a widening grin.

"So you would say them again if you had the chance?"

Stuart chuckled and looked down, then he let out a big breath of air. "I think ... ah ... this conversation has gone too far," he said. "However I feel about you, and whatever I might have said ... or want to say, I'm not the kind of man who would steal another's sweetheart."

"You aren't suggesting that Arthur owns me, are you?"

"No, but you know what I mean."

"I just wanted to make sure that you did. It would be unfortunate for us to misunderstand each other's intent," she said. "Now, could I ask you one more question, Mr. Anderson? A personal question."

"As if the previous questions weren't personal?"

"You be the judge," Annie said, raising her eyebrows, then smiling. "At the picnic on Sunday, I enjoyed your description of university life, but it seemed odd to me that you never mentioned any young women that you might know there. Was that an oversight on your behalf?"

"Not an intentional one, if that's what you're implying," Stuart replied. "And, as far as I know, there is no university requirement that states I must keep the company of young women. Do you suspect such an involvement?"

"Certainly," Annie stated. "But satisfy my curiosity, if you will. Are you involved with someone in Minneapolis, or is Stuart Anderson a free man?"

Stuart's black eyes glistened as he stared into Annie's delicate face, then he declared, "Let me assure you, Miss Harding, that I am as free as you are."

Annie studied Stuart's expression. "So, there is someone."

"Yes."

"A serious someone?"

Stuart laughed and shook his head. "Do you mean, am I in love with her?"

"Well . . . I suppose I did."

"You should ask me, then."

"Thank you, I will," said Annie, wrinkling her forehead and nodding toward him. "Are you in love with her, Mr. Anderson?"

"No."

"Is she in love with you?"

"I don't think so, but . . . I haven't asked her," said Stuart. "Perhaps you'd like to write and ask her yourself?"

Annie laughed and so did Stuart. She leaned back on the rock that she had sat upon previously and said, "I don't think you want me writing her."

"And despite what you may have said to the contrary," Stuart replied, "I don't think you want Arthur to see you here with me. If I were him, I wouldn't appreciate it."

"If you were him, you—"

The sudden clop of a horse's hooves and the sound of a buggy's wheels on the gravel road above them cut Annie's words short. For a brief moment her face flushed, then she straightened her dress again and glanced at Stuart.

"Should I hide?" asked Stuart, pointing up under the corner of the bridge. "He would never see me."

Annie hesitated, then looked up at the ridge of the embankment. "No, Mr. Anderson. I said we have nothing to hide, and I meant it."

Chapter 8

A Country Ride

"Well, well, well," Arthur Simpson called out, his blond head leaning over the iron railing at the corner of the bridge and looking down at Annie and Stuart. "I wasn't expecting this. Am I interrupting something?"

"Of course not," Annie replied, glancing quickly at Stuart as she started up the stony path of the embankment. "You're right on time, Arthur. Mr. Anderson happened to stop by, and we've had a lovely talk down by the river. Would you like a ride somewhere, Mr. Anderson? We can drop you off."

Stuart shook his head. "No, but thanks for the offer. I never got around to the reason I came down here, so I think I'll stay for a while. Thank you for the talk, Miss Harding. I really enjoyed it."

"My pleasure," she replied, turning back to Arthur Simpson as she neared the crest of the ridge.

"What does bring you down here, Anderson?" Arthur asked. "Counting the trout population . . . or something else?"

Stuart chuckled and leaned back on a rock. "I sure didn't come to count anything. I've got a lot on my mind, and I thought this might be a good place to be quiet and think things through. I didn't antici-pate anyone else being here, but life is full of surprises, wouldn't you say, Mr. Simpson?"

"I guess," Arthur replied with a nod, then turned to Annie. "Shall we be off, my dear?"

"Of course," she replied, taking his extended arm. "I can't tell you how much I've been looking forward to a ride in the country."

Arthur smiled at Annie, then turned and looked back down toward the stream. "You have a nice day, Anderson," he called out to the solitary figure below him. "I'll see you later. We do need to talk again sometime . . . soon."

Stuart waved and mumbled, "I look forward to it."

"Good, good, good," said Arthur as he escorted Annie away from the bridge and helped her up into the seat of his buggy. "Mr. Anderson thinks he has a lot on his mind now," he said. "Wait till he gets out of college and faces the real world. Unless he ends up coming home and grinding farmers' oats for his father."

Annie lifted herself up off the seat and straightened her long black dress. "I think he's wanting to make sure he's ready to face that world. But even if he did work at the mill for the rest of his life, is that so bad?"

Hopping up into the seat next to her and taking the reins, Arthur replied, "It's not bad, I guess, but it would be a shame. He's certainly capable of doing more."

"Like becoming a minister?"

Arthur nodded and smiled as he shook the reins, and the buggy wheels crunched in the gravel. "I wouldn't recommend that, as you know, but he does seem intent on pursuing it."

"Why do you speak so disparagingly about the ministry?" asked Annie, folding her hands in her lap and leaning back against the seat.

"What is there to make me think to the contrary?" returned Arthur, glancing into Annie's face. "And please don't suggest the *Reverend* Alexander Mackenzie. The man is a snake in the grass."

"You hardly know him," Annie objected. "How can you say that?"

"Ah, but I do know him," Arthur replied. "I've handled several of his financial transactions at the bank, and I am, lest ye forget, a devoted member of his flock."

"Which is a mystery to me," Annie said with a laugh. "Why do you continue to attend a church whose pastor you call a snake?"

"Because the true church of God remains the church despite the despicable men who may lead it," Arthur replied, looking straight ahead. He nodded to a man who was crossing the street in front of them, then he continued. "Should the faithful remnant allow the antichrist to drive them from the sanctuary of the Almighty?"

Annie burst out laughing and looked into Arthur's steady blue eyes.

His neatly trimmed blond hair and thin mustache reflected the bright sunshine as a slight grin pushed its way to the surface. "You even sound like a preacher," she said.

"I'm better than that," Arthur said with a smirk. "The antichrist was a favorite theme of every preacher in Chicago the last couple of years before the turn of this century. I heard enough about him to last me a lifetime. Curiously, I've seldom heard his name mentioned since."

"So, tell me why you keep coming to our church. Be honest."

"Honest?" asked Arthur, raising his thick brown eyebrows. "You're asking a lot, and I don't think you're going to like my reasons."

"I know that, but try anyway."

Arthur nodded and said, "All right. The first reason is that for at least an hour every Sunday morning I get a chance to sit and stare at a lovely young lady I see far too seldom. And that is a treat I will not sacrifice, no matter my disaffection with the person in the pulpit."

Blushing, Annie chuckled and put her hand on his arm for the moment. "That," she said, "is a poor reason, Arthur, although I am pleased by it. Why else do you come? Would you come if I did not?"

"Without question," Arthur spoke quickly. "I must."

"Why?"

"My father owns the bank, my dear," Arthur replied. "And I hope soon to take over the daily management in his stead. You realize that a respectable businessman must attend a respectable church to retain the support of the community's respectable citizens. My father told me that it was a wise investment of time, but I prefer to think of it as inexpensive advertising."

"You're serious?" asked Annie, staring into Arthur's eyes.

"Perfectly."

Annie let go of Arthur's arm and looked ahead as the buggy turned onto the road that led north out of town. Straightening up in the seat, she sighed and said, "That seems . . . dishonest . . . or something."

"Not in the least!" exclaimed Arthur, shaking his head and breaking into a wide grin. "Stopping and talking with people on the street, or my recent involvement with the city council, or my work with the school board—it's all the same, really. It all works together to build the business."

"There has to be more to it than that," said Annie. "It sounds so empty . . . heartless."

"I say that if it pays the bills, that's enough for me," said Arthur, patting the seat beside him. "How else could I afford a new buggy and a fine black mare? My daddy didn't give me this rig."

The buggy rolled down the treed lane past the last house, and the road climbed sharply as they exited the town's outskirts. Arthur made some clicking noises with his mouth as he snapped the reins twice, and the mare picked up her canter.

"So," Arthur said, looking at Annie after a long lull in the conversation, "you still don't like my second answer?"

Annie smiled and said, "No."

"Tell me," he said, "why does your father go to church? Do you think it means anything to him?"

"No," Annie spoke out before she had even thought about it. "At least, as far as I know it doesn't. He never speaks about it."

"He's just doing business, Annie."

"You don't know that."

"Why don't you ask him?"

Annie shook her head. "I would never do that. Father's got a temper you don't want to test. I would never talk to him about something that serious."

"Well, let me tell you something about your father," said Arthur. "He's all business, all the time, and he knows what he's doing. Just watch him for five minutes. Everything he does is calculated and efficient. Isn't that true?"

"Yes, I guess so."

"And that's why I think most people go to church. Everybody's out to get something for himself," Arthur stated. "I'm curious, now. You made me tell you why I go to church. I'd like to know why you go?"

The buggy had reached the crest of a wooded hill, and the road abruptly forked to the east and west. Simpson turned toward the west, and the road dipped down into a long valley that led to an arched stone bridge across Flatwillow Creek.

"Where are we going?" Annie asked, reaching up and holding her hat in place as the buggy picked up speed down the hill. "Slow down, please!"

"For a picnic, as I promised," Arthur replied. He held the reins tight as they approached the bridge, then he slowed the black mare's pace. "My mother packed us a gigantic lunch."

"But where will we have the picnic?" she asked. "I've only been up this road once, and it was shortly after we moved here."

"You'll find out soon enough," said Arthur as the buggy rolled onto the one-lane bridge. The buggy's wheels on the slender wooden planks made a hollow, ringing sound that forced him to raise his voice. "Tell me why you go to church. I must know."

Annie glanced down into the clear stream below them. "I ... ah ... I suppose it's been because I was supposed to go. It's something we do, and it's not something I would question."

"It means nothing personal to you, then?" Arthur asked. "Just a duty."

"A duty, yes, that's what it's been," said Annie. "But I hope that it comes to mean more than that. I believe it will."

"How's that?"

"I'm not sure," Annie replied, shrugging her shoulders. "I did tell you why I was going to the bridge this morning."

"And was it true? Was God there, as you said? Or did you have to settle for Stuart Anderson?"

Annie chuckled and leaned back against the seat, crossing her arms and taking in a deep breath. "There's nothing as sweet as country air, is there?"

"That depends on how close you are to a barn," Arthur replied as the buggy rolled up to the top of another steep hill. "So, was it true?"

"That Stuart was there? You knew that."

"No, that God was there."

"If I told you it was true, would you believe me?" asked Annie, looking into Simpson's face. "You wouldn't, would you?"

Arthur shrugged his shoulders twice and smiled. "Does it matter?"

"Yes."

"Why?"

"Because it matters to me. Isn't that enough?" Annie countered. "I couldn't convince you, no matter what I said, could I?"

"I'm sorry," Arthur said. "I really would like to know."

"Your lip is curling," said Annie, poking him with her elbow. "You'd like to know, but you definitely aren't sorry."

Simpson broke out laughing, then he said, "And I suspect that I'm not going to know, either."

"Correct," said Annie with a smile. "At least not today, you won't. Where are we, anyway?" she asked, pointing ahead to a long dirt driveway that led back into the woods. Through the trees she could see a wooden farmhouse that sagged in abject disrepair.

"That's the ... ah ... Sorenson place," Arthur said, slowing the buggy to a gradual stop at the driveway. "I was just out here yesterday. What a pathetic mess they're in."

"You came out to see Mrs. Sorenson?"

Arthur nodded but said nothing. His eyes were focused on the farmhouse.

"How was she doing?"

"Not good," said Simpson, shaking his head. "It's a very sad situation. I don't know where they'll go."

"What do you mean?"

"It's just a matter of time," Arthur said. A deep frown crossed his forehead. "Her husband's dead, hail took most of this year's crops, and they're nearly penniless. She keeps saying that everything's going to be fine when her oldest boy comes home from the hospital in Minneapolis, but all he's going to bring home is more bills to pay."

"You're going to put them off the farm?" asked Annie.

"No, not yet," replied Arthur, "but ... what are we supposed to do with them? They can't make their payments on the property, let alone pay the bank back for the destroyed traction engine. That's money we'll never see again."

Annie glanced quickly at Arthur, then mumbled, "And she'll never see her husband again."

"He was a stinking drunk," Simpson replied. "Folks that knew him said he was as mean as they come. Violent. Vulgar. A bully."

"So you think she's happy now?" asked Annie.

"No, she's not happy, but she's better off without him," Arthur said, taking up the leather reins and starting the black mare down the road again. "Least she won't have some brute knocking her around the house."

Annie nodded and looked one more time toward the farmhouse.

"Still, I can't imagine how terrible it is for them. Does she have any other family?"

"Just a brother in Illinois," Arthur answered. "But he can't help her."

"What can you do for them?"

"Me?"

"Or your father," said Annie.

Simpson shrugged and shook his head. "I don't know. Not much, I guess. My father says that the longer they stay there, not paying their bills, the worse it's going to get for them. What would *you* have us do?"

"I don't know," said Annie. "It just seems like there must be a way to help them."

Taking in a deep breath, Arthur said, "That's one of the things I admire about you, my dear—your tender heart. But, Annie, you must understand, the poor are a dime a dozen. I see them every day. If the bank started bailing them out, where would it all stop? We'd be out of business, and they'd be right back where they started, and who would be helped? You understand that, don't you, Annie?"

Annie nodded doubtfully but didn't answer. She just sat quietly as the road took them away from the Sorensons' place and deeper into the countryside. Gradually, the soothing rhythm of the horse's hooves and the beauty around her combined to lighten her mood, and she cried out with delight when a brilliant stained-glass butterfly floated across their path. Grasshoppers whirred in the long, dry grass waving next to the roadside, and a red-tailed hawk soared lazily across the blue horizon. Annie sighed and leaned back in her seat as the buggy rounded a corner and the road took them down a long, gentle slope toward a slender stream.

"Nice out here, isn't it?" Arthur asked, pushing back the brim of his dapper straw hat. "You know I'm a city boy born and raised, but even I could get used to this. Now, look over there to the right."

Annie followed his gesture and gave another little cry of delight when she spotted a dainty round beaver pond tucked under a small grove of trees. The burr oaks and pines cut back the midday sun and cast a delicious shadow on the water's surface. Annie saw a little green frog make its joyful leap into the water just as the buggy pulled off the road onto a narrow dirt pathway and headed toward the secluded spot.

"What do you think of it?" asked Arthur, slowing the black mare to a walk.

"It's beautiful," Annie breathed. "If that's the spot that you said was perfect for a picnic, you were right. I love it."

"I just knew you would," Arthur said, tipping his chin up toward the pond, his blue eyes flashing. "And it's all mine!"

"What do you mean?"

He pulled the reins tight, and the buggy came to a stop. Then he pointed back up toward the road. "You see that wooden post on the corner there?"

Annie nodded.

"From that post to the one on the other side of this driveway," he said, then motioned down past the pond, "and then running straight south from the posts all the way back to the ridge—all of this land is mine."

"You can't be serious," Annie said, shaking her head.

"I'm dead serious," replied Arthur. "Prettiest piece of land I could find."

"You bought it?"

"Well, not exactly," said Arthur, rubbing his chin with his forefingers. "I got lucky and worked a trade with someone who owed me some money. I forgave the debt when the title to the land was secured in my name. Let's just say I got the best of the deal."

"So it really is yours?"

"I can show you the title if you'd like."

"I can't believe it. I don't know anyone my age who is a landowner. And you're going to use it for . . . picnics?" Annie teased.

Simpson laughed and said, "Oh yes, I hope to have many picnics here. After I build my house." He pointed to an elevated spot on the property that overlooked the pond. "Right there! Can't you imagine a house with a view like that?"

"No, as a matter of fact I can't," said Annie, but her face showed that she was beginning to picture it. "How in the world can you afford all this, Arthur?"

"Well, the house may have to wait a year or two," Simpson replied. "But that just gives more time for dreaming. Just think, living out here in the sunshine without everyone in town watching every move you make. Wouldn't it be wonderful?"

Annie nodded, picturing what the view would be like from the house to the pond. "I would love the privacy, although ... I don't know ... it's a long way from the stores. My friend Elsie hates living way out in the country. Would you really want to travel all that way back and forth from the bank?"

"It's not really that far," Arthur said. "Maybe I wouldn't even go into town every day. Maybe I'd stay out here with the beavers and the chipmunks. And say, I can have your father build the house for me. What kind of house do you think it should be?"

"What do you like?"

Arthur shrugged his shoulders and smiled. "I'm really not fussy. What would you pick if it was going to be your house?"

"My house? I'm not sure," Annie said, gazing at the possible building site. "If it were going to be mine," she ventured, "I'd want it to be a little stone cottage. With a porch."

"That's what I'll do, then," Arthur said, "only I want it big. A big stone house with wide windows so I can see everything, and a big front porch so I can sit outside with a glass of lemonade and take in the view. It'll be perfect. A dream house."

"It does sound perfect," said Annie, by now completely caught in the daydream. "And you could have flowerbeds out front. And a little path built down to the pond. For the picnics," she added.

"And that reminds me," Arthur said. "Are you ready for some luncheon?" He took up the reins, then put them back down again.

"I think I am," Annie replied, looking into his handsome face, thinking that it looked softer and gentler than usual.

"Good. So am I," he said with an uncharacteristically nervous smile. "But ... ah ... before we eat, I have something for you. Guess what it is."

Annie began to blush and shook her head. "Arthur, you shouldn't—"

"Don't tell me what I should do," he broke in. "Now, guess."

"That's not fair," Annie protested. "You have to give me at least one clue."

"All right," said Arthur. "The mysterious Orient."

"The Orient? I can't begin to guess. Is it a Japanese fan?"

"Goodness, no!" exclaimed Arthur with a laugh. Then he reached into one of his trouser pockets and pulled out a small, fancy box. Holding it up for Annie to study, he said, "Try again."

"Oh, Arthur, no . . ." Annie breathed as Arthur slowly lifted the lid, revealing a perfect white pearl in a dainty gold setting. "Arthur, you can't do this!"

"But I am doing it," he stated, carefully lifting the ring out of its velvet bed. He took Annie's right hand and gently slipped the ring on her finger. "To the young lady of my dreams . . . on a perfect day . . . in a place that I hope you'll come to love as much as I do."

Before Annie could respond, Arthur reached his arm around her, took her into his embrace, and kissed her firmly on the lips. The summer breeze pushed the long brown grass in waves around them, and the dark green leaves shimmered in the trees. But nature's finest splendors went unnoticed for the moment. Arthur Simpson's long-awaited first kiss had finally come to pass.

Chapter 9

A Sniveling Coward

Stuart Anderson sat waiting patiently in the doctor's small front office, idly watching the bits of dust and lint that danced in the bright light from the window. He could almost understand some of the muffled words that Doc Jones was saying to his patient behind the closed door of the examining room, but he felt guilty when he leaned his head closer to hear. When the door handle rattled, he turned his attention quickly to the dog-eared copy of *The Ohio Farmer* magazine that rested in his lap.

"You take the hyoscine just like I said, now, right before you go to bed," Doc Jones was saying with his back to the door as it opened wide. "Drink hot water three times a day and bathe your feet in hot water before going to bed. Hop tea is good, too, when you find it's hard to get to sleep."

"And do as little work as possible, right?" Claudie O'Neill's shrill voice was unmistakable.

"That's not what I said," the doctor replied, shaking his head. "The caution to avoid overworking is for men who are doing heavy physical labor. I recommend you get outside and tone up your system. Work in your garden, help Harry with some of the light chores, and you need to cut back on how much food you're eating in the evening."

Doc Jones swung around and smiled at Stuart as he stepped into the front office. The short, portly woman followed close behind him, and the doctor's face took on a pained expression as she spoke again.

"Right before we go to bed, I have Harry wet a towel with cold water and put it on the back of my neck, then he covers my head with a dry towel," Claudie continued as she followed the doctor to his desk. "It's good for my pressure."

"Your blood pressure?" asked Doc Jones.

"My pressure."

"Claudie," the doctor said with a weary expression, "how many times have I told you that your blood pressure is perfectly normal? And *some* doctors recommend the cold towels after someone has overworked himself. Give Harry a break and don't ask him to do that."

"It feels so good that—"

"Fine, that's fine," the doctor interjected, handing her a small bottle. "If you think the towels help, and if Harry's willing to do it, it's not going to hurt you. But don't drive him crazy with all those home remedies you read about. He's got a farm to run and can't keep attending to you all the time."

"Thank you very much, Doc," Claudie said. "Your wife will send me the bill?"

"Like always," he replied with a sigh. "I wish you'd go ahead and pay when you're here, though."

Stuart kept his head down, hoping that Claudie might not notice him, but when she turned to leave, she peered at him through her thick glasses and spoke loudly, "Why, Stuart Anderson, the town hero! Stand up and let me take a look at you, son."

Reluctantly, Stuart stood up and smiled down at her. "How are you, Mrs. O'Neill?"

"Couldn't be better, son, couldn't be better," she shrilled, still taking stock of him. "My, you've grown up to be a handsome devil, Stuart. I wish I was twenty years younger. I was a sight for sore eyes back then."

Doc Jones chuckled to himself and shook his head. "Claudie," he said, "Harry's waiting outside in the wagon, and Stuart looks like he's been waiting as well."

"I'll bet the girls stand and—"

"Stuart, come on in and let's see what I can do for you," the doctor broke in, motioning for Stuart to come quickly.

"Nice to see you, Claudie," said Stuart, catching a whiff of her heavy perfume as he sidled past her. "Greet Harry for me."

"I will," she replied, turning to watch Stuart and the doctor disappear into the examining room. "Harry's in no hurry...."

Claudie's words trailed off as Doc Jones shut the door behind them and stopped to listen. He closed his eyes for the moment, and the frown on his forehead furrowed deeper as the voice in the other room continued its chatter. Stuart crossed over to a wooden chair and sat down.

"She may stand there all day waiting for you to come out," the doctor said softly. Then they both heard the front screen door slap shut, and relief flooded the doctor's face. "Thank goodness, she's gone. My apologies for not greeting you sooner."

"No, that's fine," said Stuart. "Some of the men who bring their grain to the mill will talk my leg off, too. I hate to do it, but sometimes I just have to walk away from them."

"You do understand, then," Doc Jones said, walking across the room and sitting down across from Stuart. "You also see that not everything I do here is quite a matter of life and death. I feel sorry for Harry O'Neill, I'll tell you."

Stuart laughed. "Oh, I don't know, they seem to get along just fine. Just as long as she's not asking *me* to put cold towels on the back of her neck."

The doctor broke out laughing as well. "I guess you got a point there. Now, what can I do for you, Stuart? I thought you might have left for school already."

"Tomorrow," Stuart replied. "And before I go, I wanted to ask you something. I've . . . ah . . . been thinking a lot about what you said. . . ."

"About becoming a doctor."

"Yeah," replied Stuart. "Praying a lot, too. And I think it's a matter I might at least look into. So, well, I wondered what you meant when you said you'd be willing to help me. I truly don't know where to begin."

A wide smile crossed the doctor's face, then he pressed his lips together and rubbed his chin. "Hmmm," he said, "I'm delighted to hear this, Stuart. You're not the only one who's been praying about it. So, well, the first thing you'll need to think about is getting into the university's medical school. The key to doing that will be getting your name in front of the right people, and that requires either having a wealthy family or having some other kind of connections. . . . You haven't suddenly become rich, have you?"

Stuart snorted. "You know the answer to that one!"

"Well, then, I suppose you'll have to depend on me to put your name on the desks of the key administrators," the doctor stated. "I have several friends there, and a couple of others I went to school with owe me a favor or two. You give me some time, and I'll get them on your side—provided this is what you really want to do."

"I was wondering if you could give me till Christmas to decide," Stuart said. "I need some more time to make sure it's right."

"I understand." The doctor took off his silver wire-rimmed glasses and rubbed the bridge of his large nose. "Now, if you don't mind my asking, I've been wondering about whether you might need some, ah, financial assistance."

Stuart's head tilted up and he studied the doctor's expression. "No, I don't mind your asking," he replied. "As you know, I've been working for my father, and I've saved as much money as I could, but I've used most of that for my first year at the university. This summer's pay is going to help, and my folks help when they can, but I'm still not sure where all the money will come from to get me through."

"What if I could—"

"No, please," Stuart interrupted, holding up a hand. "I couldn't—"

"Just a minute, here, before you go shutting a door to a room that you should take a look inside first," Doc Jones ordered. "Now, you're going to need to come up with some money, mark my words. And I'm getting along in years, in case you hadn't noticed. Some days, especially when I have to go out in the country and make house calls, I get so tired that I'm ready to quit on the spot. My days as a practicing physician are numbered, that's for certain. Do you see what I'm getting at?"

"Not exactly."

"My doctoring years are coming to an end for this town," Doc Jones explained, "and my concern is whether Bradford will be able to attract another doctor. Not every town this size is fortunate enough, you realize."

"I guess I do. But what—?"

"I'm going to make you an offer," the doctor said, getting to his feet and walking over to the window. He stood looking out for a moment, then turned back to Stuart. "If you're willing to sign a notarized document that states that you will return to Bradford to practice medicine for a minimum of five years, I will also sign the document stating that I will pay for two years of your medical school."

"Oh!" Stuart gasped, leaning his head back against the wall and closing his eyes. "That's unthinkable, Doc. I couldn't let you do that."

"I can do exactly what I want," the doctor replied, still staring into Stuart's face. "I love the people of this community, and I won't quit serving them until I feel satisfied with my replacement. Mildred and I have more money than we'll ever need when I retire, and I want to use some of it to make sure this town gets a good doctor."

"I know you're serious, Doc, and I don't want to sound ungrateful," said Stuart. "It's just too much for me to comprehend. I'm honored by your offer."

"You should be," the doctor said, breaking into his wide grin. "I'm only asking you to think about. And pray about it. Then you let me know. By Christmas, right?"

"Yes," said Stuart, rising from his chair. "I think I need to get outside and take a walk. My pressure's rising like Claudie's!"

Doc Jones broke out laughing and reached out for Stuart's hand. "Let's shake on it, son. You can pray about, but I think I'll start the paper work now."

Stuart squeezed the doctor's strong hand, then shook it. He looked into the kind eyes he had taken for granted all the years he'd been growing up, and he suddenly felt like shouting, but thought he better hold off until he got outside the office. "Thank you" was as much as he managed to say.

Doc Jones escorted Stuart out through the front office, but neither man spoke until Stuart pushed the front screen door and turned to say, "I hope to see you at Christmas."

"I'll be here, Stuart," the older man said, then winked. "You take care."

"I will." Stuart stepped out the door and headed down the sidewalk without thinking about where he wanted to go. The doctor's proposal was ringing in his ears, and his eyes refused to focus on anything in particular. His first inclination had been to rush down to the mill to tell his parents, but the doctor's proposal seemed too overwhelming to explain at the moment. So he stopped at the corner to the town's main street and decided to sit down for a while on the steps leading up to the three-story hotel.

This must be a dream or something, Stuart thought to himself as he leaned back on the steps and closed his eyes to the sunshine. So many puzzle pieces in his life seemed suddenly to be fitting into place, but the picture they formed was so different from what he had imagined.

Stuart sat there for several minutes, trying to wrap his thoughts together and make some sense of what he should do next. Then he heard a familiar voice calling his name. He looked down the street to see Garrit Harding walking down the sidewalk toward him. The white-haired boy had a small sack in his hand and was half skipping his way along.

"Whatcha doing up there?" Garrit called out.

"Not much," said Stuart, sitting up straight as the boy approached him on the steps. "Where've you been?"

"Getting some licorice at your father's drugstore," Garrit replied, holding up his sack and opening his mouth to reveal a black substance oozing around his formerly white teeth. "Annie likes it, too. She pays me half if I'll walk down here and buy it, but I eat most of it."

"Pretty good deal for you," Stuart said, shaking his head no when Garrit extended the opened bag toward him. "So how's your sister?"

"She's like she always is," said Garrit. "Except, she came home on Saturday with a big pearl ring. She and my mother sat and looked at it all day long. Mother says it's worth a lot of money. It must be nice to be so rich like her boyfriend."

"So Simpson gave her the ring?" asked Stuart.

"Who else?" Garrit responded, reaching down and tightening his long black shoelaces. "My father said it would take him a year to save that much money."

"Annie's happy, then?"

"It's sickening," said Garrit. "They came up the sidewalk on Saturday afternoon hugging and . . . then he kissed her. Right in front of me and my mother. Yuk."

Stuart looked down the street toward the bank, then back to Garrit. "Was it . . . did they call it an engagement ring?"

"No, that's what my father asked just as soon as Arthur left," answered Garrit. "Annie said it was to celebrate a special day or something. Father didn't believe her, but Mother did. They got in a fight about it. But they all like Arthur."

"Do you?"

"I wish he'd never come back," Garrit replied. He popped two more pieces of licorice into his mouth.

"Why?"

"He's mean, and he doesn't like me."

"How do you know that?"

Garrit looked up at Stuart and said, "He told me he didn't. And once, when he was at the house and Annie left the room, he kicked me when I got in his way. I hate him."

"Have you told Annie?"

"No," Garrit said, looking down and shaking his head. "Arthur told me that if I told Annie or my mother or father, he'd hurt me worse than when he kicked me. And that really hurt."

Stuart turned toward the bank again. "Well, I think that your sister's sweetheart has spotted us. You may want to take your licorice and head on home. I got a feeling the banker's boy isn't going to be real friendly today. Don't feel bad, Garrit. He doesn't like me, either."

Glancing down the street, Garrit quickly scooped up his precious bag of candy. "I like you, Stuart." That said, he jumped up and marched away in the opposite direction.

Arthur Simpson was striding down the street toward Stuart with a big grin on his face, buttoning his expensive suit coat as he approached. His shiny black dress shoes squeaked loudly on the sidewalk, and his deep blue eyes were triumphant. By the time he made it to the steps of the hotel, Arthur's face was flushed.

"Going to a fire?" Stuart asked, leaning forward and setting his chin on his hands.

"No!" Simpson huffed. "I told you on Saturday morning that I wanted to talk with you, and now seemed like a good time."

"Are you inviting me to your office at the bank?"

"No, I'm not." Arthur's words were clipped. "What did that kid say to you?"

"Garrit, you mean? He has a name, you know."

"What did he want?"

"He . . . um . . . offered me some of his licorice, but I don't care much for it. Were you hoping to get it from him?"

"What was he talking about?"

"Listen, Arthur," Stuart said, standing up and stretching his strong, suntanned arms. "You said that you wanted to talk with me. Garrit is a new friend of mine, and what we talked about is none of your business. If you've got something you'd like to discuss with me, say it. I'm really not in a very good mood at the moment."

"So he told you about the ring?"

Stuart took a deep breath and licked his lips. "You must have real bad hearing because I thought I just told you not to bring Garrit back into this conversation. Would you like to see whether or not I mean it?"

Simpson's expression did not change. He continued to stare at Stuart. "You would strike me here on the street?"

"Only if you want me to," replied Stuart, getting to his feet and taking a step down toward Simpson. "Would you prefer the alley?"

"I would prefer to talk like men rather than fight like barbarians," said Simpson. "Surely we can do better."

"Only if you agree to talk fair," Stuart continued, taking another step toward the young banker. "And I'll be the judge."

"Be forewarned, Anderson," Arthur said with a half smile. "I was an expert boxer in college."

"So you've told me." Stuart took another step. "Now, what is it you want to talk about?"

Simpson looked both directions down the street, then he said, "I want to know why you met with Annie down at the bridge."

"Annie already answered that," Stuart said. "Do you think she was lying? Perhaps it was a secret rendezvous?"

"Perhaps."

Stuart shook his head and started to laugh. "Boy, you are something. Annie knows that you're going to meet her at the bridge, so she plans a secret meeting with me at that very bridge on the very same morning? I wonder what you really believe about Annie. Sounds to me like you've got a problem with trusting her."

"Not anymore," Simpson sneered.

"So that ring bought her fair and square?" asked Stuart. "I'll have to get a look at it. Must be really something."

Simpson's forehead pinched down, and the muscles in his jaw tightened. Then he took a deep breath and said, "I thought you might be interested that I've done a little research into your father's account at the bank. That fire really set him back into debt, didn't it?"

Stuart's black eyes narrowed to a glare, and his knuckles went white, then he stepped up to Arthur and grabbed him by the lapels. "If I . . . ever . . . hear . . . that your bank pulls a fast one on my father, you better be somewhere out of the country, because I'll track you down. You, Mr. Banker Boy, are a bully and a sniveling coward, and I call your bluff. Go ahead and take the first swing if you'd like."

Letting go of Arthur's coat, Stuart motioned to his chin. "Give it your best, Simpson, because it'll be your last."

Arthur Simpson's blue eyes burned and he stepped forward, then he hesitated for a moment and rocked backward. Straightening his elegant coat and avoiding Stuart's eyes, he turned on his heel with an air of wounded dignity. "Good day, Mr. Anderson. I hope not to see you again."

Chapter 10

A Closed Door

Stopping at the street corner and looking south toward the Harding house, Stuart Anderson let out a groan. "Oh no," he mumbled to himself. "Why does he have to be home right now? I thought he worked all the time."

It had taken Stuart most of the afternoon to cool down after his talk with Arthur Simpson, then another two hours to decide he had to talk with Annie one more time before he left town to go back to school. His faint hope that he could avoid Annie's parents had crumbled at the sight of James Harding sitting on his front steps, reading a newspaper.

Too late to turn back now, Stuart determined, taking a deep breath and telling his feet to move forward. He strode down the street as confidently as he could. Glancing up casually, he spotted Garrit's white head poking out of one of the upstairs bedroom windows. Garrit seemed to be doing his best to wave Stuart away.

Noting that Mr. Harding had not yet looked up from the newspaper, Stuart shook his head no to Garrit, but that did not deter the lad from waving and gesturing. In fact, the boy waved harder and harder with every step that Stuart took. As Stuart turned onto the Hardings' sidewalk, he realized that Garrit was mouthing, "Stop! Not now!"

Just at that moment James Harding glanced up and let the paper sink into his lap, his stern expression darkening when he spotted Stuart. For a man who was only thirty-nine, Mr. Harding looked much older. His hair was prematurely gray, and two decades of working outdoors through the extremes of Minnesota's winters and summers had hardened and weathered his face. Brown eyes like Annie's peered out under a deeply etched brow, but his were pinched and calculating.

"Good evening, Mr. Harding," Stuart greeted. "I was wondering if your daughter was home?"

"Stuart Anderson, right?" James Harding nodded curtly but made no attempt to stand up or to shake Stuart's hand. "Yes, Annie is home. Probably up in her room."

Stuart waited awkwardly for the man to invite him in, but no invitation was forthcoming. He glanced up and noticed that Garrit was gone from the window. Then he tried again. "Sir, I wonder if I might talk with Annie for a bit. I'm leaving for college tomorrow, and I'd like to say good-bye."

Annie's father looked down at his large, muscular hand and flexed it a few times. Then he looked up and shook his head. "Sorry, Mr. Anderson, but I don't think that's such a good idea. I suggest you head on home. We don't care for any trouble here."

"What trouble?" Stuart blurted out. "What trouble could saying good-bye cause? I don't understand, sir."

James Harding chuckled sourly to himself. "I think you do, son. I heard that you picked a fight with Arthur Simpson today—right out on Main Street for everybody in the county to watch. You're just lucky he was too much of a gentleman to strike you. At any rate, I don't hold with that kind of behavior, and I don't think I want you coming around Annie again."

"But he—" Stuart caught himself, knowing that Simpson would deny everything he'd said earlier in the day. "Mr. Harding, my beef with Arthur was personal, and any attempt I make to explain would end up being his word against mine. But I assure you, sir, that I have no intentions of causing you any trouble. I only wish to be able to speak with Annie for a few minutes as a friend."

"I already told you I can't allow that," her father replied, looking into Stuart's face again. "Now, I appreciate what you done for her when the accident happened, and I always will. But Arthur Simpson was courting her a long time before that."

"But I—"

"Look, it's clear that you want to get in between my daughter and

Arthur Simpson," James Harding broke in. "It's pretty plain you'd like Arthur out of the way."

Stuart shook his head in disbelief, gazing out into the street as he gathered his reeling thoughts. While he'd hoped to avoid Annie's parents, he'd never expected to have to defend and explain the nature of his visit.

"You'd like to court my daughter, ain't that so?" James Harding demanded.

"Mr. Harding, I leave for the university tomorrow, so I hardly consider myself in a position to get in between your daughter and Arthur Simpson, although I admit that, like most young men who have met her, I would be delighted with the opportunity to court her. I would be a liar if I suggested otherwise. I would think, though, that as her father, you would be more concerned about Arthur Simpson than about me."

"What're you talking about?"

"Have you spent time with him?" asked Stuart. "Do you think you know and understand the man?"

James Harding laid the newspaper down on the concrete step. "Matter of fact, my wife and I have spent a fair amount of time with Arthur Simpson. He's a fine young man."

"You realize that—"

"No, thank you," Annie's father said, standing up and looking down at Stuart. "You keep your accusations to yourself, son. I can size up a person pretty fast, and I happen to think highly of Arthur. And by the way, he's only spoken well of you in the past. I suggest you think about that."

"I have, sir—a lot, lately—and for your daughter's sake I hope you watch Mr. Simpson very closely," Stuart replied. "Would it be possible to at least say good-bye to her?"

"I'm afraid not, Mr. Harding," said the older man. "I suggest you head on home. Please don't write her, either. Good night."

Stuart stood still and watched as Annie's father stomped into the house, the screen door slapping shut behind him. "Good night, Mr. Harding," he whispered, shook his head in disbelief, and trudged away down the sidewalk with his hands in his pockets. Glancing back at the upstairs window, he was surprised to see both Annie and Garrit peering out at him.

"Annie!" her father's voice called out from somewhere on the first floor. She gave Stuart a quick wave, then spun around and disappeared from the window. Garrit made some funny motions with his hands that Stuart could not decipher, so he simply waved back and continued down the street.

"Next thing you know, I'll run into Simpson again," Stuart muttered to himself, throwing up his hands. He shuffled his feet slowly down the street, wishing he'd stayed home after all. "What a rotten day this has been. Phew!"

Stuart had walked about three blocks when he thought he heard his name being called, and he turned to see Garrit racing after him. The boy's short legs were pumping as fast as he could go, but he was tiring by the second. When he saw that Stuart had heard him, he slowed noticeably, then walked the last half block.

"You should have . . . listened to me!" Garrit gasped through a huff and a puff. "My father's been in a bad mood tonight. He was mad even before you showed up."

"Why?"

Garrit shrugged. "I don't know. He just gets in bad moods. You shouldn't try to talk to him then."

"I think I learned my lesson," Stuart said with a nod. "Is Annie in trouble?"

"No," Garrit answered, "but she will be if Father catches her. She wants to meet you down by the west bridge."

"Tonight?"

"In just a few minutes!" responded Garrit, glancing back down the street as if his father might be following him. "My grandma's sick, and Annie's going to stay overnight at her house. It's on her way there. She'll meet you at the bridge."

"Oh, I don't think that's a very good idea," said Stuart. "Your father—"

"He's going to bed right now," Garrit interjected. "He goes to bed real early 'cause he has to get up early. So if Annie doesn't spend too much time at the bridge, no one's going to know. I have to get home before they notice I snuck out."

Garrit took off running for home before Stuart could say anything more. He stood and watched as the little boy chugged down the street, then turned and continued on his way. When Stuart reached the corner, he stopped for a moment and looked in the direction of his house. Then he took a deep breath, smiled, and turned in the opposite direction, striding quickly toward the ruined bridge.

To ensure that he wouldn't be seen, Stuart took a path through a wooded slope that led to the stream and then followed along the water's edge to a sandy point about thirty yards above the bridge. He stood quietly, watching and listening for any movement, then made a dash for a large pile of limestone rocks under the bridge. Selecting the most protected spot he could find, Stuart sat down, his heart still racing, and waited.

After about ten minutes, he thought he heard footsteps on the embankment behind him but could see no one. He stiffened when a muffled voice suddenly sounded at the edge of the bridge; someone was walking past with a dog. Stuart sat frozen in place, praying the animal wouldn't sniff him out and start barking.

Just at that moment, a gentle tap on his shoulders brought Stuart straight up from his sitting position. He had all he could do to force the yell back down his throat. He spun around to see that it was Annie who had gotten the drop on him. She was covering her nose and nearly doubled over with laughter.

"Very funny," Stuart whispered, pointing above toward the voice he'd heard moments before. "How did you get here?"

"Same way you came," Annie spoke softly as her giggles finally subsided. "I followed you through the woods, but I was a little more wary. You got preoccupied looking up the embankment. That was Mr. Greenley with old Sparkey, by the way. No reason to be nervous about them."

Stuart finally smiled. "He can hardly see anymore, and that dog can't smell. They're a real team."

Annie nodded and perched on a rock across from Stuart. He sat back down, running his fingers through his dark hair.

"I need to apologize about my father's behavior," said Annie. "Somebody stopped by the building he was working on today and told him what happened downtown this morning. He thinks Arthur is wonderful, so I guess he assumed you're awful."

"I sort of got that impression," Stuart replied with a smirk. "I wouldn't want to get your father mad at me, that's for sure."

"No, you wouldn't," Annie said, shaking her head. "He's a volcano for a temper."

"So . . . why would you risk meeting me here?" asked Stuart, searching out Annie's large brown eyes in the shadows. "If he catches you, or if Arthur Simpson finds out, you're going to have a lot of explaining to do."

Annie took a deep breath and smiled. "Seemed to me that . . . given the fact that you saved my life . . . the least I could do was say good-bye before you left. If this is the worst thing I do, I don't think my father or Arthur have much to be concerned about."

"I'd like to see you try to tell that to them," Stuart said. "I don't think they'd be so understanding."

"Is it true," asked Annie, ignoring his comment, "that it was you who picked the fight with Arthur?"

"Who did you hear about it from?"

"Arthur."

Stuart laughed and rubbed his forehead with his fingertips. "Then I guarantee that what you heard was not what happened."

"Are you saying he would lie to me?"

"Look at that pearl ring on your finger," Stuart replied, glancing down at her right hand. "I think he'd do just about anything to protect his investment."

Annie looked away, her face flushing, but she continued to speak quietly. "That, Mr. Anderson, was a very unkind accusation. I hoped it didn't happen the way Arthur said it did."

"And how was that?"

"He said you heard about the ring he gave me, and you first threatened to circulate lies about him, then you tried to provoke him into a fight in order to humiliate him before me."

Stuart couldn't restrain a chuckle or keep his head from shaking. "That's the dumbest thing I've heard yet," he spouted. "And you believed that about me?"

Staring straight into Stuart's dark eyes, Annie answered, "No, I didn't. But neither do I believe you when you say that Arthur sees me as an investment. You have misjudged him, Stuart, just as I believe that he has misjudged you."

"So you believe that he truly loves you?" asked Stuart, his eyes unyielding.

"We have never talked about love," Annie replied, glancing down at her ring. "But he obviously cares about me, and this is one way he shows it. Is that so wrong?"

"Not if his motives are honorable," said Stuart. "I, for one, do not believe they are. That's why I came to your house—to warn you. Things are not what they seem."

"Why do you dislike Arthur so?" asked Annie. "He said that he had hoped to become your friend, but that you grew hostile when you found out that he and I were . . . seeing each other."

Stuart laughed again and leaned back on his rock. "I don't mean to offend you, Annie," he stated, "but your friend is a very serious liar. On two separate occasions he has used threats to persuade me to stay away from you, and I believe he would think nothing of using blackmail if it served his purposes."

"No, no. Arthur could never do that . . . or be like that," Annie protested. "He may be a little jealous and act a little rude because of it, but he really is the finest of gentlemen. Just like his father."

"Well, one thing is as clear as this stream," said Stuart with a somber face. "Either Arthur Simpson is lying through his teeth, or I am. And I am here to tell you, as a friend, that I am afraid for you. I really do fear that he will hurt you worse than you can imagine."

Annie was staring into Stuart's eyes, but she said nothing.

"I beg you to watch his actions very closely," Stuart continued. "Listen to the words he uses . . . and his tone of voice. Never let his gifts or his charm blind you to the truth you're seeing about his life, and never let them cause you to act impulsively. He will take advantage of you if you do."

"You would put yourself to the same standard, Mr. Anderson?" Annie asked.

"If I were given the opportunity," Stuart responded.

"My parents think highly of Arthur," Annie said. "Should I discount their favor?"

"No, I suppose not," answered Stuart. "But do they speak of his character ... or of his money?"

A smile slowly crossed her delicate features. "Mostly his money, I guess. They hope I can avoid some of the problems they've experienced."

"Is that what you want, too?" asked Stuart.

"I can't imagine anyone not wanting to worry about money," said Annie. "Are you saying you'd prefer to be poor?"

Stuart shook his head no. "I should have asked whether money is all you want. Would you marry a man for his money?"

"No. Never."

"Would you marry someone for love who had no money?"

"Yes," Annie replied, then she laughed. "I'd prefer both, though, if you don't mind."

Stuart laughed, too. "Well, then, I hope ... when that day comes for you ... that you get both."

They fell silent for just a minute, and the babble of the stream beside them sounded loud in their ears.

"You know, Stuart Anderson," she finally said with a smile, "you are quite the mystery to me."

"Why is that?"

"Because I don't understand why you care about this. You're leaving tomorrow, knowing that Arthur and I will continue to see each other, and yet you nearly got in a fight with him today, and you're willing to tell me all this. I can't understand your motive. Please tell me."

Stuart rubbed his right eye, then took a deep breath and sighed. "My motive..." he mumbled and shook his head. "I guess I just can't stand by and watch you get hurt without trying to stop it."

"But why? What difference will it make for you?"

"Perhaps none," said Stuart, standing up and moving closer to Annie's face. He grinned. "Perhaps some, if I'm really fortunate."

"So your motives are less than selfless." She did not back off. "Maybe you would like to replace Arthur, just as my father said."

"My motives are as mixed as your feelings are right now," Stuart said, reaching out and gently taking her hand in his. "Can you look me in the eye and tell me that Arthur Simpson is the only man for whom you have feelings?"

Annie did not look away or pull her hand from his. She hesitated for only a moment. "I cannot deny that when I am with you my feelings are confused. But you are going away."

Stuart nodded. "So I ask only that you consider what I've asked you to do. Watch and listen with your heart. Let the truth speak above the veneer. I hope the day comes when you give me a chance."

"We'll see, Stuart Anderson," Annie whispered, a slight tremble in her voice as she withdrew her hand from his. "But now I must go."

"Thank you for saying good-bye," said Stuart. "I won't forget this night."

"Nor will I," Annie agreed. Then she leaned close to his face, kissed him ever so softly on the cheek, and whispered, "Good-night."

Part 2

Autumn Changes

Golden maples tinged with red, yellow willows bending low, brown-edged oaks—all the trees by Flatwillow Creek now speak the same stirring story, a story of good-byes.

The summer is packing to leave, and one day soon the town will wake to find it vanished. Soon, one by one, the trees will drop their leaves into the water, bowing in farewell as the leaves float off in search of the runaway season.

Through all the good-byes, the swirling waters flow true and strong. The water's gurgling even sounds like laughter, for Flatwillow Creek knows well the joys of a journey.

Chapter 11

The Bat Lady

"Miss Harding, could I see you before you leave?"

Mrs. Olson's clear, strong voice interrupted Annie in the act of closing her desk and rising from her seat. She threw a quick glance toward her friend Elsie Dale and mouthed the words "Wait for me." Then she moved against the tide of exiting students to see what the teacher wanted.

Of all the teachers she had had over the years, Henrietta Olson was easily Annie's favorite. Tall and slender, with pepper-gray hair pulled into a tight bun, she was known to be strict but absolutely fair.

"Have a seat." Mrs. Olson pointed to the dark wooden chair at the side of her desk and flashed a warm smile that softened her sharp, lean features. "I am so delighted to have you in my class again, Annie. How are you? I heard about the terrible accident."

"I'm fine now, thank you," Annie replied, returning the teacher's smile. "I hurt my head, though. Doc Jones said it was a mild concussion, so you need to keep that in mind when you grade my papers this year. I may need some special favors."

Henrietta chuckled and rested her elbows on the desk. "I'll see what I can do," she replied. "But, Annie, I also heard about Walter Sorenson and his father. That must have been a horrible sight."

"I . . . ah . . . didn't actually see them," said Annie. "When I saw the bridge breaking apart, I was trying to get my little brother out of harm's way, and I really didn't see anything after I got pulled under some of the debris. I was just fortunate to survive. Stuart Anderson saved my life. Did you hear about that, too?"

"Yes, that's what I read in the paper," Mrs. Olson said. "Stuart

Anderson was an outstanding student of mine. But I was wondering what you've heard about Walter?"

"Nothing recently. Has something happened?"

"Nothing bad," answered her teacher. "But I've heard that they're expecting him to get out of the hospital soon. He's going to stay here in town with his grandmother while he mends, then he hopes to go home."

"That's good," said Annie. "I did hear that his arm was not as badly injured as they first thought."

Mrs. Olson nodded. "They did manage to save the arm, but he'll never use it with any strength. They say it'll be nearly impossible for Walter to farm."

"Oh, that's too bad," Annie said. "His mother was depending on him to take it over."

"It won't happen. And I just know they're going to lose that farm; it's only a matter of time. But I'm hoping that something can be done to help Walter," said Mrs. Olson. "Which is why I wanted to talk to you."

"What is it?"

"I talked with Walter's grandmother, and the situation is exactly as I remembered. It seems that Walter's father pulled him out of school during his seventh-grade year," said Mrs. Olson. "She said that he can read and write and does basic math very well, but we need to help him improve. If his abilities are good enough, he could find work in an office or some job where he doesn't need so much strength in his arm."

"We, Mrs. Olson?"

The teacher smiled again. "I was hoping you might be willing to help me teach him . . . provided that Walter wants our help. I don't have a lot of time, but if we worked as a team, I think Walter might have a brighter future."

"You really think I could help?"

"Without a question!" her teacher exclaimed. "You would make a wonderful teacher, Annie. I've watched you for several years, and once you understand what's being taught, I always see you showing the other students how to do it. That's exactly what Walter needs. I know it's asking for a large commitment, but would you at least think about it?"

Annie blinked and nodded. "It's ... um ... it's a bit of a surprise," she said, then smiled. "Me, a teacher—that's something I never expected. But I will think about it, and of course I'd need to check with my parents. I really would like to do something that would make a difference for the Sorensons."

"Well, please give it some thought, and I'll let you know more after Walter returns," Mrs. Olson said. She glanced back toward the classroom door. "Looks like Elsie's waiting for you. I'm sorry to have kept you so long on the first day of school."

"That's fine," said Annie, glancing around to see Elsie standing alone in the school hallway. "We'll see you tomorrow."

"See you tomorrow," the teacher echoed.

Annie walked quickly out of the classroom to be greeted by Elsie Dale's enthusiastic hug. Elsie had become Annie's first friend after her family moved from Minneapolis, but the two young women had seen each other only twice over the summer months, and the busy first-day-of-school morning had afforded no chance for them to catch up.

"Whatever did the Bat Lady want?" Elsie asked.

"How many times have I told you not to call her that," scolded Annie as they started down the hallway toward the wide front doors of the school. "Let's go to your room. We've got a million things to talk about."

"Like that gorgeous pearl ring on your finger," Elsie commented with a sidelong glance at Annie's hand, "not to mention that cameo pendant. You've got some explaining to do, and I want to hear every detail!"

"You will, whether you want to or not," Annie replied with a laugh. "I've missed you so this summer. I wish your folks lived in town!"

The two girls had walked down the school steps arm in arm and automatically turned in the direction of downtown. Several children had stayed to play on the grassy lawn in front of the school, and the girls had to dodge a group of boys who were chasing one another. A warm breeze was whipping the flag around, and the flag's rope slapped noisily against the tall steel pole that held it.

"If my folks lived in town, though," Elsie replied, "I wouldn't be living at the boardinghouse, and we wouldn't have a place all to ourselves. My mother would try to listen in on everything."

"And my mother likes it so quiet at our house," said Annie.

"Is she still so . . . melancholic?"

"Worse, I think," Annie replied, looking down as she stepped off the sidewalk into the street.

"Your father again?"

Annie nodded. "From the minute he gets home at night he never stops getting after her. He treats her like she's his slave."

Elsie nodded knowingly and shook her head. "Are you still afraid she'll leave?"

"No, but if it wasn't for my little brother, I think she would."

"I would leave."

"Me, too, I think." Annie's voice dropped to nearly a whisper. Elsie's squeeze of her arm told Annie that her friend understood her sadness.

"So what did Mrs. Olson want? She does look like a bat, you know," Elsie said, breaking the tension of the moment.

"Don't say that. I like her a lot. She just asked me to consider something, that's all."

"That's all?" asked Elsie, bumping against Annie as they walked down the sidewalk. "Consider what? Don't you dare try to hide anything from me. I sat in our farmhouse all summer starved for news."

"Have I ever been able to hide anything from you?" Annie asked. "All right, Mrs. Olson asked me to consider helping her tutor a student who has a special need. She's not even sure if it's going to happen."

"She wants *you* to help her?"

"Yes. Do you think I shouldn't consider it?"

"No, not at all," Elsie said. "I've just never really thought of you as a teacher, that's all. Who's it for?"

"The boy who got hurt at the bridge."

"*Walter?*" Elsie gasped. "Walter Sorenson?"

"That's right," Annie replied. "His father pulled him out of school in seventh grade. Mrs. Olson hopes we can help him raise his schooling to a level where he can find an office job of some kind. His arm was badly crushed that day."

"Annie Harding, you cannot be serious," Elsie protested. "Have you forgotten that Walter is as ugly as a mud fence? He's as homely as his father was. He's tall and scraggly—"

"I've hardly ever seen him before," Annie said. "But what does that have to do with helping with his education?"

"Nothing, but ... my goodness ... his teeth are already rotting," Elsie explained with a slight shudder. "And he's got all those freckles and funny skin blotches. You can't be with somebody like him."

"Why?"

By now, Elsie and Annie had reached the corner of Main Street. Elsie pointed down toward the bank and smiled. "I'll give you one really big reason why you better stay away from someone as pitiful as Walter Sorenson. Then, if you haven't figured it out, I suggest you check out that ring on your right hand."

Annie searched her friend's face. "You're serious, aren't you? You actually think that because I'm seeing Arthur I should stay away from someone who needs help?"

"I know so."

"But why, Elsie?"

"Don't be so naïve."

"Why should my helping Walter affect Arthur? It has nothing to do with him."

"Maybe it shouldn't, but it will," said Elsie, fixing her attention on the bank. "You shouldn't do it, Annie."

"I still don't see why."

"Don't you realize that Arthur's an important man in this town? You'd make him look like he was, well, ordinary. He doesn't need that."

"And Walter didn't need to lose his father ... or hurt his arm so badly."

"Annie, somebody else can help Mrs. Olson. I'm telling you—"

"Help Mrs. Olson with what?" Arthur Simpson's musical baritone suddenly rang out from behind, startling the two young women. He broke out into a laugh and then gave a slight theatrical bow. "Good day, ladies."

"Arthur, where did you come from?" Annie asked, taking his arm and shaking him playfully. "It's not polite to sneak up on a lady like that."

"I'm sorry, but I couldn't resist," replied Arthur, nodding toward Elsie with a grin. "Welcome back to the big city, Miss Dale. It is such a delight to have another beautiful woman in this town. And you—you are looking lovelier than ever."

Elsie smiled and curtsied. "Why, thank you, Mr. Simpson. I can't tell you how much I hated being in the country all summer long. I hardly saw a soul the entire time. It's good to be back and see a handsome face again."

"Who happens to be spoken for," Annie teased.

"Elsie, did you see the ring?" asked Arthur, lifting Annie's right hand and admiring it in the bright sunshine.

"Did I go blind just because I was on the farm for three months?" Elsie returned. "It's the only thing I could think about in school today. Where did you ever find such a beautiful pearl?"

"Hawaii."

"No!" exclaimed Elsie, cupping her cheeks with her hands. "You were in Hawaii?"

"No, he wasn't," Annie corrected quickly, looking up at Arthur. "He means the pearl came from Hawaii."

"You're certain that's what I mean?" Simpson asked, wrinkling his forehead.

Annie studied Arthur's expression and replied, "No, I guess I'm not. Now that you mention it, there's a lot about your past that I don't know. You haven't ever visited Hawaii, have you?"

"Only once," he replied, standing up taller and turning his deep blue eyes on Elsie. "I've also been to San Francisco, and New York, and Washington, D.C., and Charleston."

"You're telling the truth?" asked Elsie, returning Arthur's stare. "All the places I've always dreamed about going?"

"Yes, and more."

"Arthur, don't be a tease," Annie said. "She believes every word you say."

"I assure you, I am telling the gospel truth," Arthur replied, glancing back at Annie. "You may ask my father if you don't believe me. It was his idea . . . and his money, thank goodness."

"When did you do this?" asked Annie.

"Not long before my father purchased the bank here," said Arthur. "He thought it would be good for me to get away for a while. Travel is broadening, you know."

"And did you enjoy it?" Elsie asked.

"Immensely, Miss Dale," Arthur replied with a nod. "My only regret, in the presence of such lovely company, is that I was alone. To have had such an adventure with a beautiful woman at my side would have been nothing short of heavenly."

Elsie Dale burst into giggles, and her heart-shaped face flushed with embarrassment as Arthur reached out and touched her arm, laughing as well. Annie did not join in their mirth.

"It would be hard for me to imagine," Elsie said, "that your adventure never involved female companionship, Arthur. Perhaps there was someone special in each of those cities?"

Simpson raised his eyebrows and shook his head. "*Special*, no," he said with a smug smile. "I will say no more."

"I knew it!" exclaimed Elsie.

"And what else don't we know about you, Mr. Simpson?" Annie asked, taking his arm without a smile. "Perhaps I don't want to know?"

"You don't want to know," Arthur replied, "and I wouldn't tell anyway. I believe everyone should have a few secrets."

"And every closet a few skeletons?" Elsie added.

"Not in my closet," said Arthur.

"I'll bet," Annie countered, shaking his arm, then letting go. "I don't like this at all. We're going to have a little talk with your mother one of these days, Arthur."

"Ah . . . perhaps we've taken things too far," Arthur answered, pulling out his pocket watch and making a big show of consulting it. "Time for me to get back to the bank anyway. But what were you saying about Annie helping someone?"

"Mrs. Olson asked Annie to think about helping her tutor *Walter Sorenson* when he gets out of the hospital!" Elsie blurted out before Annie could stop her. "Can you believe that?"

Arthur laughed and shook his head. "My, my, my. You'd think the woman had enough to do in her own classroom—and it's about time she concentrated her energies there. We increased her salary to three hundred and fifty dollars this year. But Mrs. Olson seems to consider herself the Queen of the Do-Gooder Club. Always poking her nose in things that don't concern her. And what a nose it is, too—long and skinny just like the rest of her!"

He laughed, and Elsie laughed along with him. Annie just looked down and lightly fingered the pearl ring on her finger.

"I was thinking that I might help her if it's all right with my parents," she declared.

The smile was quickly erased from Arthur's face, and Elsie fell silent.

"What's wrong?" Annie asked.

"Like I said, I must get back to the bank," Simpson replied with a slight smile. "I do think, Annie, that you and I need to have a nice *long* talk . . . and before you talk with Mrs. Olson, I hope. Excuse me. I have an appointment."

"You are coming for dinner on Friday night, aren't you?" asked Annie.

"Of course," Arthur said. "I wouldn't miss it . . . or our talk. Elsie, it was wonderful to see you. You're staying in the same boardinghouse for the school year, I take it?"

"Oh yes," said Elsie. "Annie and I were just on our way up there. My little room's not much to look at, but it's . . . home for now. Better than home, I guess. I can do whatever I like there."

Arthur had already started down the sidewalk toward the bank, but now he turned. "That sounds dangerous, Miss Dale. Best keep that door locked tight."

"I will, thank you," Elsie replied with a laugh as Arthur turned again and moved quickly down the street. She waited until he was out of hearing range, then she took Annie's arm and started walking her in the other direction. "What a prize! You've got the most gorgeous man I've ever seen. I could look into those deep blue eyes until—"

"Enough!" Annie exclaimed, then she laughed. "If I didn't know better, I'd say you were—"

"Smitten!" Elsie burst out, giving Annie a shove. "I would be, if he were not already courting my best friend. Annie, why in the world did you get him upset with you? He's the most cultured man in the entire county, and he's traveled everywhere! And he's so . . . charming!"

Annie nodded and said, "That he is . . . and more. And you forgot to mention that he's rich."

"All the better!" Elsie cried. "So . . . are you crazy? Didn't you see the look on his face when you talked about Walter?"

"I did, and . . . I don't know why I said what I did," replied Annie. Her expression turned somber. "I guess I've seen my father do the same thing to my mother for so long, and she just won't say what she's thinking when he does it. I'm not going to be like that."

"You'd better explain that to Arthur, then," said Elsie, stopping outside the two-story wood frame boardinghouse, "or he might get the idea you don't care about him. And if you shake him off your hook, even for a second, there's going to be another girl waiting. If I were you, I'd tell Mrs. Olson that my parents thought I was too busy to help with Walter."

"It's not going to be that simple," Annie said. "I really am going to consider doing it."

"You'd risk Arthur for an old hayseed like Walter?" asked Elsie through squinted eyes. "What's gotten into you?"

Annie shrugged her shoulders and said, "I'm not sure . . . nothing's gotten into me. It's only about my tutoring, not a choice between Arthur and Walter, for goodness' sake. But do you know, there was this other boy this summer who—"

"What?" Elsie exclaimed, looking back to make sure no one was listening. "You met someone else this summer?"

"Not exactly. . . ."

Elsie grabbed Annie's arm and pulled her up the steps of Mrs. Gunderson's boardinghouse. "Not another word until we close the door!"

Chapter 12

A Silent Partner

"Garrit," Dinah Harding said, "you may be excused. Go up to your room and play."

"Oh, can't I please go to my tree house?" Garrit begged, placing his white linen napkin carefully on his chair as he stood up. "There's nothing to do in my room."

"Fine," his mother conceded. "But don't you get into any trouble, and you stay in our yard." The towheaded boy broke into a wide grin as his mother continued. "Go to your room and change your clothes first."

"Yes, ma'am," he said as he raced for the living room doorway.

"No running in the house!" James Harding barked after his son. "One of these days that boy's going to bust something up," he groused to the others seated around the dining room table.

"He's just a little boy, Father," Annie said with a gentle smile. "He always runs when he's going to the tree house."

"Doesn't make any—"

"Mr. Simpson, can I get you anything else?" Dinah Harding interrupted, turning toward their guest as she placed her folded napkin alongside her fine china plate.

"No, thank you," Simpson replied, leaning back against the tall oak chair. "Mrs. Harding, you are a wonderful cook, and I am as stuffed as the chicken was when you brought it to the table. Did your daughter inherit your cooking prowess?"

"Actually, yes," Dinah responded, glancing at Annie. "She did most of the work on this meal, Mr. Simpson. But thank you for the compliment. May I get you some coffee and apple pie? Annie made it."

"For that," said Arthur with a smile directed to Annie, "I would find some room."

"Annie, come and help." Dinah rose from her chair, picked up her plate and her husband's, then turned to go into the kitchen.

Annie pushed her chair back, collected her plate and Arthur's, then followed her mother through the swinging oak door into the kitchen. The sink and counters were strewn with dirty pots and pans and bowls, and the massive wood stove needed a good scrubbing.

"We'll be here all night cleaning this up," her mother mumbled as she shoved an iron pot aside and carefully set the china plates on the counter. "We'd better keep your father out of here after supper. You know how he hates a mess."

"Why did you lie to Arthur about the pie?" Annie asked, setting the plates on top of the others. "Now he thinks I made it."

Dinah Harding was already busy cutting hearty wedges. "Now, you pour the coffee, and I'll take care of the pie."

"Fine," Annie said. She opened an upper cabinet door and pulled out four delicate china cups and saucers. "Why did you lie to him?" she repeated.

"What does it matter?" her mother said, glancing over at Annie as she took the enameled coffeepot from the stove. "Could you not have made this pie if you had the time after school? Haven't I taught you how?"

"Of course I could have, but I didn't."

"But you could have made it, and you did do most of the other work. We have to make a good impression."

"And what if I couldn't cook at all? Would I be good enough then?" She had poured the coffee and was lining up the brimming cups on a silver serving tray.

"I wouldn't want to take my chances," her mother said, quickly setting the plates of golden apple pie next to the coffee cups. "He's a big-city banker, Annie. He's used to the best, and I'm sure we don't come close to measuring up. Don't argue with me about this."

"Maybe he'll have to find a big-city wom—"

"Hush your mouth, now!" Dinah Harding whispered, carefully hefting the laden tray. "Come on. You get the door."

Annie stepped to the kitchen door and pushed it open, then held it from swinging back as her mother stepped gracefully into the dining room. Then Annie took her seat as her mother served the dessert and coffee.

"Ah, magnificent," Arthur declared as Dinah set a wedge of pie before him. "I had no idea you could cook so well, Annie."

Annie's narrow lips curled into a smile. "There's a lot that you don't know about me, Arthur. Isn't that true, Mother?"

"Very true," replied Dinah, raising her light brown eyebrows at her daughter. "But I suggest we save that for another time."

"I'd like to hear more now," Arthur said. He rubbed his tawny mustache lightly with his fingertip and looked expectantly at Annie's mother.

"Not tonight," James interrupted, taking a drink of coffee as Dinah sat down. "Now, what were you saying, Arthur?"

"Mmmm, this pie is as delicious as it looks," Simpson said smoothly, setting his fork down on the dessert plate. Then he sat up taller and leaned toward Annie's father. "I was just saying that I don't think the assassination of President McKinley will affect the economy in any way. Teddy Roosevelt won't let it happen. My father thinks he's far better suited for the job than McKinley was."

"Let's hope so," Annie's father replied, tapping his fork lightly on his plate. "And let's hope they do a better job of protecting Roosevelt. They say the assassin walked straight up to the president."

"The gun was hidden under his bandaged hand," Annie offered.

"Still, if it's that easy for an anarchist to kill off a president, we're in trouble," James replied. "But you were going to say something else, Arthur. Something about the building industry . . ."

"Oh yes." The young banker dabbed his lips with his napkin. "It was just that, with such a strong economy, I can't understand why you limit your business to building houses."

"I build houses because that's what I do well," James answered. "I'm able to keep one crew going pretty steady. But there's not as many houses being built here as there were back in Minneapolis."

Arthur Simpson nodded his head and leaned even closer. "Which is exactly why you need to branch out. Now, if you got into building barns, my guess is that you could triple your business in five years. And rather than actually doing the work, you could simply manage the office and hire foremen to run the projects."

Annie threw her mother a pleading look, hoping that she might say something to head off what promised to be a full-blown business discussion, but Dinah's slight shake of the head told Annie she'd better not try.

"I don't think so," her father was saying to Arthur. "It's taken me this whole first year since we moved just to get established, and—"

"But you're already the best builder in the county," Arthur broke in. "And the only builder around here who's doing barns is overpricing and cheating on his materials. You should hear old man Baxter brag when he's in my office. He's making a killing, and nobody's competing with him."

"I've seen Baxter's work," James said. "It's shoddy, and I did wonder about his materials. Looks to me like he's skimping on the big timbers."

Arthur laughed and said, "Skimping is a very kind word when it comes to what Baxter has done. He's gouging so deep it's sickening."

Despite her mother's warning, Annie ventured, "Perhaps the business talk could wait till a little later...?"

From her father's glare, Annie gathered that her question would go unanswered.

"This sounds like privileged information, Arthur," James was saying, the deep lines in his forehead creasing even deeper. "Why are you letting me in on this?"

Simpson took a sip of coffee, then rubbed his chin and smiled. "It's ... um ... not really confidential information, Mr. Harding. Do you mind if I call you James? I think we know each other well enough, don't you?"

"Yes, call me James if you like," Annie's father said with a nod.

Annie glanced at her mother with her eyebrows raised. Her father was firmly opposed to such informality.

"Well, James, what I've said about Baxter's business practices is simply a public fact," Arthur was saying. "You've seen it yourself. I'll bet it wouldn't take you five minutes of studying one of his bills to spot where he's jacking up his prices. And if you studied the materials that he states were used on a project, you'd see it doesn't match up with what's there."

"But again, why are you telling me this?" James asked.

"I'd simply like to see a good, honest business grow, James," said Arthur. "I've looked at the numbers, and you can't lose. Baxter is easy pickings."

"So, then, why don't you take him on yourself?" Annie's father continued to press.

Simpson shook his head and leaned his chin on his hand. "I'm not a builder, James. And besides, I have way too much to do at the bank. There's no way I could handle barn building as a second business. My father acts like he's going to retire tomorrow; everything that was on his desk suddenly has appeared on mine. What I'm wondering is why *you* don't want to go after Baxter? I'll bet that tomorrow morning you could build a better barn for a third of the cost."

James Harding took a deep breath and looked at his wife, then back at Simpson. "Well, Arthur, you might be right in what you're saying. But what you're talking about would take money—and a fair amount more than I've got. My business is growing, and we're profitable. I'm content with where we're at now."

"But with all due respect, sir . . ." Arthur protested. "Listen, you must pardon me if I press too hard on this; it's a weakness I have. But what if you *could* raise the capital to start building barns and could afford to hire a good foreman to run the crew. Would you do it if there was a very low level of risk?"

"Sounds to me like you had this all thought through before coming to dinner," Annie said.

"Of course, my dear," Simpson replied. "This is what I do. I look for real opportunities, and then I move to take advantage of them. So what would you say if the risk was low, James?"

Spinning the fork in his large muscular hands, Annie's father finally nodded. "Sure, I'd take the deal, but there's no such thing as low-level risk. And don't take this personal, but I won't borrow any more money from the bank. I've got a long ways to go on the loan I took out when we moved here."

"But," said Arthur, "you're ahead on that loan. I looked."

"Don't matter," James replied. "I hate being in debt, and I won't chance it. No bank loan is a low-level risk. If the economy went bust, I'd sink like a rock."

Arthur forked the remaining piece of apple pie into his mouth, chewed it slowly as if in thought, then wiped his lips with his linen napkin. "But once again, what if it really were a low risk. What then?"

"I already said I'd do it," Annie's father responded.

"So . . . how about if you brought in a silent partner?" Arthur asked, his blue eyes focused on James' face. "Say . . . someone who could bring half the funds you'd need to start. What then?"

James Harding's brown eyes pinched down tightly, and the muscles in his jaws rippled. "Why a silent partner?"

Arthur coughed and cleared his throat. "Perhaps because it wouldn't be good for this partner's other business if folks knew where he was investing his money. Trust is not easily won but, you realize, it is easily lost."

"So you want to become my father's silent partner?" Annie asked Arthur, her long slender fingers tapping the edge of her coffee cup. "Do you really think that's a good idea, even if—"

"This does not concern you, Annie," her father cut her off. "This is between Arthur and me."

Annie's eyes widened, almost as if she had been slapped, and her hands gripped the edge of the table. She did not respond to her father's censure, but she did not retreat from his cold stare.

"Yes, James." Arthur's words came between the father and daughter. "I would like to be a silent partner."

"Not as a bank loan?" asked James. "You have the money?"

"I don't have it tonight," Arthur replied, running his fingers through his gold-streaked hair. "But I can get it if it's at the level at which I think you could get started."

"What about your father and the bank?"

"It's not his idea, so he need not know a thing."

"And when would you be hoping to do all this?" James asked.

"That . . . pretty much depends on you," said Arthur. "First, we'd need to come to terms on paper. Then we'd need whatever time it takes to raise the money, find a foreman, pull a crew together, and get the word out that you're building barns. Seems to me that there's no point in pushing too hard until the winter's almost through. It'll soon be too late to start working on barns this year."

"Makes sense to me," said James.

"Arthur, I really wish we could talk about—"

"I told you it's not your concern, Annie, and I meant it," her father demanded. "Arthur and I are talking business, and you got no say in it."

"But this is really about—"

"I'm the head of this house, Annie." James Harding's voice was icy. "And I decide what's your concern and what's not. As long as you live under my roof, you'll do what I say—just like when I told you not to speak to Stuart Anderson."

"Stuart saved my life," Annie said, her cheeks flaming.

"And he used that to play on your emotions. I will not have it. Arthur, I heard that he threatened you. Is that true?"

"He did," Arthur stated. "He said he was going to circulate lies about me, try to hurt my reputation. It would be easy to do, me being new in town. Then when I refused to respond, he tried to get me to fight."

"Right out there on Main Street."

"Yes, sir."

"I . . . ah . . . heard tell you were on your college's boxing team," James said. "How'd you ever hold back?"

"I nearly didn't, sir," Arthur replied. "But not to fight seemed the honorable thing to do. Anderson's still young and impetuous, and I was so angry I was afraid I might hurt him with my fists."

"I'm afraid I might not have been so patient," Annie's father stated. "It's fortunate he left when he did."

"Yes, sir," Arthur said. "One more time and—"

"Mother," Annie broke in, pushing back her chair. "I think we should get started on the dishes. Arthur, why don't you and Father go into the living room and find some easier chairs to sit on. You can talk more business there without us ladies listening in."

"Now, that's a good idea, Annie." Her father stood and stretched. "Do you mind if I smoke my pipe, Arthur?"

"No, sir," Arthur replied, reaching inside his suit coat and pulling out two long brown objects. "Unless, of course, you'd prefer to try one of my cigars."

"Cuban!" James exclaimed, patting Arthur on the back as the two of them stepped toward the living room door. "Ah, now we're talking.

I haven't had one of those in years."

Annie piled the plates and cups and silverware on the silver serving tray, then hurried into the kitchen without speaking to her mother. She had thrown a long white apron over her Sunday dress and begun to clear the dirty dishes out of the kitchen sink when her mother came through the door with several serving bowls.

"Don't do it, Annie," her mother said, setting the bowls down on a counter and grabbing another apron from its hook on the wall. "You're overreacting."

Annie turned around, her face a mask. "Do you want to wash dishes or put away the food?"

"Please don't do it, Annie."

"Sorry, I can't hear you."

"You know what I said."

"I'm sorry, Mother. Your mouth is moving, but I can't hear you."

Dinah Harding's face reddened as she stepped toward Annie, but Annie shrugged her shoulders, turned back toward the sink, and pulled out the remaining dishes.

"Annie, don't shut me out." Dinah reached out and touched the back of Annie's arm. "I know you're angry, but you were rude in there."

"I'm sorry you were offended by my behavior," Annie said as she turned around to face her mother, her eyes smoldering with a controlled anger. "But compared to your silence, which was worse?"

"You don't understand that—"

"I understand perfectly well," Annie said quietly. "It's one thing if you want to let Father walk all over you, but how can you sit and watch him speak to me like that?"

"The two men were talking about a legal business proposition that—"

"Who cares if it's legal or not?" Annie spat the words. "Don't you see what was happening in there?"

"They're talking about a new business—"

"Mother, stop it!" Annie cried, shaking her mother. "Don't pretend you don't see it! I know that you know. This business deal is all about me, and I have no say in it whatsoever. At least you could have asked them to stop talking about it in front of us. If they want to make a deal with each other, I can't stop them, but they could have at least not done it in front of me ... and you. How could you let them do it?"

"You'd better get used to it, Annie," her mother stated flatly, her shoulders sagging. "It only gets worse. As a woman in this world, you have very little to say about anything."

"I will not let that happen to me, Mother," Annie replied. "I'd rather be dead."

"Don't say that."

"Well, how about this," said Annie, holding her hand out and taking off the gold pearl ring, then handing it to her mother. "What happens to their business deal if I give back this ring? Do you really think it's just about money, that Arthur's so interested in building barns that he would risk cutting a deal behind his father's back?"

"No, I don't," her mother replied with a sigh, looking down at the beautiful ring. "But I do think that Arthur's in love with you, and, well, he's just trying to impress your father. Is that really so terrible?" When Annie didn't answer, she pressed. "Annie, nobody's perfect. Sometimes ... sometimes you just have to roll with the waves and hope things will work out."

"Like you have?"

"No," her mother admitted, shaking her head. "I'm sorry. Perhaps I should have said something tonight, but ... perhaps I should have said something years ago. But, Annie, Arthur's not like your father; I know he's not. Please give him a chance. Talk to him. I do believe that he loves you, even though he really shouldn't have brought this up tonight."

Annie stared down at the ring in her mother's outstretched palm, then finally sighed and picked it up. "All right, I'll talk to him. But Arthur is not going to tell me how to think, even if he has all the money in the world. I won't let that happen, and I won't let Father dictate my life for me, either."

"Just be very careful, Annie. Don't provoke your father if you can help it," her mother said. "And be careful what you say to Arthur. You can react so strongly that you miss something that's very good."

"Or not react at all," Annie murmured almost to herself, "and end up missing something better."

Chapter 13

From Bad to Worse

"Good night!" Annie Harding called out to her parents as the stairway door clicked shut and she and Arthur Simpson were finally left alone in the living room. The couple sat motionless on the crushed velvet davenport as though they were required to wait until the gentle thump of shoes ascending the wooden stairs gave way to silence.

"My goodness," said Annie as she looked up at the grandfather clock in the corner of the living room, "can you believe it's after nine? I didn't think they'd ever go to bed. You certainly know how to get my father to talk."

"I had a great time with him," Arthur said, raising his thick brown eyebrows. "I'm glad we get along so well. That's important, isn't it?"

Annie nodded. "It's so rare we see him talk with anyone that it's a bit surprising when he gets carried away and doesn't want to stop. Mother nearly had to pull him out of here."

"Well, I'm glad she did," Simpson said. He grinned as he put his arm up on the davenport behind Annie and leaned his face close to hers. "Who wants to talk when you can—"

"Not so fast," Annie stated, quickly sliding over to the corner of the davenport and shaking her head. "You may have talked my father's leg off, but you didn't talk to *me*. And I think there are some things we need to discuss."

Leaning back against the velvet, Arthur crossed his arms and smiled. "I suppose you're right. Is this a discussion, though, or a lecture?"

"Which do you prefer?"

"Which one is shorter? I was hoping we could—"

"I hope you're teasing," Annie said, studying Arthur's face, "because you really don't want me to lecture you. You're not going to be cynical, are you?"

"Me? Never," Arthur answered, exhaling loudly, then uncrossing his arms. "I assume that you want to talk about the topic of our dinner conversation?"

Annie simply nodded.

"I guess I owe you an apology for that," Arthur said. "I'd been thinking about this business deal all afternoon, and the opportunity just seemed to lend itself to the moment. But it was something I should never have brought up without first talking to you about it. I could see that you and your mother were uncomfortable with it."

"So why didn't you stop?"

"I couldn't," Simpson replied. "Once it started, and your father got so excited about it, how was I supposed to pull it back? That's all he wanted to talk about the rest of the night. I really am sorry, but it truly is a great deal for him."

"There's more to it than that, though," Annie declared. "You knew that my father would get excited about this barn-building business. I don't think it was fair of you to use this to win my father's approval. I won't be the center—"

"Wait a second, now," Arthur Simpson objected. "I shouldn't have started the business conversation at the dinner table, and I'm really sorry about that. But now you're accusing me of something I didn't do. I've sat on this barn-building idea for a couple of months and decided that your father was the one builder I know who can get the job done. I plan on making a good profit, and whoever is my partner will benefit from this relationship. But I've actually held back from discussing it with your father for the very fear that my motives might be misjudged. I was hoping that you, of all people, wouldn't think this about me."

Annie stared into Arthur's face and paused, then folded her hands and blinked. Finally she said, "Well . . . you have to admit that it looks like—"

"Like I'm using the business offer to win your father's trust," Simpson interrupted, nodding in agreement. "Someone else might look at it and say that I'm using my relationship with you to secure a profitable business transaction. Either way, it looks bad."

"So what do you say it is?" asked Annie.

Simpson smiled and cleared his throat. "I'd say that . . . your father already liked me, and, if anything, this offer had the potential to get him concerned about my motives, but it didn't. Does that make sense?"

"I guess. . . ."

"On the business side, your father is the only person I would entrust myself with," said Arthur. "In that case, my relationship with you certainly benefits me, but I don't feel that I'm taking advantage of it. I can't help it if you're the daughter of the one man in the area who has the experience to expand his building operation, can I?"

"Well, no, but . . . it just doesn't seem right," Annie stated.

"I know," Arthur agreed. "I should have waited until we'd talked so you could understand. I hope it won't happen again."

Annie nodded. "You're sure?"

"I promise to try," Arthur replied, "but sometimes my enthusiasms get the best of me."

"Is that what happened when Elsie mentioned Walter Sorenson on the street the other day?" Annie asked. "You said you wanted to talk about that, and so do I. Did you hear that he's back in town now?"

"No, I hadn't heard," said Arthur. "And, yes, I had hoped we could talk before you gave an answer to Mrs. Olson."

"The Queen of the Do-Gooder Club?"

"Did I call her that?"

"You have a short memory," Annie noted with a smile. "A more appropriate question is whether or not your stomach curdled."

Arthur rubbed his thin mustache and took a deep breath. "My mouth was running ahead of my brain, I'm afraid. No, my stomach did not curdle. But is it worse than calling her the Bat Lady?"

"Only Elsie calls her that," Annie replied. "When did you and Elsie talk?"

"Oh, I saw her . . . on the street later," Arthur said. "She's right, you know. Mrs. Olson does look like a bat. Could we talk about the tutoring, though? I really don't—"

"Too late."

"Why's that?"

"I already told Mrs. Olson that I would do my best to help her with Walter," Annie answered. "I start after school on Monday. He needs a lot of help with his math, and that's where I can help him the most."

Simpson shook his head. "You couldn't wait until we talked?"

"I guess I didn't see any reason why I should," Annie stated. "Unless you wanted to pitch in and help me. You could do the math part better than I could, I'm sure."

"No thanks," Arthur said. "I'm no teacher."

"So why should I have waited?" Annie asked. "Mrs. Olson talked with me yesterday, and I couldn't see any reason to delay."

"Not even after I asked?"

Leaning her head back against the davenport, Annie said, "As far as I could tell, it was my decision and my time. I really want to do this, and I don't see how it relates to you, although it would bother me if you didn't approve of it."

"Bother as in you wouldn't proceed with it?"

"No, no," Annie replied, slowly shaking her head. "Bother as in trouble me that you could even consider this with disapproval. Whyever would someone have a problem with another person who gives a helping hand to a person as needy as Walter Sorenson . . . and his family?"

Arthur looked down at his smooth slender hands and rubbed his thumbs together. His forehead was wrinkled and his eyebrows were pressed down, then he glanced over at Annie with somber eyes. Finally he said, "You're right, a person shouldn't have a problem with it."

"But you did, and do. Don't you?"

"Well . . . you . . . caught me off-guard on the street, and—"

"How could this possibly upset you, Arthur?"

"Oh shoot," he muttered. "I don't know. I guess I'm probably way too sensitive about what people think of me. With Elsie there, I guess I thought she'd think I wasn't much of a banker if I let you—"

"Let me!" exclaimed Annie, nearly jumping off the davenport. "Let me what? I didn't realize I needed permission from you to do anything. Did you think I did?"

"Doesn't that ring mean any—"

"*Wait* a minute!" Annie protested. "This ring, as lovely as it is, is not a wedding ring, or even an engagement ring—at least, that is my understanding. But even if we were engaged, would that mean I needed to get your permission before I helped someone in need?"

"Well, at least we could talk about it," replied Arthur carefully. "A banker has a certain . . . position to maintain, and there are times when it's best not to get too close to—"

"To the people who need your help the most?" Annie retorted. "You can lend the money to someone like Walter's father to buy a farm and then an expensive traction engine, but you can't stoop so low as to pick them up when they fall?"

"Ah, it's more complicated than that, Annie," Simpson said. His forehead was wrinkled in a deep frown. "It's not about stooping; it's more about upholding the dignity of the banker's place in the community. People, especially the poor, need to maintain a certain sense of respect for the bank."

"Are we poor, Arthur?"

"Who?"

"My family," Annie stated. "Is it condescending of you to enter our humble abode here? Our house certainly doesn't match well with the mansion your father built. Might the dignity of the bank be in jeopardy because of your association with me?"

"I'd really like to not keep talking about this," Arthur said. "I think we're getting carried away."

"No, we're doing fine. You're not getting upset, and neither am I," Annie countered. "But we need to settle this. I can't be constantly worrying whether I'm behaving in a manner that you feel enhances your role as the local banker. And I'm not very good at pretending there's no problem when the problem is glaring me in the face."

"I've noticed that, especially the past few weeks."

"So, Arthur, do you consider my family poor?"

"No," Arthur spoke firmly. "Your family is certainly not rich, but you're a long way from the poorhouse. Your father runs a tight ship with his business, and his profit statements are strong for such a small operation."

"So I qualify? I simply need to learn the proper rules of who I may associate with—"

"Don't, please. You're taking this—"

"I am trying to discover exactly the type of person it's safe for someone in your position to mingle with," Annie stated. "I understand that Walter Sorenson looks bad. But where's the tolerable line?"

"Let me try another approach," Arthur offered. "It's bad for a banker to get too involved with the people to whom he lends money. If you get too emotionally attached, every time you enforce the terms of the loan agreement, it's taken personally. I couldn't live with that pressure all the time. Surely you can see that."

"That sounds a lot different from the way you reacted when Elsie was there."

"Okay, I reacted wrong ... and the fact is that I really don't like Walter Sorenson at all," Simpson replied. "But don't you see what I'm saying?"

Annie shook her head. "It almost makes sense, but ... it's too full of inconsistencies."

"Such as."

"Tonight."

"What about tonight?"

"Here you are working out a deal with *my* father at dinner in *our* house," said Annie. "Isn't your personal involvement just a bit too much? Do you maintain an equal distance with all the people you deal with at the bank, or just the poorer ones?"

"Come on, Annie," Arthur pleaded. "Please try to understand. You must see something of the truth in what I said."

"I said it *almost* makes sense," she replied. "But don't you see how impractical it all becomes in the real world? The pieces don't fit."

"Must they?"

"Not perfectly, but it won't do to pretend that pieces from different puzzles are lining up," Annie said. "A spade's a spade, Arthur."

Arthur's head slumped back against the davenport, and he closed his eyes. "All right, I surrender," he whispered. "I have no business telling you whom you can or cannot associate with, and I've grown up with a view of the poor that affects how I treat people. And I'm not sure I can change that about me. I may have inherited it." He let out a big sigh. "Anything else?"

"What do you have against Walter?"

"Oh, for crying out loud!" Simpson mumbled. "You don't leave any stones unturned, do you?"

"I'd like to know," Annie replied. "If I'm going to be teaching him, I'd like to hear what it is that you don't like about him."

"It's not a big deal, but he reminds me too much of his father, and I couldn't stand to look at that arrogant buffoon," Arthur stated. "I think he's just like his father, and if I saw that guy coming down the street, you could bet I'd head for the other side."

"You've talked with Walter?"

"No, but I talked with his old man, and his mother . . . she's one sad soul I wish I didn't have to see again." Arthur shook his head. "I don't see how Walter could avoid being like one of them, and I wish you didn't have to be around him."

"I'll see what he's like," Annie said, her delicate face brightening finally. "And if he's nice, I'll bring him by your office. You really should try to get to know someone before you get your mind so set on what he's like."

"Fine," Simpson agreed. "And I'll give him a job as soon as you've tutored him with his math."

"That's a deal I'd like to take you up on," Annie said. "You won't forget?"

"I might. It's already fading a bit for me," Arthur replied. "But let me assure you that if you stop taking me to task tonight, my memory is guaranteed to improve."

"That, sir, sounds like a bribe."

"If it works, I—"

"Just one more thing," Annie said, sliding next to Simpson on the davenport. "What did you mean when you told Elsie that there were no *special* someones in the cities you visited on your trip to Hawaii?"

"Just exactly what I said," replied Arthur. He put his arm around Annie and lightly touched her shoulder.

"But there were other someones?"

Arthur blinked his eyes slowly. "You aren't expecting me to say that you're the first girl with whom I've ever spent time?"

"No . . . but just how many someones have there been?"

"Oh boy," Arthur said with a groan. "Annie, we can't do this. We really need to let the past be the past. Sometimes it's best to keep the skeletons in the closet."

"But how many skeletons?" Annie pressed. "Why do I get the feeling that you have a long line of sweethearts behind you?"

"Annie, I give you my word. You're the only special someone I've ever had . . . or will have," Simpson said, taking her hand and stroking her fingers. "Can't that be enough?"

"If every boy in the county had courted me, would that matter to you?" Annie asked. "And would you want to know?"

"The way I feel about you, it really wouldn't matter to me," Arthur stated. "All that matters is that now you're mine."

"What would you say? A couple of dozen?"

"Come on, Annie. This is no good," Simpson said, looking into her eyes. "Let's just say there have been a lot of girls, and some of them were big mistakes that I don't want you or anyone else to have to suffer knowing about. But I can't change that, and I really don't like talking about it. Moving here has allowed me to start over without all the mess of the past. That's why I brought the ring back from Hawaii—to give to someone who is really special."

"And am I that someone?"

"Of course."

"I like that."

"Good!" Arthur exclaimed, breathing out a gigantic sigh of relief and tossing his hands up. "So, have I passed the test yet?"

"Just barely," Annie replied with a smile. "Don't blame this on me, though. You brought it all upon yourself."

"I guess I did," he admitted, then he leaned his face close to Annie's. "Now I'd like to bring something else upon myself. Let's pick up where we started the other day with the ring."

Simpson took Annie into his strong arms and gazed into her eyes. "I've waited a long time for this, my darling," he whispered, then his lips met hers in a kiss so hard and demanding that she tried to pull back. But the more she resisted and pushed against his chest, the tighter he held her, and the harder he kissed her. Then one of his hands touched her lower rib cage.

"Don't!" Annie gasped, shoving Arthur's face back with all of her strength and grabbing his hand. "Get your hand away!"

Still holding Annie in his grasp but halting his pursuit, Simpson said, "Keep your voice down, Annie, or we'll get in trouble here. What's wrong with you, anyway? We kissed the other day."

"Is this how you treated all those other girls you'd like to keep in the past?" Annie hissed, still trying to free herself from his grip. "Let go of me! Whyever would you think you can touch me like that?"

"I didn't mean to—"

"You absolutely meant it!" exclaimed Annie, finally breaking free of his grasp and scrambling out of reach. Straightening first her dress and then her hair, she asked, "What kind of a girl do you think I am?"

"I'm sorry," Simpson said, shaking his head. "I just got carried away. You're so beautiful that I have a hard time resisting. It won't happen again, I promise—unless you want it to happen."

"You really need to leave, Arthur," Annie stated flatly, not looking at him. "I don't know if this is what you expected from the other girls, but you won't get it from me. You had better continue your search elsewhere. Here," she said, slipping the fine pearl ring from her finger and handing it to him.

"No, please, don't do that," Arthur pled, waving his hand. "This has been another terrible mistake. Please try to forgive me, and we'll start over tomorrow. This night has been a disaster for me. I'm sorry."

"Please leave, then," said Annie, standing up with the ring still in her hand. "No gentleman would put me through—"

"I'll leave now," Simpson interrupted Annie, standing up as well and moving toward the front entryway. "Please don't judge me on this one indiscretion. I promise to make it up to you, and I'll never do this again. You wait and see."

"I'll do that," Annie said as Arthur Simpson exited the front door and stepped into the night's blackness.

Chapter 14

Doctor Doleful Lugubrious

Stuart Anderson stepped to his upstairs bedroom door and cracked it open, listening to the activity below as his grandmother and grandfather greeted yet another missionary who was home on furlough and scheduled to preach in their church on Sunday. The church parsonage had three available bedrooms upstairs, one that Stuart occupied during the school year and two others that were used for guests. Even after a year, Stuart was still not accustomed to what seemed to be a continual stream of visitors.

Having barely unpacked after the long train ride to Minneapolis, Stuart had hoped to be able to rest from his trip. His grandmother had met him at the station, however, with the news that their missionary friend would be arriving on a later train and that the late afternoon and evening would be spent entertaining. From the sound of her voice, Stuart knew she expected him to take part. And although Stuart usually enjoyed his grandparents' guests, he would have preferred to spend a quiet evening with his grandparents before meeting someone new.

The sound of voices and the shuffle of feet moved toward the stairway, and Stuart heard his grandmother say, "Set your bags down by the stairs. You'll be staying upstairs in the bedroom next to our grandson's room. He's going into the ministry as well."

"Oh no," Stuart mumbled to himself. "Now I'll have to explain all that."

"Stuart!" his grandmother called up the stairs. "Our guest has arrived. Come and join us."

"I'll be right down," Stuart answered with a sigh. He turned and looked longingly at the narrow bed. It seemed to beckon to him. Then he opened the bedroom door and slowly headed down the stairs. At the bottom of the staircase stood two large, severely beaten leather bags that looked as though they might disintegrate right where they had been left.

Stuart could hear his grandfather talking with the missionary out on the three-season porch, and the clatter of dishes told him that his grandmother was in the kitchen. Stuart sniffed appreciatively at the aromas that were beginning to drift down the hallway. One good side of his grandparents' constant entertaining was the bountiful supply of special meals and desserts it afforded. Turning and walking down the hallway, he stepped into the kitchen and cleared his throat to make sure he didn't surprise his grandmother.

"Stuart, come and help!" Geneva Gray exclaimed, glancing up from the red raspberry pie she was cutting. At sixty-two years old, his grandmother was nearly five feet eight and still slender as a rail. She reached up and pushed her gold wire-rimmed glasses back up on the thin bridge of her nose. "You pour the coffee, and I'll get the plates ready."

"Slow down, Grandma," said Stuart as she spun around and grabbed a plate of ham sandwiches. "You look like you're going to the racetrack. Still sneaking out on Grandpa and putting some cash on the ponies?"

"Me and the racetrack. Now, that would be the day," she replied with her soft giggle that always reminded Stuart of a teenaged girl. "Just you hush and pour the coffee."

Stuart carefully lifted the large coffeepot and filled the four crystal coffee cups that his grandmother had placed on a silver serving tray. "Slowing down in your old age?" he asked over his shoulder. "I beat you."

"I can still work circles around you, sonny boy," she replied as she finished placing the last piece of pie on its plate. "And tonight you get to do the dishes! How do you like that?"

"Same old slave driver," Stuart teased. "I'm back for half a day, and you're already going on vacation."

" 'If any—' "

" 'If any would not work, neither should he eat,' " Stuart interrupted her. "Second Thessalonians three, and your personal favorite verse to misquote."

"Bring the coffee tray and follow me," his grandmother ordered with a big smile. "And I'm not misquoting. You just don't want to obey the truth."

Stuart wasn't sure how she managed to carry four metal trays without dropping them, but he followed her out of the kitchen and down the narrow hallway toward the living room. Two wide glass doors opened out into the spacious three-season porch, where the rest of the party sat in a flood of sunshine among a jungle of carefully tended green plants.

"Ah, lunch so quickly!" Elwood Gray stood up as Geneva and Stuart entered the room. His hair, in contrast to Geneva's gray-speckled bun, was still pitch black, and he sported a neat little potbelly at the front of his otherwise lean frame. "Geneva makes certain that I never lose this," Elwood told his guest, patting his stomach for emphasis. "If you stay long enough, John, we'll put some meat back on those bones of yours. They must never feed you in India."

Setting his coffee tray down on a small oak table that was circled by white wicker chairs, Stuart smiled at the tall beanpole of a missionary who had stood to greet them. The man looked to be about Stuart's grandfather's age, with thinning white hair and deep lines etched like crevices across his forehead. Crystal blue eyes smiled from a deeply suntanned face.

"Dr. Lucas, I'd like you to meet our grandson, Stuart Anderson," Elwood Gray declared. "Stuart, this is Dr. John Lucas, who is visiting us from Allahabad, India."

"I'm pleased to meet you, Stuart," Dr. Lucas said with a gentle nod, then he took Stuart's hand and shook it firmly. "Your grandfather tells me that you recently made the news headlines."

"Looky here," said Elwood, picking up a folded sheaf of newsprint and showing the front page to his missionary friend. "'Local Young Man Saves Two Lives As Bridge Collapses.' That's my boy!"

"I only did what—"

"Exactly what the paper says you did, and we expect you to tell us the full story after we eat," Geneva broke in. "John, perhaps you would lead us in prayer."

"Certainly," the missionary replied, then bowed his head as Stuart watched with some suspicion, noticing a long grin on his face. Dr.

Lucas paused for what seemed an unusual amount of time, seeming to wait until Stuart finally closed his eyes, then he spoke slowly and softly: "Rub-a-dub-dub, God bless the grub. Amen."

Stuart smiled and peeked one eye open in disbelief, then realized by the look on the doctor's face that he'd been set up. His grandfather burst out laughing, followed by the missionary, and his grandmother quietly chuckled as she watched for his reaction and then began passing out the plates of food. Not quite sure what to make of it all, Stuart laughed along, took his plate from his grandmother, and sat down in one of the wicker chairs.

"Shame on you two old men," Geneva scolded good-naturedly as her husband and the missionary sat down. "I'd have thought that one of you might have grown up by now."

"You didn't forget after all these years," Elwood said to the doctor after he had finally stopped laughing. "Stuart, you seemed to enjoy our prayer from seminary days."

"That's . . . a new one to me," replied Stuart with a shake of his head. "I guess it works."

"Your esteemed grandfather came up with that prayer after one of our professors exhorted us to keep our public prayers short and simple," Dr. Lucas said with a big grin. "The professor had spoken to us at a luncheon held for all the seminary students and faculty, but then he made the mistake of calling on your grandpa to ask the blessing. Guess what he prayed?"

"You didn't!" Stuart exclaimed, breaking into laughter as his grandfather nodded.

"He did," the missionary said, "and the cafeteria melted into laughter. Even the ceremonious president, Doctor William Blackwell, was rumored to have told the story to several of his colleagues in the days that followed."

"The good professor was not so good-humored, though," Elwood Gray added. "For no extra fees, I received some private counsel on what was appropriate behavior in a theological gathering. Needless to say, I was never called upon to pray at any other joint meetings of the faculty and students."

"And, needless to say, the counsel did absolutely nothing to curb your uncontrollable levity," said Geneva. "You, as well as your roommate and partner in crime, were fortunate to make it through seminary. I'm glad I met you after you and your roommate parted company."

"We really weren't as bad as the stories say," John Lucas stated, taking a sip of coffee. "We just weren't convinced that everything needed to be so somber and serious. I don't think I would have ever survived in India if I hadn't learned to laugh . . . as well as weep . . . depending on what was appropriate."

"John, do you remember Professor James?" Elwood asked. "Last spring he was in town and stopped by for a visit."

"And how was old Doctor Doleful Lugubrious, as you so fittingly named him?" the missionary asked with a chuckle. "You had a label for everybody."

"He was a very nice man," Geneva broke in before her husband could comment. "Very ancient, over ninety years old, and still proud of Elwood's ministry. He was nothing like the stories you two birds told me."

"He did smile—once," Stuart's grandfather acknowledged. "It slipped."

Stuart laughed and said, "Your memory's bad, Grandpa. The man smiled the entire time he was here. Like he wasn't all there anymore."

"I can't believe he's still alive," Dr. Lucas said. "He was always sick and frail. There were classes where I wondered if he might collapse and die right on the spot."

"Shows you that you just never know about people," Geneva stated. "I'm sure the seminary faculty didn't predict that one of you would spend his life on the mission field and the other would pastor a large university church."

"Of that I am certain," her husband agreed. "They had hopes for John, but I was a doubtful one for their list."

"So how long have you been in India?" Stuart asked.

Dr. Lucas set his coffee cup down and leaned back in his chair. "Thirty-two years," he replied, "not counting the years I spent in England training as a doctor."

"Oh, so you're a medical missionary!" Stuart's interest was suddenly piqued.

Dr. Lucas nodded. "After my first two years in India, I felt I could be more effective as a medical doctor, so I left for London, where I met my wife. She passed away . . . eight years ago. Malaria."

"I'm sorry to hear that," said Stuart.

"A great loss for the kingdom, believe me," Stuart's grandfather said. "Mary Lucas was as winsome and charming a woman as you could ever meet. John, tell Stuart about her work among the fakirs. Do you know what a fakir is, Stuart?"

"No, not much more than I know about *doleful lugubrious*," Stuart replied with a smile.

"A fakir is a Hindu ascetic who practices extreme self-denial, often enduring years of horrible self-torture," Dr. Lucas explained. "Perhaps you've heard of them lying on beds of nails or holding their arms or legs in a fixed position for so long that they can never move their limbs again. The British government has outlawed the worst of their practices, but they continue to hurt themselves in horrible ways. Mary was able to rescue some of the women fakirs."

"Why would they do those things?" asked Stuart. "I've read about it in magazines."

"Come to India and perhaps you'll grow to understand it," the missionary answered. "I'm still not sure that I do, not entirely, but here's the best I can do. Hinduism, you see, is an incredibly complex religion that includes the belief in reincarnation. The Hindu devotee believes that he can make up for bad deeds in past lives and accumulate personal merit by performing penances of various kinds. Because Hindus believe that matter is inherently evil, they also believe that a person's material body is the source of most of his misfortunes in this life. What you see with the fakirs, then, are people who believe they must make war on the body to liberate the soul . . . eventually hoping to gain Nirvana, or freedom from the cycle of reincarnation. That's the goal. And the more extreme the torture, the more effective the penance is assumed to be."

"Is this anything like our concept of repentance?" Stuart asked.

"No, it has nothing to do with turning your heart from sin," said the doctor, "although sadly there have been times in the history of Christianity when similar kinds of self-torture were supported by the church. With the fakirs, the penance has more to do with accumulating merit by the very act of enduring pain. To produce physical deformities is therefore considered a mark of divine power, a holy thing. The fakirs sit as beggars before the shrines and receive offerings of food and money as a type of worship. It is pathetic beyond your imagination, Stuart."

"Tell him about that woman fakir who was converted—the one that sat in the sun for so long," said Geneva.

"Chundra Lela," Dr. Lucas spoke quietly. "She passed away soon after my wife did. Like so many Indian girls, she was married at a very young age. Her husband died tragically when she was thirteen, and his death was attributed to some wickedness on her part in a previous life. To atone for this unknown sin and get rid of the awful guilt, she spent seven years traveling on foot from shrine to shrine, visiting every important temple in India. Yet her burden only grew heavier with time.

"Deciding that she had not suffered enough," he continued, "she became a fakir, and for three years she gave herself over to self-inflicted torture, honoring the formulas in the sacred books for pleasing the gods. She spent six months, if you can imagine this, without shelter . . . in the sun all day . . . with five fires around her, perspiration streaming from every pore. Even wealthy men brought wood and kept the fires burning as an act of merit. With no clothing but a loincloth, her body smeared with ashes and her long hair rubbed with cow dung, she was worshiped by the pilgrims. At night she took her place in the temple, standing before the idol on one foot from midnight until daylight, her hands pressed together in the attitude of prayer, imploring the god to reveal himself to her."

Stuart leaned forward in his chair, shaking his head. "That's horrendous."

"It's hardly the worst, though," the doctor replied. "When the cold season came, she would go down at dark to the sacred pond and sit with the water up to her neck, counting her beads hour after hour till dawn appeared. She would cry out to her god, Ram, 'Let me see or hear or feel something by which I may know that I have pleased thee, and that my sin is pardoned.' But of course there was no sign, no response, no rest, no peace.

"My wife, Mary, found Chundra Lela destitute and nearly dead on a street corner when we were in Calcutta," he spoke with a heavy sigh. "She had come there and cut off her once-beautiful hair, offering it to the gods in the River Ganges, exclaiming, 'There—I have done and suffered all that can be required of a mortal, yet without avail!' She had finally lost faith in the idols, you see, and ceased to worship them, concluding there was nothing in her religion or she would have found it."

Dr. Lucas leaned back in his white wicker chair, his eyes closed. "I can still see Mary trudging down the sidewalk, carrying this small pile of human bones that somehow was still breathing, impossibly alive. Then with her infinite patience, my Mary nursed that tiny Indian woman back to health. With Mary at her side, in the twinkling of an eye, Chundra Lela found the peace that she could never have found in a million lifetimes of torturing herself. Whatever sacrifices it may have cost Mary and me to give our lives in service to India, seeing the transformation of that poor woman and others like her has made it seem as nothing."

"Was it even worth the malaria?" Geneva asked gently. "Was it worth losing Mary?"

"Chundra Lela stood beside me at the graveside," the veteran missionary said through a sad smile. "And dozens of other women whom Mary had helped rescue from total spiritual darkness. What can you say to that? Was it worth it?"

There was silence around the small table, then Elwood Gray answered softly, "Without a question. What a life."

"What a life, indeed," John Lucas said with a slow nod. "And now I can't wait to get back to India. It's home now."

"So you've already been to see your son in Chicago," Geneva said.

"Yes, it was a great month and a half," the doctor replied. "Martin and Ramona have four charming children who see their grandfather so seldom that they tend to adore him. It was tough to say good-bye again."

"They would adore you if you stayed all year long," said Geneva.

"I wouldn't be so sure," Doctor Lucas replied. "So, Stuart, your grandmother boasts that you're following your grandfather into the ministry. That's quite a legacy to live up to."

Stuart smiled and nodded. "Yes, sir, it is, and I'm quite sure it's one that I will never want to be compared to. Ever since I was a very little boy and heard Grandfather preach for the first time, I wanted to do the same. Listening to you today, I'm even more challenged as to what

I should do with my life . . . and confused as well."

"Confused?" his grandfather asked, sitting forward and setting his empty coffee cup on the small table. "Something wrong, Stuart?"

"Not wrong . . . so much," Stuart replied. "I'm . . . just confused is all. I was hoping we would have had time to talk about it in private, but the trains were too close together. It's sort of strange that Doctor Lucas would be here when we did talk, though. Over the past weeks, since the accident at the bridge, I've been thinking about going into medicine . . . instead of the ministry. I'm just not sure what to do . . . or what God wants me to do. Perhaps I should follow your lead, Dr. Lucas, and do both."

"No, you don't want to follow my funny trail too closely," the missionary replied, rubbing the dark skin on his neck. "I soon discovered that I wasn't cut out for preaching or teaching, as much as I aspired to it. For some reason, your grandfather and those at the seminary never managed to speak to me about it, although I think they were fully aware of it. So I merrily hopped a ship bound for India and learned the hard way."

"You wouldn't have listened if I'd said it," Elwood Gray countered. "And I thought—and think now—that you're a pretty fair speaker, or I most certainly wouldn't let you take my pulpit tomorrow."

"Telling stories, I'm fine. Having a few sermons I use over and over, that's fine," John Lucas said. "But day after day, week after week—I just don't have what it takes. I could never pastor a large congregation as you do, Elwood. Give me a roomful of sick people any day."

Stuart's grandmother had been watching Stuart since the conversation changed directions. "You discovered something different about yourself that day at the bridge, didn't you?" she asked. "I can see it all over your face."

"I *think* I discovered something," he answered, "but . . . I see the same old face in the mirror when I look. I truly don't want to disappoint you or Grandpa or Mama or Dad . . . but even our local doctor told me that he thinks I have what it takes to make a good physician."

"You've prayed about this, son?" Stuart's grandfather asked through squinted eyes.

Stuart nodded. "If there's one thing I've done, Grandpa, it's pray. Seems like I've been knocking on heaven's door almost constantly since all this came up, so I'm sure that God is well aware of my questions. I just haven't figured out what His answer is. And all I'm asking for is a simple yes or no—you'd think that wouldn't be so hard to clue me in on."

"Seems like nothing's ever simple," Dr. Lucas said knowingly. "But I'll have to tell you, as much as I hated going through them, I've discovered that the most searching, agonizing periods of my life have produced the most rock-solid answers—the kind I've never had to doubt later or revisit and wonder about them. It's worth the struggle, Stuart, although it never feels that way when you're in it."

"At this point," Stuart admitted, "I'd be happy with a simple nudge in either direction."

"What did your father say?" Geneva asked.

"He . . . really didn't say a lot," Stuart replied. "You know how proud he's been about me going into the ministry. But he said that if I keep my hands open to God, I'll know which way to walk when I need to. Mama's the one who surprised me."

"Was she upset?" his grandmother asked.

"No, not at all," Stuart said. "In fact, it turns out that she's wondered for a long time whether I have the right gifts for the ministry. I guess I've assumed that even though I'm really uncomfortable with public speaking, for instance, that God's calling would help me overcome whatever I lacked. She gave me an earful on that one to think about."

"Sounds like we need to pray for you, Stuart," Elwood Gray said. "Why don't we join together now and pray? I certainly don't want my pride about your following in my steps to get in the way of your decision. You need to do what the Lord shows you."

"Yes, let's pray," Geneva agreed, taking her husband's hand. "John, perhaps you could go first."

Dr. Lucas nodded and smiled, but not before Stuart asked, "You don't have another one of those rub-a-dub-dub ones in your back pocket, do you?"

"No," the doctor replied with a laugh. "It's your grandfather who comes up with those gems. That was the only one I remember."

Chapter 15

Providence?

"*I* thought Dr. Lucas said he wasn't much of a preacher," Stuart Anderson whispered to his grandmother, who sat next to him in a pew near the front of his grandfather's church. "Can you imagine this?"

Geneva Gray looked at the fifteen to twenty mostly college-aged people with whom her husband and his missionary friend were praying at the front of the church. She smiled and spoke softly into Stuart's ear, "It was very . . . very moving, and I've never heard John speak more profoundly than tonight. But let me clue you in on a secret. That was essentially the same sermon he gave here when he was on his last furlough, except that this time he's added some wonderful stories. They made all the difference in the world."

Elwood Gray was praying with a young man at one end of the wooden altar rail while Dr. Lucas knelt at the other end beside a curly-haired young woman. Until a few minutes before, she had been seated next to Stuart. But when his grandfather had given the invitation for anyone who felt that God might be calling them to the mission field to come forward for prayer, Catherine Bolton had been the first one out of the pews.

"Catherine is a very special girl," Stuart's grandmother whispered, noticing where his eyes were focused. "She has a tremendous heart for God."

Stuart nodded silently in agreement, watching as Dr. Lucas continued to pray with his friend. He had met Catherine at a church service during the spring of the previous school year, and the two of them had felt an instant attraction. Catherine's lively and passionate personality contrasted distinctly with Stuart's quieter, more methodical ways. In fact, Stuart had decided over the summer that the biggest reason he enjoyed her company so much was the fact that they were so different. Whatever he wasn't, she was.

"Why don't the two of you come over to the house for pie later," Geneva Gray whispered to Stuart when Catherine slowly rose from where she had been kneeling and turned toward them, tears streaking her pink cheeks.

"We'll see," Stuart replied with a gentle smile. "She may not feel much like eating pie."

Geneva nodded. "Well, if you decide to come, take your time. It looks like we won't get home for a while yet."

Stuart stood up and slipped out of the heavy wooden pew as Catherine came down the center aisle of the large, ornate Presbyterian church. Its high vaulted ceilings, exquisite stained-glass windows, and abundance of carved wood made it one of the most beautiful churches in the city. With Elwood Gray's popularity, especially among the university students, it was easily the city's best-attended church.

Holding her Bible under her arm and a small white handkerchief in one hand, Catherine glanced up soulfully at Stuart as she moved alongside him, then she looked down again. Her usually bright smile was at least momentarily subdued, and it was obvious to Stuart that she could use a quiet companion.

Stuart stepped ahead to push open the church's huge wooden doors, and the two of them slipped outside into the gorgeous September evening. Other couples were walking slowly down the sidewalk along the Mississippi River bluff, and here and there a solitary college student with an armful of books hurried purposefully down the lane. Softly diffused twilight sunshine reflected on the broad green and dark brown leaves of the maple trees that lined the street in front of the church. There was no hint yet of the coming changeover that in just a few weeks would deck the avenue with spectacular reds and golds.

As they strolled toward the river bluff, Stuart wasn't sure what to say, and Catherine continued her silent vigil, so he thought it was best to say nothing. For the moment he felt that it was just nice to walk together and to reflect on the arresting words that John Lucas had given concerning the pressing needs of the world. He had titled his message, "The Darkness of a World Where the Light of Christ Has

Never Shone," and Stuart wondered if he would ever forget the man's heartbreaking stories.

"Thank you for walking with me," Catherine finally said, glancing at Stuart with bloodshot eyes. "I wasn't . . . really expecting this to happen to me tonight. I've never heard anything like that in my life. Have you?"

"Not . . . quite like tonight, but my grandparents have had missionaries stay overnight at our house before," Stuart replied. "They didn't seem to be as passionate about their work as Dr. Lucas is, though. He told some other stories at my grandfather's house that made the hair on my arms stand up."

"It just doesn't seem possible, does it?" Catherine asked, stopping by a short brick wall and looking down on the wide river below. "How can what he said be true?"

"I don't know," Stuart replied as he leaned against the wall. "He told me he'd seen things far worse than he could tell tonight—such as the selling of young girls. That one really gets Mr. Lucas angry."

"Can you imagine?" Catherine said, her green eyes filling with tears again. "How could any parent sell their children? How twisted must their thinking be?"

"What did that verse say?" asked Stuart, pulling open his Bible to the page he had marked. " 'Alienated from the life of God through the ignorance that is in them, because of the blindness of their heart: who being past feeling have given themselves over unto lasciviousness with greediness.' That's twisted and dark, I'd say."

"Really, truly terrible," she whispered. "It's as wicked as the devil."

Catherine pulled away from the brick wall and started to slowly walk down the sidewalk again. Her face was flushed, and she reached up and dabbed the corner of her eyes with her handkerchief. Then she took a deep breath and shook her dark curls. "I've got to do something about it."

"What was that?" Stuart asked, leaning toward her as they walked.

"I said that I'm going to do something that will make a difference," Catherine spoke with resolve, walking faster with every word she said. "There's no reason why I can't. What was the missionary's wife's name?"

"Mary."

"He said she was a British nurse as well as a devoted mother," stated Catherine. "I'm training to be a nurse, so ... why can't I do what she did?"

"You think you're supposed to go to India as a nurse ... or a missionary?" Stuart asked.

"Yes. Both," Catherine replied, nodding her head and talking with her hands as she walked. "Stuart, I have to do this. I know it as sure as I know anything. Tonight, I ... I don't know, but it was so strong on my heart. I have to try. If I don't try, who will?"

"Alone?" Stuart asked. "Would you consider going alone?"

Catherine clenched her jaw and simply nodded. "Yes, I would. I sure would."

"Based on hearing one message?"

"Why would I have to hear any more about it?" Catherine protested. "Does God have to speak a second time if we heard Him clearly the first time?"

"No," Stuart agreed. "It just seems a bit rash."

"What if you're supposed to go with me, Stuart?" asked Catherine, stopping abruptly and looking into Stuart's black eyes. "Mrs. Lucas was a nurse, and he became a doctor. What if this is providential?"

"I told you that I wasn't sure what—"

"You told me that he prayed with you about the possibility of becoming a doctor," Catherine said. "Can't you see what's happening here?"

"Hold on, now." Stuart held up one hand. "You've got the cart in front of the horse on this one. I'm not sure about anything at this point."

"But Dr. Lucas first went to seminary, just like you were going to," Catherine stated. Then she placed her hand on his arm. "This is so exciting. Maybe you're supposed to take his place in India when he retires."

"Catherine, please stop!" Stuart begged. "I never said anything about being a missionary, and even if I had, you're still jumping to too many conclusions."

"Tell me that it's not a possibility," Catherine said. "I know that you were moved by what he said tonight. I could see it in your face when the doctor was telling his stories."

Stuart laughed and leaned against a big sugar maple tree. "Anything's possible, I suppose," he replied. "But that doesn't mean it's going to happen. How could I listen to him tonight and not be moved? I'd have to be dead."

"But what if you prayed about it and felt you were supposed to be a missionary . . . to India . . . as a doctor?" asked Catherine. "And I felt I was to go there as a nurse. What about that?"

Rubbing his forehead, Stuart answered, "If all of that happened— and remember that it *hasn't* happened—then I guess that would be something to consider. But as of this moment, it's not in the cards."

"Maybe you just don't want it to be!"

"No, no, that's not it at all," Stuart muttered. "Until you brought all this up a few minutes ago, I'd never even thought about it. I just don't think that God leads us in such confusion."

"You know that for a fact?" Catherine asked. "So what I felt tonight, I should not take as God's leading?"

"No, that's not what I mean. I have no idea what God may have been speaking to your heart. Anything I've said has been about me, and I'm beginning to wonder if I know anything for an absolute fact. But I surely can't go chasing every possibility that comes along. I can hardly figure out the next step in my life, let alone tell you where I'll be in ten years."

"But wouldn't it be exciting if God was calling us both to India?"

"Whatever He calls a person to . . . and wherever He directs, that's got be exciting," Stuart replied. "Are you interested in meeting Dr. Lucas?"

"I'd love to. Tonight?"

"Grandmother invited us for pie."

"You . . . why didn't you tell me?" asked Catherine, giving him a playful shove. "I'd love to talk with him. What were you thinking?"

"I was thinking that you might not want to talk with anyone tonight," Stuart answered. "Do you want to head over that way now? They're probably done at the church by now."

"Yes, let's," she replied with a smile, turning around and starting back down the sidewalk toward the church. "I'm kind of nervous, though, meeting someone like him."

"You ... nervous? Come on," Stuart teased. "You could meet the president and not get nervous."

"It's just that he's so serious," Catherine said. "What if I say something stupid or funny?"

"He'll probably laugh," Stuart replied. "Once you get to know him, he's about as intimidating as my grandfather."

"Good. That's good," she said. "I like your grandparents. They're very sweet."

"Sweet and—"

Stuart cut off his own sentence as they skirted a thick bush and suddenly came upon a young man and woman locked in a passionate kiss. The sight so caught him off guard that he lost his train of thought. Stuart stepped to his right and Catherine went to her left so they could pass the couple who were oblivious to anything but their kiss.

"And what?" Catherine asked with a bright smile, her green eyes opened wide, as the two of them came back together.

"Sweet and ... um ... kissy face," he said, breaking out into laughter. "That was nice, wasn't it?"

"Nice as in you wish that were you?" Catherine asked with a giggle.

Stuart glanced back at the couple and said, "No, I don't know her, and I didn't really get a good look at her. Did you?"

"Stuart Anderson, that's mean of you!" exclaimed Catherine. "You know what I meant."

"What did you mean?"

"I meant that we didn't see each other all summer," she replied, taking Stuart's arm. "Maybe that was the first time they've seen each other since school got out."

"Maybe."

"Well ... didn't you miss someone?"

"I did miss someone," Stuart replied, "but ... we weren't exactly on the same terms as those folks back there. I hope they're married."

"Or getting married."

"Soon."

"You only wrote me twice all summer," Catherine said. "Was life back in Bradford as boring as you said? You haven't talked much about it since you got back."

"It was pretty boring until the accident," Stuart said. "And I haven't said much about the summer because I couldn't get a word in edgewise."

"So how well did you know the girl you rescued?"

"Not very well," said Stuart. "Her family moved to our town about the time I came to school last year, so I'd really only seen her on the streets and at church."

"Is she pretty?" asked Catherine.

"Does it matter?"

"Perhaps. Is she?"

Stuart looked over to Catherine and simply nodded.

"Did you like her?"

"Catherine, she's being courted by a handsome rich fellow who has charmed his share of young ladies in his day," said Stuart. "They're nearly engaged. While I was there, he gave her a gold pearl ring that would pay my way through the university and medical school or whatever schooling I end up taking. Grinding feed all day, I was no competition for a banker's son."

"You didn't answer my question."

"You're trying to trap me."

"Correct," said Catherine. "So you did get to know her after the accident?"

"Somewhat," said Stuart. "We had a couple of good talks, if that's what you mean."

"And you liked her?"

"Should I not have liked her?" Stuart protested. "She's very nice, and I like most of the nice people I meet. I didn't care much for the charming snake who gave her the ring, though, and he didn't like me, either."

"You knew him well?"

"Not much better than I know her."

"So how did you know he didn't like you?"

"Simple. He told me."

"My goodness, you really did get involved," Catherine said as they approached the church once more. "You're not telling me the whole story, Stuart."

"There's nothing to tell."

"I'll bet—"

"Just in time," Geneva Gray called out to Stuart and Catherine as she emerged through the front doors of the church followed by her husband and Dr. Lucas. "You look like you're on your way for some pie."

"We sure are," Stuart replied. "Catherine is eager to talk with Dr. Lucas."

"How wonderful!" the missionary exclaimed as Stuart and Catherine joined them. Taking Catherine's hand in his, he asked, "And your last name is?"

"Bolton. Catherine Bolton," she answered with a warm smile. "I'm honored to meet you, Dr. Lucas. What you said tonight, I will never, ever forget. And what your wife did in India—I can't tell you how much I desire to do the same."

"Ah, that pleases me beyond words," Dr. Lucas said, starting down the sidewalk toward the parsonage. "You are training to be a nurse, then?"

"Yes, sir," said Catherine. "In India."

"In India, did you say?"

"Yes, sir."

"I am thrilled! Did you hear that?" the missionary said, turning around toward Elwood and Geneva Gray. "And how long have you been planning this?"

"Since . . . you prayed with me," Catherine said. "I knew after your first story that there was something special for me tonight. I would like very much to bring the light of Christ to some of the villages you described. After I have some experience in nursing, I'm wondering how I should go about becoming a missionary?"

"You really are serious about this, aren't you, young lady?" Dr. Lucas asked, peering into Catherine's eyes, then turning toward Stuart.

"Oh yes, sir. I am!" Catherine's face held the same look of resolve that Stuart had seen earlier.

"I think she is," Stuart added as he turned to walk up the sidewalk to the parsonage.

"Well, once you're sure of what you want to do," the missionary said, "you want to apply to a mission board. Essentially, the sooner you apply, the better. It's important that they have plenty of time to evaluate the suitability of their candidates for overseas work. Sometimes they have certain criterion they want candidates to fulfill before they will send them."

Stuart walked ahead and opened the screen door of the large white house as the group climbed the front steps. His grandmother winked at him as she passed him, and he shook his head and whispered, "Don't get any ideas."

"Why don't you all go into the living room and get comfortable?" Geneva said as she stepped into the front entry hall. "Stuart, you can help me get some refreshments together."

"Oh no, I should help," Catherine volunteered, turning around toward Stuart's grandmother.

"Not tonight, dear. You've got a lot to discuss with our friend John," Geneva replied. "Stuart will be all the help I need. He's just a little slow."

Everyone laughed, and Catherine, Elwood Gray, and Dr. Lucas strolled into the living room and sat down. Geneva quickly disappeared into the kitchen, and Stuart hurried up the stairway to drop his Bible off in his bedroom. When he came back down, he stopped outside the living room door to listen.

"That's right," his grandfather was saying to Catherine. "You've come to the right place tonight. I am on the national mission board of our church, and I can tell you a good deal about what we look for in our candidates."

"Oh, how wonderful! I can't believe how everything seems to be fitting together!" Catherine exclaimed, sitting forward in her chair. "Dr. Lucas, do you believe in providence?"

"Oh no," Stuart whispered, peeking around the corner and trying to catch the look on Catherine's face. "Please don't."

"Certainly," the missionary answered.

"Do you think that your speaking tonight was part of God's providence for my life?" she continued.

"I'm sure it could be," Dr. Lucas responded.

"And doesn't it seem like providence that your wife was a nurse and I want to become a nurse?"

"Possibly. Of course."

"Or that you trained in seminary and switched to—"

"Would you prefer coffee or tea, Dr. Lucas?" Stuart called out as he stepped from the hallway shadows into the warmly lit living room.

"Um, coffee is fine, Stuart," he replied.

"Coffee, it is," said Stuart. "And, Catherine, I think we could use your help in the kitchen after all, if you don't mind."

Chapter 16

Big Daddy

Annie paused at the front door of the tiny white clapboard house and took a deep breath. The shabby building looked even smaller up close, and despite the warm autumn afternoon, the front door and all the windows were shut tight. Pushing back another wave of self-doubt about what she might encounter, Annie reached out and knocked on the plain wooden door.

Hugging the worn math book to her chest, Annie listened but heard no movement of footsteps from within the house. Then the door suddenly swung open, giving her a start and causing her to jump.

A plump elderly woman with a stooped back and a glassy right eye stood to the side of the door, and a cloud of stale, musty air crept past Annie as if making its escape from the house.

"Come right in," the white-haired lady said with a grandmotherly smile, reaching out to shake Annie's hand. "You must be Annie. I'm Millie Gullickson, Walter's grandmother. And the eye is blind."

"Pardon me?" Annie asked as she enclosed Mrs. Gullickson's small hand in hers. "I didn't—"

"I said the eye is blind," Millie replied with a girlish giggle. "It's the first thing people wonder when they first see me, so I figure it's best to just get it over with."

"Mrs. Gullickson, I'm pleased to meet you," Annie said, stepping into the house but still looking at her host. "And I'm sorry to hear about your—"

"No, no," the old woman interrupted her, shaking her head, "don't be sorry for me. I get along fine with one eye. It's my grandson there that needs your help. Walter, come meet Annie."

Annie turned around to see the young man seated at the kitchen table with an open book in front of him and several pieces of paper that looked like written notes. Even in the dim light, Walter's smile revealed the yellow teeth that Elsie Dale had warned her about, and it appeared to Annie that a few were missing. The gangly young man stood and nodded to Annie, tugging at his oversized gray underwear shirt. His damaged left arm was tucked inside the shirt.

"I'm mighty pleased to meet you, Miss Harding," Walter said, pushing his scraggly brown hair back from his freckled face. "I'm Walter. I heard tell that you was hurt at the bridge as well."

"I . . . ah . . . hit my head, but it was nothing . . . really," Annie said. She stepped toward the table as Mrs. Gullickson pushed the front door shut behind them. "How's the arm?"

"Not so good." Walter made a wry face as he used his good arm to pull out a chair for Annie. "They done what they could, but it ain't good for nothin'. That's why we gotta get crackin' on these books. Have a seat."

"Coffee?" Mrs. Gullickson called out from behind Annie.

"Yes, please," Annie replied as she sat down beside Walter. "I see you've already started with Mrs. Olson."

"Yes, ma'am," said Walter. "She's drillin' me hard on my English, and she's got me readin' about ancient history. I like that stuff. Alexander the Great and Julius Caesar. That's fun to read."

"So you like history," Annie began, her face freezing as she caught a whiff of Walter's body odor. She turned her head slightly and continued. "And I'm hoping you like math as well."

Walter's grin returned in force. "I like math, too, Miss Harding. But I haven't done much of it in a long time, so you've gotta be patient with me. But I promise I won't waste your time. I'm just so thankful that you—"

"Let's hold the thanks until you see how I do," Annie broke in, then she waited while Walter's grandmother set a steaming cup of coffee in front of her. "I've never tutored anyone before, but if you're willing to work hard, I'm willing to help."

"We got no money to pay you with," Walter said, "but if I can get a job, I'll pay—"

"Stop, please," Annie asked. "All I'm asking is that you give your complete attention to the lessons. I just want to help you."

"You wait and see, Miss Harding. I'll be the best student you ever had," he pledged, squeezing his right hand together into a fist.

"He will, let me tell you," Mrs. Gullickson said, setting a white cup of coffee in front of Walter. "If his father hadn't pulled him out of school, he—"

"Let's don't bring Pa into this," Walter cut off his grandmother's words, the whites of his knuckles getting even whiter. "What's past is past. Today is about the future."

❖ ❖ ❖ ❖ ❖ ❖ ❖ ❖ ❖ ❖

"Annie, I can't tell you how much I've appreciated your help in working with Walter after school every day," Henrietta Olson said two months later as Annie sat down in the chair next to the teacher's large wooden desk. "What do you think of Walter's progress up to now?"

Lightly fingering the fine gold chain of her cameo, a gift from Arthur Simpson, Annie's face broke into a smile. "He's an amazing young man, Mrs. Olson. Truly. Everyone jokes about how dumb he looks, but he has to be one of the smartest people I've ever met. You tell him something once, and he's got it. As far as really practical lessons go, I've taken him about as far as I can with his math. I've truly enjoyed working with him."

"It's unfortunate that we put so much value in what a person looks like," Mrs. Olson said. "He is looking much better, though, wouldn't you say? Getting those old rotten teeth removed made a big difference."

"I'm still trying to figure out how you got the dentist to pull all of Walter's teeth and then supply the new dentures for free," Annie commented. "Doctor Gibson must have owed you a big-time favor. Or was he one of your old sweethearts?"

Henrietta Olson began to laugh, her slender shoulders bouncing up and down. "Over the years," she said softly, "one accumulates a number of favors that are owed one—and the good doctor's oldest boy, James, added significantly to my particular collection of them. That boy was simply untamable. Some folks would say what I did was collect on a favor, but I say it's just a part of my job. Walter needed his teeth pulled, and Dr. Gibson could easily fit him into his schedule and chalk it up to fulfilling his civic duties."

"But you didn't say how *you* think Walter is doing," Annie said. "Do you think he can find a job?"

"As you said, Walter's much more intelligent and hardworking than anyone would have guessed," Mrs. Olson responded. Then she stood and walked over to the tall window behind her desk. "And that's going to be part of the big problem for him when he tries to find work," she said, gazing out onto the street as she talked. "I'm afraid no one will want to take a chance on him, even though I'll promise them they're going to get a marvelous worker. On top of that, his father left a legacy of unpaid bills and deep offenses with most of the businesses where Walter might find work. I have a feeling he might have to go somewhere else to get a fair shake."

"Do you really think so?" Annie asked.

With her long arms behind her back, Henrietta Olson stepped away from the window and came back to the desk but did not sit down. "Yes, unfortunately," she said. "I've personally gone to several of the businessmen in town, and favors . . . owed or not . . . they're either not hiring or else they won't even consider Walter. If he could use his arm, he'd have no problem. But finding something in an office . . . I really do have my doubts."

"I don't know many business people, Mrs. Olson, or I'd ask them," Annie said. "My father has my mother do most of his accounting work at home."

"I do have one idea," the schoolteacher said. "Annie, I hate to ask you this, and I'm not meaning to be nosy. But you are still seeing the banker's son, right? Arthur Simpson."

"Yes," Annie replied tentatively. Even though she and Arthur hadn't gotten along quite as well during the past couple of months, her immediate thoughts flew back to the evening when she had asked Arthur to leave. "He calls on me regularly. But . . . I'm quite sure there's no chance that Walter could get a job at the bank. Arthur's father despised Mr. Sorenson, and Arthur dislikes Walter sight unseen."

"I understand that, but it's not about a job at the bank that I'm wondering," Henrietta continued as she paced back again to the window. "Did Walter not tell you what has happened?"

"No. . . ." Annie tried to think back to their last lessons and what

Walter had said. "He's been very quiet the last couple of days. Is something wrong?"

"So he didn't tell you, did he?" Taking a deep breath, Mrs. Olson said, "The bank has foreclosed on the Sorenson farm, and the family has till Thanksgiving to be out."

"Oh no!" Annie gasped. "This is terrible."

Henrietta nodded. "I knew it was simply a matter of time, but I thought that surely the bank would let them stay out there until spring. No one's ever going to move into that trashy house, so why not let them stay through the winter?"

"What will they do?" asked Annie. "Where can they go?"

"Walter told me that his mother and two young brothers are going to move in with him and his grandmother."

"No, that's not possible!" cried Annie. "The house is a crackerbox; there's no room to even turn around. They can't all stay in there."

"They have no choice," Mrs. Olson said. "They have no money. Anything that's sellable out on the farm belongs to the bank. That's why we have to find Walter a job fast. I hope that Mrs. Sorenson can also find work around town—washing or cooking or something."

"Do you think the bank might be persuaded to let them stay out there through the winter?" Annie asked, standing up and pacing around the desk. "I know they have plenty of wood cut to keep the house warm. I saw it when I was by there with . . . Arthur Simpson is the key, isn't he?"

"I hope so." Henrietta shook her head. "For the Sorensons' sakes, I hope you can persuade young Arthur to talk his father into delaying the foreclosure. The bank will derive no benefit from driving them out before spring."

"I'll go right now," Annie sputtered. "Why wouldn't Walter have told me this?"

Henrietta Olson shrugged. "I'm not sure. Probably pride. I know he'd never want you to get involved in his family problems, and you know how angry he's been about what his father's drinking did to his family. The other day he told me he feels like his father dug a deep hole, dropped them all in it, then walked away and left them to starve."

"We have to work this out, Mrs. Olson." Annie turned to leave. "There has to be a way. I'll talk with Arthur now, then I'll drop by your house later. I am so mad at him and his father that—"

"You have to be diplomatic, Annie," Henrietta warned. "Don't go in there demanding or upset. You could damage more than you fix. Use your head, not your heart."

Annie took a deep breath, then exhaled. "You're right. Calm down . . . calm down. I'd like to wring someone's neck. Calm down . . . calm down. All right, now. . . ."

With that, Annie waved good-bye and marched out of Mrs. Olson's classroom. She was glad the hallway was deserted because she was still so angry that her eyes began to tear. "Wretched moneychangers . . ." she muttered as she went out the door.

Fortunately, there were enough blocks between the school and the bank for Annie to get herself back under control. The last block she walked slowly, planning, thinking what she might say or try to say, hoping that she didn't start crying or yelling or do something embarrassing. As she approached the large glass door that opened into the bank, Annie felt confident she had hit on an approach that might work if she could just pull it off.

Annie's quick footsteps echoed off the cold white marble floor and walls as she entered the bank, nodding to the clerk who greeted her. "Good day to you," she said. "I'm just going up to see Mr. Simpson. He is in, isn't he?"

"Yes, ma'am," replied the clerk, who recognized Annie from previous visits. "I believe he is."

Nodding in reply, she hurried up the white wooden stairway that led to the upstairs offices. Walking quietly to Arthur's door, she stopped and listened for a moment. Not hearing any voices, she knocked twice.

"Come in," Arthur Simpson called out from inside.

Pushing the door open, Annie peeked in and smiled at Arthur. "May I come in?"

"Of course!" Arthur Simpson jumped up from his substantial leather chair and rounded his wide walnut desk to greet her. "I've told you you're welcome here anytime," he said, taking her hand. "How are you? I thought you were teaching after school every day."

"I'm fine," she replied, sinking into one of the smaller chairs facing the big desk as Arthur sat down in its twin. "I'm letting Walter Sorenson fend for himself today. Something more important has come up."

"Oh, what's that?" Simpson asked, his deep blue eyes shifting away from hers.

"I think you probably know," said Annie. "I just heard, Arthur. You really should have warned me."

"About the Sorenson farm?" he mumbled as she nodded. "I guess I thought I had . . . back when we went on the picnic. I told you it was just a matter of time. Well, time ran out on them."

"Yes, I remember you did say that," Annie agreed. "But why evict them now? Do you have a buyer?"

"No," Arthur replied, rubbing his fingers together as if they were cold. "Nobody's going to be interested in buying until spring, and only a hermit would move into that ramshackle house. But if we don't sell off what's there, at least the little that's left of the livestock and equipment, we won't recoup a cent. We already took a huge loss on that traction engine."

"I understand that," said Annie in a measured tone, "and I realize you run a bank and you have to make hard decisions to make money for the bank. But, Arthur, what would it cost you to let them stay out there until you get the property sold? Surely there's no reason why you can't sell off whatever is left of the livestock and equipment but still let them stay until spring. You know the only place they have to go is to Walter's grandmother's house."

"It's a roof at least," Arthur replied.

"With one tiny bedroom for two older women and three young men," Annie retorted. "Honestly, would it cost the bank to let them stay where they are?"

Arthur twisted his mouth around. "No, I suppose not. But we don't trust those people. They might destroy the buildings."

"Which are worth just about nothing and probably should be torn down anyway," Annie countered. "You told me that, too."

"I did? I don't remember," said Simpson. "But, Annie, we just can't have those people freeloading on our property."

"Won't the cost for the bank be higher, though, when people hear that these poor folks, who really have nowhere to go, were booted off the property right before winter set in?" Annie asked. "Seems to me that you're risking damage to the very reputation you've been trying to build in the community. My guess is that your customers will regard it as a heartless act."

For a moment Arthur Simpson looked genuinely stunned by Annie's words. He nodded silently, then mumbled, "You're probably right."

"Was it your decision?" Annie asked.

"Well, yes, I guess it was," he said, rubbing his fingers through his streaked blond hair. "One that I wish I hadn't had to make."

"Is it too late to reverse it?"

"Oh, I don't think I could do that. I'd have to clear it with my father, and he wanted them off the property several weeks ago already."

"So you're willing to follow through on what you know was a bad business decision even though you still have a chance to reverse that decision and protect your reputation," reasoned Annie. "I can't tell you how foolish that sounds to a nonbusiness person like me—although of course you know best. Do you think your father would agree with you?"

Simpson lowered his head. "I honestly don't know what he'd say. But I think he'd prefer to take his lumps from the community and get the Sorensons out of the way. It's been a long, unhappy chapter in the book of his life."

"But if it were solely up to you," she pressed, "would you let them stay?"

"Yes . . . at this point I think I would," Arthur replied slowly. "I think some folks will talk about this a lot. I can hear the chatter in the restaurant already. Blind Bill might even write something about it in the paper. He doesn't seem to think much of us."

Annie leaned closer and fixed her brown eyes on him. "Arthur, would you go talk with your father if I said it meant a lot to me?"

"My dad wouldn't like to hear that you were getting involved," Arthur said. "He's never allowed my mother to comment on what the bank was doing."

"I'm not asking your father," Annie said. "I'm asking you."

"I suppose I can try," Arthur conceded. "But don't get your hopes up. My father truly hated old man Sorenson. He was really looking forward to selling that traction engine out from underneath that bum, and all he got was the price of scrap metal."

"Please."

"All right, I'll—"

A loud knock on the door caused Annie to jump, and before Arthur could respond, the door opened and Arthur's father stepped into the office.

"Oh, excuse me!" exclaimed Wendall Simpson when he saw Annie in the chair across from Arthur. Tall and debonair like his son, the owner of the bank wore a stylish, expensive black suit that seemed out of place in their small rural town. "Miss Harding, I didn't realize you were here. I thought Arthur must have fallen asleep or something. Are you about finished with that report, Arthur? I have been waiting for it."

"Yes, sir." Arthur reached over the desk and grabbed a small stack of papers. Handing them to his father, he ventured, "Annie was actually here regarding some business concerns she has."

"That's wonderful," Mr. Simpson declared with a small smile. "We can use all the help we can get here. Anything I should I know about, Arthur?"

"Well, yes, I guess there is," Arthur said. "Annie is concerned that a lot of local people will feel we're being heartless with the Sorensons. Sort of a black eye that we don't need to give ourselves. She's suggesting we sell off whatever we can now but let the family stay on the property until spring rather than force them out now. Seems like a good public relations move to me."

Wendall Simpson nodded and smiled. "You know, Annie, I think you're right. As much as I disliked Andrew Sorenson, it would certainly look better to let them stay."

"So, then, we'll change the decision," said Arthur.

"No, not on this one," his father replied. "The cat's out of the bag already; can't put it back in. But I hope it's a lesson to you, Arthur. If you make a decision that you've communicated publicly, you have to live with that decision, even if it's a bad one. Especially if it's a bad one, in fact. You must never ever give the impression that you can be swayed once you've decided on something. If you do, nothing you ever say or do will be taken seriously or go unchallenged."

"You're willing for the bad press?" asked Annie, unable to sit silently. "People are going to talk, you know. This is a small community, and news spreads fast. It's the kind of story that Blind Bill likes to write about in the paper."

"No doubt he will," the banker declared. "If it sells more papers, he'll print it, that's for certain. But I can take the heat. I didn't go into this business to make friends. This is a money matter, pure and simple. You do what you can to bolster your public image, but it's dangerous to get soft."

"And if some people get caught in the middle," Annie said softly, "people who never really did anything wrong but have to suffer all the same, well, that's just too bad. Is that what you're saying?"

"It's a matter of principle, Miss Harding," Wendall Simpson explained. "Wives and children suffer every day for the stupid mistakes of men like Andrew Sorenson. Perhaps that's too bad. But if I ever let it be known that I could be swayed from a sound decision for the sake of sentiment, I'd be out of business in a minute. I don't make the rules for who wins and who loses on this earth, and I'm not about to attempt remedying all of society's problems."

"But you could ... but you won't ... make a temporary difference for *one* family that doesn't have a home," Annie spoke softly, shaking her head and closing her eyes. "If that's the principle you live by, I'm sorry, but ... I pity you, Mr. Simpson."

Wendall Simpson's face flushed, and his white knuckles crinkled the report that Arthur had handed to him earlier, but when he spoke his voice was cool and steady. "Which is why women belong at home and need to stay out of the business world," he replied, glancing at his son through narrowed eyes. "Pity is for the church and for women. Perhaps you should visit your minister and see what he can do for these poor people's plight. He seems to be especially attendant to women in need, although this one's not as young and pretty as he seems to like—"

"That's enough said," Arthur cut in, standing up to his father. "You don't have to get mean just because you don't agree with her. You've got the report you wanted."

"Don't even think about getting sentimental and reversing your decision," Wendall Simpson warned his son. "I'll come down on you like—"

"I'm aware of what will happen," Arthur stated. "You've made your point. It won't happen again."

"Good," the banker replied. "Don't forget the meeting at four-thirty. Good day, Miss Harding."

Annie did not respond as Wendall Simpson left and closed the door quietly behind him. For a moment she looked down and ran her fingers along the seam of her long green dress, twisting it into knots. Then she stood up and turned to leave without looking at Arthur.

"Annie, I'm sorry," he said, taking her by the arm.

Shaking off his hand, Annie stopped and continued to focus on the wood floor. "Is this what I can expect from you?" she whispered.

"Annie, he owns the bank. What do you want me to do? Get fired?" Arthur asked.

"You can live with that principle?" Annie continued, her bottom lip trembling as she glanced up into Simpson's eyes.

"Once he retires, I can change all this," he defended. "It doesn't have to stay—"

"If you're willing to sacrifice one person today for your bank's principle, you'll sacrifice anything, won't you?"

"This isn't my deci—"

"And you'll hide behind your father's suit while you do it," said Annie. "I have to get out of here before I get sick."

"Don't go, please," Simpson pleaded. "I'll talk to him again and see if I can—"

"Don't insult me with a lie on top of it all," Annie said, pulling open the door. "You're daddy's yes-man all the way. I should have known that."

"Annie, get back in here!" Arthur whispered urgently.

Annie turned around and stared at Arthur. "Do you think you can give me orders the way your father apparently does your mother, Arthur? You've got the wrong person."

Pulling the door shut with a loud bang, Annie stepped quickly to the stairway without looking back. As she descended the stairs, she set her chin and nodded to the cashier whose eyes were fixed upon her. Shoving open the bank's front door, Annie stepped onto the sidewalk and was relieved to see that the street was empty.

Hot tears pushed through her most determined effort to hold them

166

back and came cascading down her face. At the alleyway, she turned in and disappeared into the dark shadows. When she was finally out of earshot of the street, she ducked behind the corner of a brick building, leaned against the wall, and wept for far more than the Sorensons.

Chapter 17

How Could I Help but Love Him?

Annie Harding stood motionless on the street corner, gazing steadily at the Anderson house, wondering if she could muster the courage to march down the sidewalk and knock on the door. The November morning air was frosty, and the low gray clouds and swirling winds carried the distinct flavor of snow. For the third time since she had stopped at the corner, her cold fingers ventured up out of her deep pockets to check the top button on her heavy coat to make sure that it was still fastened.

Taking a deep draft of the cold air, Annie took one reluctant but determined step down the sidewalk, then another. Her hope that each step would get easier did not prove true, but once she was halfway down the Andersons' sidewalk, she knew there was no turning back. All that could spare her now was the slim chance that Mrs. Anderson might be away from home.

Annie's teeth were chattering as she knocked hard on the Andersons' front door. She waited and waited, but there did not appear to be any response. Partly relieved and partly disappointed, Annie slowly turned around to go home and started down the sidewalk.

The metal click of the door opening caught Annie's attention, and she glanced back as the heavy wooden door opened slightly, then wider. In the shadows a woman's head peered around the edge of the door.

"Annie Harding?" Marian Anderson's voice called out as she pulled the door open wide. She was dressed in a long white robe and slippers. "Annie, come on in. I wasn't expecting anyone this morning, so I'm not even dressed yet. But please, do come in."

"Oh, I'm sorry, Mrs. Anderson," Annie said. "I can come back later. It's not that I'm—"

"Come in, please, before you freeze to death," Stuart's mother urged. "I've been up for hours; I just don't look like it. And please call me Marian."

"Thank you very much," Annie replied as she stepped into the house and the door clicked shut behind her. The warm air and the smell of fresh-baked bread instantly greeted her.

"This is a pleasant surprise," Marian said with a smile as Annie unbuttoned her winter coat and pulled it off. "Here, let me take that."

"Thanks," Annie replied as she handed it to her host. "I should have checked with you beforehand, but I stayed overnight with my grandmother and was on my way home when I thought of stopping. Are you sure you don't mind? I don't want to interrupt—"

"No, you're not interrupting anything," Marian insisted, turning and heading down the hallway. "Come into the kitchen and let's get some hot coffee into you. I can't believe it's so damp and chilly already."

"Feels like snow," Annie said. She rubbed her cold red hands together as she followed Marian around the corner and into the kitchen. "Time to get out the mittens and boots again."

"This coffee's really hot," Marian warned, pouring the steamy brew into a china cup and handing it to Annie. "You'll want to let it cool down a bit. Have a seat at the table, there."

As Marian poured her own cup of coffee, Annie carried her cup and saucer over to the kitchen table and sank down in the chair next to the window. She wrapped her fingers around the coffee cup, letting its warmth begin to sink into her fingers, and took note of her surroundings. On the table across from her lay Marian's worn black leather Bible. Beside it was a thick leatherbound novel, the title *The Curate's Awakening* engraved on the spine. An ornate Victorian bookmark protruded from its well-worn pages.

"So now you see how I take advantage of my Saturday mornings away from the office," Marian stated as she sat down on the chair next to Annie, setting a china sugar bowl, a small earthenware cream pitcher, and a plate of thick buttered bread slices on the table as well. "Brew the coffee, get Robert off to work, get the bread in the oven, and treat myself to a good book. I should be cleaning the house, as you may have noticed, but . . . the dust seems content to simply wait for me. I say, why hurry to it?"

Annie laughed and nodded. "It does seem like an endless job," she replied, gazing around the kitchen. "Your house looks wonderful, though. Everything's so neat and tidy."

"Well, Stuart's back in school, so I don't have to chase around and pick up after him," said Marian. "I miss him terribly, but I don't miss the mess he creates. Here, have some of this bread. It's never better than when it's warm."

Annie gladly took a slice, then gingerly took a sip of her coffee, but it was still too hot to drink. Setting her cup down on its saucer, she began, "You . . . um . . . probably wonder why I've stopped by this morning, Mrs. Anderson."

Marian smiled. "Annie, you have to call me Marian. Otherwise, I feel too old, and I hate feeling old on a cold morning. And, yes, you've got my curiosity up, but I figure you'll clue me in when you get around to it. I'm in no hurry, though. If you just stopped by for us to get to know each other better, that's fine with me."

"I know it seems strange that I'd just drop in . . . we've never really talked very much," Annie said. "But something's come up, and I really don't know who I can talk to about it. Something that Stuart said to me before he left for the university made me think I could discuss it with you."

"I can't imagine what he might have said," Marian said. "But I'm a fair listener, if that can help. What's on your mind, Annie?"

"Oh my . . . there's so much," Annie replied. "So many things that are going wrong . . . things that I don't seem to be able to do anything about, but . . . I don't know. I'm just so frustrated."

"Where do you want to start?"

"Have you heard anything about the Sorenson family?"

Marian Anderson nodded. "Some people have been talking about it down at the drugstore and in the mill. We heard that the bank is forcing them off the farm by Thanksgiving. That's . . . six days from now. I didn't hear where the family was going to go."

"They're moving in with Walter's grandmother."

"With Millie? Oh, my goodness!" Marian exclaimed. "That house is barely big enough for one elderly couple, let alone add a family. How could they think that would work?"

"From what I understand, they have nowhere else to go. And to my knowledge, they'll have no source of income unless Walter gets a job. Perhaps his mother can find work, but that would be a pittance."

"Where would Walter work with that arm of his?" Marian asked, rising from her chair and pacing around the kitchen. "He'll never do a day's work with that arm."

"Not in a heavy labor job," said Annie, her face brightening a bit. "That's why Mrs. Olson and I have been tutoring him after school. He's exceptional with numbers and accounting, but it turns out he's not as strong with his vocabulary and writing."

Marian stopped midstep. "You and Mrs. Olson have been teaching Walter?"

Annie nodded. "Ever since he got out of the hospital. Mrs. Olson's been trying to find him an office job, but nobody around here is interested. She's afraid that he'll have to move to a bigger city. His father didn't make any friends in this town."

"He sure didn't," Marian agreed, taking her seat again. "I've already written off the money he owed the mill. So you think Walter would make a good accountant?"

"Mrs. Olson says he'd be wonderful if she could just get someone to believe in him," said Annie. "Do you know anyone who might be interested?"

Marian Anderson's dark eyes drifted toward the kitchen window to the barren elm trees and the snow-threatening clouds. "I'm not sure," she answered thoughtfully, lifting her now-cooled coffee for a sip. "I'd have to talk with my husband. Robert may know someone. Is that what you came to talk about, Annie?"

"No, that was just the start of it," said Annie. "I was upset about the bank forcing the Sorensons off their farm, so I tried to talk Arthur Simpson into letting them stay there until spring, but I ended up getting into a big argument with his father. It was terrible."

"Arthur Simpson—you've been seeing him for quite a long time now, haven't you?" asked Marian. "He gave you that lovely ring?"

Annie bit her lip and nodded.

"Did he get angry with you?"

"No . . . I'm not sure. I could tell his father was upset; his knuckles were white. And *I* was so mad at the two of them that I stormed out and slammed Arthur's office door."

"So do you think it's over between you two?"

"I don't know," Annie whispered, then rubbed her lips. "I'm sure I embarrassed him in front of his father."

"Do you want to keep seeing Arthur?"

"I . . . ah . . . he can be very charming and attentive," Annie said, "and I think he truly cares about me. I get confused about it, though. He can change so quickly."

Marian leaned over and met Annie's eyes. "Annie, why aren't you talking to your mother about this?"

Annie took a sip of coffee, then set her cup down on its saucer. "I can't," she said slowly. "My mother thinks Arthur's wonderful, especially wonderfully rich. And he's got my father wrapped around his little finger. They'd both be very upset with me if I told Arthur good-bye, and I think my father would be enraged. He has a temper."

"Sounds like you're in a very difficult spot," Marian Anderson said gently.

Annie nodded again. "Could I ask you something that I asked my mother?"

"Of course."

"When you think about marriage . . . how important do you think love is?"

Marian smiled and crossed her arms, then she took a deep breath. "It's . . . everything in a marriage. By that I mean real love, not just romance or sentiment. When you truly love someone, your love will carry you both through anything. If you don't have love, nothing else will hold you together."

"Not even money."

"Money's probably one of the most difficult issues in a marriage," Marian said. "Either you don't have enough, and that's a problem, or you have plenty, and it's still never enough. It's nice to have enough money to live comfortably, but the day you start loving money or thinking it's going to satisfy you, it becomes a god that you can't control. It's like a trap that's waiting to snap the second you take the bait. But it's so enticing."

Annie glanced out the window and said, "My mother said that if I wasn't careful to hold on to Arthur, every girl in the county would be waiting to take my place."

"She's probably right," Marian responded with a gentle smile. "Your Mr. Simpson seems to be quite a catch."

Annie laughed out loud. "Yes, he is. But somehow . . . lately, it's not enough. I don't know . . . What convinced you to marry Mr. Anderson—other than his being young and handsome and romantic?"

"I'll tell him you said those things about him," Marian said with a smile. "He'll like that. But oh my, what convinced me. . . ? I suppose it was a lot of things, but my decision did go beyond the romantic feelings I had for him. I'd say the things that drew me to Robert were the things we both valued. I felt that he respected me as his equal, that in love we could be partners together, that he'd always be there to support me and I'd always be there for him. And I felt certain that neither of us would ever allow something or someone else to come between our love."

"And what if your values had been different?"

"That would have been very, very hard," Marian mused, staring down into her almost-empty cup. "I can't imagine sharing a home with someone who is committed to something you're not. Seems like it would be a long, difficult lifetime."

"Like Mrs. Sorenson and her husband," Annie replied. "From what Walter has said, he apparently drank up everything they might have saved over the years."

"Sounds like torture to me," said Marian. "But it's usually not that graphic or violent. Even a quiet, respectable marriage can be very hard if your hearts aren't devoted to the same thing."

"And you feel your faith in God is the most important part of that?"

Marian let go of her coffee cup and looked up. "And how did you know that?"

Annie flashed a big smile. "Your son, Stuart, told me he'd spent a good part of a Saturday morning talking with you about his faith, and he added that he could talk with both you and your husband about it. That's really why I came over here this morning. I was . . . hoping you'd do the same for me, and I haven't been disappointed."

"Why, thank you, Annie," Marian replied. "You come any Saturday morning you like . . . as long as you wait until I've had a chance to read for a while," she added. "And yes, the center and the strength of my love for Robert is my faith in God, and that's true for Robert as well. No matter what we face or go through, we know that God is there with us. We sometimes . . . oftentimes, I suppose . . . fail to acknowledge Him or look to Him, and so we say or do the wrong thing, but eventually we apologize and forgive each other. Faith, without a doubt, is the most important issue to make sure you agree on with the person you will marry."

Annie ran her long slender fingers along the edge of the wooden table and shook her head. "It's not good," she whispered.

"What's not good?"

"As far as I can tell, Arthur doesn't believe in God at all," Annie replied, continuing to look down at the edge of the table. "At least he doesn't think he needs God in his everyday world."

"And you do?"

Annie nodded slowly and deliberately. "I didn't, really . . . before the accident. But now I do, and today I do more than ever."

"Why's that?"

"Because I need the courage to face the truth with Arthur . . . and with my parents," Annie replied, glancing up into Marian Anderson's face. "I don't have that in myself, believe me."

"What was it about the accident that changed your thinking?"

Annie smiled. "Well, the fact that I was alive certainly got my attention. But there was more to it than that. I can't explain it very well, but I know that God was there, down in the middle of the chaos and destruction at Flatwillow Creek, and He was speaking to me. Then, after the accident, your son told me that God had spoken to him through the words of the Bible, so I began reading it. It's been the most amazing discovery of my life."

"Stuart told you that?"

"We talked on the Saturday morning after he had been talking to you," Annie replied. "I was hoping to see him at Thanksgiving, and especially to thank him. Will he be coming home?"

Marian Anderson shook her head. "Unfortunately not. It's just too short of a holiday for him to come home, so he's going to friend's house for the day. She lives nearby, I guess. He will be home at Christmas, though."

"Oh good," Annie spoke softly and looked out the window. Slender yellow shafts of sunlight had found occasional breaks in the low cloud cover and appeared to be moving across the dull brown landscape. "He's different, you know."

"Good different, I hope," Marian replied with a smile.

Annie smiled again, and her delicate face lit up. "Yes, good," she said. "I've never met anyone who spoke of God as being a natural part of his life, like a person whom he knew. I wasn't sure that it was possible, but I hoped it was."

"What convinced you, then?"

Annie reached up and tapped her thumb against her chin several times, then she said, "Two really simple words made the difference, I think. I started reading the Gospels and . . . this sounds so strange to say out loud, but I think I started to fall in love with Jesus Christ. Everything He did, the words He spoke, the way He touched people in need, the way He loved everyone, even those who hated Him . . . how could I help but love Him, Marian?"

Tears welled up in Annie's large brown eyes, and she put her hand over her mouth. She closed her eyes, but several tears forced their way out and ran down her soft cheeks. "Do you love Him, Marian?" she whispered.

Marian nodded, tears spilling from her dark eyes as well. "Oh yes, Annie, I love Him . . . with all my heart. How could I not?"

Annie chuckled through her tears. "I don't know, but I don't know many people who love Him like that."

"Some do, but not nearly enough," Marian replied. "Tell me what the two words were, Annie."

Annie closed her eyes again and smiled. "When Jesus said, 'Follow me,' I knew immediately that those words were for me, that He was asking me to decide whether I would take this love I felt for Him and become His disciple. But I knew there was a cost to following Him. It's taken me several weeks to actually feel like I understand what I'm supposed to do. Do you know what I mean?"

"I think so," Marian said. "You've discovered that to follow Jesus means to obey His words, and that involves making changes in your life."

"Some very big changes . . . hard ones," Annie replied. "So many things in my life are so far from what He says they should be. And I discovered He's not about to follow me down some of those old roads where I like to walk."

"Like what?"

"Oh, you name it, I guess," Annie said, shaking her head. "I almost feel like I'm starting my life over again—or trying to learn to walk for the first time."

"So, what's been the hardest for you?"

Puffing out a mouthful of air, Annie said, "That's an easy one. Forgiving people! I see so much . . . that I hate in others . . . and in myself I see the same things. Like this situation with the Sorensons—and like the way my father treats us sometimes. I really hate that."

"There *is* a lot to be angry about, Annie. Forgiving doesn't mean you won't get angry," Marian responded. "Do you see that?"

"I think I do . . . finally," Annie replied, squinting her eyes as a large shaft of sunlight broke through the clouds and momentarily lit up the Andersons' backyard. "At least I hope I do, because I still feel angry a lot. But I really am trying to forgive people for what they're doing . . . and the way they are. You know, it's sort of funny. When you start forgiving, you feel like you understand the person better and what's making them do what they do."

"You've come a long way, Annie, if you can say that from your heart," Marian said. "There are a lot of people who never seem able to forgive—and their lives are all the poorer for it. Stuart's grandfather calls unforgiveness the devil's home on earth, and I've seen what it can do to a person."

Annie shivered at the thought. "I believe that's true, and I believe in the devil. I've felt the evil in my own heart . . . that . . . the blood of Jesus has cleansed away. It *was* evil, Marian—hateful, spiteful. Do you believe that? Have you felt that way?"

Marian ran her fingers through her black hair and nodded, then she took Annie's hand. "More than you can imagine," she whispered, tears reforming at the corners of her eyes. "What did He say, 'To whom little is forgiven, the same loveth little'? He has forgiven me much, believe me."

Chapter 18

The Dingdong

Geneva Gray sat across from Stuart at her small oak kitchen table, scrutinizing him as only a grandmother can. The rich aroma of the Thanksgiving turkey roasting in the oven and the two golden pumpkin pies cooling on one of the counters filled the room but did not seem to distract Geneva's attention.

"You have to tell her today," she was repeating for the third time, an admonition that had been previously amplified by a lengthy lecture. "I don't know what's gotten into you, Stuart, but you know better than to play with a young woman's affections."

"Grandma, why can't you believe me when I say I'm not playing with anyone's affections?" Stuart protested. "Catherine and I are nothing more than friends. I've done nothing to encourage her to think there's more."

"And what far country have you traveled from?" his grandmother scolded. "Don't you understand anything about women, Stuart? Catherine Bolton, who happens to be one of the most guileless young women you'll ever meet, believes with all her heart that you love her."

"No, she doesn't," Stuart objected, shaking his head and gesturing with his hands. "How could she? I've never hinted that I wanted to be anything but her friend. We sit together at church and sometimes we take a walk together after the evening service, and once or twice I've escorted her to a lecture or a concert. That's it."

"Sonny, you're as blind as a bat, just like your father was about your mother," Geneva railed on. "You mark my words and try opening those peepers that you claim you've got open. When you're with her family today, watch how you're being treated and listen to the words that come your way. You'll see that I'm right."

"Maybe you should come along and make sure I don't miss it," Stuart groused.

"If you listen to what I'm saying, you won't need me," she replied. "And don't go getting cross with me. I run the roost here, and just remember who cooks the meals. I can starve you out in a hurry."

Stuart laughed and stood up from his chair. "I'm sorry, Grandma. I just think you're wrong about Catherine. I've never even held her hand, let alone put my arm around her or asked for a kiss."

"And that's exactly where your thinking's way off, Stuart," Geneva explained. "A young woman as sincere as Catherine doesn't need any of those signals to attract her when you've already signaled something more important."

"But I never said—"

"But you never said you weren't," his grandmother interjected. "So unless you suddenly find yourself feeling different, you simply have to sit down with Catherine and tell her that you're grateful for her friendship, but that there's nothing more to your relationship. Going to her house on Thanksgiving says to Catherine that there's more to it, exactly as she believes. And it says the same thing to her family. You'll be shocked when you get there."

"No," he argued. "All it means is that Catherine knew I couldn't go home to see my parents, so she thought it would be nice if I had somewhere special to go to. She said that."

"And she meant it, but she didn't say all that she meant," Geneva replied. "Hey, don't you be touching my pies," she warned as Stuart picked up a fork and moved toward them. "You can have some later tonight. *After* you tell Catherine."

"All right, I will," Stuart said. "I don't think it's necessary, but to satisfy you, I'll do it."

"Good," his grandmother replied. "One more thing. Don't you dare talk to her about it anywhere other than in private."

"Why?"

"You are truly a walking, talking dingdong," she replied. "If you're brave enough to talk with her about this, you'd better be prepared for some tears. It's going to be difficult for her, but it won't be as bad if you do it privately."

"I really don't think so."

"And I know it's so."

✦✦✦✦✦✦✦✦✦✦✦

"Glenn wants to show you our horses," Catherine Bolton told Stuart after he had been introduced to her parents and her fourteen-year-old brother. As always, Catherine's dark green eyes were flashing, and her long curly brunette hair was bouncing. "Maybe we can a take a ride after we eat. Right now, though, I need to get in the kitchen and help Mother finish getting the meal ready. My folks were so excited to meet you!"

"Riding sounds like fun, if we can keep out of the wind," Stuart replied, picking up his heavy winter coat and moving toward the front door, where Catherine's freckle-faced brother Glenn was waiting. "I hate it when it snows on Thanksgiving. It's going to be a long winter again. Do you like winter, Glenn?"

"I hate it," the boy replied, pulling open the heavy wooden door and stepping out onto the cement slab. "Watch the ice. The lousy drizzle stuck like iron out here. It's real slippery."

Stuart followed Glenn out the door, carefully planting his feet on the slick concrete that was covered by a thin film of snow. A light breeze out of the cold northwest caught the falling snow granules and peppered the two young men. Stuart shielded his face as he and Glenn headed for the Boltons' small red horse barn.

The Boltons lived on the very southern edge of Minneapolis and owned a little over two acres of land. A strong white wooden fence enclosed the property, and another inner fence enclosed a small pasture and several large oak trees. The horse barn was fashioned in the familiar barn shape but was only about half the size.

"Doesn't feel like much of a day to go riding," Glenn called back as he reached for the handle of the barn door. Pushing down on the lever, he shoved his shoulder against the swollen door that reluctantly gave way to his strength, then he stepped over the concrete threshold to the instant cackle of chickens.

Stuart stepped through the doorway into a room that was home to about thirty white Leghorns, most of them roosting in their nests. "My, oh my," Stuart said to Glenn with a laugh, holding his nose. "There's nothing like the smell of chickens in a closed coop. You must be selling eggs."

"Yep," Glenn replied, closing the door with a hard shove and latching it on the inside. "In the spring we add about a hundred broilers. What a mess that is until we can let them outside. Watch out for your shoes."

Stuart looked down just as he was about to step into a clump of white-and-black chicken manure. "Oops," he said, carefully pulling his foot away. "Just what I don't need on my Sunday shoes."

Glenn laughed and unlatched the inner door that opened into the other two-thirds of the barn. Most of the space was taken up by an open pen, with a small tack room in the southeast corner and separate stalls to the side for the Boltons' three chestnut horses and one white-faced Holstein milking cow. A mahogany red Irish setter was eagerly waiting for them at the door.

"Get down, Sadie!" Glenn ordered the excited dog as the two young men entered the central pen. To the right of the doorway, a wooden ladder attached to the wall led to the haymow, and Sadie's straw bed was in the corner.

"You've got a fair amount of chores to do, I see," Stuart said as Glenn petted the dog and then made her sit.

"Dad says it keeps me out of trouble," said Glenn.

"That's what my pa said about the mill," Stuart replied. "So you keep your dog out here?"

"When the weather's bad," Glenn said. "We used to let her in the house. But one Sunday we came home from church and Sadie had knocked my mother's bird cage down. All that was left of her yellow canary was a few feathers and one claw. Sadie's slept out here ever since."

Stuart laughed and stepped over to the nearest stalls, where a curious brown head had appeared. He held out an open hand for the horse to sniff, then reached up to scratch behind her ears. She snorted, shook her head, and snuffed insistently around his pockets. "Can't fool you, can I?" Stuart said, reaching into his pocket for one of the carrot chunks Catherine's mother had given him. "I hope your folks didn't go to too much fuss with me coming here today," Stuart said to Glenn while she munched.

"No, not really," Glenn replied. "My grandparents will be here soon, but they always come on Thanksgiving. Catherine can hardly wait to show you off to them, too."

"Show me off?" Stuart questioned, his own grandmother's warnings suddenly ringing in his ears.

"Sure thing," said Glenn as he leaned against the haymow ladder and laughed. "Catherine's never had a sweetheart over to our house for a big meal like this, and she talked about you all summer long. Mother said that holiday meals are specially for times like this when couples get serious and want to meet the family."

Stuart took a deep breath of the warm, sweet-smelling air and tried to hide his sudden discomfort. "So," he asked casually, "what does Catherine say about me?"

"Well, she and Mother talk a lot about providence and whatnot," Glenn replied. "It sounds sort of stupid to me, but that doesn't stop them from going on and on. I did hear Catherine tell my dad that the two of you weren't engaged yet, but things were coming together. You think you really want to marry my sister? She makes me mad most of the time."

"I ... um ... well, your sister and I need to talk about that," Stuart muttered, then pulled out another piece of carrot for the horse. "So what time of the morning do you have to get up to milk the cow, Glenn?"

◆◆◆◆◆◆◆◆◆◆◆

"I'll be right down, Stuart. Wait there for me," Catherine said, holding up her long black skirt as she ascended the stairway and then disappeared down the hallway for her bedroom.

Stuart sat down on a chair beside the coat-tree at the bottom of the stairs and leaned his head against the wood casing. The other men had disappeared into the living room, and Glenn and his grandfather were already arguing over their game of Chinese checkers. Catherine's mother and grandmother were busy cleaning up the food and dishes from the dining room table.

"Catherine's young man is so handsome," Stuart could hear her grandmother saying above the clatter of china through the doorway.

"And to think he wants to be a doctor or a minister. That would be grand for the family, wouldn't it?"

"He's a fine boy, Mother" was the reply. "It's easy to see why Catherine thinks so highly of him."

"I just wish they weren't thinking about going to India," Catherine's grandmother continued. "Why can't they stay here?"

"That's a long ways off," Mrs. Bolton said. "We'll see what happens."

"We sure will," Stuart whispered with a deep groan. Standing up, he retrieved his coat from the hall tree, crossed to the front door, and stepped out into the cold November air. Forgetting the thin ice on the concrete slab, he barely managed to catch himself as his feet shot out from under him. "Serves me right," he whispered. "What an idiot I am. My own grandmother knows more about my love life than I do."

The cold air felt good against Stuart's hot cheeks, and he stood motionless beside the Boltons' front door as if he were awaiting a dreaded verdict. He wished he had never come for the dinner, but at least it might give him the chance to follow his grandmother's advice and talk with Catherine in private. He closed his eyes and took a deep breath of air, searching for the right words.

"Stuart, are you out here?" Catherine pushed the front door open and peered out.

"Yes, right here," Stuart said, stepping in front of the door and holding out his arm. "Don't slip on this ice."

"Whatever are you doing out here in the cold?" Catherine asked as she took Stuart's arm and stepped out onto the porch, pulling up the hood of her cape. She had changed into a well-worn riding skirt and boots. "I thought you might have snuck out to get away from my doting grandmother."

"I was just getting a little warm inside," Stuart said truthfully as the two of them walked together toward the barn. "It felt good out here."

"I'm sorry about the way my grandmother acts," Catherine apologized. "She says things before she thinks about them; it gets embarrassing at times. And the older she gets, the worse it's become. She really shouldn't have asked you how rich you hoped to be someday."

Stuart laughed as they neared the barn. "Just a second; I'll get the door." He walked over to pull the latch on the door he and Glenn had used.

"Let's use the other one," Catherine said, pointing to a door on the front of the barn that led directly into the horse pen. "Did Glenn take you through the chicken coop?"

"Yes. Why?"

Now it was Catherine's turn to laugh. "The brat does that just to watch and see if whoever he takes through there gets chicken manure on his shoes. It's all a big joke to him, and I think he feels some sadistic satisfaction after having cleaned those pens for so many years."

"He must like me, then," Stuart said, following Catherine as she pulled open the front door. "He warned me just before I would have planted my shoe on a big pile."

"That's a first," Catherine replied as they stepped into the warm moist air of the barn. "You stay down, Sadie!" she ordered before the Irish setter could jump up against her. Then she moved gracefully across the pen to the closest chestnut mare. "How are you doing today, sweetheart?" she spoke affectionately into the horse's ear and gently stroked its neck. Turning toward Stuart, she said, "The saddles are in the—"

Stuart held up his hand and asked, "Catherine, could we . . . hold off on the ride for a bit? Something has come up that I need to talk with you about, and this seems like a good time to do it."

Catherine's face lit up with an anticipation that quickly faded when she saw Stuart's somber expression. "Stuart, what is it? Did I say something in there that—"

"No, it's not anything you said or did, and it's not your grandmother or your mother," Stuart stated, shaking his head and moving closer to her. "It's about me . . . and you . . . and mostly about me."

Catherine leaned against a wooden hay manger, and a warm smile returned to her face. "Is this what I think it is?"

"I doubt it," Stuart replied, taking a deep breath as he wrapped one of his arms around one of the large wooden beams that supported the haymow floor above them. "I'm afraid I owe you a very big apology."

Catherine's green eyes searched Stuart's face, then she said, "No, you've always been a perfect gentleman, Stuart. There have been others who—"

"I don't think you understand," Stuart interrupted, "and even after I explain it, you may not understand. You see, without realizing what was happening, I'm afraid I've misled you regarding my intentions."

"How?"

Stuart looked down with a frown and rubbed his forehead. "I like you a lot, Catherine; I have since the first time we met. I've enjoyed every moment we've ever spent together. . . ."

"And I have as well," Catherine spoke softly, watching Stuart carefully.

"I know you have," Stuart continued, searching for words. "I think, though, that we're understanding each other differently. You've become a wonderful friend, Catherine . . . but that's how I view you. I wasn't thinking there was any more to it, and now I realize that you've been more serious about our relationship than I have. I'm sorry."

"Stuart, tell me exactly what you mean," Catherine said. She showed no emotion and did not move. "Is it over between us?"

Gazing up into Catherine's face again, Stuart said, "You need to know that I treasure your friendship, and I hope we never ever lose that, but I never meant to lead you to think that I was interested in courtship and marriage. I've done so, and for that I am very sorry."

Catherine looked away toward one of the dusty, cobwebbed barn windows, and in the soft light Stuart saw a few tears begin to streak down her cheeks. For a moment he wanted to reach out to her and tell her that he was making a mistake, but he held back. He didn't want to hurt her again.

"Is it the girl you rescued?" Catherine asked. Her voice trembled as she spoke.

"No, it has nothing to do with anyone else," Stuart replied. "You have to believe when I say that it's no one's fault, Catherine. You're a wonderful person, and you'll make some lucky fellow a wonderful wife. But I'm not that guy."

"Perhaps in time you—"

"No," Stuart said. "It's just not there for me. If it was, I would have known by now. But I let my enjoyment of our friendship give you hope that there was more. I'm so sorry. My grandmother warned me about this, and I didn't listen. I'm so sorry, Catherine."

Catherine dabbed at her tears, then she surprised Stuart as a smile crossed her face. "Your grandmother is the wisest of them all," she spoke in a raspy voice, then tried to clear her throat. "I was so stupid."

"What's that?" Stuart asked, stepping toward her.

With a shake of her head, Catherine looked straight into Stuart's black eyes. "This is as much my fault as yours, Stuart," she said. "It's probably mostly my fault. I ... um ... I've tried to tell myself that this was going to work, or it could work, or I could make it work, but I guess I knew in my heart it wasn't true."

She paused and swallowed, then took a deep breath and gave a crooked smile. "Stuart, you're everything I hoped I might find in a husband, and I guess I went a little overboard. Your grandmother tried to tell me—she warned me about the mystery of understanding God's providence—but I just wasn't listening. It was unfair of me to try to persuade you that God was behind it all, but even with that, I could see you weren't bending."

"So you knew," Stuart said.

Catherine nodded and said, "Hope springs eternal ... sometimes. But not today."

"I'm very sorry if I've hurt you," Stuart repeated. "I dread losing your friendship, but I'll understand if you want me to stay away."

Crossing her arms, Catherine returned her gaze out the dirty window. "No, that would be making an even worse mistake. We can't let go of our friendship because we've made some mistakes. Hopefully we'll both learn something from this. I know I will."

"I hope I will as well," Stuart said. "But I'm not sure how much to hope for. This morning Grandma called me a walking, talking ding-dong."

Catherine burst out laughing, then immediately sobered. "Stuart," she said, meeting his eyes once more. "I need to say one more thing. I think all along I knew that I was mostly in love with the thought of love rather than being in love with you. I wasn't honest with myself, and that was wrong. I've nearly destroyed something I do value. Please forgive me as well."

"I will if you'll say out loud that you forgive me."

"I forgive you, Stuart. And let's be friends forever."

Part 3

Winter Warmings

Winter, descending with a slap of December fury, freezes the laughing creek to silence. Not a sound, not even a gurgle, can penetrate the thick muffler of snow that hides the stream. Even the ruined bridge lies lonely and quiet, its mute memories silenced by a cold that denies everything but its own power.

But beneath the enveloping snow and the ice, the stream is far from conquered. It rests patiently, assured by an ancient wisdom that freedom lies ahead. It won't be that long before the sun is clothed again in strength and the snowy silence dissolves once more into glorious laughter. Until then, there's time for quiet rest, for building up strength—for winter waiting is never wasted.

Chapter 19

A Kiss in the Alley

"*E*lsie, do you want to come over to my house and finish up this report?" Annie Harding asked her friend as the other students in Mrs. Olson's class slowly filed out at the close of another school day.

"Sorry, I can't," Elsie replied, quickly putting away her books without looking up. "I have to get over to Mrs. Beldner's again. She thinks we can finish most of the sewing on my Christmas dress if we can get a few more afternoons in on it. Maybe you and I can skip lunch tomorrow and finish the report."

"We'll never get it done in time if we have to do it during our breaks," Annie protested. "And why the sudden interest in having a special dress for Christmas? Have you met someone you're not telling me about?"

"Me? Come on, Annie, what do you think?" Elsie muttered, her heart-shaped face a little flushed. "You know what I'm doing before I do most of the time. Maybe I just want to have an extraordinarily beautiful dress to spice up my dull wardrobe. It's a princess gown in deep blue chiffon and velvet pressed to look like ribbing."

"Your wardrobe is hardly dull, Elsie," Annie commented. "And you've got every boy in the school asking you to the New Year's Eve dance."

"*Boys* is right," said Elsie, standing up from her desk to leave. "I wouldn't be caught dead with one of those little pipsqueaks. See you."

"Bye," Annie called out as Elsie disappeared through the classroom door. She sat staring at the empty doorway for a few moments, then finished putting away her own books.

"Annie, do you have a minute?" Henrietta Olson asked as Annie stood up from her desk.

"Of course," Annie replied, walking up to the big wooden desk where her teacher was sitting.

"I saw you watching Elsie leave," Mrs. Olson said, tapping her pencil on her thumb. "Do you know if there's something happening with her?"

"No, not that I know about," Annie replied. "I've felt like she's been avoiding me for the last couple of weeks, but that may just be me. Why do you ask?"

"Her homework and test grades are falling off," Henrietta said. "I get the impression she's distracted with something. I just thought you might know."

"No, I'm sorry, Mrs. Olson," said Annie. "If I find something out, I'll let you know. Was that what you wanted to see me about?"

"Actually, no," Mrs. Olson responded, then a wide smile crossed the schoolteacher's usually stern face. "I believe that I have an excellent lead on someone who is interested in hiring Walter Sorenson, but I can't tell a soul until it happens. I think you'll be very pleased."

Annie's eyes lit up and she, too, smiled. "This is wonderful news, Mrs. Olson," she piped up. "You *have* to tell me who it is!"

"I can't, Annie," Henrietta persisted. "I would love to tell you more, and you'll be one of the first ones to be told. I gave my word that I would be silent, but the person in question told me I could tell you that something good was about to happen."

"Arthur!" Annie guessed out loud. "Did he change his father's mind?"

Mrs. Olson held up her hand and shook her head. "I won't let you put me to the test, Annie. We should know for certain by Friday, perhaps even by tomorrow if Walter gets back in time from seeing the doctors in Minneapolis."

"Friday or tomorrow!" Annie exclaimed, giving a small jump. "I can hardly wait. Walter will be so pleased."

"Yes, he will," Henrietta replied. "Thank you for your help, Annie. If this job comes through, Walter will be truly ready for it."

"Oh, it's been my pleasure," said Annie. "Walter's given me back far more than I've given him. It's been the most rewarding thing I think I've ever done."

"That's what teaching is all about," Mrs. Olson said, lightly rubbing her fingers over her gray hair and giving Annie a wry grin. "See how young it's kept me?"

Annie laughed. "Everyone should be as young as you, Mrs. Olson. I'll see you tomorrow. Thank you for the good news."

"You're welcome," the schoolteacher replied as Annie turned to leave. "Good-night, now."

Annie made her way out of the school building into the early December chill and stopped to wrap her wool scarf around her neck. The thought of going straight home after school seemed a bit strange after having gone to Millie Gullickson's house so regularly for the past weeks. Since the entire Sorenson family had moved in at Thanksgiving time, though, the lessons had gotten shorter. So much activity in the tiny house made concentration difficult.

Although winter had already made several ominous threats of an early arrival, there had been no significant snow, but the cold refused to make a retreat. Bundled up and in no particular hurry, Annie strolled down the streets toward home, enjoying the bright sunshine that persisted in spite of the cold. The streets were quiet except for an occasional school-age child who scooted outdoors to burn off some pent-up energy.

When she reached their house, Annie was surprised by the initial silence. With Garrit around, there was hardly a moment when chatter or noise was not coming from somewhere in the house. Hearing the floor squeak in the kitchen, Annie went to find her mother.

"Hello, Mother," Annie said as she came through the wooden swinging door. "Where's Garrit? It's way too quiet here."

"I sent him downtown to get some flour," Dinah Harding responded, glancing up from the large mixing bowl where she was creaming together a golden lump of butter and sugar. "Can you believe I ran out again?"

"Bet that made him happy."

"He was delighted, as usual," her mother said. "What are you doing home so early? No tutoring today?"

"Didn't I tell you?" Annie said. "Walter had to take the train to

Minneapolis for a checkup on his arm. He might be home tomorrow, and if he is, I heard that someone's going to announce they're hiring him. Isn't that exciting?"

"That is good news, really good news," Dinah replied, breaking an egg into the contents of the bowl, then stirring hard with a big wooden spoon. "Who?"

"That's what I won't know until Walter gets back, but I'm hoping it's Arthur and his father," Annie said. "Who else could it be?"

"I'm sure I don't have any idea," her mother said. "But I wouldn't think it could be the Simpsons. Why would they give Walter a job?"

Annie smiled a crooked smile. "Maybe . . . because . . . Arthur realizes how angry I was and now he desperately wants to make it up to me. It's possible, isn't it?"

"Possible, yes," Dinah commented. "From what I've heard about Arthur's father, though, I'd say it's unlikely. Can I get you something to eat, Annie?"

"No thanks," Annie responded. "I'm not very hungry yet. I'll wait until Garrit gets home and has his snack."

"Fine with me," her mother said. "Can you take the laundry basket that's by the stairway up to your room and put the clothes away? There's been so much humidity in the basement I didn't think some of those clothes were ever going to dry. And it's too cold to hang them outdoors."

"Of course," Annie replied, "I'll put them away now." Then she walked back out of the kitchen and down the hallway to the stairway that led to the second floor of the house. Scooping up the basket of folded clothes, Annie proceeded up the stairs and to her room, where she put away her laundry and then stayed to straighten the mess she'd left that morning. Leaning over to pick up a stray shoe, she cocked her head, thinking she heard Garrit's voice downstairs. But she hadn't heard the front door open.

Curious, Annie stepped out of her room and went quietly to the stairway to listen. The voices were coming from the dining room.

"Would you be quiet!" Dinah Harding was doing her best to hush her son. "What if Annie hears?"

"So what if she does?" Garrit objected. "If she doesn't, I'm going up to her room and tell her anyway."

"No, you're not!" his mother ordered. "You say one peep of this to her, and I'll show you how warm your bottom can get. Then I'll tell your father when he gets home."

"But I'm telling you the truth, Mother," Garrit railed. "I saw him meet with Elsie Dale in the alley behind Mrs. Gunderson's boardinghouse. He kissed her right on the lips, then he followed her into the building and didn't come out again."

"You're absolutely certain it was Arthur Simpson?" Dinah Harding asked, and Annie's heart felt like it had suddenly stopped beating. "How could you tell?"

"Easy," Garrit declared. "Who else wears a long fancy black overcoat like his? Besides, I was close enough to see his face, Mother. He was kissing Annie's best friend square on the lips! And they never even saw me watching. I'm telling Annie."

"No, you're not—"

Annie had returned to her room and slammed the door shut behind her, the noise reverberating down the narrow hallway. Now she leaned back against the door with her eyes shut and her arms crossed. From what she had come to learn about Arthur Simpson, the news that he was seeing someone else brought her little surprise. But the fact that he was seeing her best friend—and that Elsie would betray their friendship—was simply beyond comprehending. Annie wasn't sure whether to cry or laugh or scream.

"I can't believe this is happening to me," she whispered.

The sound of footsteps creaking on the oak hallway floor outside her room disrupted her thoughts. A light tap on her door was followed by her mother's voice. "Annie."

Annie stood motionless, silently leaning against the door, hoping her mother would go away.

"Annie, are you in there?"

Turning her face toward the doorframe, Annie fought to control the tone of her voice as she said, "Mother, I heard it all. Please let me be alone."

"Annie, we need to talk," Dinah Harding urged her daughter. "Please let me in."

"Mother," Annie said, "there's nothing to talk about. I just want to be alone now. Let me take care of it on my own."

"What do you mean by take care of it?"

"I'm not sure yet. You have to give me time, please."

"I'll be in the kitchen, sweetheart," her mother finally conceded. "If you need me, please come."

"I will. I promise."

As the creaking of her mother's footsteps led away from the bedroom door, Annie went to her dark oak vanity, sat down in her chair, and stared blankly into the large mirror. Blinking at her reflection, she wondered for a moment if the delicate-looking face might suddenly crack in two and then shatter. Closing her eyes again, she slowly shook her head and exhaled, then leaned her elbows on the vanity and buried her face in her hands.

But to Annie's surprise, there were no tears. Perhaps she had wept them all the day she slammed the door shut on Arthur Simpson. For a moment she felt a sense of relief that their courtship was now unquestionably over. And the stinging anger she felt welling up toward Elsie was mixed and nearly neutralized by an overwhelming sense of pity for her friend. How could Elsie possibly be willing to sacrifice their friendship for the likes of Arthur Simpson?

With the touch of the smooth pearl ring against her cheek, Annie opened her eyes and pulled her hands away from her face. Still treasuring the expensive gift on her finger, she held it up to admire the pearl's brilliant luster for the thousandth time. Then Annie noticed the cameo pendant Arthur had given her lying on the vanity next to a colorful silk scarf that had also been his gift.

Annie's focus returned to the mirror, and she stared into her own eyes. "I don't need him," she whispered to herself. Her lips pressed together tightly, and the muscles in her jaw tightened. "And I don't need anything to remind me of him."

Taking a deep breath, Annie unfolded the silk scarf and carefully laid the expensive necklace in the center. Then she slid the prized ring off her finger, studied it one last time, and placed it beside the necklace. After she refolded the scarf, she smiled and stood up. Glancing at her face one more time, Annie turned and made her exit from the room.

As much as she tried, Annie could not keep the stairs from squeaking as she made her descent. Quietly opening the closet in the entryway, she set down the silk scarf, grabbed her heavy coat, and buttoned it as quickly as she could. Leaving her mittens and wool scarf behind, Annie picked up the silk scarf and opened the front door.

"Annie!" her mother called out, coming around the corner to the entryway. "Where are you going?"

"I have an errand to run, Mother," Annie replied, holding up the silk scarf and opening it to display its contents. "It shouldn't take long."

"Not today, Annie. This is not a good idea. You're too upset."

"The whole thing has been a bad idea, and I was fooled by it for way too long," Annie said. "No sense dragging this out. I'm getting it over with now."

"But those were gifts, Annie. You don't need to give them back."

"They weren't gifts, Mother," she countered. "Arthur was buying me, and I just . . . didn't . . . see it. Or I didn't want to see it. I'll be back shortly."

Annie turned and stepped purposefully out the front door, marching down the sidewalk while her mother watched. Dinah Harding said no more, but it wouldn't have mattered if she had protested. As much as she loved her mother, Annie was not about to let anything stop her from completing this mission.

She walked briskly down the street toward the boardinghouse where Elsie rented a room. The afternoon sunshine had fled behind another low sheet of clouds, and the temperature had begun to plunge, but Annie hardly noticed the muted gray sky or the cold on her face or her hands. Crossing the last intersection and marching toward the white wooden boardinghouse, she focused on a large double set of second-floor windows, half expecting Arthur and Elsie to be standing at the window watching for her. But she saw no faces, no sign of movement. Without hesitation she pulled open the heavy wooden door, climbed the rickety stairway, and hurried down the familiar hallway to Elsie's door.

Stopping in the dimly lit hallway, Annie took a deep breath, then listened for voices in the room. In the silence that followed she wondered if Garrit might have been wrong about what he thought he'd seen. Perhaps Elsie had gone to Mrs. Beldner's as she said and this was all a big mistake. She turned to leave, but then the muffled sound of a man's laugh from within Elsie's room dispelled all doubt.

Raising her hand, Annie rapped on the door and held her breath, unsure of what she was actually going to do if it opened. When no one answered, she tried again but knocked harder and summoned her courage to call out, "Elsie, come to the door. I know you're there."

This time Annie heard Elsie's agitated voice and some rustling around in the room. The dreaded sound of soft footsteps toward the door made Annie's heart beat loudly in her head, and for a second she wished she had simply turned away without ever having knocked. The metal lock on the door rattled, then the white-painted door opened slowly. Elsie peeked out through the narrow slit.

"Annie!" Elsie exclaimed, pulling the door open another couple of inches and offering a strained smile. "I wasn't expecting you. Mrs. Beldner wasn't well, so I couldn't have a fitting. What are you doing here?"

"This is the first time I've ever had to give a reason for coming to see you, Elsie," Annie replied, carefully burying the silk scarf in her coat pocket. "I was hoping we could talk."

"Now?"

"You're not going to invite me in?"

"I was just sort of busy now and—"

"It's all right, Elsie. You can let me in for a minute," Annie said, not taking her eyes from Elsie's worried face. "I'd really like to talk with Arthur as well."

A gasped "Oh no!" escaped Elsie's lips, and her gaze dropped straight to the floor. She closed her hazel eyes as she leaned hard against the door. Then she slowly opened it wide to reveal Arthur Simpson sitting calmly on Elsie's old brown davenport.

"Come in, come in," Arthur said, nodding pleasantly toward Annie. "We were just talking about you."

"I'm sure you were," Annie replied, stepping into Elsie's room and stopping in front of Arthur. "And what exactly were you saying, Arthur? You were probably telling Elsie how much fun it was to pull the old pearl ring trick on me. I'll bet that's worked on every girl you've wanted so far. Expensive but effective—business as usual."

Arthur shrugged his shoulders and glanced at Elsie. She was standing with her back against the closed door and her arms crossed. All it took was one look from Annie, and the tears began to pour down her face.

"I'm sorry," Elsie sputtered. "I'm so very sorry."

With Elsie crying behind her, Annie turned to Simpson and said, "Only you could stoop this low, Arthur. You fooled me with your charms and your gifts and the smell of money, but never again. I wanted to bring you a little something special to make sure you never forget me."

Annie reached her hand into her coat pocket, and when she did, Arthur Simpson flinched back against the davenport and cried, "No, please don't—"

Drawing the silk scarf out with a look of utter disdain, Annie chuckled. "Why, you disgusting coward. You keep this up, and someone . . . someday . . . just might pull a gun on you."

After she lifted the gorgeous pearl ring out of the scarf, Annie took Arthur's hand in hers, slipped it onto his little finger, and jammed it on as far as she could. "You were probably wishing you already had this to give to Elsie, eh?" She pulled out the cameo pendant, reached the gold chain around Arthur's neck and clasped it in the back, then took the colorful scarf and stuffed it into the upper pocket of his suit coat. "That should about do it, don't you think?" she spoke softly in his ear. "Should save your valuable trinkets for whoever's next on your list.

"Elsie," Annie continued, "are you looking for a good used cameo?"

When her friend did not respond, Annie said to Simpson, "Is this how you get your entertainment in a little town? Pull the wool over our eyes, destroy friendships, bait little traps, and get us to fall into your arms so you can take what you want? You're pathetic and disgusting. Don't ever knock on my door again."

Simpson took a deep breath, leaned back, and crossed his arms over his chest. "You've already forgotten the matter of the loan with your father, Annie. Perhaps I'll have to—"

"You think you're the only one who can play tough," Annie spoke with a sudden menacing look in her large brown eyes. "You've got one minute to get out of this room, or I'll scream bloody murder. One minute."

Arthur sat looking dumbfounded at Annie's command, then glanced at Elsie, who had remained by the door. "You're not *that* stupid," he railed. "It's your word against ours. Two against one."

"I believe it's against the rules for Elsie to have any men in this room," Annie declared, stepping back toward the doorway. "If I scream, guess who's going to find out about it, and guess who's going to look real bad to his precious community. And if I go outside this room and start telling people what the banker's son was really doing in Elsie's room, my goodness. People talk too much, you know. I hate rumors, don't you, Arthur?"

"You're bluffing," Arthur replied, reaching up and trying to unclasp the gold necklace.

"I'll count down the last twenty seconds, then I'll scream so loud the whole town will come running," Annie persisted, staring into Arthur's deep blue eyes. "Nineteen, eighteen—"

"Get out now, Arthur!" Elsie cried, pulling herself away from the door and then opening it.

"Thirteen, twelve, ele—"

"Arthur, go!" Elsie spat the words. "She's not bluffing!"

Simpson jumped up from the davenport, pulled the silk scarf from his pocket and tossed it on the floor, then stomped angrily to the door. "You'll be sorry for this, Annie," he growled. "I make people pay, and I'll make you pay for this."

"Three, two—"

"Out!" Elsie cried, putting her hands on Arthur Simpson's back and shoving him into the hallway, then slamming the door shut.

Elsie leaned her head and body against the door, holding the handle as the tromp of Simpson's black leather shoes sounded down the hallway. "Annie, I'm so sorry," she whispered. "I don't know what I was thinking."

"I think you did, Elsie," Annie said quietly. "I think you figured having Arthur was worth risking our friendship, and I don't understand that at all." She gazed around the familiar room. "This isn't the first time he's been here, is it? That looks like his sweater on the chair there. How long has it been, Elsie?"

Elsie took a deep breath and stepped away from the door. "About a month. I feel so rotten—"

"Save your breath, Elsie," Annie broke in, moving to the door and opening it. "I should have seen it coming. Let me warn you, though. Arthur Simpson will make you feel like a queen, but then he'll use you like a rag. Maybe he already has. Then he'll toss you away."

She stepped out into the hall, pulling the door shut behind her. "Run for your life, Elsie," she said back over her shoulder, "while you've still got it."

Chapter 20

When the Heart Goes Silent

Annie Harding walked slowly down the long school hallway and watched as Elsie Dale wrapped a long black scarf around her neck, pulled on thick woolen mittens, then shoved open the heavy school door and slipped out alone into the cold wintry air. For the first time since she had met Elsie, an entire school day had elapsed without either girl speaking one word to the other. The few times that Annie had noticed Elsie looking her way, it appeared that Elsie's eyes were bloodshot and teary. But as quickly as Elsie had escaped the confines of the school, Annie could only wonder if she might be meeting with Arthur Simpson again.

Pulling a small slip of paper out of her coat pocket, Annie unfolded it and read for the sixth time the message that Mrs. Olson had left on her desk during the class break for lunch: *Marian Anderson came by and asked if you could stop at the mill today on your way home from school.*

Annie's thoughts had immediately flown to Stuart Anderson. Perhaps he was already home for Christmas. But that wasn't likely; he wasn't supposed to be home for at least a week or two. Now Annie's thoughts roamed back to her conversation with Marian some weeks before. Marian had told her how important it was for couples to share the same values. How right Marian had been, and how lucky Annie had been to get away from Arthur Simpson after being fooled for so long.

Shoving the slip of paper back into her coat pocket and pushing open the school door, Annie squinted hard as the dazzling sun reflected off the fresh layer of brilliant white snow. After holding back for nearly three weeks, the dull gray clouds had finally delivered the first big snowfall the night before, blanketing the community with nearly six inches. The air had changed to extremely dry and cold, and an afternoon breeze chased Annie as she hurried down the snow-packed sidewalk.

The Anderson feed mill wasn't exactly on her usual route home from school, and Annie continued to wonder what it was that Marian would want to see her about. Turning at the corner toward downtown, Annie had to walk straight into the northwesterly wind that funneled down the long street. Annie pulled her red scarf up tight around her cheeks and wished that Marian had picked a better day to get together.

When she reached Main Street, Annie turned west and continued the last few blocks as fast as she dared to walk on the slippery side-walks. Although the wind was no longer in her face, her eyes continued to water until she reached the steps that led up to the office of the feed mill. Swabbing the corners of her eyes one last time with her green mittens, Annie marched up the steps, pushed open the door of the mill office, and stepped inside.

Expecting to see Marian Anderson at the back desk where she had told Annie she usually worked, Annie was shocked to see the lanky frame of Walter Sorenson seated there instead. He looked up and flashed a wide smile that showed off his new white dentures. With his fresh haircut and a new white long-sleeved shirt and tie, he looked like a different person.

"Walter!" Annie exclaimed, squinting as her eyes tried to adjust to the relatively dark office. "Whatever are you doing here?"

"What's it look like, Annie?" the tall farm boy replied, standing up and stepping out from behind the large wooden desk. "Do you like my new clothes and shoes?"

"But how could you afford all that, Walter?" Annie asked, taking a few stunned steps toward Walter. "And what are you doing—?"

"Annie!" Marian Anderson called out as she and her husband entered the back of the mill office through the door that led down a hall-way to the Andersons' other business, the town drugstore. "I was hoping you'd stop by. Isn't this wonderful?"

Annie looked baffled at Marian's radiant smile. "What's wonderful? Why is—oh my goodness, you didn't?"

"Oh yes we did," Robert Anderson declared, reaching up and wrapping his arm around Walter's wide shoulder. "We'd like to introduce you to our newest employee, Walter Sorenson. He started as an accountant this morning, and if he works hard and can handle the pressure, he'll be taking on more. I expect a lot from anyone who comes with as high a recommendation as this young man did."

The freckles on Walter's face looked like they were about ready to pop off, along with the buttons on his new white shirt. Beaming a smile from ear to ear, he nodded toward Annie. "I couldn't have done it without your help, you know."

Annie was so shocked by the image before her that she hardly knew what to think. She started to laugh, then took off her mittens and tossed them up to the tall ceiling. "Hallelujah!" she cried out, rushing to Marian Anderson and hugging her. "Thank you! Oh, thank you!"

Marian returned Annie's hug and said, "Don't you go thanking us yet. If Walter doesn't work out, we're going to make you come in and take his job. He'd better be as good as you and Mrs. Olson said he was." Then Marian burst into laughter.

"Why didn't you tell me?" Annie asked. "I never dreamed—"

"That would have been no fun at all," Marian broke in, still laughing. "Besides, we had to wait until we could talk to Walter and see if he was interested."

"Are you kidding!" Annie exclaimed. "I would have killed Walter with my bare hands if he had said no to you!"

All four of them laughed, and Annie kept staring at the transformation that had come over Walter.

"It's no business of mine," she finally asked him, "but how could you afford the new clothes? Your grandmother didn't sell her crystal goblets—"

"No, of course not," Walter interrupted, glancing down at his new shirt and pants and shiny black leather dress shoes. "You know I couldn't afford these duds, but they came with the job. I was told I better take good care of them, because it's the only outfit I don't need to pay for myself."

"I don't believe this!" Annie cried. "Does Mrs. Olson know?"

"Of course," Marian replied. "She thought it would be fun to set you up today."

Annie laughed and shook her head, then she grew serious again.

"Marian, what does this mean to you? You're going to have Walter do your work?"

Marian smiled and nodded. "He'll take care of all the records for both businesses, and we think he can fill in whenever we need help in the drugstore."

"But what will you do?" Annie asked.

"Oh, I'll be around here some of the time," said Marian. "It'll take a while to show Walter the ropes, although he's already catching on to my bookkeeping system. And there's always something else that needs doing around here that never gets done. But I . . . um . . . I'm going to spend more time being a housewife . . . at least for a while. I've been at this job for a lot longer than I originally hoped, and it's time for a change. Besides, I have a pile of books I want to read!"

They all laughed, but the approaching sound of wagon wheels and a team of horses outside cut short their visit. Robert Anderson went to the window and peeked out, then grabbed his heavy coat and hat.

"You'd think the snow would keep the farmers away, wouldn't you?" Robert grumbled as he buttoned his coat. "It's like they wait until the worst day just to torment me. If I—"

"You'll have to get used to the complaining around here, Walter," Marian broke in as Robert pulled on his hat and ducked out the door with a quick "Excuse me."

"I think I can put up with it," said Walter, a big smile seemingly permanently etched on his face. "If I do good at this job, we'll be able to move out of Grandma's house."

"Did your mother find work yet?" Annie asked.

"Nothing regular," Walter replied with a sigh. "She can cook and clean and she's real good at sewing, but nobody seems to be looking for a regular housekeeper, and she don't have room to do much sewing at Grandma's."

"It may be that I'll have some steady work for her in a few months," Marian said. "That's if things work out."

"You'd hire a housekeeper?" Annie asked, a bit puzzled.

"No, no," Marian replied with a shake of her head. "I've got an idea I've been thinking about . . . a small business that might have some possibilities. If I pursue it, I'll need at least one person to help me. And I've already talked with Walter's mother, and she'd be perfect."

"What kind of business?" Annie responded.

Marian glanced at Walter, who was still smiling, then she said, "Until I decide, it's a secret, and don't try to squeeze it out of Walter. I haven't even started to explore whether there's any chance I could make it work. Not having to do the bookkeeping should mean I can try some new things, don't you think?"

"Of course," Annie said. "I didn't realize you were such a business person, though."

"Neither did I," Marian commented. "But I've been involved with the store for so long that it gets in your blood. Maybe after a couple of days at home I'll be content with that. We'll see."

"Well, I do need to be going," Annie replied, looking up at the large wooden clock on the wall. "Walter, congratulations. I couldn't be happier for you. This is the best place in the world for you."

"Someday I hope to be able to thank you proper," Walter said. "I'd like to repay—"

"Don't . . . you . . . *ever* say another word about paying for something," Annie interrupted. "Today was all the reward I need, believe me. And, Marian, you and Mr. Anderson are wonderful."

"No, we're just shrewd business people who got a good tip on a smart young man and grabbed him," Marian said. "I just know this is going to work out well for everyone."

For the first time since she stepped into the mill office, Annie noticed that Walter was holding his damaged arm with his good arm. That reality, contrasting with his almost childish grin, brought tears to Annie's eyes. She glanced away and swallowed hard.

"I need to go," she spoke softly, quickly glancing back at Marian and Walter with tears clouding her vision. "Good-bye."

Annie spun around and barely heard the voices behind her saying "Good-bye" as she exited the mill office. The frigid northwestern wind grabbed at her as she descended the steps to the sidewalk, tossing the ends of her red scarf back up into her face. But neither the cold nor the wind nor the taunting scarf could erase her smile of unabashed delight.

Smiling and waving good-bye to Robert Anderson, who was working inside the grain mill, Annie turned and headed down the sidewalk toward home. The sun was already low on the hills that seemed to close in on their small town with the first blanket of white snow. Annie walked quickly, her eyes watering first from joy and then, once again, from the unrelenting breeze. The frosty air brushing her warm cheeks felt good for nearly the entire walk home, but by the time she reached the last block, the chill had overcome the waves of emotions that had welled up within her.

Dashing up the front steps to their house, Annie pulled open the heavy wooden door and ducked into the warm entryway. Quickly shutting the door behind her, she pulled off her coat and scarf and reached up to hang them in the closet. As she did, she felt a light tap on the back of her leg and turned to see her brother.

"Garrit," she said. "How was school?"

"Shhh," he whispered with a grimace across his face. "Father's home, and he's in a really bad mood."

"Why's he home?" Annie spoke softly. "What's wrong?"

"The snow and cold," Garrit explained. "He had to quit early. But I don't know why he's so mad. Just don't get in his way."

Annie nodded, knowing exactly what he meant. They had learned long ago that the only safe thing was to stay clear of their father until his bad humors subsided. And the trick was always to figure out when that was. Oftentimes the best signal was listening to the tone of his voice when he spoke with their mother, but even that had fooled them on occasion.

"Where is he now?" Annie asked, listening for voices in the house even as she whispered.

"He's in the living room," Garrit replied, pointing around the corner with his pudgy finger. "Come the other way."

Garrit led the way around the corner of the hallway, but her father had apparently heard her come through the front door.

"Annie," James Harding's voice ordered, halting both Annie and Garrit in their tracks.

"Go on!" Annie whispered to Garrit, who looked up into her face with concern but turned reluctantly and sped away toward the safe refuge of his bedroom.

Annie took a deep breath, then slowly turned and made her way back toward the living room. As she stepped through the doorway, she was surprised to find her father standing by the large set of living room windows rather than sitting in his chair with his pipe in hand. The deep lines across his forehead told Annie all she needed to know.

"You're late," he barked, a glare pinching his brown eyes down tight. "Where have you been?"

"I ... um ... stopped by ... Mrs. Anderson left a message that I should stop by the mill on my way home from school," Annie stuttered. "I'm sorry. I didn't know you'd be waiting for me."

"What did she want?"

"It was just that ... the Andersons have hired Walter Sorenson as their accountant," Annie replied, not being able to hold back her smile, even though she knew her father disapproved of her helping Walter. "He was so happy that—"

"I'll *bet* he was happy," her father snapped, his graying hair flashing nearly white in the window's bright sunlight as the last rays of the day beamed through. "You spend all your time with that stinking bumpkin while your best friend is stealing your man right out from under your nose. It's all over town, what happened. You should have heard the men in the saloon laughing about it. What's the matter with you, anyway?"

Annie looked away and closed her eyes, totally unprepared to discuss what had happened between her and Arthur Simpson with anyone, least of all with her father. What she wanted to do was run to her room, but Annie knew she had no choice but to answer him as best she could. "What did you hear, Father?" she asked quietly.

"You know what I heard," James Harding nearly spat the words. "Elsie Dale has been charming the young banker for weeks, they say, and you never noticed a thing. You're not going to let it happen, Annie."

"What?"

"I said you're not going to let that hussy take him away from you." Her father bit off the words, the muscles of his weathered face tightening. "You're going to get him back."

"He's gone, Father," Annie said firmly, shaking her head in disbelief. "He's not the man I thought he was. I could never love him."

The knuckles on her father's large hands whitened as his fists clenched. "Young lady, you'll *never* . . . *ever* do better than Arthur Simpson . . . at least not in this town. That man could give you everything you ever wanted. You find a way to take him back from Elsie Dale . . . or else."

"Or else what?" Annie challenged, a sudden resolve rising up within her mixed with an uncontrollable swell of tears. "I would gladly remain single rather than spend my life with that man."

"Then you'll move out just as soon as summer comes," James Harding ordered. "You'll be through with school then. If you're so foolish about love, then it's time you learn to face reality. Make your own way."

A steady stream of tears was glistening Annie's red cheeks, but there was no sense of yielding in her voice. "I think I know what this is about now, Father," she addressed him. "You're afraid . . . that Arthur will pull his backing out of your business deal, aren't you? This isn't about me. This is a business matter for you."

Her father's glare did not flinch, but he did turn to look out the window. "Simpson wouldn't dare pull out," he growled.

Annie closed her eyes and shook her head, then wiped some of the tears away. "But I'm your insurance, aren't I?" she muttered softly. "How could you stoop so low? Don't you have any love for—"

"What do you know about love?" James Harding snapped, turning his angry eyes back on Annie, then moving across the room toward her. "I ought to show you what—"

"James, stop!" Dinah Harding screamed, rushing into the living room from behind the dining room door, where she'd been listening. She cut in front of Annie and stood before her husband. "This is enough! She's our daughter, for heaven's sake!"

"She's a fool," he continued to rant, the smell of whiskey strong on his breath. "And she gets all her stupid ideas from you. If you think I'm going to sit back and let her—"

"You say one more word to Annie about Arthur Simpson," Dinah Harding warned, her soft brown eyes turned to flames, "and I'll take the children and we'll leave you tonight. I'll do it, James. I will not let you destroy their lives, no matter what it costs."

The flexing of his jaw muscles was the only visible change in James Harding's face, but for the moment he was silent. Then he took a deep breath but said nothing.

"Annie, go to your room now," her mother ordered without turning around.

"But—"

"Go."

"This is still my house," James Harding spoke in a firm but somewhat subdued tone as Annie turned to leave the room. "She moves out when school's done."

"After what you've said," Dinah Harding spat, "why would she want to stay?"

Those were the last understandable sentences that Annie heard that night. She rushed to her bedroom, locked the door behind her, then curled up on her bed and covered her head with a pillow. Many more angry words filled the living room below her, but it may as well have been a room on the other side of the world. Long before the house went totally silent for the evening, something went silent in Annie's heart.

There was no dinner that night except for some leftovers James Harding managed to find in the kitchen. Annie and Garrit remained locked in the safety of their rooms. Later Annie heard her mother crying in her parents' bedroom, but she couldn't risk confronting her father again that night. And her mother never came to Annie's room, as Annie had hoped, even though she knew that would also risk her father's anger.

Annie's own tears finally subsided, and all she could do was pray. Moving out of the house at the end of the school year sounded like a release from prison, but she had no idea where she would go or what she would do. For the moment, she found, it was enough to simply realize that God was still with her and that He cared about them all, even her father, who was the hardest of all to forgive.

Early in the evening she fell into a deep sleep, still wearing her white blouse and black skirt. But her dreams were chaotic and troubled, and she woke suddenly at midnight with soft moonlight streaming across her bed. Listening to the house's silence, an eerie sense of dread threatened to steal over her heart. But then the pleasant memory of Walter's smile earlier in the day encouraged her to believe that something better was ahead for her as well.

Chapter 21

Merry Christmas!

"So you really think Grandpa isn't disappointed?" Stuart Anderson asked his grandmother, sliding back in his chair as she set his breakfast plate down on the kitchen table. It was still dark outside, although the winter morning sky had begun its slow process of brightening the horizon.

"How many times does he have to tell you that he's delighted with your decision? If you refuse to believe him, why should I waste my breath trying to convince you?" Geneva replied, picking up a cup of coffee from the counter and setting it down next to Stuart. "Now, if you're going to catch the train, you'd better eat up. Do you really think your mother is going to appreciate being surprised like this?"

"Of course she is," Stuart replied, cutting his fried eggs. "If she knew I was done with classes a day ahead of schedule, she'd want me home. So she'll be glad, even if it means a little shock when I sneak up on her."

"Little, I bet," his grandmother said. "Knowing you, you'll go for the heart attack."

"Probably," Stuart agreed. "You take what life gives you, right? Mama needs something to keep her life from getting dull."

"Just don't push it, young man," Geneva replied, taking a sip of coffee. "And you be careful with that box of Christmas presents. If you lose my—"

"I know, I know. I'll be careful with it, Grandma," Stuart said. "Is Grandpa up?"

"Not yet," she answered. "He can't seem to shake that cold, so I figured it was best that he sleep in for once. I'm glad you could catch a ride to the depot with your friends."

"I wish I could talk with him once more before—"

"Stuart," his grandmother interrupted, "I'm not going to say this again. You have to follow where your heart is leading, and you just can't worry about what anyone else thinks. This is not a matter of whether being a missionary is better than being a pastor, or a pastor is better than a doctor, or a doctor is better than a blacksmith. It's a matter of being open to God's direction and getting the training you need to do whatever it is that He wants you to do. Becoming a doctor will never diminish what God can do through your life as long you are obeying Him. You are going to talk to Dr. Jones, right?"

Stuart nodded. "Yep. First I surprise my mother, then I stop by the doc's office."

"And then you stop looking back. Correct?" Geneva said. "Say yes, Stuart, or don't come back to torture me anymore."

Stuart laughed and nodded, but a knock at the front door cut short his response. "Time to go," he said, taking a last sip of coffee and jumping up from the table. Then he kissed his grandmother on the cheek, wished her a Merry Christmas, and dashed out of the kitchen.

Slipping on his heavy winter coat, Stuart gathered his brown leather suitcase and the box of Christmas presents that his grandmother had packed. Then he pushed open the front door and scooted down the slippery sidewalk to the horse and carriage that waited in the semidarkness. Stowing his luggage with the other cases piled in the back, he climbed into the carriage with a group of students who were also heading for the train depot.

Stuart's train was waiting at the gates when they arrived, so he quickly said good-bye to his friends and purchased his ticket. Even though the large depot clock showed there were fifteen minutes before the train would leave, Stuart hustled through the gates and stepped up into a passenger car that was nearly empty. By the time the train pulled out, only a few more people had boarded.

Two laboring steam engines slowly pulled the heavy train out of the downtown depot and chugged along the frozen steel tracks through the city's south side, then finally began to pick up speed as streets and closely built houses gave way to open fields and barns. Stuart sat watching the eastern sky as the shimmering red sun crept up over the silvery snow on rolling hills. Pine-fringed ridges and dark, tangled stands of burr oaks stood strong against the clear blue sky.

Thundering down a long straight stretch, the train passed empty white pastures that in early September had been bright green and filled with herds of black-and-white dairy cows. In the flying pictures framed by the windows, the occasional white farmhouses melded with the white snowbanks and long lines of wooden fences disappeared over the rolling countryside. Then the train slowed its speed as the tracks began to zigzag through the lowering valleys and approached the first of what seemed to Stuart like an unending number of stops at sleepy small towns whose lifeline was the railroad.

It was a little after one o'clock in the afternoon before the train chugged into the small depot in Bradford and came to a halt. Located two blocks from Main Street, the depot handled a great deal more freight business than passengers. Even though he was a day early getting home, Stuart found himself scanning the dock, relieved to see no one waiting for him. Grabbing his suitcase and box from the overhead racks, he jumped out of the passenger car, walked around the depot office, waved a greeting to the manager, then headed down the street toward the mill.

In the rush to leave his grandparents' house, Stuart had forgotten his winter cap, and the frigid breeze soon made him wish he had ear flaps to turn down. By the time he reached the mill, his ears were fiery red and the pain was excruciating. But with both hands full, there was little that Stuart could do except try to walk faster. Fortunately for him, there were no customers at the mill, so he knew he could go straight in and surprise his mother at her desk.

Ascending the steps to the mill office, Stuart set down the leather suitcase outside the office door, quietly turned the handle, then shoved the door open and jumped through. "Merry Christmas!" he cried, holding the box of presents high over his head as he landed three or four feet into the office. As his eyes worked to adjust from the bright outdoor sunlight to the dim corner of the office where his mother worked, Stuart made out two people at her desk, but neither was shaped like his mother or his father.

The box of Christmas presents slowly sank to Stuart's chest as his embarrassment rose. And then the heat from the potbelly stove began to thaw his ears, sending shooting pains from his head to his toes. Setting down his box and grabbing his ears, Stuart bent over and let out a moan.

"Stuart, are you all right?" A young woman's voice finally got through to Stuart as the pain began to subside. He immediately identified the voice as coming from Annie Harding, even though his eyes were only now making out the two forms. "Santa's a little early this year, isn't he?" she continued. "Looks like he'd better get a cap next year when he's delivering presents."

There was little that Stuart could do except laugh, but he did manage a distraction when he stepped back to the office door, picked up his suitcase, and brought it inside. Then he closed the door and peered back into the dark corner.

"You'll have to excuse me, Miss Harding," Stuart said, still unable to make out the man who was seated at his mother's desk beside Annie. "I . . . ah . . . thought I would surprise my folks by getting home a day early, but it looks like I made a slight miscalculation. Where's my mother?"

"She's at home, I think," Annie responded with a chuckle. "Isn't that what you said, Walter?"

Stuart's eyes finally made a sufficient adjustment to see that Annie's words were true, although he could hardly believe that the young man in front of him with the finely trimmed hair and neatly pressed shirt and a tie was Walter Sorenson. "Is my mother sick?"

"No, I think she was going to bake some Christmas cookies this afternoon," Walter offered, flashing a toothy grin that also surprised Stuart. "She's been talking about you coming home for days. Merry Christmas to you, Stuart."

"Um . . . Merry Christmas to you, as well, Walter, and to you, Annie," Stuart managed doubtfully, then he added, "Look, I really hate to sound rude, but why are you sitting at my mother's desk? Is my father around?"

"Not right now, he's not," Walter replied. "He was picking up some freight that was supposed to be on the train. I'm surprised you didn't see him out there at the depot."

Stuart chuckled to himself and took a deep breath of the warm office air. "Let me try again with the other question. Why are you at my mother's desk?"

"She didn't write you?" Annie asked.

"Not about Walter sitting at her desk."

"Your mother no longer works here," said Walter, still grinning. "Your father hired me to take her place, and she's been training me on the job."

"What? Come on, that's ridiculous!" Stuart was incredulous. "Now, a joke's a joke, but I think you'd better move away from her desk before my father returns. Those bookkeeping records are confidential."

Walter nodded in agreement, and Annie said, "Stuart, it's just as Walter says. He's been hired to take your mother's place."

"My father fired my mother?" Stuart sputtered, then he started laughing. "This is all a big setup, isn't it? How in the world did they ever find out that I was coming early?" Stuart asked, watching for any hint of reaction on Walter's and Annie's faces. "Did my grandmother wire my parents to warn them that I was on my way this morning and hoped to surprise my mother?"

"I have no idea. I just got here myself," Annie replied, glancing toward Walter. "Did Marian say anything about a telegram?"

Walter shook his head and shrugged his shoulders. "Not to me, she didn't."

"Marian?" Stuart said. "You call my mother Marian?"

"She said I had to," Annie replied, laughing, as Stuart gently rubbed his ears and shook his head.

"I . . . ah . . . still call her Mrs. Anderson," Walter added. "She's been my boss, and it wouldn't be proper for me to call her by her first name, although she told me I was supposed—"

"All right, all right," Stuart broke in, holding up his hands and laughing. "You've had your fun. You almost had me believing for a second here. Now, where's my mother? Is she hiding in the back there?"

"We told you. She's at home baking—"

"Come out, come out, wherever you are!" Stuart called out, cutting off Annie and walking to the back of the office to check the hallway that led to the drugstore. Peering down the dark corridor, Stuart turned around and said to Walter, "I can't believe how they decked you out just to fool me. Those teeth even look real."

Walter burst out laughing. "They're brand-new dentures, Stuart. And the clothes came with the job. Not bad, eh?"

Stuart glanced down at the ledger that was on the desk in front of Walter and realized that not a single line resembled his mother's fine handwriting. Although the ledger was still meticulously neat, the handwriting represented a definitely heavier stroke that was harder to read. He gave a crooked smile, then turned to Annie. "What is going on?"

The handle on the wooden door to the office rattled, and Stuart turned around to see his father step into the office, stomp his feet on the thick rag rug, and begin to unbutton his coat. Stuart chuckled as Robert Anderson squinted to try to focus in on him.

"Stuart?" his father asked, stepping toward him and beaming a smile. "Stuart! Goodness, me! What a surprise! When did you get here?"

Robert gave Stuart a huge hug and pat on the back, then he asked, "Have you seen your mother yet? She'll be shocked."

Stuart smiled and nodded. "No, I'm just a little confused, and I never imagined you could act so well. I came jumping through the door like Santa Claus, thinking I'd surprise Mama really good, and these folks here nearly fooled me into believing that Mama has quit. Did Grandma wire you this morning that I was coming? You're all pretty convincing, Dad."

"Well, thank you," his father responded, running his fingers through his graying brown hair and nodding. "I didn't realize I was acting, and . . . no . . . your grandmother didn't wire us this morning. I had no idea you were coming. I'm not sure how I didn't see you at the depot, but I guess I wasn't looking."

Wrinkling his forehead, Stuart glanced quickly at Annie, who immediately burst out laughing when their eyes met. That set Walter off, as well, and Robert Anderson joined in, although he seemed nearly as baffled as Stuart.

Reaching over to the ledger, Stuart flipped back several pages and stared at the point where the handwriting had changed dramatically. He looked into Walter's guileless smile, and then over at his father. "Walter works for you . . . doing the bookkeeping that Mama has done since forever?"

Robert Anderson nodded. "He sure does. Walter's very good, and we felt we were fortunate to hire him before somebody else got him. Your mother got the inside story from Walter's tutor, Annie Harding, and it paid off."

"You tutored Walter?" Now Stuart turned toward Annie, whose big smile reflected her immense enjoyment of the moment. "And you call my mother Marian?"

"Yes, and yes," Annie replied, her eyes sparkling. "It was Mrs. Olson's idea—not calling your mother Marian, but tutoring Walter. She heard Walter's arm wasn't getting any better, so she asked me to help him catch up with his schoolwork so maybe he could get an office job and support his mother and brothers after the bank kicked them off the farm. And then nobody would hire Walter, but your parents did, and he's doing wonderfully, and—"

"You really are serious?" Stuart asked again, interrupting her breathless account. He turned toward his father. "What's Mama going to do at home?"

"Be a housewife, she claims," Robert Anderson replied. "Read some books, get a garden going like she always wanted, visit with the neighbors—things like that. I'm not inclined to believe this is going to last long, but maybe she'll surprise me."

"Actually," Annie said, "she says she's working on a new business idea. I don't think Marian is your ordinary housewife."

"I think you're right about that," Stuart agreed, still trying to take in all the information that had been dumped on him in the last few minutes. "When did the bank take back the farm?"

"At Thanksgiving," Walter answered, his face losing its smile for the first time since Stuart had jumped through the doorway. "I guess they couldn't wait for spring to get us out of there. If I hadn't gotten this job, I don't know what my family would have done. Starved, maybe."

"Doesn't surprise me, but I did wonder what was going to happen. You talked with the Simpsons about it?" Stuart asked, turning to Annie, but from the way her face had fallen he wished he hadn't. "I'm sorry, it's none of my—"

"It's all right. Yes, I did try talking them into an extension . . . and failed," Annie interrupted Stuart. "It's not my favorite subject to talk about. Let's just say that someone got her eyes opened . . . and someone else showed his true colors."

"Gray, like a rat," Walter added, surprising them all. "The same color as his father."

Stuart grinned and nodded to Walter, then he turned to Annie and said, "You might recall that Arthur Simpson wasn't my favorite—"

"I recall that quite vividly," Annie said with a small smile. "You warned me to watch and listen, but I'm sorry to say that it took me a while to see the truth. The glimmer turned out to be not so golden after all. Your mother was a real help to me."

"My mother, whom you call Marian," Stuart mused. "Now, how is it that you and she got together?"

"I knocked on her door one Saturday morning," Annie replied, "and since then she's been Marian Anderson, my friend and teacher who listens to my personal woes."

"Mama let you in on a Saturday morning?" Stuart asked, glancing at his father with his eyebrows raised. "That's sacred time for her."

"She told me that . . . and I figured that I'd used up my only chance." Annie smiled again. "I've tried to avoid that morning since then."

"How can so much happen in four months?" Stuart asked, turning again to his father.

"You haven't heard half of it yet," Robert Anderson replied, "but your mother will have to clue you in, and she's going to be very upset if you fiddle around here too long without seeing her." He ducked toward the hallway. "Now, if you'll excuse me, I need to tend to some things over at the store, and . . . I do believe my new accountant has a fair amount of work that you're distracting him from."

"Work, work, work, just like always," Stuart teased. "I get the point, but I'm going to stop by and talk with the doc first. I'm taking him up on his offer."

"Wonderful!" his father exclaimed, then he walked over to Stuart and gave him a bear hug. "I think it's right for you, son. Your mother and I are very excited about it. So's the doc. He must have asked me a dozen times if you'd written us about it. By the way, your mother's trick didn't work, did it?"

"Sending me a pencil, an envelope, and a stamp," Stuart said. "No, I thought Grandma was writing often enough to cover for me, and I didn't want to spoil my perfect record from last year. I did use the pencil, though."

"You'd better not tell your mother that," Robert Anderson said with a chuckle. "She actually thought she might dupe you into writing a letter. I told her she was dealing with the impossible. But . . . if you'll excuse me, I do need to keep moving here. I'll see you tonight, Stuart."

"I'll see you then," Stuart echoed as his father turned and walked down the hall. "I guess I better get moving as well."

"Me too," Annie said. "I almost forgot why I came over." She pointed to a box she had laid on Walter's desk. "Mrs. Olson asked me to drop off some lefse for her. I hope your family likes it."

"Are you joking?" Walter responded, lifting the lid and peeking at the pile of flat pastries made from potato dough. "I think I'll snitch a few pieces before my brothers and I start fighting over who gets the most. I'm obliged to you for bringing it over."

"Better thank Mrs. Olson, and keep up the good work, Walter," Annie said. Then she followed Stuart to the front door, where he stopped to gather his belongings.

"So school is out?" Stuart asked.

"We just got out today," Annie replied. "Are you staying here through New Year's Eve, or will you go back early?"

"No, I'll stay here the whole time," Stuart replied. "Why would I go back early?"

Annie gave him a crooked smile. "Just curious, I guess. Back at Thanksgiving time, your mother mentioned you were going to a friend's house for the day. I thought that maybe you . . . and her—"

"Nope," Stuart interrupted her. "Catherine and I were good friends, and I hope we still are. But I sort of messed up and let her think that I was courting her when I wasn't. It wasn't all my fault . . . but I don't think her Thanksgiving Day was one she's going to remember with fondness."

"So you're—"

"Yes, very."

"Do you sort of mess up a lot?"

"I hope not," Stuart replied with a chuckle. "Once was plenty. As long as my grandma is around, she's going to be cracking me with a stick if I do it again. She set me straight on this one, believe me."

"So there's no one else at the university—"

"No. How about you?"

"No."

Stuart smiled, his black eyes flashing. "Is the town still having the New Year's Eve dance?"

She nodded. "They are."

"I . . . ah . . . might you be interested in going with me?"

She nodded again. "I would."

"And banker boy is out of the picture?" he continued.

"Out of my picture," Annie echoed. "He'll be there with my best friend, though."

"Now, that's a low blow!" moaned Stuart. "Why doesn't that surprise me?"

"I have to face it every day in school," said Annie. "It's been pretty terrible."

"And will your father approve of your going to the dance with me?" Stuart asked. "I don't think I charmed him on our last encounter."

Annie shrugged, her face unreadable. "He probably won't approve, but . . . it won't have anything to do with you or me. And it really doesn't matter anymore. That's too long a story to tell right now."

"So what are you doing tomorrow?"

◆ ◆ ◆ ◆ ◆ ◆ ◆ ◆ ◆ ◆ ◆

Only Annie was close enough to hear the soft knock on the Hardings' front door a few days later. Annie was in the living room reading a book that Mrs. Olson had lent her for over the Christmas holiday when the knock came, and for a moment she felt panic that she might have misunderstood the time when Stuart said he was going to arrive. Jumping up from the davenport, she straightened her skirt and hurried to the door.

"Mrs. Sorenson! What a surprise!" Annie exclaimed as she pulled open the door and saw Walter's mother standing there in her worn winter coat with a carpetbag in her hands. "Come on in. Should I get my mother?"

Gladys Sorenson stepped into the entryway. "No, Annie, it's you I've come to see."

"Me?" Annie questioned. "Here, let me take your coat."

"No, I shouldn't be staying," the woman replied, tucking a few loose strands of gray hair back under her hat. "I've just stopped for a moment to drop off something for you."

"For me?"

"For you," the older woman said with a smile and a nod. "It's just a little something from Walter and me for your Christmas."

"No, you—"

"Here," Walter's mother said, holding out the carpetbag to Annie. "Open it and see. And don't be fussing about it."

Annie took the bag from her and stared into Mrs. Sorenson's steel-gray eyes. Then she looked down and slowly opened the top of the bag. Reaching in, she gently lifted out a thick white muffler intricately knit-ted of the softest wool. Tucked in below the muffler were a pair of soft gloves and a matching hat. "Oh, Mrs. Sorenson, you shouldn't have. It's truly lovely. You made these yourself? I've never seen this pattern before."

"Made it up," the woman replied with a proud nod, then she spoke softly, "I never cared much for living on a farm, but I can sew and knit with the best of 'em. The wool's from our own sheep—or they used to be ours. The wool was about all we took with us when the bank sold the place."

"Mrs. Sorenson, this is really too much," Annie whispered, her throat beginning to choke up. "I think you should—"

Gladys Sorenson reached out and took one of Annie's hands, then looked down and shook her head. "We ain't got much, Annie," she said, "but if it weren't for you and Mrs. Olson, we wouldn't have nothing this Christmas. And who knows what would have become of Walter.... I've never seen him so happy, in spite of his arm."

"And I heard you found steady work at the hotel," Annie said.

"At least till spring," Mrs. Sorenson replied, glancing back up, tears rimming her eyes. "Thanks to Mrs. Anderson. She got me in, you know."

"No, I didn't know," Annie said. "Doesn't surprise me, though. She's helped me more than I can tell you."

The gray-haired widow nodded knowingly. "She's got a way, that woman. She told me God could take all the bad things we've been going through and bring good out of them. I . . . truly thought she was a fool,

I did, until I saw the smile come back to my Walter's face. Then I knew
... I knew she was right. God bless her."

Tears continued to fill Gladys Sorenson's eyes, and she turned
quickly to go, but Annie reached out and wrapped her arm around the
older woman and pulled her close.

"I'm so sorry for all you've gone through," Annie whispered in the
widow's ear as her own tears began to fall faster and faster—tears of
joy and sorrow and somehow, strangely, release and healing.

"I'm so sorry ... about ... it ... all."

Chapter 22

The Christmas Dream

Annie Harding sat on a chair in front of the dressing table in her room, staring into the mirror as she brushed her hair, the long, silky strands falling nearly to her waist with the end of every stroke. The creaking of footsteps on the hallway's wooden floor caught her attention, and she laid down her brush when she heard a light knock on her door.

"Annie, may I come in?" her mother asked quietly.

"Of course," Annie answered, turning in her chair as Dinah Harding opened the door and quickly stepped into the bedroom, then closed the door behind her.

"How are you coming?" her mother asked as she walked close to Annie and sat down on the corner of the bed.

Annie smiled and took a deep breath. "I'm sort of . . . taking my time. Stuart won't be here for another half an hour."

"Do you need any help?" Dinah asked. "I could braid your hair if you're finished brushing, unless you're going to roll and pin it."

"No, I don't want to look like Elsie tonight," Annie responded, sliding her chair back next to her mother and then turning her head. "I'd love for you to braid it, though. It's so much easier when you do it."

Dinah Harding carefully separated the fine gold strands and skillfully began weaving them together. "You really like Stuart, don't you, Annie?" she asked.

Glancing into the mirror at her mother's soft brown eyes, Annie flushed and nodded slightly. "Is it that noticeable?"

Her mother smiled. "You've had a dreamy look in your eyes ever since he arrived. Your father even noticed it at supper. Things are getting pretty obvious when that happens."

"Was Father upset?"

"Not that I know of, but ... who knows?" Dinah replied, shaking her head. "He doesn't say much to me."

"Why aren't the two of you going to the dance tonight?" Annie asked. "You did last year."

"That was last year," her mother said tersely. "Things are different now."

"Is he gone already?"

Dinah nodded. "He probably won't be back from the saloon until after midnight." She dropped a strand, deftly snagged it up with her little finger, and continued braiding in silence.

"Was Father like this when you first married him?" Annie asked after a minute.

"The drinking, you mean?"

"Yes."

"No," Dinah said. "He seems to go in spurts. When you were little, he drank pretty heavily for a few years. Then he stopped for a while. About the time Garrit came along, it got bad again. You don't remember that?"

"Sort of ... the smell, I guess."

"Well, your father hid it well," Dinah explained. "I suppose you were usually asleep. This time around, he doesn't seem to be trying to cover it up."

"I really hate it, Mother," Annie said, "especially when Garrit sees him. Father can get so scary."

Dinah Harding nodded. "Yes, it's bad this time. I just hope he quits soon ... or at least slows down."

"How much does he know about Stuart and me?"

"Not much," her mother answered as she finished the long braid, then tied it with a red ribbon. "Stuart's been here two evenings, and you went to his house on Christmas night. He knows you're going with Stuart to the dance tonight."

"So you haven't told him the rest?"

"That you two have gotten together every day since Stuart got home? No. I figured it would be best that he didn't know. But if he does find out, he may not care. I think the only thing that's on his mind right now is the worry that Arthur will not come through with the money like he promised."

"As if Father needed another business to get underway," said Annie. "He's never here even when he only has one business to run."

"I keep hoping that the money *will* fall through," Dinah said, leaning back on Annie's bed. "Your father will kill himself trying to make everything work. I dread it."

Annie turned around in her chair and looked at her mother's weary face. "There's been a lot to dread lately around here, and I know that my situation with Arthur only made it worse. I never said it, Mother, but I can't tell you how much it meant to me the night you stood up for me. You were very brave. I get the feeling that Father's drinking . . . that maybe he feels he's paying you back . . . or all of us back. I don't know. I'm sorry that I ever brought Arthur Simpson into our house."

"It wasn't your fault, Annie," her mother spoke softly, pursing her lips and glancing toward the bedroom window. "What I did wasn't the least bit brave. If I was brave, I would have packed our bags a long time ago and gotten us away. I . . . just couldn't do it. But I won't let him destroy your life . . . or your brother's."

"Do you think he'll change his mind about my leaving?"

"I don't think so," Dinah said. "But it's probably for the best, though I dread that as well. At least you can be close by for the summer."

"Is Father aware that Grandma said I should come stay with her?" Annie asked.

"No," replied Dinah. "She thought it would be good to make him sweat it out, wondering if you'd have anywhere to go."

"Grandma was so angry with him," Annie said. "She told me she really told him off one day when he stopped by to see how she was doing."

"She told me that, too," Dinah said, "and I hope she did, but I guess I doubt it. I think a lot of the time she tells us what she wishes she would have said instead of what she actually said."

"Well, I'm just glad I can stay with her this summer."

"Me too," Dinah replied, leaning forward and taking a deep breath. "I better let you finish getting ready. Don't want to make Stuart wait."

"Oh, a little waiting might be good for him," Annie said, looking back into the mirror, a smile lighting up her delicate face. "You know, give him more time to anticipate. . . ."

Her mother laughed and took Annie's arm. "I am so happy for you, Annie," she whispered. "Stuart is truly a wonderful young man. I wish I had seen through Arthur Simpson's disguise sooner. I was wrong about him."

"But so was I," Annie said. "So wrong . . . for so long. I really can't believe I was so foolish. Poor Elsie. At least I warned her."

Dinah Harding nodded her head and stood up to leave. "Don't give up on her, Annie. She's going to need a friend when Arthur gets tired of her."

"I know," Annie said. "So you and Garrit are going down to the church?"

"Yes," her mother said with a bright smile as she crossed to the bedroom door. "Pastor Mackenzie thought the children would need something special to do on New Year's Eve while everyone else is out celebrating. Garrit can hardly wait for all the games they've got lined up to play. I suspect it'll be mostly mothers and children who show up. Martha Mackenzie is still visiting her mother in St. Cloud."

"I know Garrit will love it," Annie said. "And it will be nice for you to get out."

Her mother lingered just a minute, a wistful look on her face. "That's what Pastor Mackenzie says. He's a good man, Annie. He's been a real help to me in the past few weeks, with your father's drinking so much worse. He prayed with me about it before church last Sunday."

Annie's eyes brightened, her momentary tinge of alarm replaced by a hope that her mother might share her recent spiritual journey. "Oh, Mother, I've been praying, too, and . . . things have been changing. I just know things will get better. . . ."

But the soft hope Annie had seen in her mother's eyes vanished behind her familiar expression of stoic suffering. "Well, dear, I'm sure it will be a wonderful evening. But you must get ready now." The next second she swept out the door and closed it behind her.

Annie stared after her mother for a moment, but then, seeing her new dress laid out on the bed, was reminded of what she was doing. She took great pleasure in slipping the beautiful red gown over her head, even though she'd tried it on many times over the past few days.

When her mother heard that Stuart had invited Annie to the dance, she and Annie had rushed downtown to find fabric and a pattern, then Dinah had worked long nights at her treadle machine to get it ready in time. Standing in front of the mirror, enjoying the fine embroidered silk braid and ruffles and tucks in the London smoke-cloth dress, Annie was even more grateful for her mother's artistry. She hoped Stuart would like it.

Dabbing on a special French perfume that her mother had let her borrow, Annie took one last long look in the mirror, ran her slender fingers down her soft cheeks, and whispered, "I think I'm in love, and I think I like it." Pressing her lips together, she pinched her cheeks a couple of times, blew herself a kiss, then turned and headed out of her room.

When she came to the living room, Stuart was already there waiting with her mother and brother.

"That took you forever, Annie," Garrit piped up as she stepped through the doorway. "What were you doing up there?"

"Garrit, hush!" scolded Dinah Harding.

"But Stuart's been—"

"Do you want to stay home with me tonight, young Mr. Harding?" his mother broke in.

"No, but . . ." The boy's voice trailed off.

"Annie, you look beautiful," Stuart exclaimed as he stood up from the davenport. "The dress is—"

"Mother made it," Garrit broke in again. "You should have seen them race around here to—"

"Garrit, one more word and I'll ring your sweet little neck," Annie cut in. Then she turned to Stuart with a smile. "I'm glad you like the dress. Mother did in fact make it, just as Mr. Mouth has announced."

"It's wonderful," Stuart said. "You do beautiful work, Mrs. Harding."

"Thank you, Stuart," Dinah replied. "I enjoyed doing it. Now, you two go enjoy your evening so Garrit and I can get going as well."

Stuart picked up the long black dress coat that Annie's mother had laid on one of the chairs and helped Annie slip into it. Then he handed her the white muffler and gloves that Mrs. Sorenson had made for her.

"Why are you wearing Mother's coat?" Garrit asked. "You smell like her, too."

"Because I'm pretending to be Mother, can't you tell?" Annie replied, shaking her head at her brother. "We'll see you later."

"Good night," Stuart called out as he followed Annie around the corner and into the entryway. Annie waited at the front door for Stuart, who held it open as Annie stepped out into the bright wintry night.

"What a gorgeous night! Look at the full moon!" Annie exclaimed as Stuart came alongside her and held out his arm. A southerly breeze had blown for two days straight, bringing with it warm moist air and a welcome reprieve from the frigid December. The fluffy white snowbanks had shrunk, and even the icy sidewalks had partially cleared. Moonlight streaming through the leafless trees glittered on the snow like diamonds in front of them.

"Maybe we should just go for a walk and not bother with the dance," Stuart said, pulling her close as they ambled down the sidewalk to the street.

"You don't want to go to the dance?" asked Annie. "I thought you liked—"

"I do like to dance," he answered. "But I hate the idea that I might have to share you with somebody tonight. You know how it goes."

"You don't like to share?"

"Not you, I don't," Stuart said. "And especially not tonight. I have to go back to school in a couple of days, and I can't stand to think of it."

"Maybe we should go for a walk and then go back to my house for a while," Annie suggested. "Nobody's going to be home until ten or so. You wouldn't have to share."

Stuart laughed and shook his head. "I don't think that's a good idea . . . at least not tonight. Not the way I'm feeling right now."

"And how's that?"

"Like . . . I shouldn't be in your house alone with you, no matter how much I'd like to be," Stuart murmured as Annie looked up into his dark eyes. "And you know better, too."

"I certainly do," Annie said. "I just thought I'd test you and see. You passed."

"Good," Stuart replied with a warm smile as they crossed at the corner and continued down the street. "I keep wondering when I might flunk and this all will come crashing down on me."

"Are you really concerned?" Annie asked, stopping for the moment under a large elm tree that stood gaunt against the moonlight and the dark blue sky.

"That the Christmas dream will end?" Stuart took Annie's gloved hands in his and held them tight. "That you'll pinch me and tell me to go back where I came from? I came home figuring that Arthur Simpson had proposed to you by now, and instead I find myself walking down the street with you at my side. It's all been too good to believe, don't you think?"

Annie smiled and whispered, "This is one dream that doesn't need to end, Stuart. One kiss will keep it going, for tonight at least."

"At least," Stuart whispered, taking her into his arms. Her lips met his in tenderness and warmth, and the kiss seemed to have no end, although it was not the first in recent days and would not be the last.

"See," Annie spoke softly in Stuart's ear as he continued to hold her. "You're still dreaming."

Stuart nodded and held her tight. "It's a good one, but . . . I don't think we're really being honest about this."

Annie's eyes misted over. Then she looked up into Stuart's face. "I think you're right, Stuart. But I want you to say it first, and I want to see it in your eyes."

"I've never said this before to anyone."

"Good," Annie replied. "And you'll never have to say it to anyone else."

Gazing tenderly into Annie's brown eyes, Stuart said the words. "Annie Harding, I love you with all my heart. Can you find it within yourself to love me back?"

"I don't have to look very far," Annie responded without blinking. "I think I fell in love with you when you spoke those words in my ear at the bridge—'Wake up, sweet beauty!' It just took me a while to figure out my heart."

"And what does your heart say now?"

"It says I love you, Stuart Anderson," she said softly, tears forming at the corners of her eyes and spilling out. "My rescuer and my love."

This time Stuart needed no coaxing. He bent down and kissed

Annie firmly on her waiting lips, with passion and fire welling up within. Her tears mingled with their kiss, strengthening their embrace.

The sound of a door opening suddenly snapped the couple back to reality, to the sidewalk on which they were standing. An elderly man stepped out from his front door and stared at them from the steps. "What's going on out there?" he called in a high-pitched voice. "Are you all right?"

"Yes, we're fine, Mr. Amunson," Stuart called back. "I was just kissing my girl here, and I told her that I loved her. Is that all right with you?"

"Carry on," the old man replied, giving them a wave and stepping back into the house. "Good night."

"How could you say that to him?" Annie cried, giving Stuart a playful shove, then he slipped on a patch of ice and nearly fell. "Serves you right if you land on your backside. This is personal, Stuart."

Stuart straightened up but continued to laugh. Finally he said, "You don't know Mr. Amunson, do you?"

"No. Why?"

"He's as deaf as a rock," Stuart replied, laughing again. "But he's got eyes like a hawk, and he watches the street all the time. I forgot that he'd probably see us."

"You are a terrible tease," Annie said as she started to walk down the sidewalk again. "I think we should go to the dance for a while before somebody else catches us."

"Or maybe to your house?"

"Forget that," Annie responded with a laugh, taking Stuart's arm again as they walked. "I'm not sure that standing on a city street is safe with you tonight."

"Guess you're right about the dance," Stuart admitted. "Besides, my parents are going to be there, and they'll be looking for us."

They turned at the next corner and headed for the town hall, where the dance was always held. The building housed several city offices along with a large open room that was used for a variety of community events. Both Stuart and Annie were quite familiar with the spacious room with its high ceilings and massive fireplace at one end.

When they reached the front doors, they could already hear the music playing inside. Several couples had arrived just ahead of them, and the hallway was clogged with people taking off their coats and trying to find hangers. Stuart took Annie's coat, then turned to begin his own search.

"I'll be right back," Annie told Stuart above the din. "I need to check my hair. Someone may have messed it up."

"You look fine, just a bit rumpled," Stuart teased. "I'll meet you by the fireplace."

"Good," Annie replied, leaving him behind.

As Annie disappeared down the hallway, Stuart heard the front doors open behind him and glanced back to see Elsie Dale and Arthur Simpson step inside. Arthur immediately spotted Stuart and smiled, then he went to help Elsie with her coat. Elsie's sleek new dress high-lighted her mature figure and caused several men's heads to turn. Even Stuart, whose head was already turned, couldn't help but notice.

Elsie marched down the hallway without speaking a word to Stuart, although he was aware that she was watching him. He finally managed to find two free hangers, quickly loaded his and Annie's coats on them, and found a place for his hat. Then, as he turned to go down the hall-way, he found himself face-to-face with Arthur Simpson.

"Well, well, if it isn't my old friend Stuart Anderson," Simpson crooned, pulling off his own expensive leather hat and placing it care-fully on a shelf above the hangers. "Rumor has it that you managed to finally get what you wanted this summer."

"Get?" Stuart asked, bristling inwardly. "If you mean whether I've tried to purchase someone ... with a pearl ring, for instance ... no, that's just a rumor. I don't have a tin ring, let alone one of gold and pearl. Hey, it's good to see you, too, Simpson. How've you been?"

"Not too bad," Simpson replied, taking a single hanger and placing first Elsie's coat and then his own coat on it. "I saw you take a look at Elsie. Not bad, eh?"

Stuart shook his head and blew out some air. "Elsie's always been beautiful, but I didn't notice the old smile I used to see. I'm sure you're treating her well."

"The best, of course," the young banker said with a Cheshire grin. "Just as long as we understand who's in charge, my women never com-plain of lacking a thing."

"Sounds like a wonderful life," Stuart said. "I'll bet all those Simpson women tell you how much fun it is to know who's in charge."

"You might be surprised, Anderson," Simpson returned coldly, leaning against Stuart and speaking quietly. "For the record, I find you an annoying little country bumpkin. You should ask your young lady whether she enjoyed the taste of my kiss."

Stuart leaned back against Arthur Simpson and discreetly grabbed the lapel of the young banker's perfectly tailored suit. "You better step back, Mr. Simpson, or I may lose my dinner all over you. You ran away from me on the street once before. Perhaps you'd like to venture outside now and get this over with. I'm a little out of shape, but you look even worse. Shall we?"

Arthur Simpson smiled and shook his head. "You can't get me to play your game, little man. I can make you crawl on your belly if I want. And I could take back that silly little Annie Harding, too, if I wanted her. I snap my fingers, and people who owe us money at the bank bow down. I suggest you watch your tongue, or I'll cut it off. I have ways of shortening legs at the knees, Stuart. Would you like to try me?"

"I didn't start this conversation, and I'm not looking to try anyone, but you have a way of bringing out the worst in me," Stuart replied, leaning hard against Simpson's wide shoulder. "I warned you before, and I'll say it again. There's always a way to take a big guy down, and when he goes down, he doesn't get up."

Bringing his face up close to Arthur's, Stuart added in a hoarse whisper, "Don't . . . ever . . . threaten me or my family or Annie. God is my witness. You will come down."

Chapter 23

Tracks in the Snow

Sitting quietly at her school desk, Annie Harding ran her fingers lightly across the opened edge of the letter she had received from Stuart on the previous day. It was the third in the three weeks since he had returned to the university, a flurry of correspondence she counted as nearly miraculous, considering his sorry record for writing his own mother. Annie kept the latest letter with her at school, and between assignments she would often carefully open it and reread its treasured words.

Today, however, even the anticipation of rereading Stuart's letter could not quell the feeling of queasiness in her stomach. Walking to school that morning, Annie had hoped that her headache and nausea would go away, but instead it had worsened. After two hours of increasing discomfort, she was regretting that she hadn't listened to her body's signals and simply stayed in bed. Then she suddenly felt a wave of chills course through her body, followed by a contrasting wave of feverish heat, and she knew there was no point in attempting to stay in class.

Gathering her letter and a writing assignment she could work on at home, she walked to the teacher's desk, where Mrs. Olson was busy grading a history test from the previous day. The teacher looked up, a frown of concentration frozen across her forehead, but she relaxed and smiled when she saw Annie.

"Mrs. Olson," Annie spoke quietly, "I'm feeling pretty sick. I need your permission to go home."

"What's wrong?" the gray-haired teacher asked. "You look all flushed. Is it the grippe? A lot of the younger children have been coming down with it."

"I guess it is," Annie replied. She rubbed her forehead and pressed her fingers against the sinuses behind her eyes. "My head hurts. I have the chills. I feel like I need to throw up. And it's getting worse. I'm quite sure you don't want me spreading this around."

"Can you make it home?"

"I think so," said Annie, wishing she lived blocks closer. "May I go?"

"Certainly," Mrs. Olson said. "I'll let the school office know. You don't need to stop and tell them."

"Thank you, Mrs. Olson," Annie said. She swallowed hard, her throat beginning to hurt as well. "I don't think I'll see you for a few days. Say hello to Walter for me if you stop to see him."

"I will," her teacher responded with a smile. "He's doing fine. You get going now and stay in bed until it clears. Do you understand?"

Annie nodded and whispered, "Believe me, I will."

As she left the room, Annie stopped and whispered to Elsie Dale that she was sick and going home. Elsie nodded but said nothing. It seemed to Annie that no matter how hard she tried to mend her friendship with Elsie, she still got the cold-shoulder treatment. Even when she'd stopped by Elsie's boarding room to give her a Christmas present, there had been no invitation to come in and talk, just a polite "thank you."

Annie wrapped herself tightly in her heavy winter coat, donned Mrs. Sorenson's warm hat and gloves and scarf, then made her way quickly out of the school building. Turning down the sidewalk, she saw with relief that the morning's snow had let up. The warm moist air of Christmas vacation had left the day Stuart kissed her good-bye at the small railroad depot, and even now that the bright winter sun had appeared from the clouds, the temperature had only managed to climb slightly above the zero mark.

She walked as fast as she dared across the snow-packed sidewalks and streets, and before long she had turned down the street in front of her house. One set of fresh footprints preceded her on the newly fallen snow, a man's large size with a long stride. Annie followed the lone footprints for a while without thinking anything about them, but she stopped, surprised, when they turned onto the sidewalk that led to her house. The prints led straight to the Harding front door and then disappeared.

"This is strange," she whispered to herself, knowing that her father had left early in the morning to work on a farmhouse several miles north of town. "Who would—" Then a sudden image from the past summer startled her—a mental picture of Pastor Mackenzie walking away from her house. It left behind an eerie, sickening feeling that had nothing to do with her other physical symptoms.

Staring at the house for a moment, Annie made her decision and walked quickly up the sidewalk but did not go to the front door. Instead, she followed the sidewalk around the side of the house to the kitchen door. Pausing to listen, she grasped the large round metal knob and cautiously twisted it open, then pushed her shoulder against the door and slowly swung it open. She stepped into the kitchen and carefully closed the door behind her, frozen in place as she listened for the sound of voices in the house, for any sound at all.

At first she heard only the thumping of her own heartbeat in her head. Silence filled the house, but the footprints that led through the front door had not led out the back door. Glancing around the kitchen, Annie untied her heavy shoes and slipped them off, then tiptoed in stockinged feet across the shiny waxed floor. When she was almost to the kitchen door, the floorboards cracked loudly, freezing her in place again. She paused, holding her breath, and thought she heard voices somewhere inside.

Annie moved to the swinging oak door that led to the dining room and pressed her ear against the crack as she ever so slightly nudged the door open. The sound of muffled voices seemed to be coming from the living room. Annie let the door close and stood still in the kitchen with her eyes closed, her fingers twisting the buttons on her coat. Did she dare go through the dining room to the living room door? Should she? If the situation were innocent, as she hoped it was, what would she say if she were discovered? Or if the situation was as she dreaded, what would she do?

As she waited, a wave of nausea swept over her, and she thought she would be sick right on the spot. Annie trembled as it passed, holding her hand over her mouth, then she breathed deeply. She knew that the next wave of nausea might not be so kind. Taking another deep breath, she pushed the swinging door open and did the impossible, willing her left foot forward first, then her right.

Carefully holding the door until it swung shut silently behind her, Annie moved noiselessly around the dining room table and crept along the wall to the living room doorway. Large beads of perspiration had already formed on her forehead and began to streak down her face. Then, as she stopped at the doorway, for a second she felt faint. Squeezing her eyes together, she pressed her hands against the wall and took several short breaths. Slowly her head cleared and she got her bearings again, then she straightened herself and listened to the voices that were no longer muffled.

"You truly think there's a chance he'll change?" Pastor Mackenzie was saying. His voice sounded strained and pressing.

"I don't know," Annie's mother replied. "I keep hoping."

"Even though he's taken to the bottle again? Is it still as bad as it was?"

"Worse. This is the worst I've ever seen him."

"Has he . . . has he struck you?"

There was a long pause, and Annie strained to hear. Finally her mother said, "He's shoved me twice since Christmas, but it's been worse in the past . . . when he's drunk."

"What about the children?"

"No, he leaves them alone."

"So far."

"He knows I'll leave if he goes after either of them."

"Why don't you leave before he hurts you?"

"Where would I go? What would I do?" Dinah Harding asked. "It's not that simple."

Annie thought her mother's voice trembled, and she could resist no longer. Slowly she peeked around the corner and spotted the pastor and her mother sitting on the davenport. Dinah Harding was leaning forward with her face in her hands, and Pastor Mackenzie had his arm around her right shoulder.

"You don't have to be so unhappy," he was saying. Annie drew back behind the corner of the doorway before one of them had the chance to glance her way. "You deserve better than this, Dinah. I can help."

"I can't, Alexander. I've told you that."

"But you can. No one needs to know."

Dinah Harding did not respond immediately, and Annie was about to risk peeking again when another wave of nausea swept over her. She leaned hard against the wall and held her breath, perspiration still streaming down her face. As the seconds ticked by, a fresh sense of relief came as she managed to temporarily escape the grasp of her illness.

"No one will ever know," the pastor continued to press. "You need someone to love you the way I can."

Annie pressed her fingers into the wall and shook her head in restraint. "No!" she whispered. "Don't listen to him."

"You know that I love you, don't you? Who else has been here when you needed someone?"

"But this is different," Dinah Harding spoke softly. "You shouldn't have come."

"You asked me to come. Your note said—"

"But I didn't mean . . . if I had thought your intention was to—"

"My intention is to give you the love that your husband is incapable of," the pastor interrupted. "Isn't it what you really want? Tell me it's not why you wrote that note."

"No . . . I . . . you misunderstood," Annie's mother sputtered. "I wrote the note because I needed to talk with someone, and you're the only one I have. But I didn't mean for . . . I didn't mean any more than that."

"But can't you see how much he's deprived you of. . . . how much you're missing even now? Tell me that you've never thought of me in this way. You have, haven't you?"

"Yes, but I didn't—"

"Are you happy with the love he brings you?"

"No, but that doesn't—"

"Yes, it does. It has everything to do with it," Pastor Mackenzie urged. "You have to stop letting that husband of yours dictate what your life is going to be like. If you won't leave him, at least let me provide the love he won't."

"Can't you just hold me?" Annie's mother begged. "Why must it be more?"

"Because love is so much more than that. Let me show you."

Annie's hands had started to tremble, and she felt the same sensation in her legs. She took a deep breath and peeked around the corner again.

The pastor was massaging her mother's back, and her face was still buried in her hands. Annie thought her mother's shoulders and back looked tense and rigid.

"Just relax, love," the pastor said. "You're going to enjoy—"

"Please don't," Dinah Harding protested weakly, shaking her head. "I can't—"

"Relax!" Pastor Mackenzie spoke firmly, running his hand down her spine. "I know what you really need."

"Stop! I can't do this now!" Dinah Harding cried, reaching back and grabbing his arms. "This is wrong!"

Annie could take no more, but before she could think of what she was going to do, she knew she was going to be sick. Rushing to the kitchen door, she slammed it open and let out a very loud moan as her stomach heaved. Annie dashed across the kitchen to the sink, then she lowered her head and let go. Behind her Annie was aware of voices from the other room, but for the moment she didn't care about anything except getting rid of the contents of her stomach.

"Annie!" her mother called out, hurrying into the kitchen. "What's wrong?"

For the moment, Annie could not even look up. Tears had filled her eyes as she remained bent over the sink, her arms shaking, with the worst taste imaginable in her mouth. She heard the rattle of glasses in the cupboard followed by the pouring of water into a cup. Annie also thought she heard the dining room door swing quietly shut.

"Here," Dinah Harding spoke softly to Annie. "Rinse your mouth out with water. You'll feel better."

Annie partially straightened up, then took the glass in her right hand and lifted it to her lips. Taking a mouthful of water, she swished away the bad residue and spit it out, then she took a deep breath and leaned back over the sink.

"Did you get sick in school?" her mother asked.

Nodding her head, Annie whispered, "I started feeling sick and got permission to leave. I think it's the grippe. My head aches. I've got the chills. And now this."

"Why didn't you come in the front door?"

"I saw someone's tracks in the snow," said Annie, leaning back again and taking another sip of water, "and it seemed like a better idea to come in the back."

"Looks like it was," her mother said. "I'm glad you made it to the sink, but I had better get this all cleaned up. Are you feeling better now?"

"Yeah," Annie responded, stepping back and finally unbuttoning her winter coat. "Who's here?"

"Oh, it's . . . um . . . Reverend Mackenzie," her mother mumbled, not looking up from scrubbing the sink. "He stopped to drop off some music."

"He left?"

"Yes, when we heard you being sick, he excused himself," Dinah answered. "Listen, why don't you go up to your bed. You're as pale as a ghost. I'll come up as soon as I've finished cleaning this up."

Annie simply nodded her head and whispered, "All right," then she walked slowly out of the kitchen and up to her bedroom. She felt a little worse with every step and changed from her school clothes to her nightgown as quickly as she could, then crawled between the covers and sheets just as the chills hit again. She lay shaking under the heavy blankets while her teeth chattered. Her forehead was cold and clammy and her throat was very sore.

By the time her mother entered the room with a hot cup of black tea, Annie's chills had subsided and she was lying motionless for fear that any movement would prompt another wave of the shakes. As Dinah Harding crossed the room and set the steaming cup on the end table by her bed, Annie prayed that she would have the right words to say to her mother.

"Here's some tea," Dinah said gently, leaning over and feeling Annie's forehead with the palm of her hand. "You feel feverish. I should probably go heat up the water bottles and see if we can get you to break a sweat."

"Why don't you wait with that," Annie suggested as her mother sat down on the edge of her bed. "I hate lying here packed with hot water bottles, sweating like a Trojan. Maybe the tea will help."

"Not much ever helps cure influenza," her mother said. "A couple of days in bed is about all you can do."

"Or a couple of weeks. At least that's how I feel right now," Annie said, closing her eyes and feeling overwhelmingly tired.

"You drink that tea before you fall asleep," Dinah Harding said, picking up the cup of tea and handing it to Annie.

Annie had to sit up in her bed to drink, and as she pulled herself up and took the cup, she moaned as she felt her entire body start to ache. Lifting the cup to her lips, she took a sip and swallowed hard as it burned against her tender throat. Then she held the cup securely between her chilled hands and stared with large eyes at her mother.

"What?" Dinah asked. "Is something wrong?"

"That's . . . what I was going to ask you," Annie replied. "Why did you say the reverend was here?"

"He had some music . . ." her mother said, pausing as she looked into Annie's eyes, then she quickly glanced away. "It's for Sunday. A new hymn he wants me to try."

"Mother," Annie spoke gently, "I know why he was here. I listened from the dining room."

Dinah Harding closed her eyes and covered her face with her left hand, then she started to stand up.

"Please don't leave," Annie begged, reaching out and taking her mother's arm. "I heard him. He's a horrible, wicked man. It wasn't your fault."

Her mother sat back down on the bed and began to weep quietly, but it didn't take long before she was sobbing. Annie set the cup of tea back on the end table and put her arms around her mother, holding Dinah with as much strength as was left within her. Feeling something of the despair that had driven her mother to the pastor, Annie began to weep as well.

"It wasn't your fault, Mother," Annie repeated as Dinah's sobs finally began to subside. "He took advantage of you. He was going to—"

"It was my fault, Annie," her mother mumbled, shaking her head back and forth. "I knew all along what he really wanted, but I kept hoping that he might really care. I played right into his hands. I'm so ashamed of myself."

"How could you do—"

"I . . . at first I just needed someone to listen to me," Dinah replied.

"I'm sorry for what you heard said about your father. It's just been so bad, and I thought . . . it felt so good to talk about it, and to feel like it wasn't my fault. But it went further than that, and . . . I knew it was coming, but . . . I couldn't seem to say no, either. If you hadn't come when you did, I don't know what would have happened. How can you forgive me, Annie?"

"We have to stop him, Mother," Annie declared, feeling a surge of adrenaline drive back her fatigue. "He's preying on women like you. The rumors are true."

"No, Annie. No!" her mother gasped. "If your father discovers any of this, he'll kick me out or drive me away. We can't let that happen to our family, Annie. Please. It'll destroy us."

Dinah Harding pulled back to peer into Annie's face, and Annie knew she was right. No matter whose fault this was, her father would surely take it out on her mother. Annie had seen him do it on lesser issues than this.

"You have to promise me that you'll never go to him again—for any reason," Annie warned.

"I promise it'll never happen again," Dinah replied, closing her eyes again. "I am so sorry that you had to be involved. It makes me sick that you saw us together. I won't blame you if you hate me for it."

"Please, don't say that, Mother," Annie said, taking her mother's arm once more. "The pastor was leading you into this with his lies. Every word he said was meant to trap you. I just thank God I got sick. Maybe this is *why* I got sick. He was intervening in your behalf."

Dinah Harding opened her eyes and looked at her daughter. "Do you really think that's possible, Annie? That God would do something like that, I mean."

"I mean it with all my heart," Annie stated with a confident nod. "That's what I was trying to tell you the other night. I also know God can forgive our sins, and there's no sin too great that He can't forgive. Do you believe that?"

"To be honest," her mother said, "I don't know what I believe anymore. If the pastor can do what he did, who can believe anything?"

Annie shook her head. "Oh, Mother, please don't confuse Reverend Mackenzie with God! There's no resemblance, not even if the pastor uses all the right spiritual words. He's a liar and a fake, and I hope and pray someone blows the whistle on him. Think of all the women he may have hurt—or is hurting now."

"You stay clear of him, Annie," Dinah warned. "He's dangerous."

"But he'll keep coming after you," Annie protested. "We have to do something. . . ."

"And lose everything?" her mother replied. "How could I possibly risk that?"

Chapter 24

Two Can Play
the Game

"Annie, you have to take the cake to the church for me," Dinah Harding repeated herself. "The wedding's this afternoon, and they're setting up the lunch this morning. The women's circle is expecting me to bring this."

"I hate to go in there alone, though," Annie replied. "Can't it wait until Garrit gets home from Tommy's house?"

"No, it can't wait for him. He might not come home until after lunch," her mother said. "You should be all right. There will be several women at the church working on the wedding preparations. Just drop the cake off quickly and get out of there."

"I can't stand to look at the pastor anymore, Mother," Annie stated, shaking her head as she picked up her heavy winter coat and began to button it. "He makes me sick."

"And that makes two of us," Dinah said. "But I can't go back in there and chance another encounter with him. Sooner or later he's going to try again. I know he will."

"He has to be stopped," Annie said sharply. "Think of all the other women he's pulled this on. And they're all afraid of what he might do to them."

"I can't do it, Annie," her mother said. "I've thought and thought about it, and I hate what I let happen, but if your father finds out ... well, he just can't find out, that's all."

"Maybe there's another way," Annie said softly as she picked up the cake.

"I warned you already, Annie. Don't you get close to him," Dinah Harding said firmly. "He twists things, manipulates situations, and

241

pretty soon you start believing he's right. Stay away from him."

"I just meant that maybe there are other women who would come forward if they knew they weren't alone," Annie explained. "If we watch him closely, I'll bet we can find some candidates."

"Just . . . please . . . stay away from it," her mother replied. "He won't go down without taking others with him."

Annie just shrugged and flashed a lopsided smile at her mother. "Well, I'll be back shortly. If I'm not home within an hour, send in the troops." She pulled open the wooden door and winked at her mother, then she stepped into a blustery day of dull gray clouds and a few snow-flakes being whipped about in the air. "What a lousy day for a wedding," she muttered to herself as she headed down the snow-packed sidewalk, holding the cake tightly.

Annie did not know the couple who were getting married, although she did know the bride's youngest sister from school. Neither Annie nor her mother had made plans to attend the ceremony, so she hoped she could avoid the family as well as the pastor. Hurrying down the street with the cake in hand, she wondered what she would say if she did see him.

She reached the white wooden church and climbed the front steps, thinking how strange it was that she would feel the need to pray for protection as she entered it. Of all the buildings in town, this should be the safest, but instead, the sight of it only brought Annie a renewed sense of dread. The majestic stained-glass windows and graceful steeple could not make up for the fact that a predator lurked within its walls.

Pulling open the church's large wooden door, Annie immediately let out a sigh of relief as she spotted two church women busy decorating the center aisles of the sanctuary for the wedding. She waved at them, then followed the enticing food smells down the stairway to the basement. The door opened to a large cafeteria that held more than a dozen long decorated tables. Beyond that was the church kitchen, where Annie assumed that three or four of the women from her mother's circle group were busy preparing food for the reception. One of the tables was loaded with a variety of baked goods that had been dropped off.

Annie slowed her pace, soaking in the room's rich aroma and welcomed warmth as she crossed the woodplank floor to place her mother's cake on the table. Setting the chocolate cake next to a large tray of iced gingerbread, Annie stopped to admire the elaborate baking that some of the women had done. Then she glanced through the large serving window that opened into the kitchen and saw Pearl Tienter, the bride's sister, standing by the sink and talking to someone Annie could not see from where she was standing. She stepped around the corner of the table and looked again, this time spotting Pastor Mackenzie. He appeared to be alone in the kitchen with Pearl.

"Oh no!" Annie gasped, stepping back around the table where the pastor could not see her. "Pearl, get out of there," she whispered, then began to cut across the large meeting room to make her own escape. Almost to the door, Annie stopped and looked back, even though she knew that she couldn't see into the kitchen from where she was standing now. Staring at the blank serving window, she finally sighed and turned around. No matter how much she wanted to get away, she couldn't leave Pearl alone in the kitchen with the pastor.

Taking a deep breath, Annie trod slowly over to the window, then stopped to listen in on their conversation, but they were talking so softly that she couldn't hear what was being said. With her hand on the wall, still listening in silence and wondering what she should do, Annie was suddenly struck by an idea that nearly took her breath away. *What if I set a trap for him?* she thought.

The sudden sound of footsteps from the entry above the stairway forced Annie to act before she had time to formulate a plan. Stepping to the large open window, she leaned into the kitchen and said, "Pearl, how are you? Pretty exciting day, eh? I just dropped off a cake for the lunch." Then she turned to the pastor and smiled. "Pastor Mackenzie, good morning, I didn't see you. Helping with the lunch, are you?"

"No, no," the handsome minister replied with a warm smile. "Just making sure that everything's ready for the big day."

"My goodness, I didn't realize you had to supervise everything," Annie said. "That's pretty impressive, isn't it, Pearl?"

Pearl nodded. "There's a lot to do here, that's for sure."

"I'm sorry I missed your visit the other day," Annie said, turning back to the pastor. His dark eyebrows rose, but he continued his pleasant smile. "You caught me at an unpleasant moment. I was hoping that we could talk, too, but as you probably heard, I wasn't feeling very well."

"You sounded very ill," Pastor Mackenzie responded, then he turned to the other young lady. "Pearl, if you'll excuse me, I should keep moving. It was nice to talk with you. See you this afternoon."

"Yes, thanks. I can hardly wait for the service," Pearl said as the minister went to the kitchen door.

"Have a good time, Pearl," Annie offered as she stepped back from the window and heard the kitchen door swing open.

Pastor Mackenzie strode across the floor to meet Annie, running his fingers back through his dark hair and clearing his throat. Annie took a few steps his way but had all she could do to remain composed. She crossed her arms and did her best to smile.

"I'm sorry you were so sick," he said in his strong preaching voice. "I did peek into the kitchen, but then I thought I best leave. I didn't mean to run out on you or your mother. Was it the grippe?"

"Yes," she replied, shaking her head. "Not very pretty, was it?"

"You must have come through the back door," the pastor continued. "That seemed odd."

Annie's hands squeezed down on her arms, and for a second she lost her train of thought. Then she said, "It was odd, but I saw your footprints going into our house, and I was afraid I might get sick at any moment. I thought the back door was a better choice."

"So it was . . . so it was," Pastor Mackenzie intoned, pressing his lips together and nodding. "You must have come into the dining room. The door was still swinging when I got to it."

"I came in to see who was visiting, but then I got sick," Annie said. "When I heard your voice, I hoped I'd have a chance to talk with you, but . . . so much for that."

Annie could feel the pastor's dark eyes searching hers for what she knew, and the anger she felt rising up inside her fueled her resolve to execute the very sketchy plan she had devised. "It's about my father," she spoke softly, glancing around the room. "My mother said that she's had several helpful talks with you about him. I . . . um . . . I have a very hard time with my father. I was hoping that . . . you could . . . would perhaps . . . extend the same guidance to me. I can't take much more, Pastor."

"Now?" he asked, still staring into her eyes, but his expression had warmed to a caring look. "I really should—"

"Oh, I'm sorry," Annie apologized, leaning toward him and placing her gloved hand on his arm. "I didn't mean now. No. You've got more important things than some silly girl who—"

"Surely not more important," the pastor broke in, sliding his hand on top of hers. "But . . . the wedding is most pressing, and I still need to attend to matters upstairs. Should we schedule something for next week? Monday, perhaps?"

"No, I think later in the week would be better for me," said Annie. The strong scent of his cologne was nearly choking her. "But I'd rather drop in when I can do it without my mother knowing about it. She gets . . . so nervous about things like this; she's afraid my father will find out. I'd rather she not know . . . or anyone else. Of all people, I'm sure you understand."

"Where would you like to meet?" he asked.

"I'd thought I'd come here—to your office," Annie stated. "Or do you have somewhere more confidential? My parents cannot find out about this."

Pastor Mackenzie smiled again and looked back at the kitchen window. "No . . . I . . . ah . . . the church is probably best. I . . . sometimes arrange to meet people where they feel most . . . relaxed. But we can't meet at your house."

"Not unless my mother is gone," Annie said. "Would you come if I can arrange it?"

"If you're comfortable with that," he replied. "But the church office might be best. You decide."

"Once I find out what my mother's plans are, I'll let you know."

"How?"

"I'll either stop by the office . . . or leave you a note," Annie said, slipping her hand back away from his arm. "I feel better already, Pastor."

"That makes me very happy, Annie," he said with a nod. "I look forward to our talk. I hope it goes well for you."

"Thank you so much," Annie replied, staring into his eyes. "I'll be in touch."

"Very good," he said, reaching out and lightly touching her shoulder. "Greet your mother for me. She and I didn't finish our discussion the other day. Tell her I hope to have another chance to meet with her. Good day."

Annie could only nod and take her leave. Her legs felt stiff as she trudged up the stairway, and she noticed that her arm trembled as she pushed on the church's heavy front door. Snowflakes swirling in the doorway greeted her, bringing a splash of refreshing cold to her red cheeks and clearing her raging thoughts. "What in the world did I just do?" she whispered to the snowy gray clouds as she marched down the steps of the church.

But there was no answer given. No answer was required. She knew full well what she had done, and what she was going to do. With every step home, she grew bolder . . . and felt sicker. The smell of the pastor's cologne seemed to fill the air.

♦ ♦ ♦ ♦ ♦ ♦ ♦ ♦ ♦ ♦ ♦

"You *are* going to church with us," James Harding ordered, pushing his chair back from the dining room table and standing up, towering over Annie. "And you're sitting with us. Just like always. No more excuses."

Annie glanced angrily at her mother, who offered no response other than silent resignation. She knew that the chances had been slender that she could convince her father to let her stay home, but she hadn't expected him to get so upset. The thought, just the notion of enduring an hour and a half of the Reverend Alexander Mackenzie was more than she could bear. She wondered how it was possible for her mother to sit so passively and face the same torture.

Her father turned and left the room. He appeared to be satisfied that his words had been understood and would be obeyed.

"What's wrong, Annie?" Garrit spoke softly, tugging on Annie's white blouse. "I thought you felt good again."

Annie looked down at her brother and ran her fingers through his tangled white-blond hair. "I'll be fine, I hope. Someday . . . soon," she whispered to him. "Now, let's go brush your mop and get you spiffed up for church."

♦ ♦ ♦ ♦ ♦ ♦ ♦ ♦ ♦ ♦ ♦

Feeling like every nerve in her body was on edge, Annie had purposely sat on the outside seat of their pew. Every time Pastor Mackenzie looked in her direction, Annie's skin started to crawl but she refused to look away. She would not let that man intimidate her. The more she was forced to listen to his hollow religious words, however, the more she wanted to stand up and scream. As he launched into a sermon titled "The Garden of the Soul," she could take no more.

"I have to leave," she whispered into her mother's ear. "I'll meet you downstairs by the coatracks afterward."

"No, your father—"

"I'm sorry, Mother," Annie interrupted, leaning against her mother's shoulder. "Tell him that I really am sick, because I will be if I sit here another second."

That said, Annie quickly made her way out of the pew and headed down the outside aisle. She felt every eye in the church was following her exit, but she really didn't care. If her father followed her, she was willing to face whatever he might say. And if he was upset, she would take whatever punishment he doled out.

Emerging into the foyer, Annie escaped down the inside stairs and stepped into the cherished silence of the large, empty meeting room. "This is better," she whispered to herself. Then she recalled that occasionally one of the mothers would bring down a restless child and let him or her run around the room. Deciding that the kitchen might afford her even more solitude, she crossed the room and disappeared behind the swinging wooden door. The kitchen's large service window was closed, giving her the maximum privacy.

Two mismatched chairs were pushed against the back wall of the kitchen, and Annie sat down on what appeared to be the more comfortable of the two. She stared out one of the high kitchen windows at a barren elm tree silhouetted against the dark morning clouds and wondered if the sun would ever shine again. Then she heard the kitchen door swing open and her stomach tightened, feeling the approach of her father's wrath. She turned to see Marian Anderson coming through the door instead.

"Communing with the trees, I see," Marian said with a smile as she approached Annie. "This is a strange place to spend your Sabbath."

Annie laughed out loud, partly in response to Marian but more out of sheer relief that she wasn't encountering her father. "I . . . ah . . .

guess I wasn't in the mood for church this morning," she said, sliding her chair over so Marian could take the other one. "Sometimes an ugly chair in an empty kitchen isn't so bad."

"What's wrong?" Marian asked as she sat down next to Annie. Her dark eyes flashed at Annie despite the kitchen's dim light.

"Just . . . not in a good mood," Annie replied weakly.

"I think it's something more," Marian stated. "I was right behind you, even if you didn't notice me. You looked like you were being tortured."

Rubbing her forehead, Annie chuckled. "I thought I was doing better than that."

"It was the way you were twisting your fingers," said Marian. "I thought you might have broken a couple of them right off. What's wrong? Do you want to talk about it?"

Annie looked down at her long fingers and shook her head, considering what to say, if anything at all. Could it be that Marian's following her out of the church service was an answer to her prayers? Her intention had been to tell no one about her plan. However, she was still unsure as to how she would pull it off. Perhaps she needed help.

Looking back into Marian's face, Annie smiled and exhaled a big breath of air. "Marian, if there's anyone I'd like to talk with, it's you. But I have a problem that's so big I can hardly imagine that anyone would believe a word I say about it. It's just not fair to pull you into it."

Marian nodded. "Some things you have to face alone. But other things were meant to be shared. Some things are so overwhelming they threaten to topple over on us. I can't tell which this one is, but I'm here to listen and help if you need me."

Annie ran her fingers down along a seam in her dress and felt a sense of relief in the other woman's presence. "No one can ever hear a word of what I tell you," she spoke softly, looking up and scanning the kitchen.

Marian nodded, then she shocked Annie by saying, "What did the pastor do to you?"

"How did you know?" Annie gasped before she checked her words.

"Every time he looked at you, I could see the muscles in your back tense up," Marian explained. "Did he do something to you, Annie?"

Annie shook her head at first, but then nodded. "Not to me, not yet," she whispered, pulling at the fabric of her skirt and twisting it into knots. "He tried ... I saw him trying to ... commit adultery ... with my mother ... in our house. He doesn't know that I know, but my mother does."

"You can witness to it?"

"Yes, I saw him with my own eyes, Marian," Annie replied. "I heard his words. If I hadn't distracted them, I can't tell you what might have happened."

"Oh, Annie, you have to come forward and confront him," Marian urged. "Your mother's not the first, I'm sure of that. But no one will talk. If you—"

"Marian, I can't do that!" Annie cried, her voice trembling. "If I could, I would have stood up this morning and screamed it out to the whole church. I hate him. I hate what he's done. But if my father discovers what my mother has been involved in, our family will be ruined. I cannot do it. Please don't ask me, Marian."

Silence followed Annie's plea, and Marian sat back in her chair, still staring into Annie's eyes.

"It's all right, Annie, I understand," Marian replied gently, raising her fine dark eyebrows. "Somehow he's been able to do this again and again and to keep his victims quiet. I suppose he uses the same kind of fear of discovery over and over—it's like blackmail. I wonder if Martha has any idea. . . ." She had fallen to musing, but now she snapped back to attention. "But, Annie, what did you mean when you said that he hadn't done anything to you *yet*? That doesn't quite make sense."

Annie finally smiled. "I think I'm going to need your help, Marian."

"Has he blackmailed you as well?"

"No—or like I said, not yet. And he's not going to get a chance, if everything works out right," Annie said. "Marian, I've set a trap for him, just like he did to my mother. But I haven't figured out how I can make it work alone. Will you help?"

Marian gasped. "Oh, Annie, you used yourself to bait a trap, and he's already falling for it? Annie, do you know how foolish that was? You have no idea what that man is capable of doing."

"I know it sounds foolish, and maybe it is," Annie agreed. "But the opportunity came, and I just had to take advantage of it. I need your help, Marian, I really do. But I'll try it alone if I have to. I will not let him destroy my mother or our family. I can't let him do that. So what about it? Will you help me spring the trap?"

"It doesn't sound like I have much choice," Marian said. "Tell me exactly what you have in mind."

Chapter 25

Throwing Caution to the Wind

*T*he first light of dawn had finally begun to drive back the dark wintry night. Annie Harding sat in a chair next to her window, staring at the faint outlines of trees and housetops, her heart filled with anxiety. She was certain she had not slept a wink that night; she wondered if she had slept all week. For the thousandth time, she thought through her plan, wondered whether it could possibly work, and recounted the hours left to go. "I'm so glad Marian will be here," she whispered into the dawn.

After school on the previous afternoon, Annie had delivered a perfume-scented note inviting Pastor Mackenzie to visit at her house on Friday afternoon. She had slipped it under the door of the pastor's office at the church, then left quickly. She knew that Pastor Mackenzie always prepared for his Sunday morning sermon on Thursday afternoon, and unless it was an emergency, he took no appointments. Mrs. Tavington, an elderly woman who volunteered her work as the church secretary, was only there on Fridays, so no one else was in the church at the time to see Annie come or go.

It had been Annie's grandmother who inadvertently provided her with the opportunity to lure the pastor to her house. Whether the older Mrs. Harding had slipped a bit mentally, or whether she had simply lost interest in housework, her house seemed to be in constant disarray these days. For several weeks, therefore, despite the old woman's protests, Dinah Harding had dedicated Friday afternoons to cleaning her mother-in-law's house. And Garrit was to go over to his grandma's house directly from school.

Marian Anderson had given one condition to helping Annie, and it was the piece of the puzzle that worried Annie the most. "If anything goes wrong, if there's even the slightest hint that this isn't working . . . or if it looks dangerous to proceed," Marian had warned, "you either stop it . . . or I will. I will not, for any reason, let something bad happen to you, no matter how strongly you feel to the contrary. Agreed?" The problem in agreeing with Marian was the high risk that something *could* go wrong at any moment, and who knew how the pastor would respond. One wrong move, and the whole plan could collapse.

The sudden loud ringing of her father's alarm clock shook Annie out of her reverie, and she quietly returned to her bed. It would be another hour before her mother knocked on her bedroom door, waking her for school. Pulling the covers up around her neck, Annie tried to relax, hoping she might even drift off for a few minutes. But whenever she closed her eyes, all she seemed to see was the handsome, sickening face of Reverend Mackenzie.

When Annie was eating her breakfast later, her mother asked, "Annie, are you sure you can't come to Grandmother's after school? If we all pitch in, it wouldn't take the whole afternoon."

"No," Annie replied, a shot of adrenaline surging through her body. She was glad that her father had left for work already. "I promised I'd meet Marian Anderson this afternoon and help her with a project. If that falls through, I'll come. And next Friday shouldn't be a problem."

"It's not fair," Garrit grumped, pushing his scrambled eggs around his plate. "Why should I have to—?"

"Because I told you to," his mother broke in. "You come immediately after school, or you're in big trouble. Annie, are you okay?" she added. "You look really tired."

"I'm fine," Annie replied. "I didn't sleep well . . . haven't slept well lately. You know how it is."

Dinah Harding nodded but said nothing, and Annie was relieved that her mother said very little else before they left for school. She could only hope the rest of the day was so quiet.

School, as she anticipated, was nearly as unending as her sleepless night. The big clock behind Mrs. Olson's desk ticked and ticked and ticked but never seemed to move. By midmorning, Annie was nodding off to sleep at her desk. Over and over her head dipped, but try as she did, there was no way to keep her eyes open. After finally sinking into a refreshing nap, she opened her eyes and found herself looking up straight into the bewildered face of Henrietta Olson.

"Would you like a pillow?" Mrs. Olson asked, breaking into a smile as the rest of the class broke into laughter. "Should we wake you for lunch, or would you prefer to sleep right through? Maybe we could find a cot in the office?"

Sitting up straight, her face changing colors from a pale wintry white to a summery sunburn red, Annie shook her head and took a deep draft of air. "I'm sorry, Mrs. Olson. I slept poorly last night. It won't happen again."

"And you think you're the only one tired this morning?" her teacher asked, gazing into Annie's face. "Perhaps you could stay after school and redeem the last hour you've lost?"

"I promise it won't happen again, Mrs. Olson," Annie pled, hoping to find some latitude in her teacher's strict sense of fairness. "I have a commitment that—"

"Then take my words as a warning, Miss Harding," Mrs. Olson stated. "Your first commitment is to this class. Break that commitment again, and you'll be late for whatever else you have planned after school."

Annie had no problem keeping awake the rest of the school day.

✦✦✦✦✦✦✦✦✦✦✦

It was just after three o'clock in the afternoon when Annie quietly closed the front door to their house behind her and stopped to listen. The silence she was hoping for was the silence that greeted her. Quickly hanging up her coat, hat, and scarf, she hurried up the stairway to her bedroom, then peered from out her window at the empty street. She was anticipating that Marian Anderson would arrive at any minute, but there was no sign of her yet.

Annie crossed over to her dressing table and sat down in front of the mirror. She looked into her round brown eyes and hoped that Pastor Mackenzie would not see the same fear in them that she could see. Straightening several blond tendrils that had slipped out of her pins, Annie prayed again that God would give her success. She took no pleasure in any of this, especially knowing the potential it carried for damaging her own family. Nevertheless, Annie felt strongly that what she planned was the right thing to do.

She had talked with Marian about changing into her nicest dress and loosening her hair, but Marian had felt that both would be a mistake. Better to give the pastor exactly what he would be expecting, Marian had told her, and let him show his true colors on his own. If he was truly the type of person they thought he was, he would create his own downfall. For good measure, though, Annie did dab on a bit of the violet-scented toilet water she had received for Christmas.

A loud knock at the front door startled Annie, and she realized she should have been watching closer to make sure it was Marian and not the pastor arriving early. Annie hurried down the stairway, ran over to the living room window, and carefully peeked around at the front door. "Marian!" she exclaimed with a sigh of relief, rushing to open the door.

"I'm sorry I'm late," Marian apologized as she stepped into the front hallway and turned around to scan the street one last time before closing the door. "I shouldn't have stopped at the office. Walter had found some invoice errors and needed help sorting them out."

"We should be fine," Annie said, following Marian into the living room. "How do I look, Marian? Are you sure that this is good enough?"

Marian smiled. "You're a beautiful girl, Annie," she assured her, gazing at Annie's delicate shapely form in a simple white blouse and long cranberry skirt. "My guess is that he'll fall all over you. Whatever you do, you can't give him an excuse to say later that he was tempted or coerced into this."

"And what if he doesn't do anything?"

"Then we let him go," Marian reasoned. "But it's not going to happen that way. I know it's not."

"How?"

"Because he's gotten away with this for so long that he's no longer being cautious," said Marian. "He wouldn't have put his hand on yours in a public place if he was concerned about getting caught. And with all your neighbors watching, he'd never visit you or your mother in your own home unless he's already thrown caution to the wind. He either thinks he's invisible or he's lost control of himself, and I suspect he thinks you're an easy mark because you're younger."

Annie nodded and returned to the frosty living room window to look out, although she wasn't expecting the pastor for at least five more minutes. She crossed her arms, feeling chilled in spite of the furnace heat radiating up through the large metal grate in the floor.

"Nervous?" Marian asked, coming alongside her.

"Yes, very," Annie said, eyes focused on the street.

"Good."

"Good?" Annie asked, looking into Marian's face. "My teeth are starting to chatter. I'm afraid I'm going to fall to pieces."

"Of course you are," Marian stated reassuringly. "And that's exactly what he'll be expecting. He knows how vulnerable people are when they talk about their problems, especially for the first time. He likes that. If you're too smooth or too calm, he might notice."

"You're sure?"

"Absolutely," Marian replied. "Now, where am I going to be?"

"Right behind the dining room doorway," Annie said, pointing her finger and walking across the living room. "You should be able to hear everything from here."

Marian stepped into the dining room and looked around. "Good," she said. "Now, remember, the best thing you can do is to get him to talk. Once he feels he's in control, I think he'll move quickly. And remember I'm right here with you. If anything goes wrong, I step in."

Annie nodded, then stiffened at the sound of a quiet knock on the front door. "He's early!" she panicked. "What is he—"

"It's all right," Marian said, taking Annie's hands. "He just couldn't wait any longer. Nothing's changed. Take your time, Annie . . . and remember, I'm here."

Taking a deep breath, Annie turned slowly, wondering how she could have ever thought of trying to do this alone. Even with Marian Anderson a few feet away, she could barely shuffle her feet toward the front door. But they did move, even though she felt as if there were lead in her shoes.

As Annie approached the entryway, a louder knock rattled the front door, causing her to jump with fright. "Oh!" she gasped, shaking herself and forcing herself forward. Grasping the door handle, she felt her hand tremble and closed her eyes. "Dear God, help me," she whispered. Then she turned the large round brass knob and pulled open the door.

"Come in, Pastor." Annie managed a slight smile as he stepped quickly through the doorway into the relative darkness of the entryway. She closed the door behind them and immediately felt as if she were in a small cage without an opening. "May I take your coat?"

"Thank you, Annie," Reverend Mackenzie murmured as he slipped the long heavy coat from his shoulders and handed it to her. Then he stepped around the corner into the living room and disappeared from her view without saying a word.

Marian! Look out! Annie wanted to scream as she struggled to get the coat on a hanger and into the closet, but there was nothing she could do but hope. Hurrying around the corner, she was relieved to see that he had gone to the living room window rather than look into the dining room.

"This seems like a good place for us to talk," the pastor said gently, turning to Annie. "Your mother isn't home, correct? I know you were concerned that she not know we had talked."

"No, she and my brother are at my grandmother's," Annie replied. "They won't be home until after five."

"Very good," the pastor said with a smile. He walked back across the room toward Annie. "Why don't we sit down and get started. I believe you wanted to talk about your father."

Annie nodded and sat down on the davenport, then Pastor Mackenzie sat down next to her. Trying to move to her right, she bumped against the crushed velvet arm of the davenport and felt the room creeping in on her. The strong smell of his cologne surrounded her again, intensifying her feeling of claustrophobia. For a moment she struggled not to run from the room.

"Are you all right, Annie?" the pastor asked, watching her obvious discomfort. "If you'd rather not—"

"I'm all right," Annie said, taking a deep breath and forcing a smile. "I don't like talking with anyone about my father, but I know you have talked with my mother. She's told you the whole story, right?"

"I think she has," Pastor Mackenzie responded. "I'm sure it's nearly as difficult for you to face his anger as it is for your dear mother. Has he struck you at times—perhaps when he is drunk?"

"No, never," Annie said, glancing toward the dining room doorway. "But when he's home, which is not often, he treats us all very harshly. There are times when I don't think I can take any more, Pastor. I wish

I could just leave today and get away from it."

"Please—call me Alexander," the pastor said, patting her on her left arm. "I'm here to help you through this. What you've described sounds like what your mother has stated. But why don't you leave? Most girls your age would have been long gone by now. Married, perhaps."

"I want to finish school, for one thing," Annie answered. "And I do feel like my presence here helps protect my mother. Do you really think my leaving home is the best way to solve this problem?"

"No," he replied, shaking his head. "But I really don't believe that your father is going to change for the better, no matter what you do, so you shouldn't concern yourself too much about him. The real solution lies within you . . . not in your father."

"What do you mean?" Annie asked, swallowing hard and rubbing her hands together. "If you knew how much it hurts to have—"

"No, no, no," the pastor broke in, placing a large, smooth hand on top of hers. "What I'm saying is that the pain is truly inside you, and you alone know how much it hurts not to feel your father's love. But the solution lies also within your heart, and your father cannot stop that. It is possible . . . and I've seen it work in other lives . . . it's possible for you to know what it feels like to be loved unconditionally—whether your father loves you or not. Is that what you're looking for—to know that you're loved?"

Annie looked up into the pastor's dark eyes and read much more than the concern she thought she heard in his voice. She nodded and said, "I . . . um . . . that sounds too wonderful to be true. I suppose I would give anything to know that kind of love. But I've never heard it described as you have. How do I find it? Is that what my mother is looking for?"

"Yes, she has a deep hunger—"

"Has she found it yet?"

"No, not yet," he said, shaking his head, "but she's very close. She hasn't broken free from your father's controls yet, but she will . . . and soon. You seem stronger than she is, Annie . . . as if you've already broken away from him. You don't need to wait for this, and neither does your mother. This love can be yours—right here and right now. Are you willing?"

The pastor's warm hand still covered Annie's hands and was making her skin crawl. "I want to know what this love feels like, Alexander," Annie whispered, pleading with her eyes. "What do I do?"

His right hand moved from her hands to her back and settled on her shoulder, sending chills up and down her spine. Every muscle in her body tightened, and she could not restrain a shudder that left her trembling.

"You feel the love already, don't you, Annie. Go ahead and relax. This is to enjoy," Pastor Mackenzie urged her. "I've counseled many women who were looking—"

"Enough!" Marian Anderson called out loudly as she stepped out from behind the dining room doorway, causing the pastor to jump straight up off the davenport. She marched over toward him. "You filthy, rotten dog. How can you speak in God's name and not be struck down with lightning? How many women have you deceived with this sham you call love?"

"Listen here, woman! This is none of your business," the pastor demanded. He had risen to his feet and now towered over Marian Anderson. "I suggest you leave—immediately!"

Marian Anderson shook her head. "No, Pastor, I believe you're the one who's leaving. And not just this house. I'm suggesting that you leave *town*—immediately."

"I came over to counsel this young woman at her request," Pastor Mackenzie protested, pointing a finger at Annie. "She begged me to keep this totally confidential, and you have broken that trust. Perhaps I'll need to speak with Annie's father regarding the nature of my discussions with her mother and herself."

"No!" Annie gasped before Marian could intervene, and a smug smile crossed the pastor's face.

"You're playing with the wrong deck of cards, Mr. Mackenzie," Marian replied, unshaken. "I heard every shameful word you spoke to this seventeen-year-old girl. And unlike what you've managed to pull off in the past, you have no way to keep my mouth shut. I suggest that you don't doubt my sincerity."

"My, aren't you the fiery one, Mrs. Robert Anderson," the pastor said with a sneer. "I always wished that you and I—"

"One more word from you and I slap your face," Marian shot back, sticking her finger in his ribs, backing him up. "Two more words and my husband will teach you a lesson you'll regret for the rest of your life. You're a coward, Mr. Mackenzie. I know your type, and you're all the same. Robert, come on out!" she called, waving toward the dining room door.

Alexander Mackenzie spun around, and Annie saw the fear in his eyes as he focused on the open doorway. As the seconds ticked by and no one appeared, the pastor's red face went to crimson. The muscles in his jaw flexed, then he swallowed hard and turned to face Marian. "I can change, you know," he spoke softly. "If you give me—"

"That's not for me to decide, and you know it," Marian Anderson declared. "It's time for you to repent and confess your sin to almighty God, Mr. Mackenzie. I pray that He has mercy on your soul for the evil you have done to people in this town. But be assured that I will go to the elder board and repeat the indecent proposals you made to a young lady in my own hearing and what you have done to others who have gone before her."

"It'll be your word against mine," he countered, shrugging his shoulders.

"It will be *our* word against yours," Marian corrected him. "And when we speak, how many other women will stand up behind us? But if the church fails to act, rest assured that I will go door to door and tell every person who will listen to me what you've done. And if you appear at the front of the church next Sunday morning, you'll have to raise your voice to be heard above mine, and I assure you that my voice will be *loud*."

"And you're willing to risk the reactions of some of the husbands when their wives' stories are leaked out by an unnamed source?" Pastor Mackenzie asked, turning his gaze on Annie.

"Hiding in the darkness is always more damaging than coming to the light," said Marian, "even if it means risking the pain. If the truth of God prevails over your lies, what is the risk?"

"And maybe you should consider your own risk," Annie piped up, surprising both the pastor and Marian Anderson.

"What are you talking about?" he asked.

"Do you have any idea how angry someone like my father will be with you if these stories get out?" Annie questioned, her voice suddenly energized. "Yes, he will be angry with my mother, and that could be terrible . . . but when he comes looking for you, you'd better hope he doesn't have a gun. And even if he doesn't, he might use his hands."

Annie's brown eyes glared into the pastor's dark ones, but he quickly glanced away. Turning slowly, he walked from the living room and disappeared around the corner into the entryway. The last sounds they heard were the banging of a wooden hanger in the closet followed by the front door opening, then shutting.

Marian Anderson went to Annie and hugged her tightly, then she whispered, "It's over, Annie."

Chapter 26

In the Night

Annie Harding sat in the church pew next to her brother, Garrit, and glanced across the center aisle to the place where Marian and Robert Anderson were seated. For a woman on a mission, Marian Anderson seemed the picture of calm serenity.

Annie felt anything but serene. From the moment Pastor Mackenzie had closed the door of the Harding house on Friday afternoon, she had dreaded this Sunday morning. There was not a shadow of doubt in her mind that if the pastor attempted to open the morning worship service Marian Anderson would take action, even if it meant having to explain herself to the board of elders later. Annie's stomach had been turning in knots the entire morning, despite Marian's assurance that God would take this terrible situation and turn it into something good.

Looking back down the pew at her mother and father, Annie wondered what good could possibly come to them. She had only recently understood how far apart they had grown—how desperate her mother was to be loved, and how bad her father's drinking had become. Just the night before, he had come home shouting and swearing and had barely made it out of bed to get to church. It seemed so hard to believe that the two people she loved most in the world could have come to this point. But as dearly as she wanted to tell her mother what had happened on Friday afternoon, Annie had not whispered a word of it to anyone.

When the Hardings entered the sanctuary, Annie had noticed Arthur Simpson sitting alone toward the back of the church and thought it odd that Elsie Dale was not beside him. He had given Annie the strangest look when she walked past him, something in his eyes that she hadn't seen since the day she found him in Elsie's room. Looking back now, she realized he was staring at her. Annie turned around quickly.

The door to the choir loft clicked opened. Annie held her breath and squeezed her hands together, but it was only the men and women of the choir making their usual entrance. On most Sunday mornings the pastor preceded them, but occasionally he was delayed and did not come out until immediately before the service started. Taking her cue from the choir's entrance, the organist began to play the prelude music.

Everything looked like a typical Sunday morning, but Annie noticed that one of the men in the choir, Leonard Caldwell, who was also the head of the elder board, was watching the back of the church closely. She glanced to the back but did not see anything unusual except for Arthur, who nodded at her. But the longer the organist played, the more Leonard fidgeted, and the deeper his frown became. Finally he whispered something to the man next to him and quietly made his exit from the choir loft.

"What's going on?" Annie heard a woman behind her ask. Other muffled voices seemed to echo throughout the congregation, and it wasn't long before most of the members were gaping about, discreetly, of course. A few of the other elders and deacons exited the sanctuary. The pastor was seldom late, and he had never missed a Sunday morning service except when he was ill, but he was well past the point of being late this morning.

When the organist finally quit after having repeated the prelude music four or five times, the church began to buzz. Annie looked across the aisle again, and this time Marian Anderson was quietly talking with her husband. Marian looked over at Annie and nodded with a reassuring smile, but Annie was not prepared to start smiling yet. Whatever was going on, she didn't like what she was feeling.

Above the restrained din of the congregation, Annie felt her heart sink into her shoes at the sound of the door to the choir loft clicking open again. Tall and gaunt and somber-faced, Leonard Caldwell reentered alone, but instead of taking his choir seat he walked straight to the pulpit. The confused organist began to play the prelude again, but he held up his hand toward her to stop.

Absolute silence now swept the congregation, and every eye was riveted on the head elder. With a strained look on his face, he scanned the sanctuary, rubbing his forehead and looking very much like he wished he wasn't the poor soul who was the center of such rapt attention.

"I have a difficult announcement to make," he started, running his hands out on the corners of the wooden pulpit and leaning forward. "It appears that our service this morning will need to be canceled."

A wave of murmurs and the shaking of many heads in disbelief broke the speaker's concentration. He raised his hand for silence and waited, then he announced loudly, "For reasons we are unaware of at this time, Pastor Mackenzie seems to be absent from us this morning. It was reported that one of the neighbors noticed the back door of the parsonage was left wide open early this morning, but they didn't check on it later. A couple of men have gone to see if everything is all right. Richard, what did you find?"

This last question had been directed to the back of the sanctuary. Another round of mutterings and the swishing sound of garments against the wooden pews filled the sanctuary as the entire congregation swiveled to look back. Richard Lancaster stood behind the last row of pews with his heavy black winter coat still on and waited for the rumblings to die down.

As Annie turned to look back, she felt her mother's eyes upon her. She looked over, their eyes locked, and Annie was aware that her mother knew something. She held her breath and wiped her wet hands on her skirt.

"They're gone!" Richard Lancaster called out in a booming voice that seemed to shake the sanctuary. "No one's at the parsonage, and most of their belongings are gone. There were ..."

Richard Lancaster held up his hands for silence, but the gesture had no affect on the overwhelming buzz that drowned out his strong voice. It appeared that two hundred people were all trying to talk at the same time. Some were voices of shock; others seemed outraged.

"Annie!" Garrit called out, tugging on her dress and stretching up toward her ear. "I hope he's gone for good. I didn't like him, did you?"

She could only shake her head noncommittally and be glad that Garrit's small voice was easily swallowed up by the surrounding noise. But even with her father speaking something loudly to her mother,

Annie was aware that Dinah had noted the exchange. Despite that surveillance, Annie couldn't resist a glance across the aisle at Marian Anderson, whose calm demeanor told no story. Marian was listening closely to Robert Anderson and responding to his questions.

"Please, let him finish!" Leonard Caldwell cried out, banging the wooden pulpit with his fist as the noise level finally started to subside. "This is important."

Richard Lancaster took a deep breath and spoke loudly, "There were heavy wagon tracks in the driveway that led to the back door. It appears that in the middle of the night they loaded up what they wanted to take and just left. They didn't even bother to close the door after them."

The stunned congregation remained relatively quiet as Lancaster finally finished his announcement, then they turned slowly back toward the head elder, who remained stuck to the pulpit. His expression was nearly as dazed and confused as any of the church members.

"I don't know what to say, really," Leonard Caldwell spoke out, his hollow eyes seemingly to sink even deeper into his skull. "I'm sure there's an explanation for all of this, so I caution you against falling into idle rumors that are bound to follow. Before we close this service, though, is there anyone here who might know something about this? What I mean is factual information that you would be willing to state to the board of elders—not hearsay."

The few members who were still whispering suddenly stopped, and no one moved in the entire congregation. A heavy silence hovered over them, and Annie closed her eyes as her mind raced. Despite all the arguments that raged inside for her to remain silent, Annie desperately wanted to stand and declare the truth.

However, she didn't have to torment herself long, and neither did anyone else who might have felt constrained to speak out. Annie clutched her skirt as she heard Marian Anderson's voice.

"Mr. Caldwell," Marian said in an even tone, "it was my full intention to meet with you and the elder board at your next meeting, which I believe was scheduled for Monday night. Given what has happened this morning, I wish now that I had come to you directly on Saturday. I believe I have the information that explains the pastor's exit in the night. Would you like me to meet with the elders now before stating it to the congregation?"

"No," Mr. Caldwell replied quickly. "If you have something to say that will silence the rumors that I know are coming, please do. The board of elders will still want to meet with you, though, and report anything else to the membership that seems appropriate."

Along with every other member of the congregation, Annie focused upon Marian Anderson, who stood in her pew facing the head elder. Annie felt lightheaded and nauseous and began to shake involuntarily, dreading the moment when Marian would have to mention her name.

"What I have to say is straightforward and simple," Marian declared, looking back around the congregation. "Rumors have circulated for more than two years concerning our pastor's fidelity to his wife, and this past week I was involved in a situation where Pastor Mackenzie did indeed make a brazen, immoral approach."

Marian Anderson had to pause, even though it was evident that she wanted to continue. If someone had fired a cannon into the congregation, the shock couldn't have registered higher. Heads were shaking and mouths could not be held in check for the moment. It was as though, finally, someone in the church was brave enough to speak what others knew to be true, and the floodgates opened wide.

"I was deeply offended by our pastor, and I confronted him to his face about his specific sin," Marian continued. "When I spoke with him, he gave no indication of repentance. Indeed, he threatened that if I went to the elders, I would simply be pitting my word against his. I told him I was willing to take that risk, that without a question I would be going to the elder board, whether he repented or not. I also reminded him that, if I stood up, there might be others who would come forward to witness against him.

"While I feel it is inappropriate for me to repeat the specific nature of what I faced, I do believe it was lascivious, unclean behavior on his part. It was unbecoming of any Christian man, and certainly for a married man and one who has accepted the call to be a minister in God's church. And now I believe the evidence shows that the Mackenzies have run away rather than confront the truth."

Annie exhaled heavily and felt an incredible wave of relief rush through her as Marian finished and sat down. The assembled multitude seemed content to breath a collective sigh. As bad as the news was, there was an immediate sense that Marian's words were absolutely true and that at least a partial justice had already prevailed.

Eyes turned back to Leonard Caldwell, who was still staring at Marian Anderson. He nodded thoughtfully and finally said, "I . . . appreciate your honesty, Mrs. Anderson. I realize those words were difficult to say, and I'm sorry for whatever you've had to endure regarding this. We, the elder board, will meet with you immediately and try to bring this matter to a rapid close. We need to give the pastor an opportunity to clear his name, of course, but . . . I suspect we've heard the last of him.

"I want to close this service with an admonition that each of us leave this morning with our own prayers for Alexander and Martha Mackenzie, as well for anyone in our community who may have been hurt by what apparently has gone on here. And pray, too, for what we need to do about the future of our church. Please exit quietly, and please do pray."

Annie did not look at her mother or even at Marian Anderson but simply rose and headed for the back of the church. A number of people remained in their seats. Annie couldn't tell whether they were praying or simply too stunned to move; she was just glad they were leaving the aisle clear for her quick passage. The sooner she got away from the church, she suspected, the better she would feel.

As she descended the basement stairs to get her coat, Annie heard Arthur Simpson's baritone voice behind her, "What's your hurry, my dear?"

With a sick feeling in her stomach, Annie reluctantly turned to face her former sweetheart. She realized that the disgust she felt toward him was really the same disgust she had felt for the pastor. "What is it to you, Mr. Simpson?"

"Oh, I always liked those flashing brown eyes," the banker's son said, his thin mustache curling up as he smiled. "You truly are a beautiful woman, Miss Annie Harding."

Annie didn't answer, only turned and continued to the coatracks with Arthur following behind. She grabbed her long coat and slipped it on, but Simpson was next to her as she began to button it. She could feel his closeness, but she refused to look his way.

"I was . . ." Simpson whispered, "I was actually wondering if you and young Mr. Anderson were really as chummy as you looked the last time I saw you together. You see, I've been missing you, and I'd be interested in getting together if—"

"You did it, didn't you?" Annie snapped, glancing up at Arthur Simpson, then quieting down as other church members began to slowly filter into the basement for their coats.

"What's that?"

She stepped away from the coatracks, and Arthur Simpson followed her out into the middle of the basement floor where they could talk without being heard.

"You jilted Elsie, didn't you?" Annie asked.

"I . . . um . . . didn't think you were interested anymore, but I'm pleased to see that you are," Simpson replied, buttoning his expensive black dress coat and smiling toward some people passing by. "Miss Dale and I are no longer seeing each other, if that's what you mean. But it was never serious, nothing like you and I were. I just could never stop thinking about you, Annie, even when I kissed her."

Although she was fully aware of the other church members moving about in the basement, Annie's reaction was immediate and uncalculated. Swinging her arm up with more power than she would have dreamed she had, Annie slapped Arthur Simpson's cheek so hard he was rocked by the force. She had all she could do to restrain herself from following the slap with a furious kick, but Garrit's cry of "Annie!" from somewhere near the coatracks restrained her.

Without speaking another word or even looking at Arthur Simpson, Annie marched across the basement floor and ascended the stairway with hot tears pouring down her cheeks. Ducking her head, she pushed open the front door to the church and stomped down the concrete steps. Glancing down the street toward home, Annie hesitated. Then she turned and started down the sidewalk in the opposite direction—toward the wooden boardinghouse where Elsie Dale lived during the school year.

As her tears cooled in the cold wintry air, Annie quickened her pace across the crunchy snow-pack. With every step away from the church came a gnawing realization that slapping Arthur Simpson in a public place might not have been a good idea. Certainly it would not go without retribution. But there was no taking back her actions now, so Annie just shook her head and walked on.

Entering the boardinghouse for the first time since before Christmas, Annie climbed the stairs and walked down the long, dark hallway to Elsie's room. Lightly knocking at the door, Annie wiped away the remaining tears in her own eyes and resolved to save whatever energy and concern she had left for her friend.

Annie heard the shuffling of feet toward the door, then she heard a very soft "Who's there?"

"It's me, Annie. Open up, Elsie. Please."

The door lock rattled open, then the handle turned and the door opened slightly. Elsie's hazel eyes were bloodshot, and her lovely auburn hair was spilling out in every direction. "Annie, I can't see anyone. I'm not feeling well, and I haven't even dressed yet."

"I talked with Arthur, Elsie," Annie replied. "Please let me in. I want to talk."

The door swung open and Annie stepped into the room. Elsie was clothed in her heavy bathrobe and thick wool socks. The room was cold, although the big metal steam heater under the window was sputtering out a fine mist. An opened brown whiskey bottle sat on her kitchen counter, evidence that Simpson had recently been in the room.

"You warned me, Annie. And . . . I knew you were right, and I knew this was coming," Elsie said, her usually vibrant face now deadpan as Annie sat down on one of the room's few chairs that was not covered with clothes or other belongings. "I appreciate you stopping by, but I really don't want to talk about this. Did you leave church early on my account?"

Annie shook her head. "No. That's another bad story, and one I'd like to not talk about, either. But I had to come over. I've missed your friendship, Elsie, and I'm here to see if we can't get back what's been lost."

Elsie walked to the window and looked out through the frosty glass. The clouds had finally parted, and the bright morning sunshine poured into the room to surround Elsie in a warming envelope of light. Her full lips curved slowly into a sad smile. "I'd like that, Annie . . . I really would. But . . . this is so ugly. I'm ugly. Uglier than ugly. What I've done, how I've treated you—it's beyond that, Annie. Give me some time to recover from this. Maybe someday...."

"How about today?" Annie pressed. "I'll give you five minutes if you need it, but that seems like a waste of time. Elsie, I know what happened to you, and ... I know why you did what you did. I felt so foolish to have been so charmed and deceived by Arthur Simpson. I looked into his face this morning, and I hated the day I let him kiss me. I hated that I had ever considered living my life as his wife, that I let his money and his gifts blind me to what he really is. But I did those things, Elsie; I can't change that. And he'll always have that against—"

"But you didn't cut off your best friend to do it," Elsie said.

"I didn't have to," Annie answered. "You weren't in the way."

Elsie turned slowly, a sad silhouette in the bright sunshine. "You mean ... you might have ... if I—"

Annie walked over and placed her hands on her friend's shoulders. "Oh yes, Elsie, I could have done that. I look back at the lies I believed about that man, and ... it frightens me."

Elsie finally raised her eyes and met Annie's. "Did Arthur get ... intimate with you?" she asked.

"No," Annie said, suddenly fearing for her friend. "He tried, and he wanted to, but I made him stop. He thought that pearl ring would give him license to do whatever he wanted. Did he try that on you?"

Elsie grimaced and nodded, then went to the counter and grabbed the whiskey bottle. Taking it to the sink, she tipped it over and poured the remnants down the drain. "Yes, he did, and he nearly won," she spoke softly. "He got me to drink some of this stuff, then he made his move. I was so woozy I could hardly think ... let alone fight him off."

"What happened? He didn't—"

"No, he didn't, but he would have if I hadn't remembered how you got him out of this room," Elsie said, smiling shyly. "I couldn't see straight, but I knew I could scream ... and we both know the only thing he seems to fear is damage to his reputation. I went crazy on him, and he left in a hurry. I knew he'd never come back. He'd had as much fun as he was going to get, and that was all he cared about."

"Oh, Elsie, I'm so sorry for you," Annie said. "You didn't deserve it—warning or no warning. That man toyed with both of us."

Elsie nodded and turned her face away, then her shoulders began to shake. Annie jumped up from her chair and put her arms around her friend as the sobs began.

She would not arrive home until late in the afternoon, but when she did, it would be with a friend whose absence had been felt for far too long.

Part 4

Spring Stirrings

Finally exhausted, the long winter sputters its last desperate snowbursts, then retreats with a grumble before the certain approach of Easter. Snow crystals tucked deep in the crevices of countless hills melt and join their brethren with a joyous rush into the lowlands. Soon tiny creeks are roaring like mighty rivers.

Flatwillow Creek, impatient with the confinement of its banks, protests with an exuberant splashing and swirling beneath its bridges, and young boys brave their parents' stern disapproval to follow the tumultuous waters downstream. But parents, too, feel the exhilaration of the rushing creek and hear the promise in the water's roar.

When Flatwillow Creek sings its spring song, who can stay away?

Chapter 27

Spring Is in the Air

Standing alongside Stuart Anderson's parents on the wooden platform at the train depot, Annie squinted her eyes as she gazed down the shiny silver railroad tracks. Dressed in her favorite long white dress, she relished the warm spring sunshine and the strong afternoon breeze as it did its best to renew her winter-dulled sensibilities. The southerly breeze reminded Annie of the one that had blown in their faces the night of the New Year's Eve dance, the night that Stuart had kissed her in the darkness and told her he loved her.

Now it was almost Easter, and she hoped that his arrival on this fine day might entail something on an equal par with that evening. She also longed for the chance to talk to him face-to-face about all that had occurred in the months since he had last been home—although she was not yet sure how much she wanted to tell him about what she and his mother had done to stop Alexander Mackenzie.

The rumors about the pastor's sudden departure were only now beginning to die down, although nearly two months had passed. Only a few facts had been actually confirmed. The pastor had evidently paid a handsome sum of money to a freight hauler to take one large wagonload of household possessions from the parsonage to the train depot in the middle of the night. The freight hauler was not a church member and had not inquired about the reasons for the night move. Pastor Mackenzie and his wife had then purchased tickets to Chicago and had been the only passengers who left on the southbound train early Sunday morning.

No one seemed to know where the missing pastor had gone from there. The church's denominational office had not been able to locate him, and no letter or word had come from him with any explanation for what had occurred. A report that the Mackenzies had been seen by a family member in Kansas City remained mere speculation. It was nearly universally believed that Alexander and Martha Mackenzie had headed west to start a new life in a place where no one knew him for the reprobate he was.

As for Marian Anderson, after her bold announcement in church that Sunday and her meeting with the elders, she had said little more about the situation. She had, however, become something of a heroine to women in the church. It was rumored that several married women had come to Marian for help, having been caught in the pastor's web of darkness, although Marian never spoke a word of such confidences.

And now, with the welcome arrival of the robins and the familiar sound of Canada geese chasing Old Man Winter northward, the church's focus had begun to switch from what caused their pastor's mysterious disappearance to the task of finding a replacement for him. For several Sundays, church elders led prayer services, a retired preacher from a nearby community traveled to Bradford a few times, and of course a search committee had begun their work. But Easter was fast approaching, and progress was slow. This was a second reason Annie Harding was waiting at the depot with the Andersons.

"Can you believe how beautiful that crabapple tree is?" Robert Anderson was saying. The small tree across the railroad tracks had dared an early bloom, and its shimmering pink-and-white blossoms sent a delicious aroma wafting toward the group on the platform. "I'll bet your dad will want to cut a few branches for the house," Robert added to Marian.

"Annie, I just know you'll love my parents," Marian Anderson said, shielding her eyes with her hand and staring down the still-empty tracks. The board of elders had asked Stuart's grandfather to come and preach at both the Good Friday service as well as on Easter morning. "I hope you get to spend some time with them while they're here."

"I almost feel like I know them already," Annie replied. "Stuart has told me a lot about them in his letters."

Marian shook her head and smiled at Annie. "He writes you every week since he went back to school, and he hasn't managed to write me once in two years," she said. "Can't you speak with him about that?"

"He says it's like father, like son," Annie replied with a laugh, then glanced back down the tracks at the sound of the train whistle echoing down the valley.

"There's probably some truth in that," Marian added. "Robert, do you remember all those letters you wrote me when you took that logging job up north the winter before we married?"

"I sure do," he replied, getting a bit red in the face, then pointing down the tracks as the first locomotive emerged from the woods puffing its black smoke. "Here she comes."

"I was thinking that Annie might like to read some of those letters," Marian teased. "They were so romantic that I saved them in a special box."

"I've saved Stuart's as well!" Annie exclaimed. "He must be like his father—very romantic."

"Ah . . ." Robert complained, stepping forward away from the women and waving off their laughter. The train rolled closer, and another long shrill whistle pierced the perfect spring air. He pushed a small luggage cart to the edge of the wooden platform and waited.

Annie watched the big steam locomotive as it slowed its approach to the depot, belching out a continuous stream of dark smoke. She thought of Stuart's many letters—sometimes two a week—and felt a quiver of delight at the constant love they expressed. And she thought of how close she had grown to Stuart's parents, especially Marian. In a sense, Marian had become almost more of a mother to her than her own mother. Her door was always open for a visit, and Annie had found many reasons to stop by after school.

As the locomotive rolled past them, Annie could see Stuart waving from the steps of one of the passenger cars. She and Marian waved back, and as the train shivered to a halt, Stuart jumped down from the steps and quickly helped his father pull his grandparents' leather suitcases from the car and load them on the cart. Then he turned and ran for Annie, scooping her up into his strong arms and spinning her around and around.

"Stop!" Annie cried, holding on for dear life while breaking into laughter. "Everyone's watching, you wild man."

Stuart laughed and set her down again on the platform, his black eyes focused only on hers. "And they love it," he whispered, "like I love you." Then he pulled her tightly into his embrace and kissed her long and fervently.

"That's quite enough!" Elwood Gray called out, banging his simple wooden cane down on the depot platform as he walked toward them with his wife on his arm. "You're making my old heart pump too fast."

"Oh, go right ahead!" Geneva cried as she shook his arm playfully. "You can't hurt his heart," she told the others. "It's barely ticking most of the time anyway."

The four older adults laughed, and Marian Anderson reached over and tapped Stuart on the shoulder as he pulled away from Annie with a huge grin. "Hello! This is your mother speaking," she said. "Is this the way you always introduce people to your grandparents?"

Stuart laughed and shook his head, then he said, "Annie's not just anybody, Mama. And neither are you." He pulled his mother to him in a big bear hug, then kissed her on the cheek before turning to his grandparents.

"Grandma and Grandpa," he announced with a smile and a little bow, "I'd like to introduce you to the lovely Miss Annie Harding, of whom I have spoken on occasion." Turning to Annie, he bowed again. "Miss Harding, these are my grandparents, Elwood and Geneva Gray."

"On occasion!" Geneva Gray snorted, her gold-rimmed glasses glinting in the bright spring sunshine. "Annie Harding, you are all my grandson has talked about for three full months. We're very pleased to meet you."

"The pleasure is mine," Annie replied, shaking Stuart's grandparents' hands. "I was just telling Marian . . . Stuart has written me so much about you that I feel I know you already."

"Did he tell you that Elwood is famous for walking around the house in his long underwear?" Geneva teased, watching Annie's eyebrows rise, then breaking into great laughter.

They all laughed together, and Robert Anderson rolled the cart past and said, "I think we better get home before we create a public disturbance. If we get any crazier out here, kissing and talking about underwear, a certain famous preacher just might not be preaching tomorrow night after all."

"How about if Annie and I walk home?" Stuart asked as they headed for the horse and carriage. "We've got some catching up to do."

"Dinner's at five sharp," Marian said.

"And if I'm a second late?" asked Stuart.

"You miss out on a mighty fine meal," his mother replied. "The rules haven't changed, buddy boy."

"I didn't think so," Stuart said. "We'll see you all later, and I won't be late."

Annie and Stuart walked straight across the street as Robert Anderson loaded the luggage onto the back of the carriage. Holding out his arm for Annie to take, Stuart led her down a side street and headed toward his father's mill.

"Where are we going?" Annie asked, looking up at the green buds on the elm trees that were just breaking open into leaves.

"Where do you think?" Stuart replied. "Where's the only place around here where we've ever been able to meet alone?"

"The old west bridge," she spoke softly. "Not much to look at, but it is our place, wouldn't you say?"

They walked on, slowing their pace and chatting small talk as they went, mostly about Stuart's grandmother and how excited she got about the chance to ride the trains. Passing the mill, Stuart surveyed the building but showed no interest in stopping. When they came to where the iron bridge had been, they stood at the top for a while, watching the usually clear and placid creek as it rolled and roared and foamed several feet above its summertime level.

"So they're going to start building the new bridge this spring?" Stuart asked as they climbed down the embankment and found a big limestone slab near the edge of the swirling water.

"That's what they say," Annie replied, trying to get comfortable by resting her back against Stuart's arm. "I hope they build the next one a bit stronger."

"I'm sure they will," said Stuart. "No one was even dreaming about the weight of traction engines when they built the first one. They probably should have replaced that bridge a few years ago."

"They don't have any choice now," Annie said. "People are getting really tired of having to drive all the way around to the other bridge."

Stuart nodded and stared absently at the stream. "You forget how relaxing it is to sit by a stream," he said finally, breathing in deeply. "There's something about the pace of living in the city. It just never stops. There's always something going on, someone stopping by, something to get done right away. I really get sick of it. I can't tell you how good it feels to be here."

"Yes, you can," Annie replied, leaning against him and looking into his dark eyes. "I'm not going anywhere, and I can tell you it feels mighty good to have you here." Then she kissed him—first on the cheek softly, then on the lips slowly, enjoying the closeness after being apart for so many months.

"Whew!" Stuart said, breaking into a grin. "Now I remember why I came back here after all. That was good. Don't get me started, though."

"Why's that?"

"You know, and I know, and we both know it's no good to throw more wood on the fire," Stuart replied.

"There's plenty of water right here," Annie teased, glancing across the stream. "I could always toss you in. With the snow melt, it would cool you off in a hurry."

Stuart laughed and shook his head. "It might work, but I doubt it," he said, walking around a little to work off some steam. "So," he said while he walked, "tell me the real story about the pastor leaving town."

"Didn't I write about—"

"You wrote, but you didn't tell me what truly happened," Stuart said. "And my mother wrote me about it, and guess what? She's hiding something, too. She played her cards a little better, but I got the feeling you both really want to tell somebody about this."

"She did tell you, didn't she?"

"She didn't really tell me anything, but her letter gave me the impression that she would if I pressed it." He sat back down beside her and met her eyes. "One thing you need to know about me, Annie, is that I really hate secrets. I know that my mother wasn't alone on this thing. The pastor would never have dared to approach her. Something else got her involved."

Annie looked away and rubbed her forehead, and any trace of a smile was erased. "Stuart," she spoke softly, "some secrets are better left buried and dead. I haven't told anyone what I know, and it's better that way."

"It was your mother, wasn't it?" Stuart asked as Annie flinched at his words. "Annie, please trust me. Our secrets will be real secrets. But I can't stand being in the dark."

"What makes you think it was my mother and not yours?"

"Anyone who got away with what he did for as long as he did was very careful about whom he chose," said Stuart. "He had to find women who he knew were susceptible and whom he could silence once he had them. He could have never gotten that far with my mother."

"And he could have with my mother?"

Stuart shrugged. "I'm not meaning to accuse your mother of anything. But I am very aware of some of the struggles she's had with your father. She's a lonely woman, and I think she'd be a target for a man like him. And she's certainly lovely enough to get his attention."

"You sound like a detective."

"Am I right?"

Annie nodded and pressed her lips together. "She came so close to falling into his trap," she said. "I don't think she even realizes just how close she came. And you're right, the pastor never came after your mother. But she did help me spring a trap on him. He seemed to think that if my mother was vulnerable, I would be as well. He was wrong . . . but I could never have done it without your mother."

Stuart bristled and sat up straight. "Mackenzie came after you?"

"On a run," Annie replied with a shudder. "But I went to him first, knowing he couldn't resist. What he never expected was for your mother to be listening to every filthy word he said. I had foolishly thought I could trap the pastor without anyone's help, and fortunately she intervened. When my knees started to buckle, she stood and was fearless."

"And then she told the story in such a way that people thought he had approached her?"

Annie nodded. "But every word she said was true, and there was really no reason that anyone needed to know any more about it, unless the pastor had stayed and tried to defend himself. Then it could have gotten ugly. But it didn't. Your mother spared me . . . and my family . . . from a lot of grief and sorrow. She's an amazing woman. I've come to love her a great deal."

"From her letters, I would say that she feels the same about you," Stuart said. "Which . . . makes me glad."

"And why is that, Mr. Anderson?" she asked, leaning her head against his shoulder.

Stuart sat quietly for a minute, then he said, "It . . . um . . . makes me glad to see the two women I love the most in the world becoming friends. That's nice, don't you think?"

"I prefer it over being enemies, that's for certain," Annie joked, then grew quiet. "I feel very fortunate, Stuart, both to be your mother's friend and to be loved by you. Your love means more to me than anything in the world."

"Oh my!" Stuart gasped, putting his arm around Annie and holding her tight. "I still can't believe that any of this has happened to me. One man's terrible misfortune leads to another's treasure. How do you figure that?"

"I really don't try," Annie said, shaking her head. "If I tried to make sense of everything I see, I'd be in a sanitarium by now. You have to face life the way it is, not the way you hope it will be or think it should be."

"Tell me how things are with your father," said Stuart. "Has he changed his mind about making you move out when you graduate?"

"No. If anything, things are worse with him," Annie spoke softly. "He's still drinking, and I wish I were wrong, but he doesn't seem to want to have anything to do with any of us. I'm sure I'll have to move out."

"Well, then, I think I know the answer to this, but . . . Do you have any idea what your father thinks of me?" Stuart asked.

Annie shrugged. "He never says anything about it, never asks me about you. Maybe he . . . thinks that if he keeps the pressure on about my having to leave, I'll still get back together with his old friend Arthur Simpson. Who knows? Father and I haven't talked in a long time."

"So what do you suggest I do?"

"What do you mean?"

"I need to talk with your father," Stuart replied. "But if he's not talking with you, what chance is there he'll talk with me?"

"You're planning on talking to my father?" Annie asked, pulling back from Stuart's embrace. "About what?"

Stuart chuckled and reached down to take Annie's hand. "I thought . . . after I had first asked you, that I would need to ask him for permission to marry you. I know this is going to sound crazy, and maybe it is crazy, but I can't wait any longer to find out. Will you marry me, Annie?"

Annie's eyes had widened as Stuart spoke, then they filled with tears. "Oh, my goodness, Stuart!" she exclaimed as the tears poured out and trickled down both cheeks, then she buried her face into his shoulder. "I would marry you today if we could. Don't you know that?"

Stuart closed his eyes and tears of joy ran down his own face. "But what if the best thing is to wait until I'm trained as a doctor," he muttered, swallowing hard. "Would you wait for me, Annie? Please say yes."

"Yes, I will," Annie whispered into his ear. "I will marry you, Stuart Anderson, if it takes a lifetime. But I'd prefer tomorrow."

"I have no ring," Stuart said, kissing Annie on the cheek. "And I don't know how I'll ever approach your father."

"It doesn't matter," said Annie as his finger lightly touched her lips. "Everything else has worked out for us so far. There's no reason to doubt now."

Stuart nodded and said, "I love you, Annie Harding. Nothing will ever come between us."

That said, Annie's delicate red lips rose to meet Stuart's with a strength and desire that could have warmed the snow-fed waters of Flatwillow Creek.

Chapter 28

The Angels Rejoice

*A*nnie paused at the bottom of the wooden stairway and listened to the complete silence of the house. She had slept in late, even for a Saturday morning, having been out with Stuart until well past midnight the night before. They had attended the Good Friday church service and then stayed at Stuart's house talking with his parents and grandparents until Marian Anderson had finally declared it was time for everyone to go to bed.

The layer of dust on the steps of the stairway and the lint rolls at the sides of the hallway reminded Annie of the housecleaning chores she needed to do before she would be allowed to spend the rest of the day with Stuart. But they also caused her to wonder where her mother was. Usually Dinah was busy cleaning and cooking by this hour on Saturday, and the relative quiet of the house told her that something was different.

Stopping in the living room, Annie found the windows wide open and a wonderfully crisp spring breeze pushing the white curtains back and driving out the stale remnants of winter. She drank in a deep draft of the refreshing air, full of earthy smells, clean and dry. The songs of a pair of robins and a cardinal from somewhere in the front yard drew her to one of the living room windows. She gazed out into the clear morning sunshine but did not see her mother.

Annie walked through the dining room and into the kitchen, but it was empty as well. There were no messy mixing bowls full of flour and sugar on the counters, no bread dough rising slowly in metal tins, and the oven was not heating. Everything was neat and tidy, and even the dirty dishes had been washed and put away. The back door had been left open, and Annie could see that the screen door was unlocked.

Stepping to the kitchen sink and looking out the window toward Garrit's tree house in the huge backyard maple tree, Annie was surprised to see her mother sitting alone at their roughhewn picnic table. Her back was toward Annie, and the playful wind tugged at her hair and dress and teased the pages of the book she was reading. Annie's forehead drew up in a baffled crease. It was rare to see her mother with a book, and rarer still to see her reading at the picnic table when there were chores to be done.

Annie watched her mother for a while, wondering what could be so captivating as to break her mother's rigid Saturday morning baking ritual. Then she wondered if it might be connected to her father's sudden departure from last night's church service. He had disappeared in the middle of Elwood Gray's extraordinary sermon on the crucifixion of Christ. Annie had not seen him leave, but Stuart's grandfather had said he looked like a man who was standing too close to a fire and couldn't take any more heat.

Finally deciding to see what was on her mother's mind, Annie opened the screen door and let it slap behind her as she passed through it. Dinah Harding turned and smiled, her brown eyes squinting against the sunlight. For a moment her mother's smile and the way she was sitting at the table reminded Annie of years past, of the tea parties they had had when Annie was a little girl, and of far happier times in her mother's life. She silently prayed that better days might lie ahead.

"I thought you were going to sleep the whole day away," Dinah teased. "You didn't exactly rush home after church last night."

"No," Annie replied, shaking her head. "Was Father—" She broke off, surprised to see that the book her mother was reading was the old family Bible. She sat down at the table across from her and said, "We went to Stuart's house and talked until about twelve-thirty. It was a lot of fun, but I couldn't wake up this morning. It's going to be late again tonight, I'm sure."

"I can't tell you how happy I am for you, Annie," her mother said quietly. "You're in love with Stuart, aren't you?"

Annie took a deep breath and nodded. "But how did you know?"

Dinah Harding laughed and pushed back some of the long stray hairs that were blowing across her face. "I'd have to be blind not to notice, Annie," she replied. "Every time you get a letter, you light up like a Christmas tree. And now that he's home, I've never seen you so happy. Has he told you that he loves you?"

"Many times, Mother," Annie said, smiling as her mother took her hand. "The first time was . . . the evening when Stuart and I were walking to the New Year's Eve dance," Annie answered. "Do you remember how beautiful it was? It had to be the most romantic night I've ever seen. We stopped beneath a tall elm tree in the bright moonlight. Then he declared his love for me . . . and kissed me in a way that I didn't think possible."

"And you never bothered to tell me?" her mother asked, lightly rubbing Annie's hand. "You didn't think it would be important to me?"

Annie shook her head and said, "I . . . guess I thought the less said about Stuart around here the better. I know that Father is still hoping I'll go back to Arthur Simpson. And I know you like Stuart, but . . ."

Dinah Harding snorted. "Arthur Simpson!" She shook her head and swallowed hard. "Annie, it was wrong of me ever to encourage you toward Arthur, especially when it was so obvious that you didn't love him. I guess I hoped that if you could marry into a wealthy family you could avoid some of the hard things I've experienced. That was foolishness. Arthur Simpson would have made you the most unhappy person in the world. I pity whomever he finds to marry him."

"Elsie was fortunate to escape when she did," Annie said. "Arthur only knows how to use people for what he wants at the moment. Once he's done with them, he crumples them up and tosses them away like a scrap of paper."

"He and Alexander Mackenzie were cut from the same material," her mother said, glancing away from Annie's face and staring toward the distant hills. "My father used to warn me about men like them. 'Look out for those dirty dogs,' he'd say. Annie, I am still so ashamed by what happened, by what I did . . . and that you were affected by it."

Annie glanced down at the Bible and said, "Is that what this is about? I couldn't believe you weren't busy in the kitchen when I came down this morning."

Her mother smirked, then smiled and replied, "I've . . . been spending a lot of time reading the Scriptures since the pastor left. After last night's sermon, I finally began to put some pieces together. I don't think I've ever heard anyone speak as clearly as Stuart's grandfather. For the first time I began to hope that it really was true—that I could be forgiven for this sin of mine that seems to haunt me most of my waking hours. I'm looking forward to hearing him again on Easter morning."

Closing her eyes, Annie swallowed hard and squeezed her mother's hand. "There is hope in God, Mother, but there is no hope apart from Him," she whispered. "I know that absolutely. I've seen it working in my life. Mother, Jesus can never ever fail us. But we have to come to Him."

"Seems like He's doing a fair amount of the coming himself," her mother replied, glancing down at the page. "I've read and reread the crucifixion scene in each of the Gospels this morning. He really didn't leave anything undone, did He?"

Annie shook her head slowly. "I nearly started shaking last night when Mr. Gray shouted out, 'It is finished!' I felt totally free from all the sin and condemnation and guilt that I've ever known. Totally free, because He took it from me."

"I'm still working on that part," Dinah Harding said, pressing her lips together. "All of my life I've thought I knew what it meant to believe. It's quite a shock to discover you knew nothing at all."

"What about Father?" Annie asked. "Did you talk with him after the service?"

"No," her mother said. "Something that Stuart's grandfather said really set him off during the service. Did you see him leave?"

"No, but I noticed he was gone long before the sermon was over."

"Gone, and I doubt he'll come with us tomorrow morning," Dinah Harding said. "Your father's not one to admit he has a need. He ends up trying to drink it away."

"Did he go out drinking last night?"

Annie's mother nodded. "I can't help him, Annie. Not now, at least. I know I've failed him, too, but until I put my own life together, there's nothing left inside me for him. I'm not sure that I'm willing to forgive him yet, and I know that's a problem. Jesus said—I just read it." Quickly she flipped back a few pages in the Bible. "Here it is. 'If ye forgive not men their trespasses, neither will your Father forgive your trespasses.' I don't know that I have it in me to forgive your father."

"I know," Annie spoke softly, swallowing hard again. "But, Mother, God knows how hard it is. He understands completely. He watched His only Son die at the hands of murderers! But He did it, Mother. He extended His forgiveness to them . . . and to us, who would have done the same thing. His forgiveness transforms our forgiveness."

Dinah Harding smiled. "You're quite the preacher yourself, aren't you, Annie?" Then she sobered. "Oh, Annie, pray that I can believe that—what you said about forgiveness. And please, stay close to me. I don't want anything to drive us apart again."

"Oh, Mother, I don't want that, either." Annie stood up, walked around the table, and locked her mother in a fierce embrace while the thin Bible pages fluttered in the wind.

"Well, now," Dinah said when they finally pulled apart. "Is there more to your story about Stuart that you haven't told me?"

Annie nodded and whispered, "There's much to tell, if you don't mind that the housecleaning won't get done."

"There's nothing inside that can't wait," her mother replied. "And I want to know everything, so don't rush it. I've got a lot of catching up to do."

◆◆◆◆◆◆◆◆◆◆◆

Stuart Anderson glanced toward the back of the sanctuary, where the ushers had already begun setting up wooden folding chairs, and muttered to himself in wonder. It had been several years since the church had been packed for any Sunday morning service, but his grandfather's Good Friday sermon had quickly become the talk of the community, bringing people out for this Easter morning service whom Stuart had never seen in church. Annie and Stuart watched the last front pews fill up, then noted the concerned expression of the ushers as they redirected the flow of people to the chairs temporarily set up in the back.

"We prayed for your mother this morning," Stuart whispered to Annie, noting that Dinah Harding was sitting with Garrit toward the back of the church. Annie's father was not with them.

"So did I," Annie said, leaning against his shoulder and speaking softly. "I think she's ready to respond, although she got very quiet around the house this morning when my father refused to come."

"It's too bad he left when he did on Friday night," said Stuart. "Maybe he would have gotten some help if he had stayed."

"Maybe my mother's the one who needs the help right now," Annie responded. "Without Father here, at least she doesn't need to be concerned about what he's thinking. She's so looking forward to your grandfather's sermon. Does he always preach like he did the other night?"

"Well, that was a high point," Stuart answered, glancing to the front of the church as Elwood Gray quietly made his entrance through the choir loft and sat down next to the pulpit. "But he's always good." Stuart loved to watch his grandfather's quiet confidence as he approached a congregation. There was no pretension or pride, just a complete sense of assurance that the words he would speak were true to God's Word and would change lives if he faithfully delivered them.

By the time Elwood Gray began to preach, all the folding chairs had been taken, and a number of people were standing in the back. One of the ushers propped open one of the large front doors to the church, letting in a gentle flow of fresh air to help keep the packed sanctuary from overheating. Although Stuart tried to concentrate on the sermon, his attention seemed to keep drifting to pray for Annie's mother. It seemed to him, as his grandfather moved deeper into his message, that every word was chosen for Dinah Harding.

"The apostle Peter said that 'he that believeth on Christ shall not be confounded,'" Elwood Gray was saying. "Peter tells us that we will never be disappointed nor ashamed if we put our faith in Jesus Christ. All that Christ has promised to be, He will be to those who trust Him. If Christ is the promised Savior, He will surely save. Believers shall never be forced to confess that they made a mistake in trusting Him. The most childlike confidence in Christ Jesus is nothing more than He deserves. It is always the highest wisdom to place everything in His hands and leave it there for time and eternity. To risk all with Jesus is to end all risk. Faith is as safe as the throne of the Eternal."

Elwood Gray paused and took a drink of water from a glass that was set behind the front ledge of the pulpit. His dark, piercing eyes scanned the congregation, and he took a deep breath. "That does not mean, however, that there are no special enemies that will try to damage our faith. There are times when a person's sins rise up before him like exceeding great armies. It is relatively easy to believe in Jesus when you are not conscious of any great sin, but true faith is not confounded even when it groans under a grievous sense of sin.

"Have you ever had times in which all the ghosts of your dead and buried sins rise again and come marching upon you, armed in their weaponry? How can you respond? 'He that believeth on Him shall not be confounded.' Though the whole horde of his sins march by, the believer cries, 'They are all gone into the tomb where Jesus was laid, and the blood of Jesus has cleansed me. There is not one of them left. My sins sank like lead in the mighty waters, for God has cast them all into the depths of the sea.' "

Stuart glanced back and could see that Dinah Harding's complete attention was fixed on Elwood Gray. Garrit's white head was leaned against her arm, fast asleep, but it appeared to Stuart that there were no adults suffering with the same drowsiness.

"There will come other troubles besides this," his grandfather continued, "yet in these also, Christians shall not be confounded. Believers shall be tried when the natural desires of the flesh break loose into vehement lustings, and corruptions will seek to cast them down. There will come personal losses, business trials, and domestic bereavements. What then? As sure as the Word of God is true, the Lord shall sustain the believer under every tribulation. And He will sustain even to the end, when death will come to us. Loved ones will wipe the cold sweat from our brows, and we shall gasp for breath, but even then we shall not be confounded, for our last breath will echo the precious name of Jesus."

Stuart marveled at the sense of authority that seemed to accompany the words of his grandfather. He had never sensed the presence of the Lord in a church service quite like he did this morning. Annie had taken his hand and was squeezing it tightly, as if she could wring out some extra truth from the message they were hearing.

Elwood Gray said, "We read the four Gospels with delight and perceive the exceeding beauties of Christ's matchless character. There was no fault in our Beloved, and we worship Him alone. He is a lamb without blemish and without spot. He completely fulfills the just requirements of the law and presents to God a perfect righteousness on our behalf."

At that point Stuart's grandfather paused and let a long silence wash over the sanctuary, an occasional cough and shuffling of feet only accenting the hush. Then Elwood continued in a quiet voice that seemed to echo in the silence, "This morning is our opportunity to accompany our Lord to the Garden of Gethsemane. There every drop of blood pleads with us that we should trust Him. There His sighs and cries and throes of anguish all plead with us that we should rely upon Him. Regarding Him as the Son of the Highest, we see an overwhelming argument for faith, for who can doubt the merit of that work that begins with the holy Son lying prostrated in Gethsemane, exceedingly sorrowful, even unto death.

"But do we trust Him, brethren?"

Stuart's grandfather closed his eyes and shook his head for a moment, then he went on. "Come with me now and see Him seized by His captors and delivered to the high priest, to Herod, and to Pilate. How they pour contempt upon Him! How the smiters scourge Him! How His enemies mock Him! His lowest shame, His worst desertion, His bitterest griefs, His dying pangs all say to us, 'Cannot you trust Him?' Then with tears in our eyes we stand at the cross of Calvary and see those blessed hands and feet nailed to the tree that He might be made a curse for us. Can unbelief live after this? Surely it must die!

"O Son of God," the elderly preacher cried, "You have triumphed over our unbelief upon the bloody tree! Now You lead our captivity captive, and we bow before You, fully assured that You are mighty to save. We feel constrained to cry, 'I must believe. Those nails have crucified my unbelief. That spear has slain my doubts.'"

Even before Elwood Gray had reached the end of his sermon, Stuart could see and hear the effect of the powerful words throughout the congregation. Several church members had leaned forward in prayer and covered their faces with their hands, and some were in tears. In the sudden silence of the moment, the apparent conviction of sin seemed to intensify, and a few people began to sob.

"Trust Jesus Christ to save you!" Elwood Gray called out above the growing din. "Sink or swim, throw yourself into the sea of Jesus' love. You shall see the glory of God in your pardon, in your new creation, in your being sustained under temptation, in your being lifted up at the day of judgment to receive an acquittal and being pronounced faultless before His presence with exceeding great joy. I have known myself as defiled and corrupt, but I see the day coming when I shall be wearing a crown, bowing before the eternal throne, unblemished. My soul leaps at the very thought that I shall tread the streets of gold and see Jesus' face and bow before him—I, who was once filled with sin and temptation, filled to the brim with the vision of God. You and I will meet in that place, and what a wonder it will be that we should have ever gotten there. Trust in Jesus now."

Stuart glanced back as his grandfather ended his sermon and saw that Dinah Harding was one of those whose tears had given way to sobs. "Annie," he whispered, "I think your mother needs you."

"Dear Jesus," Annie spoke softly as she turned around and instantly stood up at the sight of her mother broken in remorse. Tears of concern and pain poured forth as she made her way to her mother's side, and tears of joy would triumph before the service was ended, for today was a marvelous day for the angels to rejoice.

Chapter 29

One Rotten Apple Left

Annie held the crumpled note in her hand and stopped at the street corner to stare up at Arthur Simpson's second-story office window. She had not been inside the bank since her argument with Simpson and his father over their treatment of the Sorenson family, and she had hoped to never go inside the bank doors again. Slowly unfolding the note for the fifth time since her brother had delivered it to her, Annie read it one last time: *Have some distressing news from your friend Pastor Mackenzie. Please stop by my office today and put my concerns to rest.*

No matter how strong the sense of dread that filled her, Annie knew she had to face Arthur Simpson and find out what he had discovered. If Simpson had somehow uncovered the truth of the pastor's departure, the question was not whether he would use the information against them but *how* he would use it. She had no reason to hope he would spare her.

Despite the knots in her stomach, Annie pressed forward. She had considered talking with Marian Anderson or even asking the older woman to come to the bank with her. But then she had decided first to find what they were up against. With Marian present, Arthur Simpson might never tell her the truth of what he knew or what he wanted.

Crossing the dusty street, Annie pushed open the bank's large glass door and stepped inside. The gleaming white marble floors and the distinctive smell of the building evoked queasy memories of her previous visit. Walking quickly to the freshly painted wooden stairway, Annie ascended the stairs and stopped to knock gently at Arthur Simpson's door.

"Come in," Simpson's deep baritone voice called out from inside the office.

Annie took a deep breath, turned the doorknob, and stepped into the familiar plush office. Although she had seen Arthur regularly at church, her heart lurched at the sight of him sitting in his leather chair behind his large walnut desk. This was definitely his world, one that he could control and manipulate, and his power in this room was very real.

Simpson glanced up with a practiced smile and set the piece of paper he was reading back down on the desk. Getting to his feet and quickly rounding the corner of his desk, he reached to take her hand. "Annie, so good of you to come so quickly." Instead of releasing her hand, he covered it with his other hand and held it while he continued. "I thought you might take a day or two to get up your nerve to see me. So many unfortunate things that didn't work in our past. Please," he gestured, "have a seat."

Annie did not smile, but she did sit down in one of the tall chairs that faced Arthur's desk. "Your note said that you have distressing news concerning the pastor," she began. "Is there some reason why you would contact me? I hardly knew the man."

"Hardly knew the man . . ." Simpson replied, raising his eyebrow and nodding his head. Then he chuckled. "That's not the way I understood it, Annie. But it's been so long since we've talked, let's not rush into that. I'd like to know how you've been. I hear rumors about you and Stuart Anderson these days."

"I asked you why you had Garrit bring me the note," Annie spoke firmly. "I'm not here to talk about anything else."

"Very well," Arthur said, lifting the paper back up and handing it to Annie. "I thought you'd want to see this for yourself. The pastor seemed to think of you on a more intimate level than you're indicating here."

"What are you talking about?" Annie asked, taking the paper and fearing the worst. She recognized the heavily slanted handwriting; she had seen it many times on notes from church and Sunday school certificates.

Arthur Simpson leaned back in his leather chair and kept talking as Annie read. "Quite a list of names the reverend has written there, wouldn't you say? You and your mother are down toward the bottom of his list. Your mother is an attractive woman. I can see why he would take interest in her. But that you and Stuart's mother would set the poor fellow up like that. Hmmm ... that's very clever. I would have never thought you had it in you. In fact, I become more impressed with you every day."

Annie's face remained expressionless as she finished the brief letter, then she reached forward and set it back on top of the desk. "How did you get this?" she asked, staring hard into Simpson's deep blue eyes. "No one knows where the pastor and his wife went."

"He came to me via the mail," Arthur replied. "If you're going to leave town, the middle of the night is a poor time of day to withdraw any personal savings or records you might have in the vault. And the good reverend had a fair amount tucked away here."

"So you blackmailed him into telling you the women he'd been involved with and why he left town?"

"Well, that's a little harsh, don't you think?" Simpson asked. "I simply wrote him back and told him that without better identification, I couldn't release the funds in his savings account. Now, who else could provide the exact details found in that letter? It resolved all my questions about the validity of the source. I was simply doing my best to uphold the integrity of my father's bank."

Annie finally smiled. "Those are probably the most truthful words I'll ever hear you say. The ethics of your conduct here and the integrity of this bank are probably on an equal plane, as you say."

"So we have a bit of a temper, do we?" Arthur commented, running his finger across the edge of his desk. "That's something new and interesting since we broke up. I like it."

"I couldn't care less what you like, Mr. Simpson," said Annie. "Can we finish this so I can go and be sick somewhere else?"

"Finish?" he asked. "You were expecting more?"

"You're wasting your valuable time."

"Oh, I see," Arthur said. "You're wondering what I plan to do with the information I've received from our mutual friend, the good Pastor Mackenzie. Perhaps you were thinking I was going to send the letter to Stuart Anderson's grandfather and ask him to pray for these unfortunate women who fell under the pastor's charm?"

"No, that would have been the last thing I'd expect of you."

"So what did you expect?"

Annie took a deep breath and studied Simpson's handsome face. "My guess is that you'll tuck it away in your safe and use it only when you're in trouble of some kind," she said. "You have enough names there to string this out several years, I'm sure."

"We think alike," Simpson replied, his expression brightening. "That will come in handy, I'm sure, when we work together in the future, don't you agree?"

"No, we don't think alike," Annie replied. "But I know enough about you to know what you're thinking. And I have no plans to ever work with you."

"Which is why I asked you to stop by today," Arthur said. "You do realize, of course, how easy it would be for me simply to drop a rumor about your mother's involvement with the pastor. Funny how fast a story can spread through a small town, isn't it? This would never work in Chicago."

"A rumor's just a rumor."

"Until it becomes a fact," Arthur continued. "I'll bet that more than one of your neighbors saw the pastor come and go from your house. It won't take much fuel to get a nice hot fire going, will it? If that doesn't work, I'll toss out another—"

"And what will it take to keep you quiet?"

"Just two things," said Arthur. "I've heard that your father was upset with you when you broke off our relationship. I heard he's kicking you out of the house when you graduate, and you'll be on your own. Is that true?"

"That's true."

"Well, I want you to come work for me as soon as school is over," he said. "I need an assistant who can handle some of the secretarial and detail work for me, and I can't think of anyone I'd rather share the office with. What do you have left of school? A week?"

Annie nodded.

"Good, good!" Arthur exclaimed. "How about you start working on the following Monday? I'll have an office all set up for you."

Not answering his question, Annie asked, "What's the other thing you want from me?"

Arthur leaned forward in his chair, placing his elbows on the desk. "This one is not so easy, I know," he said quietly. "But I want you to agree not to see Stuart Anderson again. I want him out of your life. I should never have given you up so easily."

"You think you can have me back?"

"Certainly."

"And if I refuse to do either?"

"The rumors will fly, most assuredly," Simpson replied. "I don't think your father will be in the best of spirits if that should happen. How unfortunate that your mother might have to raise young Garrit without a father."

"And if I choose to let that happen?"

Simpson shrugged his shoulders and said, "Then we both lose, I guess."

"And if I blow the whistle on what you're doing?" Annie asked.

"No one will believe a word you say, and you know that," Arthur replied, picking the piece of paper up again. "Without this, you have no case against me. The rumors will accomplish exactly what I intend, believe me."

"Why are you doing this?" Annie asked, showing some emotion for the first time with a shake of her head.

"Why not?" Arthur replied. "I made a mistake with Elsie, and I'm sorry for that. I want to start over."

"You call this starting over?"

"I'm only asking you to come work here and to get rid of Stuart."

"Is that all?" Annie mocked. "And if I did that and you still don't get what you want, what will you ask next? Why not just get it over with and tell me that I have to marry you?"

"Because I want you to choose that," Arthur said. "And I believe that you will if I give you time."

Annie stared into Simpson's face in disbelief, then she said, "You've had your way for so long you think whatever you touch is yours. If you're looking for love, Arthur, you'll never find it this way. You need to know that I love Stuart Anderson with all my heart, and I have every intention of marrying him. I could never love you."

"You could try."

"And you think Stuart will just walk away from this?" Annie asked.

"You're afraid of him, aren't you? There was something about Stuart Anderson that you couldn't beat, and it frightened you. What will you do when he knocks your door down?"

"I'll show him your name on the pastor's list."

"I've already told him the whole story. He knows the truth, and his mother can verify every word of it."

Arthur opened a desk drawer and pulled out some more papers. He smiled again and said, "You might be surprised at the number of difficulties that can come up over a loan. That fire that Robert Anderson had a few years ago really set him back here at the bank. That was before my father bought the bank, and it was a loan that shouldn't have been made. That drugstore just isn't paying out enough."

"And you would call the loan due?"

"Not if everyone cooperates and does what they're told."

"With you holding all the cards."

"Looks like a full house to me," Arthur replied. "But I'd rather you did't force me to play them. I'd hate to see either your family or Stuart's family suffer over something the two of us can handle together. What do you say?"

"I think I should go have a chat with your father."

Arthur shrugged and held up his hands. "Be my guest. But of course it's your word against mine, and I don't think he's forgotten how you felt he handled the Sorenson deal. He doesn't care much for women who criticize him."

"Does he love your mother?" Annie asked. "I've heard he drove her to drink, but I never see her."

Arthur's smile was replaced by a solemn frown. "You never see my mother because she was accustomed to good society and hasn't adjusted to narrow-minded small-town people. And she does drink, sometimes too much. But she's home by herself most of the time, so I don't see that it harms anyone. From what I hear, the question is whether your father loves your mother. Does he?"

"I can't speak for him," Annie replied coldly. "I know he loved us once upon a time and that the love of money has done something terrible to him. He's been drinking, too. Based on what I see and feel, I would say he's abandoned the love he had for us."

"Maybe he'll straighten up if Elwood Gray comes back again and leads another revival in the church," Arthur said with a smirk.

"I really hope so," Annie said. "My mother's life was changed by it."

"We'll see how changed it is when the rumors start flying and your father dumps her and your brother out on the street," Arthur said. "How can you believe that hocus-pocus?"

"You saw the power of God change so many lives that morning and you still make fun of it?" Annie asked. "I'm warning you, Arthur, don't cast contempt on God's mercy. He can bring you down so low ... so fast ... that you won't know which train ran over you."

Simpson laughed out loud and shook his fist defiantly. "You have no idea what I've done and gotten away with. If God is real, He's had all kinds of opportunities to get me in the past. He must either be a bad shot or else very ignorant of what's going on."

"Or very patient."

"I couldn't care less," Arthur stated. "What I want from you is an answer. How would you like me to deal with this letter, Annie?"

"Right now?"

"Yes."

"I can't answer that."

"I think you can ... and better," Simpson said. "One of my cashiers downstairs tells her mother every crazy story she hears. That woman has a lot of friends who love to chatter."

"I can't answer you now," Annie replied. "Give me a week."

"Now."

"If you believe this will last for a lifetime, Arthur, what's the rush?" Annie asked. "One week. I'll be done with school then and able to answer."

"All right, I'll give you a week," Arthur conceded. "But if I haven't heard by four o'clock next Friday afternoon, I start talking. Fair enough?"

Annie stood up and walked out of Arthur Simpson's office without turning around.

◆ ◆ ◆ ◆ ◆ ◆ ◆ ◆ ◆ ◆ ◆

Marian Anderson sat staring out her kitchen window as the late afternoon light began to slip away. She was still holding Annie's hand after a long and very difficult story had been unfolded. Annie had been relatively composed when she arrived and started to tell Marian about her encounter with Arthur Simpson, but the more she told, the more she fell apart.

"What can we do, Marian?" were the last words the young woman had asked before she collapsed into sobs. Now that Annie's tears had been dried, Marian searched for an answer.

"I don't know that there's much we can do but pray very hard," Marian finally said softly.

"Arthur has us, doesn't he?"

Marian nodded solemnly. "It looks and feels that way. He could hurt your mother beyond imagination, and that could push your father over the edge. And if he starts rumors about your involvement, even though they're absolutely false, they could follow you the rest of your life."

"He'll do it, too. There's nothing inside him to stop it."

"I know."

"What about your bank loans?"

Taking a deep breath, Marian Anderson said, "What he said was true. With what we lost in the fire, Martin Dozier shouldn't have given us a loan. But he liked Robert. I wish Martin had never sold out to Arthur's father."

"So the bank could take your business?"

"It might cause some uproar around town," Marian replied, "but on paper I'm sure they could make a financial case for such a strange move. Or they could twist and bake the numbers however they want. If a banker's dishonest, you don't have much chance. The fact is, we're slowly paying that loan back."

"Marian, I'm so sorry that I've—"

"Don't speak such nonsense," Marian said. "There's one rotten apple left in the barrel, and we have to get him out."

"How, though?"

"First, we pray . . . and keep praying," answered Marian. "And second, we refuse to let Arthur Simpson bring us down to his level. No matter what it costs us, we have to take our stand with God and absolutely refuse to compromise what we know is true. You have a week before you are going to answer him with a resounding no. God would never ask you to sacrifice yourself for such a vile man."

"But he—"

"Mr. Simpson reminds me of Haman in the book of Esther," Marian continued. "Do you remember him?"

"The wicked man who hated the Jews and coerced the Persian king into signing their death warrant," Annie answered quickly. "The story of Esther has become one of my favorites."

"Mine as well," said Marian. "And it reminds us that God can turn the whole situation upside down."

"But that was a long time—"

"Not so long ago," Marian countered. "And that's what we have to believe. He can do it again. Why not?"

Annie smiled for the first time since she had arrived. "If we just had some damaging information on him, maybe we could—"

"That's it!" Marian exclaimed. "Or maybe that's part of it."

"What's it?"

Marian withdrew her hand from Annie's and closed her eyes to pray. Annie had seen the same look on her face once before when they were praying for Annie's mother on the Saturday night before the Easter service. Marian did not speak but squeezed her eyes tightly and then covered her face with her hands. Annie closed her eyes as well and began to pray.

The two women had not prayed long when Annie opened her eyes and saw that Marian Anderson was staring out the kitchen window again with a different look in her eyes.

"That didn't take long, did it?" Marian whispered. "Annie, I think I know what I'm going to do."

Chapter 30

Cook the Goose

"Guess we're a little early," Robert Anderson said, glancing at his pocket watch as he sat down next to Annie on a wooden seat outside the railroad stop. "Hope you don't mind."

"No, I've been so worried about this that I couldn't stand to wait around the house any longer," Annie replied. She reached down and straightened the pleats of her pale yellow dress. "I've got one more day left before I have to talk to Arthur Simpson. If Marian didn't uncover something on her trip, I just don't know what I'll do. I truly wish I had the faith she does, but I don't. Not yet, at least."

Robert laughed and said, "Most of us don't. But if it's any comfort, Marian wasn't always like this. Seems like it was some of the hard times we've experienced that made the difference for her. When we went through the fire at the drugstore—I think that's what really did it. She determined that with God's help, we could survive the loss. And she was right."

"Until Arthur came and—"

"Arthur nothing," a familiar voice broke in from over Annie's shoulder.

"Stuart!" Annie cried, jumping up and turning to nearly leap into his arms. "What are you doing home?"

Stuart and Annie embraced tightly, then he kissed her so long and hard that someone inside the small railroad office began to tap on the window.

"Whew!" Stuart exclaimed as he let Annie go and the two of them sat down next to Stuart's father. "That was enough right there to make the trip worthwhile."

"Why didn't you tell me you were coming?" Annie asked.

"That would kind of ruin the surprise, wouldn't it?" Stuart responded with a bright smile. "It's your graduation tomorrow night, right?"

"Yes."

"I couldn't miss that," Stuart said. "Besides, I got a telegram from some strange woman in Chicago that said I needed to be here today."

"Marian," Annie said. "She told you what Arthur has done?"

"No, but Dad filled me in after I got here," Stuart replied, his dark eyes showing some smoldering fires. "It's lucky for Arthur that my mother is coming home today, because I'm ready to make this a day he'll never forget."

"I'd like to have a few moments face-to-face with him as well," Robert Anderson added. "College boxer or not, I'm afraid I might hurt him real bad. Someone needs to teach that boy a lesson."

The distant sound of a train whistle from the south pulled Robert up from the wooden seat. He walked to the edge of the platform and stared down the long ribbon of steel tracks that seemed to shimmer in the bright afternoon sunshine. "She's early," he called to the young couple, who were already being distracted with another kiss that lasted nearly until the train pulled into the station.

A light breeze from the wrong direction grabbed the black smoke from the two powerful steam engines and rolled it in billowing clouds toward Annie and Stuart, causing them to cover their faces. As it passed by them, the long train shuddered to a halt and the roar of the engines dropped. Robert Anderson had already spotted his wife and was waiting to take her hand as she stepped down from the train sporting a stylish new hat.

Robert and Marian Anderson kissed and embraced, but not quite with the same intensity that the younger couple had demonstrated. Then Marian said something to Robert, who turned and grabbed a railroad baggage cart and headed down to the car that held the luggage. Marian waved for Stuart to come as well.

"Help your father!" Marian called out above the low rumbling of the idling engines.

Stuart ran down the line of cars and joined his father as they waited for someone to open the doors to the baggage car. Marian walked over to Annie and gave her a warm hug.

"Well, I did it!" Marian exclaimed. "How do you like my toque with the satin bow?"

"It's grand," Annie responded with an admiring smile. "You look like a Gibson girl!"

Marian shook her head and said, "I'm too old for that. But I'm not too old to start a new business. Look!"

Annie turned toward where Marian was pointing and saw Stuart and Robert stacking what looked like a dozen round hat boxes onto the baggage cart, along with what appeared to be bolts of fabric and ribbon.

"You're going to do it!" Annie said. "You and Mrs. Sorenson."

"Yes," Marian proclaimed. "My sister in Chicago has the most elegant hat shop I've ever seen. She says that if we do quality work and keep up with the styles, she can sell as many hats as we can provide."

"And Mrs. Sorenson will make the hats?"

"She was a milliner in Brooklyn before she married and the two of them moved here to Minnesota to try farming," Marian said. "I can take care of the bookkeeping and help her with the basics, but she'll do the real skilled work. And if this goes well, she'll be a lot better off than the cooking job she's got at the hotel."

"You're wonderful!" Annie cried, giving Marian another hug. "But did you find out anything about the Simpsons? Looks like you spent most of your time on the hat business."

"Yes, indeed I did," Marian replied. "It only took me a day and a half to track down what I hoped I might find about young Arthur. Just as I thought, he's been a very bad boy. I knew that the Simpsons didn't move here just to enjoy the quiet of a small town. Remember what I said?"

"Where there's smoke, there's fire?" Annie repeated.

"What we have is quite a blaze," Marian said, sitting down on the wooden seat and opening her large carpet bag. She reached in and pulled out what appeared to be an old yellow newspaper with *Chicago Daily News* printed in bold letters across the top.

Annie stopped at Arthur Simpson's door and listened for voices inside. Stuart waited calmly behind her and nodded to her as she reached out to knock on the dark wooden door. The bank was so quiet that her raps rang out and seemed to echo down the hallway.

"Yes," Arthur called out. "Come in."

Opening the door quickly, Annie stood in the doorway and smiled at Arthur. "Today's the day, right?"

"Why, yes, it is," Arthur said. "You had me worried. I thought you weren't going to show."

"Whyever would you think that?" Annie said, shaking her head and leaning against the doorframe. "Don't tell me you don't trust me. I thought you and I were . . . friends again."

"There's nothing that would make me happier," Simpson replied. "But after what you pulled on the pastor, I've been a little nervous about this. Please come in. That hallway has ears."

"It really does," said Annie, glancing back at Stuart and smiling. Then she turned back to Simpson and said, "I hope it's no problem, but Stuart Anderson just happened to surprise me and came home for my graduation. I asked him to come along for our chat. Do you mind?"

Simpson's slick smile gave way to an angry glare as Stuart stepped into the doorway behind Annie. "He stays outside," Simpson ordered. "This is between you and me, Annie."

"I don't think so," Stuart said. He followed Annie into the office and stopped to gaze around at the room's expensive decor. "My, oh my. Your daddy set you up with all these fine trimmings?"

"The building belongs to my father, as well as all the office furniture." He stood up from his leather chair as if to challenge Stuart. "Now, please leave before I—"

"Call your daddy and let him bail you out of a jam?" Stuart suggested. "Maybe you should try to grow up for five minutes and handle things by yourself for once. Actually, I think you'd better sit down—now. I've been in a very bad mood since I got home yesterday, and there's something about your face that brings out my bad side. Would you like me to expand on that?"

"No, not here," Simpson muttered, sitting back down. "Maybe we can meet later."

"That would give me great pleasure," said Stuart. "But I don't think it's going to happen. Anybody as yellow-bellied as you are would never show up. So let's just see how our little talk goes here."

"Fine," Arthur snapped, his face flushed and tense. He tugged at the tight collar of his white shirt and stretched his neck. "So, Annie, what's your answer?"

Annie simply stared at Arthur Simpson and then smiled. "You are truly a handsome man, Arthur," she finally said. "There was a time when I thought I was the luckiest girl in Minnesota to be with you. Are you still going to build that big stone house out past the old Sorenson farm?"

"Probably," Simpson said with a half smile. "What does that have to do with our arrangement here?"

"How about that fine pearl ring that I returned to you?" Annie continued. "Does that come with the deal as well?"

"I . . . um . . . didn't get it back from Elsie," Simpson sputtered. "What does—"

"Could you get it back?" Annie pressed. "I'm not going to come cheap, you know."

"I could try, but it's been so long that—"

"You have to do better than this," Annie said. "You see, I truly love Stuart, and I need to know just how far you'll go to get me back. How about making me a vice-president when you take over the bank? I think I've got a lot to offer here, but I want to make sure you'll cooperate."

"Wait a minute," Arthur ordered. "You're the ones who better—"

"How about we make a counter offer?" Stuart said. "We think we can put something on the table that's even better than what you offered."

"I only have one offer," Simpson snapped, "and that stands as I gave it."

"What if I offer myself to you for seven years of service," Stuart said, "and in exchange for that I get Annie. You must remember the story of Jacob and Rachel. I want to do the same. Seven years of free labor is a very good deal for you."

"Get out of here," Simpson barked. "That's so stupid that I can't believe it."

"But it's very romantic," Annie added. "All you did was offer me a job as your secretary. You'll have to admit that's not very enticing."

"All right, stop the games," Simpson demanded. "You've had your fun with me. Now, tell me your answer. And by the way, I've decided to add Stuart's mother's name to the pastor's list. She'll be second on the list to have some charming rumors circulate. What's her name?"

"Marian Anderson," Stuart said. "M-a-r-i-a-n. And she seems to really dislike you, Arthur. You played the wrong card when you let her get into the game. She is one—"

"What are you talking about?" asked Simpson.

"After you told me your terms for keeping your mouth shut," Annie said, "I went to Marian and told her the whole story. She got very upset with you, just as she did when I told her what Pastor Mackenzie was doing. You see, Arthur, Marian may be a quiet woman, but she's somebody you don't want to have mad at you. And Marian is mad, Arthur. Oh, she got angry."

"So what?" Arthur said. "If I take action on their loan, she won't be able to do a thing about it."

"That's true," Stuart piped in, nodding at Simpson. "You can twist your numbers around and put my parents out of business tomorrow, and it'll stand up in a court of law. But you see, my mother got so upset that she decided to visit your old stomping grounds and see what it was that caused your family to leave Chicago in the first place. It didn't take much digging to discover your legacy."

"You were a naughty boy," Annie added, leaning forward. "A very naughty boy who got his daddy into some very hot water."

"Hot enough to cook his goose," Stuart added. "I'll bet the old man was really mad at you. And now you're pulling the same stunt again. How do you think he's going to like that?"

"You're bluffing," Simpson retorted. "We moved here because of my mother's health. She was suffering from—"

"Stop the violins!" Stuart cried. "I could just cry all over the office for you. Mommy's health, was it? I thought the newspaper said something about a banker's son who was convicted as a minor of blackmailing certain of his father's customers."

"That's a lie and you know it," Arthur protested. "You're not going to turn the tables on me!"

"Oh, is that a fact?" Stuart said. "Isn't your father's office the one next to us here?"

"Yes, but—"

"Time to see what Daddy's up to these days," Stuart said, leaning toward the wall and banging on it with his fist. Then he called out loudly, "Father, I need your help!"

Even with the wall between the offices, they could easily hear the sound of a heavy chair being pushed back and the tromp of heavy feet across the floor. The sound of a door slamming in the hallway was followed by a loud knock on Arthur's door.

"Come in, Father," Stuart called out before Arthur could react.

"What in the world is going on in here?" Wendall Simpson growled as he pushed the door open and stepped into his son's office. "This is a place of business, not a fun house."

"Oh, we're working really hard with Arthur on a deal," Annie said. "Your son tried to blackmail us, Mr. Simpson. Can you believe that?"

"No, I can't," the tall man spoke firmly. "My son would never do that. I think you'd better leave now or face charges of slander."

"Why don't you ask Arthur what he's been up to?" Stuart asked, looking at the banker's son.

"They're lying, Father," Arthur said. "Anderson is jealous because Annie has fallen in love with me again and he's out of her life."

Annie and Stuart looked at each other and then burst out laughing, angering the elder Simpson even more.

"I want you out of here immediately, or I'll have one of my book-keepers go for the sheriff," Wendall Simpson commanded. "You're not going to disrupt our business with your—"

"Bring the sheriff in?" Stuart rubbed his chin. "I like that idea. I'm sure he'd be interested in the little piece of news my mother stumbled on in Chicago. I suspect that you must be suffering from a severe loss of memory, Mr. Simpson."

"What are talking about?" the banker asked.

"Oh, surely you remember this?" Annie asked, pulling the yellow newspaper from her bag. "Your name is spelled W-e-n-d-a-l-l, right? I just want to make sure we have the facts straight. One would never want to make a false accusation if one could help it."

As Annie held up the newspaper, Arthur's face blanched. "Where did you get that?" he hissed. "You can't blackmail me. I'm the one who—"

"You're the one who got caught with his fingers in the piggy bank, so to speak," Stuart stated. "Last night I sat and thought about what you had done. Made me wonder what the folks in this community would think about having a crook in such a vital position in their bank. Funny that you never thought to inform your bank customers regarding this serious matter, Mr. Simpson. You actually trust this bum after what he pulled on you?"

"That's none of your business," Wendall replied. "I can—"

"But your dandy son made it our business when he tried to blackmail us," Stuart said. "I suggest you listen very closely to the new terms of this deal. And if you can't bother to listen, I'll have the sheriff here so fast your head will spin. We've got two witnesses and a prior conviction. That should interest the law."

"I'll pay you to bury this story," Arthur pleaded, reaching into one of the drawers of his desk. He pulled out what looked like a small metal money box. "If you want, I'll—"

"You're not getting off that easy this time," Stuart broke in. "This isn't about hush money. It's about you coming clean. I want you to start by apologizing to Annie."

"But I didn't mean—"

"Apologize!" Wendall Simpson barked, breathing heavily. "Now."

Arthur looked away from his father's glaring eyes to Annie's stoic gaze. "I . . . um . . . I'm sorry for what I've done," he said.

"What exactly did you do?" his father asked.

"I tried to force Annie to leave Stuart and come back to me," Arthur muttered. "I . . . used Stuart's father's loan to try to leverage the deal."

"You idiot!" the banker roared. "You drove us out of one city already. This time . . . I'm not bailing you out."

"I also want you to let Annie's father out of whatever terms you set regarding the loan you suckered him into," Stuart continued.

"You worked a deal behind my back?" his father asked, shaking his head.

"It was my own money—"

"Such an arrangement violates the integrity of this bank, and you know it! I told you to never work a deal on the side!" Wendall Simpson demanded, banging his big fist down on the walnut table. "You're going to let him have that money. It's dirty."

"But I need—"

"Not a word more!" his father ordered. "I don't care how much money it was. Miss Harding here better not ever come to my office and tell me her father ever heard another word about what he owed. You write it off. Do you understand?"

Arthur Simpson blew out a big breath of air. "Yes, sir."

"We have one more thing to discuss," Annie said. "But I think it might be more appropriate if you tell Arthur, Mr. Simpson."

"I'm not leaving town, if that's what you mean," Arthur stated, sitting up in his chair. "You can't expect that—"

"You're leaving just as soon as you can pack your bags," Wendall Simpson interrupted his son. "And you'll tell your mother exactly why."

"Where will I go?" Arthur pleaded.

"Wherever you want to go. I really don't care," his father said, his anger subsiding into a determined resignation. "But you'll never work in my bank again, and you'll never live where I live. Your mother and I have mollycoddled you enough. Now it's time for you to face life on your own. Pack your belongings and vacate this office."

"But I—"

"You have fifteen minutes," the banker said quietly, "before I call someone to put a new lock on this door. Whatever's not out of here by then will stay with me."

"If you'll excuse us," Stuart said as he and Annie stood to leave.

"Miss Harding." Wendall Simpson held out his hand. "I am very sorry for what my son has put you through. If there's anything that I can or should do, please let me know."

"Thank you. I will," Annie said. Then, as she returned his handshake, she surprised him by asking, "Do you remember Andrew Sorenson's wife?"

"Yes," the banker responded, not meeting her eyes. "I remember we talked about her. I guess I didn't handle that very well."

"No, I suppose you didn't," Annie said. "I wonder if now you might be able to help the Sorensons find some better housing. Perhaps a personal gift from an anonymous source?"

Wendall Simpson pressed his lips together and nodded. "I think that's a very good idea. And I do apologize for the attitude I brought to our previous discussion. For some reason, my son here seems to bring out the worst in me. Please forgive me."

"I do forgive you," Annie replied before turning to the banker's son. "And good-bye, Arthur. You have a chance to start over and do things right. I suggest you recount your steps and see where you're headed."

Chapter 31

For a Lifetime

"Annie, something's wrong with Father!" Garrit exclaimed as he poked his blond head into her bedroom.

"Father's home?" Annie asked. She handed the box she had just finished packing to Stuart, then crossed her arms. "He said he wouldn't be here to help me move."

"I know," said Garrit. "But he's acting real strange, like somebody died or something. He and Mother are talking at the kitchen table, but ... well, I think you better go see."

"I don't live here anymore, Garrit," Annie said, reaching down and picking up an armful of dresses that were still on their hangers. "It's really not my business."

"I think it is," Garrit countered. "I heard them talking about you. Please, Annie. You have to at least try."

"Stuart, come with me," Annie said as she moved toward the bedroom door. "I don't want to face Father alone again if he's upset."

"I don't think he's mad," Garrit said. He stepped back into the hallway so Annie and Stuart could get by him. "He had a piece of paper in his hand that he was showing Mother."

"Oh no!" Annie gasped, clutching her dresses tightly as she stopped on the stairway and glanced back at Stuart. "What if—"

"No chance," Stuart broke in before she could say more. "Simpson wouldn't dare go against his father."

"Who wouldn't?" asked Garrit, who was following close behind Stuart.

"None of your business," Annie said. "Garrit, please go to your room or outside. It's better that you not hear what we're going to talk about."

"I promise—"

"No, please, just do it," Annie interrupted him. "This is really important to me."

"Will you come and get me if it's all right?" Garrit asked.

"Yes. I promise," Annie said as he turned around.

Stuart followed Annie into the living room, where they set the dresses and the box down, then they tiptoed through the dining room and stopped at the door to the kitchen. Annie pushed the swinging door open a crack and peeked in toward the kitchen table. Her mother was sitting with her back to Annie, and her father was across from her, looking straight at the kitchen door.

"Come on in, Annie," James Harding called out before she could let the door close.

"Oh no!" she whispered as she stepped back from the door.

"It's all right," Stuart urged. "Maybe this is my chance to talk with him."

"Oh my," Annie groaned. "Are you sure?"

"I've put this off too long," he answered.

Annie reached out and took Stuart's hand, kissed him lightly on the cheek, then took a deep breath and pushed the swinging door open. The two of them stepped into the kitchen and walked slowly to the table. Dinah Harding turned toward them and smiled, although her eyes were red and puffy from crying.

"Are we interrupting something?" Annie asked.

"Yes," her father said, his pinched brown eyes staring up at her. The weathered lines carved across his forehead seemed even deeper than usual. "But it involves you both, so I'm glad you came down. Have a seat."

Annie sat down next to her mother and saw a look of uncertainty in her eyes. Stuart took the other wooden chair at the table but continued to hold Annie's hand. In the center of the oak table was a short letter that Annie could see was signed by Arthur Simpson.

James Harding rested his elbows on the table and covered his mouth with his large hands, staring silently at the letter for a while. Then he smiled tentatively, the first smile that Annie had seen on her father's face in weeks. He cleared his throat and finally said, "It . . . um . . . it looks and sounds like I owe you both a very big apology."

"What?" Annie asked, wondering if she had heard him correctly.

"This letter was delivered to me this morning," her father said, reaching out and pushing the letter across the table to Annie. "It seems that my faith in young Simpson was unmerited . . . and has colored my thinking badly. He says that he tried to use blackmail to separate you and Stuart and that the start-up loan he made me was a ploy at the time to win my confidence in him as a suitor. Annie, your mother tells me that it was even worse than the letter describes."

Annie glanced at her mother, who nodded to her, then she turned to her father and spoke softly. "Arthur was very deceptive, Father. I mistook his gifts and attention for love, and when I finally saw that Stuart's warning about him was true, I had to end our association. But I never expected to face Arthur's vengeance. He was willing to destroy the Andersons' businesses as well as pull the loan out from you. Stuart's mother was the one who saved the day."

"So I hear," James Harding said, looking at Stuart. "Simpson's already left town. Did you know that?"

"No," Stuart replied. "We knew his father was adamant about his leaving, but I wouldn't have thought it would happen this fast. Perhaps a change of location and this sudden change of heart will afford him a new start."

"Perhaps," Annie's father replied. He paused and ran his finger over his gray mustache as he looked out the window. "I'm afraid, though, that it's my heart that needs the changing," he whispered, then looked back at Annie, his eyes softening. "I've been . . . apologizing to your mother, Annie. It's not just the drinking, although that's been a nightmare for all of you, I'm sure. But I . . . ah . . . I can't tell you how ashamed I am of the way I've treated her. Why she's stayed with me, I don't know. But I've failed your mother in every way, I've hurt her . . . with my words and actions, and I feel like I surrendered my soul to making money. What I've done, what I've been—it's been eating me up all morning."

James Harding reached out and took his wife's hand, bringing an immediate gush of tears from both Dinah and Annie. His muscular hand enveloped hers, and his lips trembled as he said, "When Stuart's grandfather preached on Good Friday, I ran away from the service because I couldn't stand to hear the truth about me. I've sinned against heaven ... and you, and I'm asking you to forgive me. I've asked God to forgive me, and now I'm asking you."

Tears streaming down her face, Dinah Harding squeezed her eyes shut and whispered, "Yes, James, I forgive you. I failed to love you, as well, and I let the anger I felt toward you turn to bitterness. I let you drift away, and it was only God's intervention that kept me from even deeper sin."

"Something changed at Easter, didn't it?" James asked as Dinah smiled and nodded. "I knew that what I walked away from that night was the exact thing that had changed you. I was so full of myself that I couldn't ask for help, but I was dying inside."

"We were both dying, James. Both failing each other," Dinah said, rubbing her husband's hand. "But ... God has given us a chance to start over."

"That's what I want, but I'll need your help," he said. "I think I've warped the man I once was. You think God can straighten me back out?"

Dinah nodded. "I think so."

"Father, I know He can," Annie breathed.

James Harding took a deep breath and shook his head. "Annie," he said, lifting his free hand. "As a father, I can't explain how I could treat you the way I did ... trying to force you to stay with Simpson. I told myself that a rich young man was the way for you to escape having to struggle to make ends meet, and that lie made all the other wrongs seem right. I know it's asking a lot, but ... can you forgive me?"

Annie laughed and cried at the same time, still holding Stuart's hand with one hand and applying her white handkerchief to her face with the other. "Only if you don't kick me out of the house!" she sputtered between short breaths of air. Then she laughed some more.

"God, forgive me," her father lamented. "How can you forgive me? That wasn't even human."

"So I can stay?" Annie asked.

"Of course you can stay," James Harding replied. "But now I'll have to apologize to my mother. She was so looking forward to your coming to live with her this summer. I think she was offering her place to get even with me."

All four of them broke into laughter. It was true. Annie's grandmother had actually fixed up a bedroom especially for her and had even started baking again.

James Harding then turned to Stuart and said, "I'm afraid I haven't exactly given you a chance, Mr. Anderson, but I'm not completely blind. I can see that Annie and you love each other, and what I see makes me happy, despite how I've acted. I trust we'll get to know each other better, but from what I can see my daughter's made a wise choice. I'm very sorry that you've seen me as I've been. Hopefully it's the worst I'll ever be, and anything from now on will be an improvement."

Stuart choked back the lump in his throat and reached out his right hand to shake James'. "Thank you, sir," he said. "I've been hoping for the chance to talk with you about Annie, but I never expected it would be like this. To tell the truth, I've been afraid to broach the matter of my love for Annie with you, but I should have done it anyway."

"No, it was probably wise that you didn't try," James replied. "I truly believed that I knew more about this than Annie did, so your reception would not have been a pleasant one. So, now, tell me what I've been missing."

"Well," Stuart responded, squeezing Annie's hand tight, "your observation is absolutely correct. I love your daughter, sir. She's more than I ever dreamed of finding. I've come to ask you for her hand in marriage."

For a moment James Harding's weathered face hardened, then he smiled and chuckled to himself. "I guess that tells me what I've been missing," he said. "My, oh my, how could I have been so far away from things? Do you love Stuart, Annie?"

"You know I do, Father," Annie said, swallowing hard. "I can't imagine loving anyone more than I do Stuart."

"For a lifetime?" her father asked, looking from Annie to Stuart. "You promise your love for a lifetime? Even if your spouse turns out to be like me?"

A resounding "yes!" came from both Annie and Stuart.

"What do you think, Dinah?" James asked as he smiled at his wife. "You know this part better than I do."

Dinah Harding's smile lit up her pretty face as she looked from James to her daughter. "I think they make a wonderful couple, James, and I don't believe it was only the accident that brought them together. I couldn't be happier for you, Annie. You've made a very wise choice in Stuart Anderson. And, Stuart, I'd be very pleased to call you our son-in-law. I can't tell you how thankful I am for what you've already done for us—you and your whole family. We're deeply in your debt."

"I didn't—"

"You certainly did, and I don't want to hear you denying it," Dinah broke in on Stuart. "We've missed out on so much already. I really hope we can make up for it somehow. Will you be coming home to work for your father this summer?"

"Yes, in a few weeks school will be over," Stuart said. "And after that I hope to spend so much time here in the evenings that you'll be happy to see me leave."

"Which brings up something else we wanted to ask you about," Annie said, glancing quickly at her mother and then her father. "You realize that until half an hour ago, I thought I was on my own and that my decisions were my own. That I had to learn to live with the choices I was making about my life. That's what you said."

"Yes," James Harding assured her. "I said it . . . and I meant it, although I wish I hadn't said it the way I did. But you are eighteen now, and your mother and I agree that what you decide about your life is really up to you."

Annie looked into Stuart's eyes, and he nodded knowingly.

"I know that this is going to seem rushed . . . really rushed to you," Annie began, "but Stuart and I want to get married before school starts in the fall."

"You mean this fall?" her father asked.

Annie nodded and said, "Yes. We've talked about mid-August with Stuart's parents."

"This fall? They agree about this fall?" her mother asked.

"Yes, but they were surprised as well . . . at least sort of surprised," Stuart replied. "My mother said she saw it coming, and my father thinks extended engagements are a bad idea. I have so much schooling ahead of me that we really don't want to wait. We feel it's better to go through it together."

"We would have talked with you sooner," Annie said, "but the way things stood, it didn't seem like something we could discuss and—"

"That's my fault, Annie. You don't have to apologize," James Harding said. "I would have done the same thing if I were you. What other options did I give you?"

"So you think it's all right?" Annie asked, looking at her father and then at her mother.

Dinah Harding stared into her husband's eyes and murmured, "I was seventeen when we married . . . and very much in love. The problems we've had in the past years had nothing to do with how young we were when we married. We've let other things creep in and crowd out our love, and I hope you can learn from us never to do that. . . . So I'd say that if you feel you're ready to be married, you have my blessing. But it's not going to be easy if Stuart's going to school."

"We know," Annie agreed.

"We'll both have to work, and I'll only be able to handle part-time work," Stuart said. "But I believe we're ready."

James Harding rubbed his eyebrows and closed his eyes, then chuckled to himself and shook his head. "Oh my!" he muttered. "One minute I'm kicking you out of the house, the next minute we're talking about you getting married. I think my head hurts . . . or my heart, if it's still in there. You have my blessing, as well, for what it's worth these days."

"It's worth everything," Annie whispered, blinking back tears again and taking her father's hand. "I love you, Father. It's so good to have you back."

Her father covered his face with his hand and simply nodded.

"And I still love you, James," Dinah Harding said softly. "We need to wipe the slate clean and start over again."

"I'd sure like to try," he responded, taking a deep breath and looking at her with moist eyes.

✦✦✦✦✦✦✦✦✦✦

"And this is where it all started," Stuart Anderson said, wrapping his arm around Annie as they walked slowly out on the shiny new steel bridge over Flatwillow Creek, then stopped to look down upon the very spot in the quiet flowing stream where Annie had nearly died.

Annie shaded her eyes from the late summer's evening sun that was glaring off the upstream water. For a few moments she watched a pair of dark blue barn swallows playfully swoop and dive just inches above the surface of the clear water, then she said, "It's still so lovely and peaceful here . . . but it's not the same, is it?"

"The bridge?"

"No," she spoke softly. "The bridge has certainly changed. It's so much bigger and stronger. But it's the place I'm talking about. It just doesn't feel the same to me."

"Perhaps it's because we've changed," Stuart suggested. "Nothing ever really stays the same, especially people . . . especially us."

"Maybe you're right," she said. "Maybe it's not the place."

"Look at that!" Stuart said as a small school of minnows suddenly leapt in the water directly beneath them, followed by a big swirl in the current. "There must be a big brown trout lying in there. I should get my fishing gear and—"

"Not on the night before your wedding, mister," Annie interrupted him and squeezed his arm. "The trout can wait, but I can't. I get you to myself for the rest of this evening. What did you think of what your grandfather said at the rehearsal?"

"The text he's going to use in the wedding sermon?"

"Yes."

"I think it fits us perfectly," Stuart said. "But then again, I think it's going to get a resounding response from a lot of hearts."

" 'Behold, I am the Lord, the God of all flesh: is there any thing too hard for me?' " Annie quoted, closing her eyes and leaning back against Stuart's chest. "Just think of all that's happened in the past year, Stuart. Nothing is too hard or impossible for God."

"Not even in your father's life."

"Or my mother's life, or Walter's life, or my own life . . ." Annie added. "And it all began when you kissed my cheek and whispered in my ear. I hope your kisses never lose their power, Stuart."

Stuart laughed and held her tightly. "I don't see their strength waning," he said. "As long as I'm kissing you." He leaned back a little and placed a gentle finger under her chin, tilting her face toward him. "And you're the only one I ever hope to kiss this way," he added.

"That's the promise you make tomorrow."

"And it's the promise I give you now."

As the last rays of evening sunshine touched down lightly upon the western hills that sheltered the bridge over Flatwillow Creek, one more kiss was given as a covenant of their undying love. Their future, though uncertain, rested in the hands of their heavenly Father, and that assurance was enough to carry them through a lifetime. And indeed, as the years would unveil, it was more than they dreamed or imagined.